FATAL

Michael Palmer

arrow books

Published by Arrow Books in 2003

5 7 9 10 8 6 4

Copyright © Michael Palmer 2003

First published in the United Kingdom in 2003 by Century

Arrow Books
The Random House Group Ltd
20 Vauxhall Bridge Road, London SW1V 2SA

Random House Australia (Pty) Limited
20 Alfred Street, Milsons Point, Sydney,
New South Wales 2061, Australia

Random House New Zealand Limited
18 Poland Road, Glenfield, Auckland 10, New Zealand

Random House (Pty) Limited
Endulini, 5a Jubilee Road, Parktown 2193, South Africa

The Random House Group Limited Reg. No. 954009
www.randomhouse.co.uk

A CIP catalogue record for this book is available
from the British Library

Papers used by Random House are natural, recyclable
products made from wood grown in sustainable forests.
The manufacturing processes conform to the environmental
regulations of the country of origin.

ISBN 0 09 946237 0

Typeset by SX Composing DTP, Rayleigh, Essex
Printed and bound in Great Britain by
Cox & Wyman Ltd, Reading, Berkshire

For
Nicholas Aleksander Palmer
Believe it or not, once upon a time your grandpa wrote
this book.

And for
Dancia Damjanovic Palmer,
Jessica Bladd Palmer,
and Elizabeth Hanke

For taking such good care of my boys

Acknowledgments

One of the most pleasurable things for me about finishing a novel and knowing that soon it will be in stores and libraries and homes around the world is to take some time to reflect on the help I have received in getting to this point.

Jane and Don, thanks for being there for me as always, every step of the way.

Bill Massey, thanks for so skillfully editing the manuscript. Nita and Irwyn, Andrea Nicolay, Kelly Chian, and everyone else at Bantam Books, thanks for shepherding it through the arduous path to publication.

Lieutenant Cole Cordray, Dr. Stanton Kessler, Dr. Pierluigi Gambetti, Dr. Erwin Hirsch, Rick Macomber, Barbara Loe Fisher, and Kathi Williams, thank you for your technical assistance. Bill Wilson and Dr. Bob Smith, thanks for what you've given to me and so many others.

Daniel, bless you for your website and your ideas; Mimi, Matt, and Beverly, thanks for the readings.

And Luke, wonderful, magical Luke, thanks for understanding that sometimes Dad had to say, 'We'll play later.'

Prologue

It had started with a sore throat.

Nattie Serwanga remembered the exact moment. She had been having dinner with her husband, Eli, when some green beans hurt her going down. At the time, the two of them were talking about whether Nadine would be a better choice to name their daughter than Kolette. The discomfort was the beginning of a cold, she thought. Nothing more.

But despite treatment from the doctors in the clinic, the sore throat had gotten progressively worse. Now, nine days after that first scratchy pain, Nattie knew she was sick – really sick. The pounding headache told her so. So did the chills and the sweats and the fiery swelling in her throat that the antibiotics had done nothing to help. And beginning at three this morning, there was the cough.

Across the raised glass counter, the kids from the hospital day-care center were lined up for lunch. Chicken nuggets and spaghetti. Pudding for dessert.

'Hi, Nattie Smattie.' . . . 'Me first, Nattie. Me first.' . . . 'Ugh, not spanetti again.'

Winking at an adorable four-year-old named Harold, Nattie forced a few drops of saliva past the burning in her throat and filled his plate. A moment later, without enough warning even to raise her hand, she was jolted by a vicious, racking cough –

the worst yet. Droplets of her saliva sprayed over the contents of the trays in front of her. She stumbled back but caught herself before she actually fell. Each hack drove a six-inch spike into her brain.

'Damn,' she muttered, regaining her equilibrium. She was tough – tough as nails, one of her sisters liked to say. But this infection was tough, too. Instinctively, she slid her hands beneath her apron and pressed them against her womb. For a few horrible, empty seconds, there was nothing. Then she felt a sharp jab on her right side echoed immediately by one on the left. Despite the headache and the cough and the hot coals in her throat, Nattie Serwanga smiled.

At forty, married seven years, she had begun to believe it was her sad destiny to remain childless. Eli, who came from a family of ten children, desperately wanted kids. He had all but given up, though, and had begun talking about taking in foster children or even adopting. Then the miracle.

'Nattie, are you okay?'

Supervisor Peggy Souza eyed her with concern. Nattie's smile this time was forced. A piercing ache had materialized between her shoulder blades.

'I'm . . . I'm fine,' she managed. 'It's just a cold that doesn't want to dry up. I been to my obstetrician – twice.'

'He give you something?'

'First penicillin, then something stronger.'

She decided to leave out the part about sending her to an infections specialist if she wasn't better soon, or all the questions about the trip she and Eli had just taken to see his family in Sierra Leone.

'You wanna go home?'

Nattie gestured to the crowd on the other side of

2

the counter. A number of nurses and doctors were now lined up behind the kids.

'After the rush, maybe.'

The trip to Africa had used up the last of her vacation. She had been saving up her sick days to use in conjunction with maternity leave. With any luck she would be able to work until the last week and then take almost three months off. There was no way she could leave work just now.

'Well, I tell you what,' Peggy said. 'Why don't you wear one of these surgical masks until you're ready to leave? That was some nasty coughin' you were doin'.'

Nattie turned so that Peggy couldn't see her fumbling with the strings of the mask.

What in God's name is happening to me?

The next ten minutes were a blur of pain and poorly suppressed coughing. Still, Nattie managed to finish serving the children and even to make a dent in the staff, each of whom, she knew, had almost no time at all for lunch. Now, in addition to the unremitting pain, she was experiencing spasms and fullness in her rectum.

Please God, take care of my baby. Don't let anything happen to her.

'Nattie? . . . Nattie!'

'Huh? Oh, sorry, Peggy. My mind just wandered.'

'You were just standing there starin' off into space. I think you need to stop for the day an' . . . Nattie, look over here at me.'

'What?'

'Your eyes. They're all spotted with blood.'

'What are you talking about?'

'The white part of your eyes. There's, like,

3

patches of blood all over them. Nattie, you'd better get to a doctor right now.'

A sudden, strangulating tightness in her rectum made it impossible for Nattie to speak. Panicked, she nodded, then hurried as best she could to the rest room. The masked face staring back at her from the mirror looked monstrous. From under her paper hair-covering, clumps of her ebony hair were plastered to the perspiration on her forehead. Below that, the whites of her dull, almost lifeless eyes were nearly obliterated by splashes of bright crimson. She untied the top strings of her mask and let it flop over onto her chest. The inner surface of the mask, spattered with blood, looked like some obscene piece of modern art.

Another spasm from below – a white-hot spear thrusting up inside her.

This is bad. Oh, this is bad.

She hobbled into the stall. Her clothes were drenched with sweat. A viselike cramp in her lower belly was followed immediately by explosive diarrhea. Heavy drops of perspiration fell from her forehead.

Eli . . . oh, honey, I'm so sick. . . .

Nattie struggled to her feet. Behind her, in the bowl, was a hideous mix of stool and curdled blood. *More blood.* All she could think of was the baby. She tried again to feel the kicking in her womb, but she was shaking so hard, she couldn't tell. Eli would know what to do, she thought. He was always the calm one. She fumbled in her pocket for some change to call him at work. Nothing. The phone in Peggy's office. She could call him from there.

Lurching from side to side, unbalanced by her pregnancy, Nattie braced herself against the wall and moved ahead. Sweat was pouring down her now, stinging her eyes and dripping off her nose. Twice she was stopped by rib-snapping salvos of coughing. Her hand and the wall beyond it were speckled with crimson.

'Nattie? . . . Nattie, just lie down! Right there. I'll call the ER. Jesus, look at her!'

Peggy's voice seemed to be echoing through a long tunnel.

'My baby . . .'

Nattie sank to one knee as pain exploded in her head. A white light bathed the inside of her eyes. She felt her bowels and bladder give way at the moment her neck jerked back. She knew she was falling, but there was nothing she could do about it.

'She's having a seizure! Call the ER!'

Peggy's words were the last thing Nattie heard before a darkness mercifully washed away the pain.

Chapter 1

Belinda, West Virginia

'Matt, this is Laura in the ER. . . . Matt?'

'Yeah.'

'Matt, you're still asleep.'

'I'm not.'

'You are. I can tell.'

'Time zit?'

'Two-thirty. Matt, please turn on a light and wake up. There's been an accident at the mine.'

Matt Rutledge groaned. 'Friggin' mine,' he muttered.

'Dr. Butler has activated the disaster protocol. Team B is it tonight. Matt, are you awake?'

'I'm awake, I'm awake,' he pronounced hoarsely, fumbling with the switch on his bedside lamp. 'Nine times seven is fifty-six. The Miami basketball team is the Heat. The fifth president –'

'Okay, okay. I believe you.'

From college, through medical school and residency, and now into his life as an internist, it had always been a chore for Matt to shut his mind down enough to fall asleep – but not nearly the challenge of subsequently waking up. Laura Williams knew this trait of his as well as any nurse, having worked with him in the ER of Montgomery County Regional Hospital for two years before his decision to switch over to private practice. She and all the other nurses had adopted the policy that Dr. Matthew Rutledge wasn't definitely awake until he could prove it beyond a reasonable doubt.

'Light on? Feet on the floor?'

'I'm up, I'm up. Hold on for a second.' Matt tossed the receiver onto the bed and pulled on a pair of worn jeans, a CAN AEROSOLS NOW T-shirt, and a light sweater. 'Was it a cave-in?' he asked, tucking the receiver beneath one ear. He sensed a tightening in his gut at even saying the words.

'I think so. Ambulances are out there, but no one's been brought in here yet. The man from the mine just got here, though. He says he thinks ten or twelve are injured.'

'Man from the mine?' Matt pulled on a pair of gym socks. Two toes – the little one and the fourth – poked through a hole in the left one. He briefly considered a replacement, then pushed the toes back in and went for his boots instead.

'He called himself the safety officer, something like that,' Laura said.

'Tall, black hair with a white streak up the front?' *Sort of like a giant skunk*, Matt wanted to add, but didn't.

'Exactly.'

'That would be Blaine LeBlanc. He's a very important person in Mineville. Just ask him. Laura, thanks. I'm up and dressed and on my way.'

'Great. The first rescue unit won't be here for a little while, so drive slowly.'

'I know. I know. Motorcycle equals donorcycle.' He pulled on his boots. 'I won't go over five, I promise. The rest of the team on their way in?'

'All except Dr. Crook. So far he hasn't answered his phone or his pager.'

Please let it stay that way, Matt thought. Robert ('Don't ever call me Bob') Crook was a carriage trade cardiologist. One of the senior medical citizens in the multispecialty Belinda Medical Group, he had been the most vocal in opposition to Matt's move from the ER into their practice. Ultimately, though, those who thought a well-liked, Belinda-born-and-raised, Harvard-trained internist and ER specialist might just help fill the desperate need for a primary care doc won out over Crook, whose main objection (spoken) was that Matt was an arrogant weirdo who didn't dress or look like a doctor, and (unspoken) that he had once turned down his daughter's invitation to the prom.

'Well, I should be there in ten minutes.'

'Make it fifteen.'

'Okay, okay.'

'And Matt?'

'Yes?'

'Nine times seven is sixty-three, not fifty-six.'

'I knew that.'

Matt set the phone down, pulled his dark brown hair back into a ponytail, and secured it with a rubber band. For as long as he and Ginny had known each other, he had worn his hair short – not exactly a crew cut, but almost. And by her decree, she was the only one allowed to barber him. Since her death, he hadn't done more than trim his sideburns. The stud in his right earlobe had followed a year or so later, and the tattoo on his right deltoid a few months after that. It was a masterful rendering done from a photograph of the

8

white-blossomed hawthorn tree in their yard – Ginny's favorite.

The five-room log cabin the two of them had designed together was perched on a bluff looking out across the Sutherland Valley at the Allegheny Mountains. Pulling on a denim windbreaker, Matt stepped out onto the broad porch where, toward the end, Ginny had spent most of her time. In fact, only the tattoo artist in Morgantown had kept him from having the porch etched permanently into his arm instead of the hawthorn tree. ('I can dig the sentiment, man, but believe me, the aesthetic is just bogus.')

Anytime Matt began doubting his decision to come back to West Virginia – and of late those times were increasingly frequent – he needed only to walk out the front door of the cabin. This was Ginny's kind of night. There wasn't a single cloud in the new-moon sky. Directly overhead, the eternal river of the Milky Way shimmered across the blackness. The chilly late-summer air was, as always, tinged with a hint of smoke from the huge coal processing plant adjacent to the mine. Nevertheless, it was still sweet and fragrant with the scents of lavender, linden, wild orchids, wild roses, St. John's Wort, and hundreds of other kinds of blossoms.

Country roads, take me home, to the place I belong. . . .

Matt looped around the cabin to his one-car garage and fired up his maroon Harley Electraglide. In addition to the hog, he had a 900cc Kawasaki roadster and a 250cc Honda dirt bike, all of which he could pretty much maintain himself. The Harley was his choice for cruising, and the jackrabbit-quick roadster for those days when he wanted to live a bit

9

more on the edge. The Honda, in addition to being a thrill a second in the woods, was invaluable in making house calls to a large portion of his practice, inaccessible by any but the most primitive road.

As he rolled down the gravel drive to State Highway 6, Matt started feeling the first rush of adrenaline at what the next few hours might hold. This accident was hardly the first he had dealt with courtesy of the Belinda mine, although at ten to twelve injured it would be the biggest. Over the years, there had been bruises, gashes, strains, sprains, and fractures too numerous to mention. There had also been a few deaths. But the only other time disaster team B had actually been called in proved to be a farce. An underground train known as a maintrip had derailed deep in the mine. Twenty members of team B had milled around the ER from two until three in the morning before word was received that instead of the thirty to forty casualties originally reported, there were none.

However, this new disaster, Matt sensed, was the real deal.

The six-mile ride to the hospital was along a serpentine road for which the motorcycle seemed expressly created. Matt leaned into the familiar turns with a rhythm that had become second nature. He wondered if this latest disaster was yet another monument to the Belinda Coal and Coke Company's cutting safety corners wherever possible. Despite the constant pressure for modernization and improved safety that he and a few other brave souls tried to keep on the mine owners, little had changed. BC&C was persistently unwilling to do anything but the barest minimum to ensure the well-being of the miners. It was that way

10

with the massive conglomerate today just as it had been that April night twenty-two years ago when the ceiling of Tunnel C-9 – the tunnel cutely nicknamed Peggy Sue – caved in, crushing to death three miners, including shift foreman Matthew Rutledge, Sr.

Chapter 2

The ER at the modern, 120-bed Montgomery County Regional Hospital had a patient capacity of twelve, including rooms specially equipped for orthopedics and pediatrics, as well as room 10, the 'crash' suite for major medical or surgical emergencies. Two surgeons and a GP were waiting by the nurses' station when Matt arrived, but he knew there were at least two or three more clinicians around, plus a radiologist. In addition, almost certainly poised over in the lab, was Hal Sawyer, the chief of pathology and Matt's uncle. Hal, part mountain man, part community activist, part playboy, all scholar, was Matt's mother's brother, his godfather, and the major reason he had decided on a career in medicine. Over the twenty-two years since the cave-in of Tunnel C-9, Hal had been as close to a father as Matt had.

Matt hadn't been in the ER more than a minute when a pickup screeched into the ambulance bay bearing the first casualty. He waved off the other docs and accompanied two nurses to the truck. If the miner, muddy from a mix of limestone, coal dust, dirt, and perspiration, was any indication of the carnage in the mine, it was going to be a long night. His bloodied leg, fairly effectively splinted between two boards, had an obvious compound fracture of the femur. A grotesque spike of bone protruded through a tear in his coveralls midway up his thigh.

Matt followed the litter to the ortho room. Out of the corner of his eye he saw mine safety officer Blaine LeBlanc, dressed in pressed chinos and a hundred-dollar shirt, speaking to the driver of the pickup while making notes on a clipboard. Too late for Matt to avoid eye contact, LeBlanc turned toward him. His face was pinched and pallid. Matt flashed on what the humorless mine officer might be thinking.

Oh, no, here we go again. Another goddamn crusade by Dr. Do Little. Well, go ahead and try causing us more trouble, asshole. No one pays any attention to you anyhow. . . .

LeBlanc shook his head derisively, and Matt responded with a cheery thumbs-up. As long as Matt continued his efforts to make BC&C own up to its safety shortcomings and corner-cutting, they would be enemies.

Brian O'Neil, the orthopedist on team B, reached the cast-room door simultaneously with Matt. At six-three, O'Neil was two inches taller than Matt was, and a couple of years older. He had added two or three dozen pounds to the hard-nosed linebacker he had been at WVU, but at forty he was still a hell of an athlete. He was also a top-notch surgeon and Matt's closest friend on the medical staff.

'You first,' Matt said. 'I take enough of a pounding from you under the hoop.'

'Since when did Gunner Rutledge ever mix it up under the hoop? You'd need a map just to show you where under the hoop is. Get a line in please, Laura. Normal saline. Usual bloods. Type and cross-match for six units. Portable films of his chest and leg. As soon as Dr. Gunner here has finished examining him, give him seventy-five of Demerol and twenty-five of Vistaril I.M.'

'We're on it,' Laura Williams replied, unflappable as always.

'You know, pal, Laura and some of the other nurses were betting that you'd sleep through this one.'

'They may still be right. Seeing you here on time makes me think I might be dreaming.'

Together, they moved to the bedside and assisted the nurse in cutting away the young miner's clothes. He might have been nineteen or twenty, with reddish hair and wide, feline eyes. His narrow face was etched with pain, but he forced his lips tightly together and took the jostling to his shattered leg without a sound.

'I'm Dr. O'Neil, the orthopedist,' Brian said. 'This is Dr. Rutledge. He's a veterinarian, but he's a damn fine one. We're going to take good care of you.'

'Th-thanks, sir,' the young man managed. 'I'm Fenton. Robby Fenton.'

'What in the heck happened down there, Robby?' O'Neil asked as Matt began a rapid physical assessment.

'It was Darryl Teague, sir. He . . . he went berserk. He's been actin' a little tetched for a while, but tonight he was operatin' the C.M. an' he jes went off. You know what a C.M. is – a continuous miner?'

'That monster machine that scoops up coal and puts it onto the conveyor belt?' Matt said.

'Exactly. Twelve ton or more every minute.'

'You never cease to amaze me, Dr. Rutledge,'

O'Neil said. 'No wonder you don't date even though people tell me you're the prime catch in the region. You scare all the women away with your vast knowledge.'

'Don't pay any attention to him, Robby. He's lucky he's a darn good bone doctor, or no one would even talk to him. Go on.'

'Well, early on in the shift Teague got into a shovin' match with one of the guys, Alan Riggs. I don't know what it was about. Teague's been like that for a while – pickin' fights, complainin' that people were out to get him, that sort of thing. Well, a bunch of us broke it up between him and Riggs. Then, a little while later, Teague goes after Riggs with the C.M. He runs right over him, I mean right over him. Then he goes on an' takes out maybe half a dozen supports. That's when the roof caved in. How are the rest of the guys?'

'We don't know yet, Robby. You're the first arrival.'

'Alan's got to be dead. You shoulda seen it. Blasted Darryl Teague. I don't usually wish nobody no harm, but I hope he got hurt but good.'

'Dr. Rutledge, we need you,' Laura Williams said from the doorway.

Matt had been so mesmerized by Robby Fenton's account that he had completely forgotten about the deluge that was about to hit. Now the ER was in beehive mode. Six of the beds were occupied by miners in varying degrees of distress and pain. Technicians, nurses, and physicians were in constant movement, but the chaos seemed organized and nothing looked out of control.

'We don't need your internist skills right now,' Laura said, 'but we sure could use your ER talent.

15

There's a lac in three. A beauty. I've ordered skull films, but they're going to take a while. He's low on the triage totem pole.'

Matt stopped in the on-call room and quickly changed into scrubs. He was on his way to room 3 when Blaine LeBlanc intercepted him. A New Yorker with a dense accent, LeBlanc was a fit fifty, just an inch or so shorter than Matt, and broader across the shoulders. His thick, jet hair was slicked straight back and held in place with something from a tube. His trademark white stripe, an inch and a half across, glistened beneath the fluorescent overheads.

'What did that kid in there tell you?' he asked.

'Nice of you to inquire after the lad, Blaine. He has a compound fracture of his femur. That's when the ol' thighbone is sticking out through the skin. He won't be pushing coal for you for a while.'

'Back off, Rutledge. What did he tell you?'

Matt met LeBlanc's icy stare with one of his own. The man was potentially dangerous. Of that, Matt had no doubt. It was possible that before Ginny died, he had held his contempt for LeBlanc and BC&C in better check. But with her gone, he simply didn't care. A lifelong health nut and nonsmoker, Ginny had no family history of lung cancer. She was only thirty-three when the diagnosis was made, and her tumor was an unusual cell type – the kind of unusual cell type that might, *might*, have been caused by some sort of toxin.

No one could deny that BC&C's coal processing plant was awash in carcinogenic chemicals. Whether they were handling and disposing those toxins in a safe, legal manner was another story. Matt had plenty of theories and some hearsay about illegal

'What's the deal with your qualifying to collect disability?' Matt asked.

'We get full salary so long's we have sick time available. Then it's a month waitin' period before the disability kicks in. With a doctor's note sayin' the problem is work-related, we start collectin' disability immediately with no loss of sick time. But I'm –'

'Shhhhhhh.'

Matt selected dissolving sutures for a careful, layered closure, and fine, 6-0 nylon for the actual skin. Then he donned magnifying goggles and a new pair of gloves. Mickey's lined, weathered face showed every day of three decades in the mine. But there was no way he was going to leave the ER with anything but the thinnest of scars from this one.

'You're out for two weeks,' Matt said. 'I'll give you the note. In fact, make that three weeks. And if you have any kind of a headache, any kind at all, we'll tack on a few weeks more.'

Twenty minutes later, he was halfway done with a closure that would have satisfied a movie star, when Laura Williams, breathless, called to him from the doorway.

'Matt, Dr. Easterly needs you right away in the crash suite. You'll have to finish in here later.'

Matt placed some saline-soaked gauze over Shannon's wound and set the sterile drapes aside. Then he stepped back from the table, flexing some of the tightness from his neck.

'Mickey, you hear that?' he asked.

'Don't worry about me. Who's he got to see, miss?'

'A man named Darryl Teague,' Laura replied.

19

'Some sort of heavy equipment fell over on him.'

'Let 'im die!' Mickey Shannon snapped.

Considering that every bed in the ER was occupied and most of those patients were being attended to, there was quite a crowd working in room 10. One glance at the overhead monitor told Matt why. Heart rate 140. Blood pressure 80/40. Oxygen saturation only 89 percent. Jon Lee, the nurse working beside the gurney, caught Matt's eye and made a brief thumbs-down sign. It seemed as if Mickey Shannon's and Robby Fenton's prayers were being answered. Somewhere beyond the wall of technicians, nurses, and GP Judy Easterly, Darryl Teague was on the verge of checking out.

'What's up?'

Startled, Judy Easterly swung around, then came over to him. Not the most energized or enthusiastic of doctors under any circumstance, she was currently in her seventh or eighth month of pregnancy, and looked as if she would have chosen to be anyplace in the world at that moment other than where she was.

'This is the guy who caused all this,' she whispered.

'I know,' Matt whispered back. 'Is he bleeding somewhere?'

Easterly thrust out her gravid belly and arched her back, trying to relieve some tightness somewhere.

'Not that I can tell,' she replied, still whispering. 'He drove some piece of heavy equipment over two guys. No one knows why. One of them's dead. The other's up in the OR right now, and I don't think he's going to make it. After he did that, he knocked down some supports and the roof collapsed. He was trapped beneath a load of rock. The rescue guys said his BP was all right on the way in. I think the triage nurse assigned him to me because he looked pretty good when he got here.'

'Not anymore. Obvious fractures?'

In addition to the usual sources of hidden blood loss – the chest and abdominal cavities – a fractured leg, or even an arm in some cases, could cause enough bleeding into muscle to throw a victim into shock.

'None,' Easterly said. 'He's moving all extremities. Joe Terry was just hanging around waiting for the OR to be ready for his case, so I had him put an arterial line in.'

'Nicely done.'

Matt meant the compliment, although it was also obvious that except for the arterial line, Easterly hadn't been nearly aggressive enough with a man this hurt. At the moment she seemed close to tears.

'You know,' she said, 'if I had known I was going to end up with this sort of crunch in the very guy responsible for the disaster, I would have stayed home.'

'Listen, Judy, why don't you go ahead home right now,' Matt said. 'You've got things under reasonable control here, and it looks as if you and the kid could use some rest.'

Easterly started to protest, then suddenly thanked him.

'Bloods are off for the usual labs plus six units,' she said rapidly. 'I ordered a portable of his chest and abdomen. I really appreciate this.'

'Just name your kid after me,' Matt said.

'Matthewina,' Easterly said. 'I think she'd like that. Hey, thanks. Good luck.'

Before Matt could even respond, she was gone. It was just as well. She clearly had other things on her mind and was already hovering between not-much-help and downright dangerous. He glanced again at the monitor and moved into Easterly's spot at the bedside, across from Jon Lee. Then he stopped short, staring down in disbelief at the man whose insane rage had just killed one and possibly two co-workers. Darryl Teague's face was covered with fleshy lumps, at least twenty of them, some pea-sized, but some quite a bit larger, and one, just in front of his left ear, approximating a walnut. Almost certainly they were neurofibromas – bundles of nerve tissue mixed with spindly fibrous cells. Cause: unknown. Cure: none known. Darryl Teague was well on his way to becoming an Elephant Man.

Even more startling to Matt was that Teague was the second case of such a condition he had seen in the past four or five months.

'Laura, Dr. Hal Sawyer is part of our disaster team. Could you please call him in the lab and ask if he can come over as soon as possible.'

'You've got it.'

Matt quickly turned his attention to the miner. Teague was conscious and still breathing on his own, but his skin was mottled and his lips were a grayish purple.

'Jon, anything ordered for his pressure?'

'Nothing yet, Doctor.' Lee's tone made it quite clear that he was grateful for the change in medical command.

'Hang some dopamine, standard drip. Run it

22

wide open until we see what happens. Get a catheter in him and keep his volume up.'

Laura Williams returned. 'Dr. Sawyer will be over shortly,' she said.

Matt peered up at the EKG monitor. The size of the beats on the tracing appeared much smaller than normal. He filed the information away for the moment and began an efficient exam. Teague's heart sounds were muffled and distant. There was tenderness in the center of his sternum – enough tenderness to cause the semi-comatose man to cry out when the spot was pressed. His belly was soft and not the least bit tender. His lungs were clear. Legs, arms, unremarkable. Skull and scalp also normal, except that there were a dozen or more neurofibromas hidden beneath Teague's long, strawlike, dirty blond hair.

In short, there was no evidence for bleeding anywhere. So why was Teague in shock?

The likely answer at the moment centered around trauma to the miner's breastbone, and beneath it, his heart.

'Laura, where's Dr. Crook?' he asked.

'On his way in. Turns out his beeper was accidentally shut off, and his phone wasn't working. The Sandersonville police went out to his place and woke him up.'

Sandersonville was twenty minutes from the hospital and Crook was hardly the sort who would simply jump into a pair of sweats and race on in – especially when there was no definite indication in any of the victims that a cardiologist would be needed.

'Dr. Rutledge?'

Lee gestured at the monitor – 70/30.

'Prepare to intubate him, Jon. Anesthesia around?'

'In the OR.'

'Radiology?'

'Same. She's doing some sort of procedure with Dr. Terry.'

Inwardly Matt groaned. He had intubated dozens of patients, many of them critical, so that was no problem. But his ability to interpret an ultrasound was average at best. In a life-and-death situation like this one, he would want a radiologist's opinion.

'No problem,' he said. 'Get me a seven-point-five tube, please. Laura, could we talk out there?'

The nurse looked at him curiously.

'Of course,' she said.

'Jon, just shout if you need me.'

Matt walked Laura to the nurses' station. She was a straight-laced grandmother in her early fifties, traditional in her approach to medicine, and a damn fine nurse. She was never comfortable with Matt's open style, manner, and dress, and she had said so on several occasions. Still, over the years, they had managed to co-exist with few problems. Now, he knew, he was about to put their mutual respect to the test.

The commotion in the ER seemed to have leveled off, and the moaning from the injured miners was much less.

'How's he doing?' Blaine LeBlanc asked as they passed.

'Later,' Matt said.

'You talk to me before you do anything heroic, you hear? That . . . that weirdo killed one and maybe two of my men.'

24

'Sure, Dr. God,' Matt said. 'I'll be certain to consult with you.'

He turned his back on LeBlanc and spoke softly to the nurse. From what he could discern, blood was building up between the lining of Teague's heart and the heart muscle itself. The resultant constriction of the heart muscle was keeping it from filling properly between each beat.

'Laura, this guy's got a pericardial tamponade.'

'How do you know?'

'That's what it's got to be. We need to stick a needle into it and drain the blood.'

'Can't we wait for Dr. Crook?'

'Unless we can be sure he's going to be here in the next five minutes, the answer is no.'

'What about some tests? An ultrasound?'

'Radiology is in the OR. I don't trust the tech or me to read one with certainty. Besides, I don't think we have time. This kid is going out.'

'Maybe that's for the best,' Laura said.

'Now, don't let us get started on that,' Matt said. 'Please get me a pericardial drainage kit.'

'Matt, I don't like this at all. How many times have you done this procedure?'

'A few during my residency,' Matt lied. 'I can do it.'

'Pressure's not reading,' Lee called out. 'EKG is showing many extra beats.'

'Please,' Matt said, heading back to room 10.

'If you're ordering it, I'll be right there with the kit.'

'Remember what I told you,' LeBlanc said as Matt passed him.

Matt knelt at the head of Darryl Teague's bed and skillfully slid a breathing tube down his throat and between his vocal cords. The respiratory tech then hooked the tube to a breathing bag and oxygen, and began to pump. Teague's chest expanded much more than it had been, but his blood pressure only rose to 50.

'Nice intubation, Doctor.'

Hal Sawyer stood just inside the doorway. With his dark hair graying at the temples, his carefully trimmed mustache, his gold-rimmed glasses and knee-length lab coat, Uncle Hal looked as professorial as did any medical school dean. In fact, he did have a clinical teaching position at one of the medical schools, but for the most part he stayed pretty close to Belinda, where he was chief of pathology (there was one other full-time pathologist) as well as the Montgomery County medical examiner. Hal was also erudite, well-read, and adventurous. He seldom spoke up at hospital staff meetings, but when he did, people generally listened.

Never married, Hal didn't seem to lack for company. His latest girlfriend, Heidi, was a pretty, young thing he had met on some sort of rafting trip. The gossipers in Belinda went on about his personal life, but he never seemed to care, just as he didn't care when the rumors started going around some years ago that he was gay. Hal was very much his own man, and Matt credited him with fostering his own sense of independence.

'Hey, Hal,' Matt said, 'thanks for coming over. This is the guy who went berserk in the mine and caused this nightmare. People say he's been acting paranoid for months. Paranoid insanity coupled with diffuse neurofibromatosis of the face and scalp. Ring any bells?'

'Just like that cliff diver.'

'Exactly. His name was Rideout. Teddy Rideout. And where did he work?'

'As I recall,' Hal said, palpating the lumps, 'he, too, was a miner.'

'He was most definitely that. BC and C, to be exact.'

'My, my,' Hal said.

Some months ago Matt had been cruising on his Harley down a particularly winding mountain road when Rideout sped past him on the inside, traveling much faster than the road ahead would tolerate. A minute or so later, Matt came upon the shattered guardrail and saw the car lying on its roof several hundred feet below. Rideout lay well beyond resuscitation. His striking facial lumps were identical to Teague's, and subsequent discussion with his family revealed a history of rapidly progressive paranoia and irrational, aggressive behavior. At the man's autopsy, Matt wondered out loud to his uncle if Rideout might be toxic from something at the mine.

Hal had promised to run some extra tests, which came back negative. It was Hal's belief that the man was one of a kind – a very unusual case, but just a single fluke point on the graph of life.

Well, Matt thought now, *here's dot number two*.

'I'll see what I can dig up about Mr. Rideout,' Hal said. 'I don't recall anything unusual in the autopsy except for those neurofibromas, which were only of interest because of their numbers, not their microscopic appearance.'

'Here's the kit,' Laura said, setting the tray marked PERICARDIOCENTESIS down on the stainless-steel stand.

'Any sign of Crook?'

'He could be here any minute. Are you sure you –'

'But he's not here now. This guy's BP is back down to zero. He's firing extra beats. I say we go.'

'Suit yourself,' Laura said coolly.

In fact, Matt had attempted pericardial taps a number of times as the last gasp maneuver in cardiac arrest patients who were about to die despite the most heroic resuscitative measures. But never had the procedure located any unsuspected pericardial blood. And never had any of the patients survived.

'Need any help?' Hal offered.

'Will Robert Crook to stroll into the ER right now,' Matt said. 'I just don't think we can wait.'

Beyond Hal, just a few feet outside the door, Matt could see Blaine LeBlanc, watching, waiting.

'I'm still not getting any pressure at all,' Lee reported. 'Ventricular extra beats in pairs.'

Sometimes you just got to do what you got to do, Matt was thinking.

He attached a four-inch-long, wide-bore cardiac needle to a 20cc syringe and hooked an alligator clamp to the base of it. He would know he was wrong about there being pericardial blood only after he had driven the heavy needle through the tissue-thin pericardial membrane and into the base of Teague's heart. The electrocardiogram would react immediately to the trauma, and hopefully, he would have time to stop and withdraw the needle before any major damage was done to the cardiac muscle. Hopefully. But if he pierced the muscle and hit a coronary artery, the resulting heart attack would give Teague almost no chance at all.

Matt forced the needle through the skin at the V formed by Teague's left lower ribs and the tip of his sternum. Then he angled it toward his left shoulder. Keeping the pressure constant, he advanced the needle through the diaphragm toward what he envisioned was the base of the heart.

Slowly . . . slowly . . .

'Lots of extra beats,' the nurse reported.

'Are you hitting his heart right now?' Laura asked.

Matt checked the monitor.

I sure hope not, he thought.

'No,' he said assuredly.

'Are you sure?'

Without warning, the syringe filled with blood.

Yes!

Matt switched the three-way valve on the syringe to empty and injected its crimson contents into a small glass cup. Then he withdrew another 25cc of blood from Teague and squirted it into a larger beaker.

'How do you know you're not drawing blood directly from his heart?' Laura asked.

The woman simply wasn't going to let up.

Hal stepped forward.

'Ms. Williams,' he said calmly, 'it looks very much like Dr. Rutledge knows what he is about. There is one way to tell right here where that needle tip is. If that blood Dr. Rutledge just removed was sitting in this man's pericardial space, it probably won't clot. If it's directly from the ventricle of the heart, it will.'

'How long will that take to know?'

Matt ignored the question and drew off another syringeful. Teague's condition remained unchanged. To his left, Lee tried again to hear a pressure, then shook his head gravely.

'If he's in shock and you might be taking blood from his heart, won't that make the situation even worse?' Laura asked.

Back off! Matt wanted to scream. The nurse was quite obviously protecting herself against Robert Crook's certain onslaught.

I tried to reason with him, Dr. Crook, really I did.

Matt slid a thin plastic catheter through the needle and into what he hoped was the pericardial space. Then, carefully, he withdrew the needle and fixed the catheter in place with a single suture through the skin of Teague's chest. Blood oozed from the catheter opening and soaked an expanding stain into the sterile drape. For several seconds there was nothing but a tense silence.

'Pressure's still zero,' Lee reported at the moment Robert Crook charged into the room.

A rotund, ruddy-faced man, Crook had dense, sandy-gray brows that always looked to Matt like giant woolly caterpillars about to do battle. Along the margin of his left jaw were several fresh clots from where he had nicked himself shaving, as well as a tiny, bloodstained flake of tissue paper. His response to the emergency at MCRH had clearly been to charge into the bathroom and break out his razor and shaving mug.

'Rutledge, what's going on?' he demanded.

Matt shrugged.

'He lost his blood pressure and I couldn't figure out why. I decided he had a pericardial tamponade, so I tapped him.'

'You . . . *tapped* him?'

'Still no pressure,' Lee called out.

'Be sure the dopamine is open all the way,' Matt ordered.

'It is.'

'Did you see pericardial fluid on his echo?' Crook asked, ignoring the sterile field and the thin catheter in order to listen with his stethoscope.

'I . . . wasn't able to get an echo. No time.'

Crook erupted.

'Jesus Christ! How can you be sure you've stuck that needle into his pericardial space and not into his friggin' heart?'

'I did what I thought was right,' Matt responded as steadily as he could manage. 'I did what I thought was needed, and I did it the best I could.'

'The best you could? Rutledge, you're not a doctor. You're a goddamn cowboy. A loose cannon. And I want you to know that I fully intend to report your actions to –'

'Wait,' the nurse cried out. 'I hear a pressure. It's loud and clear at sixty. . . . No, now it's eighty. It's eighty.'

At that moment, Darryl Teague lifted one arm and turned his head.

Chapter 3

'Mornin', Kim,' Matt said to the efficient, empathetic clerk of the ICU.

'Good morning, Doctor' was the chilly reply.

Matt considered confronting the woman. Kim West had always been at least cordial to him, if not downright friendly. But there was no sense in singling out her rudeness. The Belinda Coal and Coke Company was the lifeblood of the valley. In one way or another, all of Montgomery County was linked to it. Over the three days since he saved the life of Darryl Teague, the coolness toward him on the streets of Belinda had grown increasingly unpleasant. Teague had never been a favorite son of the town, and now two young men were dead because of him. And because of Matt, he wasn't. The gas station, Scotty's Diner, the dry cleaner – wherever he went, there were whispers and tension, even in the hospital, where people should have known better about the choices doctors should and should not be making.

Within hours of the incident in the ER, Robert Crook had sent a memo to the entire hospital staff decrying Matt's behavior and judgment. He even speculated that poor technique in doing the pericardial aspiration had placed the man in as much jeopardy as had the accident itself.

Teague was officially Crook's patient, and the

cardiologist had gone out of his way to involve an internist other than Matt in his care. Still, Matt had made it a point to visit Teague twice a day since the disaster. Helping to save a person's life forged a connection only those who had been in that situation could completely understand.

Ignoring the distasteful glare from one of the older nurses – a miner's mother, Matt recalled – he went directly to room 6. The lights were out, save for a dim fluorescent over the bed. Teague, his monstrously deformed face battered and bruised, lay on his back breathing shallowly and irregularly on a ventilator. He was unconscious, as he had been since shortly after his transfer up from the ER. From what Matt could tell, there was no decent explanation for his lapse into a coma. Initially, blunt head trauma was the likely suspect, and that certainly remained a possibility. Still, there had been no order for an MRI or CT scan, or even for a consultation with the neurologist. Robert Crook certainly wasn't going to win any Doctor of the Year award for his attention to this case, although he might well receive a good citizen medal from the townsfolk.

Matt stood in the gloom, looking down at Darryl Teague.

What happened to you, Darryl? he asked silently. *What did you and Teddy Rideout inhale? What did you drink? What did you rub onto your skin?*

Matt took Teague's wrist and checked his pulse, which was quite strong. The torn vessel that had caused the nearly lethal cardiac tamponade had clotted, and the narrow drain, which had been placed under the pericardial membrane, had been removed. Now, to all intents, Teague's mysterious coma was all that was standing between him and a transfer out of MCRH – probably to some prison hospital. Matt did a brief neurological check. Nothing alarming – no focal signs that would suggest a slowly increasing hemorrhage between the skull and brain. He reached up and gently touched the hard, fleshy lump above Teague's left eyebrow, then the one on his chin. Had the man ever bothered to see a doctor for this bizarre condition, or did his rapidly progressive mental illness prevent him from acting rationally?

'What's the deal, Darryl?' Matt whispered. 'Come on. Wake up and tell me. . . . What's the deal?'

He picked up the bedside phone, hesitated, then called the pathology lab. In seconds his uncle was on the line.

'Hal, how're you doing?'

'Well, I don't have half the town wanting to tar and feather me for just doing my job, if that's what you mean.'

'There's a nurse right outside who'll be happy to smear the first glob on me. Listen, Hal, I'm here in Teague's ICU cubicle. You may already know this, but he's been in a coma since right after he was moved up here from the ER. I'm wondering if someone's medicating him.'

'Why?'

'First *if*, then *why*. Is there any way you could have one of your techs draw an extra tube and run a drug screen on it?'

'Without telling Crook?'

'That's the idea. I would draw it myself, but there would be hell to pay if a nurse walked in on me while I was doing it.'

'I'll do it, nephew, but I expect a pouch of premium tobacco next Christmas. No more ties.'

'You sure? I think I still have three or four left in my closet.'

'I'm sure.'

'Okay, no more ties. Thanks, Unk.'

Matt's office occupied the first floor of a shingled old two-family just off Main Street, near the center of town. He parked his Harley by the garage in back and entered through the rear door. The moment he stepped inside, he could hear an animated exchange coming from his waiting room. The voice, a woman's, was strident and shrill. Responding to her, evenly, civilly as always, was Mae Borden, his office manager and receptionist.

'Now, Mrs. Goodwin,' Mae was saying, 'I'm not trying to convince you not to switch doctors, but I do think you owe it to your husband to think things through.'

Matt stopped just short of the door to his office and leaned against the wall in the hallway.

'Charlie's the one who made me come,' the woman said. 'He's very upset about what happened in the mine.'

'You mean Dr. Rutledge saving that boy's life?'

'Yes. The two men Teague killed were friends a Charlie's. An' the mine's been closed for three days now because a the damage Teague did down there. That's money outta everyone's pockets.'

'I understand. Tell me something, Mrs. Goodwin. If your husband had been the one driving that equipment that night, would you have wanted Dr. Rutledge to do all he could?'

'Well, I . . . I suppose I would.'

35

'And has Dr. Rutledge always given you two the best of care?'

'A course he has.'

'And you want to switch doctors?'

'Well, I –'

'Mrs. Goodwin, supposin' I keep your records here until Charlie comes in and speaks with me – or better still, with Dr. Rutledge. I'm not supposed to say this, but I know for a fact that the two of you are among his favorite patients. He'd hate to lose you.'

'Well, the truth is, I'd hate to lose him, too.'

'So?'

'Mrs. Borden, I was really hopin' you'd talk me outta this. I'll tell Charlie if'n he wants to go through with it, he's got t' come in an' face Dr. Rutledge hisself.'

'I suspect he'll be relieved you didn't do it.'

'I think he will, too. Thank you. Oh, thank you so much.'

Matt heard the front door open and shut.

'It's okay, Matthew,' Mae called out. 'She's gone. You can come in here now.'

Matt entered the modest waiting area and kissed his office manager on the cheek.

'I have some Eskimos I want to sell refrigerators to,' he said. 'I think you're just the woman for the job.'

'No thanks. I can't stand the cold.'

'Bless you for saving my practice.'

'Oh, it's not been that bad,' Mae replied in her melodic, Alabama drawl. 'Six attempted defections so far, only three successful ones.'

Mae had been Matt's office manager since the day he entered practice. She was in her fifties, but her

36

silver hair and conservative manner and dress added a decade to that. Over the years, the two of them had become bound by their differences as well as by a total devotion to the practice and their patients. In addition to making the best pot of coffee in town, Mae was a wizard at squeezing in any patient who needed to be seen, and at 'adjusting' a bill for anyone who couldn't pay.

'I'm afraid this Teague business has made me a few enemies around town, Mae,' Matt said.

'Correction, sir, people in town like you and respect the kind of doctor you are. Many of them sympathize with you because of the losses you've endured. But they're losing patience. Since you came back here to practice, your attempts to get the mine fined or even shut down for safety violations have already rankled a whole bunch of people. It's made you an irritant in some quarters and the butt of jokes in others. Saving Darryl Teague has merely pushed the envelope.'

'Mae, come on, now. Stop mincing words. What do you *really* think?'

Mae smiled in spite of herself.

'Very funny,' she said. 'But it's not so funny when people won't come to see the best doctor in the valley because they think he's always crusading to take away their livelihood.'

'I'm not crusading to take away anyone's livelihood. It's just that –'

'Matthew, open your eyes,' Mae cut in. 'Ever since Ginny died, you've had blinders on. You were already writing letters to the mine safety people and trying to make every injury in the mine a federal case. After she passed away, you just haven't let up. And what have you got to show for it? Nothing.'

'Ah-ha!' Matt said. 'Now, that's where you're wrong.' He raced into his office and returned with a stack of magenta paper. 'I have these to show for it, fresh from the copy store.'

He set the sheets on Mae's counter and passed one over.

WANTED
INFORMATION ON ILLEGAL TOXIC WASTE DUMPING OR STORAGE AT ANY MINE IN MONTGOMERY COUNTY

$2,500 REWARD
FOR INFORMATION LEADING TO MSHA OR EPA ACTION
COMPLETE CONFIDENTIALITY GUARANTEED
REMEMBER, IT'S YOUR HEALTH
The Healthy Mines Coalition

'Lord,' Mae groaned. '"Healthy Mines Coalition"?'

'I thought that sounded better than Matthew Rutledge, M.D.'

'Matthew, when are you going to see the light? You can't hurt these people. They have more money than we could ever dream of, and more influence in high places than they need to brush off a fly like you. Going against them, you can only hurt yourself.'

'Mae, Ginny died of a type of cancer that only shows up one in a million times in female nonsmokers her age. Now along comes two cases of a totally unusual syndrome in two men who both just happen to be miners. How can you not believe that BC and C is responsible? Do you have any idea how many barrels of toxic petrochemicals they generate converting coal into fertilizers or paint, or especially coke? Where are they?'

If nothing else, Matt had done his homework. The production of coke, the derivative of coal that was essential to the production of iron and ultimately steel, was, to his mind, a major culprit. With enough plant space, equipment, and technology, certain types of coal could be utilized nearly 100 percent. But various by-products of production – creosotes, tars, pitches, and many other hydrochemicals – if not generated in sufficient quantities to be commercially valuable, had to be disposed of safely, or else stored. It was in this area that Matt believed the powers at BC&C were cutting their most dangerous corners.

Shaking her head more in frustration than disapproval, Mae handed the fliers back to him.

'You have five minutes before Jim Kinchley,' she said. 'I sent him over to the lab for routine bloods and an EKG.'

'Perfect. Mae, don't worry. We'll do fine.'

Mae smiled thinly and returned to her business.

Matt repaired to his office and began working his way through the pile of lab reports and charts on his desk. As usual, Mae made sense, he was thinking. When was the last time one of his letters to the editor had actually been published? And what about the abortive town meeting he had held where there were only seven attendees, including his mother, uncle, and two homeless people who were clearly there for the coffee and cookies?

He looked up just as a scarlet tanager alighted on a branch of the white oak outside his window. For a minute, maybe even longer, the magnificently colored little songbird perched there, motionless, looking, it seemed, directly at him.

Ginny?

The bird remained fixed in its spot.

Ginny, is that you?

From the doorway, Mae Borden cleared her throat discreetly.

'Matthew, are you okay?'

'Huh? Oh, sure. I'm fine.'

He glanced back at the tree, but the tanager was gone.

'You were thinking about your wife, weren't you?'

'No, I mean yes. Yes, I was.'

'I thought so.'

'You know, Mae, it's been almost four years and the feelings haven't really changed inside me at all. If anything, I miss her more than ever. First it's a cloud that reminds me of her, then a scene in the woods, or the way a woman on the sidewalk looks from behind. Just now it was a bird – a tanager. Only this time it didn't just remind me of her, Mae, I had this powerful feeling it *was* her. No matter how hard I try, I can't seem to get my brain around how long forever is. I keep thinking that some director's going to walk into the room, clap his hands, and announce that this scene is over and we get to move on to the next – the one where she's waiting at home to tell me about her day with the kids at school.'

Mae crossed the room and set her hand on his shoulder.

'You have every right to hold fast to the memories of her,' she said, 'so long as they don't blot out the life you have left to live. With your dad gone, and your mother, bless her soul, getting more and more . . . sick, and the hours you spend working here and in the hospital, and now this mine thing, I wonder sometimes how you do it. The trick is to have those memories remind you not of what life was, but of how wonderful it can be again if you'd allow it.'

'I hear you.'

'I hope you do.'

Mae walked around to the corner of the desk and picked up the stack of magenta fliers.

'You going to throw those away?' Matt asked.

'No,' she said, her tone and expression bittersweet. 'I'm going to put them up all around town. Who knows?'

As she left Matt's office, the phone was ringing. Through his open door he heard her answer it.

'Dr. Rutledge's office . . . When? . . . Any idea why? . . . I'll tell him right away. . . . Thank you. Thank you for calling.'

She set the receiver down and moments later appeared at the doorway.

'Matthew, that was Janice in the ICU. Darryl Teague just had a sudden cardiac arrest. They tried resuscitating him, but nothing worked. He's dead.'

Chapter 4

It was the second straight day of unremitting rain. Nikki Solari hated running in this kind of weather, but today she was considering doing it anyway. It had been more than a week since her roommate and close friend, Kathy Wilson, had stormed from their South Boston flat. A week without so much as a word – to her or to their mutual friends. The police had been surprisingly little help. Nikki had filled out the appropriate forms and brought in some photographs, but so far, nothing.

'. . . Miss Solari, try to relax. I'm sure your friend will turn up.'

'It's *Doctor* Solari, and why are you so sure?'

'That's the way it is with cases like this. Everyone worries and the missing person just shows up.'

'Well, this missing person is an incredibly talented musician who would never leave her band in the lurch, which she has. She is a wonderfully dependable friend who would never do anything to upset me, which she has. And she is an extremely compassionate and kind woman who would never say anything abusive to anyone, yet before she disappeared she had become abusive to everyone.'

'*Doctor* Solari, tell me something honestly. Were you and Miss Wilson lovers?'

'Oh, Christ . . .'

Nikki desperately needed to wrest the worry

from her brain, if only for a while, and the only ways she had ever been able to do so were running, making music, and performing autopsies.

It was eleven in the morning. One more hour until lunch. She could go out and splash through a few miles then. She stood by the window of her office watching the cars creep down Albany Street past the modern building that was the headquarters of the chief medical examiner and his staff. This was her third year as an associate in ME Josef Keller's office. She was fascinated by the work and absolutely adored the man. But the past week had been hell. She glanced over at her desk. There were reports to be read, dictations to do, and several boxes of slides to review, but the concentration just wasn't there.

'Hey, there, beautiful, you've got a case.'

Without waiting for an invitation, Brad Cummings strode into the office. Divorced with a couple of kids, Cummings was the deputy chief medical examiner. He was athletic, urbane, and, in the eyes of perhaps every woman in the city except Nikki, handsome. She found him smug, self-absorbed, and way too pretty – quite possibly the absolute antithesis of what she was looking for in a man.

'Where's Dr. Keller?' she asked.

'Away until one. That means I'm the boss until then, so I get to say who gets what case, and you get this tubber.'

'This what?'

'Sixty-six-year-old guy had a coronary getting into his Jacuzzi, smacked his head on the side, and went for the eternal swim. He's just eight months post-bypass surgery. I spoke to his doctor, who said he was on *mucho* cardiac meds and undoubtedly had an MI. So, he's really just a "View". You don't have to cut on him at all. And that means we have time to go have lunch at that place on Newbury Street I've been telling you about.'

'Brad, I don't want to go out with you.'

'But I thought you broke up with that drip you were dating.'

'Correction, that drip broke up with me. And I'm not interested in starting up with another one.'

'She digs me. I can tell.'

At the best of times, Nikki had precious little patience for the man.

'Brad, you have more than enough scalps hanging on your lodge pole without mine. And I'm sure there are plenty more where those came from. We'll keep getting along fine so long as you keep things on a business or collegial basis. But I promise you, Brad, call me beautiful again, or sweets, or honey, or babe, or anything other than Nikki or Dr. Solari, and I'll write you up and hand it over to Dr. Keller. Clear?'

'Hey, easy does it.'

Nikki could tell that he stopped himself at the last possible instant from adding 'babe.'

'I'm going to get started on the new case,' she said.

'I told you, this is a straightforward View. No scalpel required, just eyeball him and sign off.'

'If it's all the same to you, I'll make that decision after I've seen the guy.'

Nikki didn't add that there wasn't a chance in the world she would pass on this case regardless of how open-and-shut it was. Here was the perfect opportunity to get her mind off of Kathy for a few hours without getting soaked on the streets of Boston.

'Suit yourself,' Cummings said. 'Three days.'

'What?'

'Three days. That's how long the dude's been in the water. He's a little, um, bloated. Sure you don't want to just View and then skidoo?'

'Have a good lunch, Brad.'

Nikki changed into scrubs and located the remains of Roger Belanger on the center of three stainless-steel tables in Autopsy Suite 1. The daughter of an Italian and an Irishwoman, she could easily trace her thick, black hair and wide (some said sensuous) mouth to her father, and her fair skin, sea-green eyes, slender frame, and caustic wit to her mom. At her father's urging, she had tried to follow his rather large footsteps into surgery. But after a year of residency, she switched to pathology, realizing that her desire to have a life outside of medicine was precluded by spending most of it in the OR or on rounds. Not once had she regretted her decision.

Belanger was hardly the most unsightly corpse Nikki had ever examined, but neither was he at all pleasant to look at. Overweight and nearly egg-bald, he was extremely bloated and discolored, with purplish marbling of his skin. His flaccid limbs were well past rigor mortis. The white scar from his bypass ran the length of his breastbone.

Good-bye for now, Kath, she thought as she began to focus in on the details of the body. *I'll let you back in in two hours.*

'No matter how obvious a case is,' Joe Keller had reminded her on more than one occasion, 'no matter how apparently open-and-shut, you must make no assumptions. Process is everything. If you stick to process, step by step, you will seldom have to explain having missed something.'

Step one: Read over as much information as you can lay your hands on about the subject. Step two: Inspect every millimeter of the skin.

Nikki used the foot-activated dictation system as she went.

'. . . There is a well-healed three-inch scar in the right lower abdominal quadrant, possibly from an appendectomy; a ten-inch scar less than a year old down the mid-anterior chest; a ten-inch scar of about the same age on the inner right thigh, probably from harvesting a vein for his bypass; and a well-healed two-inch scar just below the left patella, probably from the repair of a laceration many years ago.

'There is a single contusion just above and behind the right ear, with discoloration and some swelling, but no depression of the bone beneath. There is a nickel-sized abrasion just beneath the right mandible that –'

Nikki peered at the innocent-looking scrape. It was the only place on Belanger's waterlogged body where skin was actually scraped off. She put on a pair of magnifying goggles and illuminated the area with a gooseneck lamp. The abrasion was actually a perfect hexagon. And in the center of the shape were ten tiny bruises perfectly forming the letter 'H.' She photographed the area, then proceeded with her meticulous examination.

Process is everything.

An hour later, she had accomplished two major things. She had in fact managed temporarily to drive her concerns for Kathy Wilson from her mind, and she had come within one final step of proving that

Roger Belanger had been murdered. She stripped off her gloves, grabbed the Boston Yellow Pages, and made a call. Minutes later she paged Brad Cummings.

'Jesus,' he said, the dishes clinking in the background, 'this pager goes off so infrequently, it scared the heck out of me.'

'You almost done?'

'We were just waiting for our flans.'

Nikki didn't want to go anywhere near who 'we' was.

'I need you to pick something up for me and come back to the office, Brad.'

'But –'

'No buts, no flans. Just go to Mulvaney's Pool and Patio on Route 9, right after the mall. You know where that is?'

'Yes.'

'They'll have a package waiting in your name. Eleven ninety-five plus tax. I'll pay you back. Hurry.'

For the next forty-five minutes, Nikki finished collecting her specimens and waited. Inexorably, her concerns for her friend reemerged. The two of them met almost three years ago at a folk club in Cambridge. Nikki had been a classical violinist from age three when her father enrolled her in a Suzuki method class. She played in chamber-music groups right through college and medical school when time allowed, and was reasonably satisfied with what she got from her music – that is, until she heard Kathy Wilson and the Lost Bluegrass Ramblers play. Kathy sang lead and played strings – mandolin, guitar, and bass – with astounding deftness and heart.

Nikki had heard bluegrass before, but in truth she had never paid much attention to it. That night, the Ramblers, and Kathy in particular, brought her an exhilaration that had long ago vanished from the music she played and listened to. After the performance, she waited by the dressing room door.

'I don't collect autographs,' she said once Kathy had emerged, 'but I wanted to tell you that I love your voice and your energy.'

'Jes doin' what comes naturally. You play the fiddle professionally?'

'Hardly. How did you –'

'You've got a fiddler's mark right there under your jaw.'

Nikki knew the reddish-brown mark and the small lump beneath it, caused by long-term pressure from her violin's chin rest.

'It became permanent sometime during college,' she said. 'I play mostly chamber music.'

'Eyes and necks, that's how I judge a person. Eyes and necks. An' yours tell me you care a lot about people an' about music.'

Half an hour later, Nikki was drinking beer with the band and sharing intimate details with Kathy about her laughable lack of judgment when it came to choosing men. A week after that, Kathy gave her a lesson in bluegrass. Over the two years that followed, Nikki developed into a reasonably proficient bluegrass musician, good enough to sit in with the group when they weren't touring.

'Girl, you're capable of hittin' on all cylinders when you put your mind and soul to it,' Kathy said. 'But you gotta learn how to shut out the extraneous – especially all them folks who want a piece of you.

Do that an' you'll feel your feet start floatin' off the ground when you play.'

From day one, being around Kathy was an adventure in spontaneity. Nikki had friends – close, good friends – from college and before, and two from medical school. But from their earliest times together, often talking and giggling from the end of a show until breakfast, Kathy and she were sisters.

'I've had it with men,' Kathy moaned after she and her bassist boyfriend had broken up for the third and last time. 'Pass the beer nuts is all they're about.'

'That and apologizing for leaving the toilet seat up again.'

'But only after you've gone for another unexpected dip.'

The night of that conversation, a year ago, they decided Kathy would move into Nikki's second-floor flat in South Boston. The deal was one-quarter rent and utilities for Kathy plus weekly lessons for Nikki. Kathy had been religious about giving them, too, when she and the band weren't on tour. She was a treasure, absolutely irrepressible and in love with life in general and her music in particular. Not at all shy about grading every man Nikki dated, she once told a lawyer he simply wasn't interested enough in anything but himself and his BMW to have designs on her friend. They were in a gritty club, one of Kathy's and Nikki's favorites, and the man was fidgeting uncomfortably as if battling the desire to wash down the furniture and probably some of the patrons as well. Often outspoken when she was sober, Kathy had consumed, perhaps, a beer or so too many.

'Give it up, Counselor,' she said suddenly, as

Nikki sat watching in stunned silence. 'I know this woman here's beautiful, an' I know she's smart, an' I know she'd look great at your office Christmas party, to say nothin' of in your bed. But I am the guardian of her chastity, and I'm tellin' you what she's too damn nice to say: There ain't no set of car keys you can produce is gonna get her to where you want her to be.'

Not highly educated in any traditional book sense, Kathy was a patient listener, wildly funny when she wanted to be, and always philosophical in an earthy, homespun way. The perfect roommate – at least until the mood swings began.

It might have been four or five months ago when the sleeplessness started. Two, three, four in the morning, she would be pacing the apartment or walking the streets. Then a day or two or even three would go by without her coming back to the apartment at all. Soon after, her meltdowns began at home and with the band – rages that could neither be predicted nor controlled. Nikki begged her to see a doctor and even arranged for several appointments, none of which Kathy kept.

Finally, maybe six or seven weeks ago, odd lumps began appearing on her face – the first two just above her eyebrows, then one by her ear and another on her cheek. She wouldn't let Nikki touch them or even talk about them until ten days ago. In a rare, totally lucid moment, she sank onto a chair in the kitchen, buried her face in her hands, and sobbed.

'Nikki, what's happening to me? . . . Where has my mind gone? . . . Where has my music gone? . . . Why are they doing this to me?'

Her sobbing became uncontrollable. Nikki held

her tightly and felt the fear and confusion in her body. Beneath her hair she could feel more lumps – solid rather than cystic, slightly movable, not tender that she could tell. Lymph nodes? Some weird kind of firm cyst? Neurofibromas? It was impossible to tell. Nikki begged her to come with her to the ER. Finally, Kathy agreed to see Nikki's doctor the next day. But at the appointment time, she was nowhere to be found. She came back to the apartment once more that Nikki knew of, then vanished again.

'Nikki, how are you doing?'

Dr. Josef Keller had entered the autopsy suite and now stood beside the bloated corpse of Roger Belanger. Nikki had covered the open thorax and abdominal cavities with moist towels. Keller, a German Jew whose family had fled the Holocaust, was a year or two from retirement, but was still vibrant, curious, and energetic. Still, the strain of overseeing a department responsible for the evaluation of more than fifty thousand deaths statewide each year was taking its toll. He limped from arthritis in his hip and had a back condition that made it painful to bend over the cadavers for long.

'I'm glad you're here,' Nikki said. 'This is an interesting case.'

'I thought this man had a coronary,' Keller replied, with still the hint of an accent.

'Well, I think he was murdered.'

'Murdered? Have you been watching reruns of that pathologist show – um, what was his name?'

'Quincy. Nope. I may be wrong, but here, look at this.'

First Nikki showed him the bizarre abrasion beneath Belanger's chin.

'A ring?' Keller asked, immediately on top of things as usual.

'I think so.'

'With diamond studs forming the initial.'

'Exactly. There's more.'

Nikki handed over the otoscope – the tool used by physicians to examine the ear canal and drum. More often than not, she had found residents and even board-certified pathologists omitting this part of the postmortem exam. *Process*.

Keller took his time, murmuring to himself as he examined Belanger's ears by turning the large, violet head from one side to the other and back and inserting the otoscope into the external ear canal.

'Ruptured, with flakes of dried blood,' he said finally. 'Both eardrums were ruptured shortly before his death.'

'I haven't been to see his Jacuzzi,' Nikki said, 'but I would bet it isn't at least five feet deep.'

Five feet – the minimum depth where the pressure on the drums, if not equalized, could cause rupture.

'You are postulating that this man did not drown in his tub?'

'I am. I think he drowned, all right, but I think someone he was swimming with – someone with the initial "H" on his ring in diamond studs – dragged him underwater by the throat – maybe to the bottom of a pool – and then brought him home and put him in the tub.'

'An argument?'

'Perhaps.'

'And the water in his lungs and stomach?'

'I'm waiting for –'

'Home is the hunter, home from the kill. Oh, hi, Joe.'

'It's home from the *hill*, Brad,' Nikki said. 'Did you pick up the package?'

'I did. What do you need chlorine test strips for?'

'I think your "tubber", as you so quaintly put it, actually drowned in a pool.'

'But then how did . . . murdered?'

'You are exceedingly sharp,' Nikki said. 'No wonder they named you Brad.'

She dipped one of the strips into the water from Belanger's stomach. In seconds the tiny indicator square had turned faint purple.

'I am most impressed,' Keller said. 'I shall call our friends at the station house and let them know. This is quite fascinating . . . quite fascinating indeed.'

He limped back to his office.

'Good thing I insisted you do a full autopsy on this guy,' Brad said.

Nikki glared at the man, but honestly couldn't tell if he was being serious. The overhead speaker kept her from finding out.

'Dr. Solari, are you still in there?'

'Yes, Ruth, I'm here.'

'There's an outside call for you. I'm going to transfer it.'

Seconds later the wall phone rang. Brad held his ground as she passed, forcing her to squeeze between him and Belanger's autopsy table.

'Grow up,' she said.

'She digs me,' Brad said.

This time Nikki ignored him.

'Pathology, this is Dr. Solari.'

'Nikki?'

Nikki felt her heart stop.

'Kath, where are you, honey? Are you all right?'

Kathy Wilson's voice was that of a small child.

'Nikki, I'm so cold. . . . They're after me and I'm so cold.'

There were traffic noises in the background, now a car horn. She was calling from a pay phone.

'Kathy, stay calm. I'm going to help you. You're going to be all right.'

'Why are they trying to kill me, Nik? . . . Why am I so cold?'

'Hey, what gives?' Brad Cummings asked.

Nikki snapped a finger against her lips then waved him out of the room.

'Get out,' she mouthed.

'Okay, okay. You know, you're really very touchy today. You must be having your –'

'Out!' This time she shouted the word. Pouting theatrically, Cummings left. 'Kathy, listen, just tell me where you are and I'll come right over and get you. . . . Kath?'

'You're just like all the others, Nikki. You want my music to stop. . . . Is that why they're after me? Because they want my music to stop?'

Her singsong voice was haunting and vague. Nikki imagined her on some street corner, huddled at a pay phone kiosk in the pouring rain. She cast about for some way to alert the police and maybe have this call traced.

'Kathy,' she tried, 'look around and tell me what you see.'

'Nikki . . . Nikki . . . Nikki. You sent them, didn't you. You sent them to silence my music. I'll get you for this, Nikki. I'll get you if it's the last thing I do.'

'I love you, Kathy. You're my friend. I would never do anything to hurt you. In your heart you know that. Honey, you're not thinking clearly right

54

now. You've got to come home. Let me help you.'

'Help . . . me. . . .'

'Kathy, just tell me what to do.' There was a prolonged silence.

'Kathy?'

Nikki waited for another thirty seconds before slowly setting the receiver in its cradle. Then, making no attempt to deal with the cadaver of Roger Belanger, she burst into tears and raced from the room.

Chapter 5

It was a gray, blustery day – a day totally befitting a funeral. Matt was one of just twelve mourners at the graveside service for Darryl Teague. The other eleven were relatives of one sort or another, all of whom lived in the hills north of town. The irony was hardly lost on Matt that in clear view of the dreary, overgrown cemetery were the tall hills that housed the BC&C mine.

But the day held another irony.

It wasn't until he stepped off his Harley and approached the rectangular pit that he realized this was the first funeral he had been to in nearly four years. The last one was his wife's. Matt recalled that day with painful clarity – the crowd, the limousines, the flower-bedecked hearse bearing what remained of the woman he had all too happily pledged to love until death did them part. Only death hadn't ended his love for her. Not at all.

The ill-kept cemetery, bordered by an irregular row of shrubs, was at the center of a broad, rolling, treeless field. Teague's grave, on the far west side, was marked by a hastily erected, rough-cut chunk of marble with the initials 'D.T.' crudely chiseled into it. Nothing more.

Virginia McLaren Rutledge
Beloved Daughter, Sister, and Teacher
Beloved Wife of Matthew Rutledge

Matt stopped by his mother's house three or four times a week, but he visited Ginny's grave nearly every day, often leaving a leaf or sprig of her hawthorn tree, sometimes a flower. Sometimes he would stay only a few minutes, but others he would sit for an hour or more by her stone, reading or just staring off across the valley. Each visit seemed to strengthen the bond he felt with the only woman, save his mother, he had ever truly loved. Of his friends and family, only Mae Borden knew how often he went to the Saints and Angels Cemetery.

'Matthew,' she had said several times in one way or another, 'we all miss her and love her, but we love you, too. It is time for you to pick up the pieces and move on. You have room in your heart for Ginny *and* for someone new. I know she wouldn't have wanted you to spend your life this way.'

Matt would respond with a shrug or a grunted acknowledgment, and head off. There was no sense in discussing something that simply wasn't going to happen.

The gaunt preacher performing the ceremony for Darryl Teague had little to say. To his credit, he made no attempt to lie. He called Darryl a carefree, playful child who had grown away from God and had become an angry and troubled young man at the time of his death. He read some bible passages, and issued appropriate words of consolation to Darryl's parents and sister.

'God works in mysterious ways,' he said as four men grasped heavy ropes and prepared to lower the plain pine box into the gaping maw in the earth. 'God works in mysterious ways.'

There were rumblings around the hospital that

Matt was the last person known to have been in Teague's room before his heart stopped irretrievably. But no one could come up with a sensible explanation for why he might have saved the man's life one day and taken it just a few days later, so natural causes became the consensus around town.

Hal Sawyer's autopsy contributed little to solving the mystery. As Matt suspected, Teague's cracked sternum was the cause of the torn vessel that had resulted in his near-fatal tamponade. Beneath that fracture, the heart muscle was bruised. It was certainly the sort of injury that could have caused electrical instability and irregular rhythms in his heart. Hal signed the man out as a fatal arrhythmia secondary to a cardiac contusion secondary to accidental blunt chest trauma. The lumps over Teague's face and head were nothing more than neurofibromas. The brain itself was grossly normal, leaving Hal with no immediate explanation for Teague's coma. Full toxicology studies would not be available for another week or two, but a preliminary screen had shown none of the depressants Matt had wondered about.

A sharp gust of wind whipped across the field, swirling dust around the small assembly of mourners, who were singing a hymn Matt vaguely remembered from his youth. He found his thoughts drifting to his father. BC&C had been found blameless in the cave-in that killed Matthew Rutledge, Sr., but Matt, only fifteen then, had heard rumors of safety funds diverted, corners cut, and even men paid off.

'We will close our service with the twenty-third psalm. Pallbearers may lower the casket as we recite,

"The Lord is my shepherd, I shall not want. . . ." '

No one except Matt had even suggested that Ginny's bizarre cancer was tied to the mine.

'You yourself said that there are several hundred of these types of lung cancers around the country every year,' BC&C president Armand Stevenson had said to him. 'And with each of those cases, I am sure there's a factory close by, or a lab of some sort, or even a mine. I know you're frustrated, Dr. Rutledge. Your wife has just died. I know you're angry and want to blame us. Well, BC and C is not to blame. I repeat, the company is not to blame for your wife's death any more than it was to blame for your father's.'

' ". . . He restoreth my soul. . . ." '

Matt watched as the casket was slowly lowered down onto the floor of the grave.

Someone from the mine killed you, Darryl, didn't they? . . . Why? . . . What did you know? . . . Had you stayed alive, what could your body have told the world about them?

' ". . . Yea, though I walk through the valley of the shadow of death . . ." '

Matt forced his careening thoughts aside and joined the others in the final lines of the psalm. When the service was over, he accepted heartfelt thanks from Teague's family for having tried to save his life, then took a long, slow walk out toward the hills and back. Ginny would have wanted him to keep pushing for answers. Now she was joined by Darryl Teague and Teddy Rideout. Their conditions were different, but maybe the toxins responsible were different, too.

Well, don't worry, Gin, he thought. *Sooner or later, one way or another, we're going to nail them.*

The one way or another clearly did not include the offering of a $2,500 reward. Matt had printed three hundred of the magenta fliers. Mae had posted half of them around Belinda, and he had tacked up the other half in the adjacent towns. Within twenty-four hours, nearly all of them were gone. There had not been one response. So much for the Healthy Mines Coalition. *Another battle lost,* Matt thought, *but not the war. Not the goddamn war.* He swung the Harley around and headed back to his office. Patients were waiting.

As it turned out, there was a message waiting for him as well – a message from Armand Stevenson requesting that Matt come to the mine offices to meet with him and some of those in the company responsible for health and safety. Mae was smiling as she passed the note over.

'Yes!' Matt exclaimed, pumping his fist.

'I thought you might be interested in going, so I cleared you for tomorrow afternoon,' she said. 'You're due out there at one.'

'It seems a bit presumptuous of you to assume I was interested in going,' he said.

'I know, I know,' Mae replied.

Matt kissed her on the cheek and settled in his office to await his first patient of the day. Not a minute later, his uncle called.

'Hey, Hal, we are officially off dead center. I'm going out to the mine tomorrow to meet with Stevenson.'

'I know. That's why I'm calling.'

'What do you mean?'

'I just ran into your friend Robert Crook. He told me Stevenson had invited you out there. Crook's going to be there, too, as the head of the physician advisory committee for health and safety.'

'Any idea what they want?'

'None, but I'm calling to urge you to keep your cool no matter what.'

'You mean you think I shouldn't tell them up front that they killed my father and are probably responsible for my wife's death as well, and now they're poisoning miners?'

'Something like that. Matt, you've got a reputation with those people as a hothead. Try not to give them any reason to fire back at you.'

'Not to worry. I'm going to be just like Mr. Rogers. "Oh, it's a beautiful day in the neighborhood, a beautiful day for a neighbor. Would you be mine?" . . . See, I'm practicing up.'

'Seriously, Matt, those people hold all the cards in this community. I should think by now you would have figured that out. I just want you to go easy – have them view you as a responsible man.'

'I'll do my best, Hal. I promise. Listen, thanks for calling. Give Heidi a hug for me. And don't worry. Responsible is my middle name.'

At twelve-thirty the following afternoon, Matt placed his two overstuffed BC&C files into a gym bag, strapped it onto the Harley, and headed west out of town. Hal only wanted what was best for him, but he was a worrier. This meeting was, perhaps, the first real break he had gotten. He wasn't about to screw things up.

Next to medicine and motorcycles, the thing Matt knew most about in the world was coal. He had learned about it at the knee of his father, and later on the Internet and in the library. He knew that the Belinda Coal and Coke Company, and indeed the town itself, owed its existence to a huge deposit of semibituminous coal, first discovered in 1901 deep within the tall hills west of the town. Semibituminous coal, also called smokeless coal, was found at only three sites in the state. Smokeless coal was relatively free of impurities, making it the choice for generating steam and also for producing coke. The founders of BC&C had the foresight to construct coking and chemical plants near the mine, as well as a rail spur to speed their products wherever they needed to go.

The entire BC&C operation was located on a vast, dusty plateau, and was completely surrounded by several miles of nine-foot-tall chain-link fence, much of it topped with barbed wire. Matt had been to the mine just once since his father's death, on a guided tour he and Ginny took shortly after he started work in the ER.

Today, he was an anticipated guest. The uniformed guard at the visitors' gate greeted him by name before he could introduce himself and directed him to the sparkling two-story cedar and glass headquarters. Blaine LeBlanc's assistant, Carmella Cassetta, was waiting for him in the carpeted reception area. A former coal-face miner herself, she was attractive in a hard-featured way, and had married one of the execs in the company. Over the years, Matt and she had met on a few occasions and had gotten along reasonably well.

'Matt, it's so good to see you,' she said warmly, extending her hand.

He tried unsuccessfully to read something into her being the one chosen to greet him. He gestured at the spectacular six-foot-square photos of BC&C

scenes – historic and modern – that adorned the lobby walls.

'Thanks. This is quite the building.'

'It makes a good first impression. We do a lot of business here – national and international. Well, we should hurry on over to the conference room. They're waiting for you. I think you'll be very excited with what they have to say.'

You mean they're going to let me live?

'I'm looking forward to whatever it is.'

As they neared the door to the conference room, an elderly black woman approached from the other direction pushing a linen-covered cart with coffee and Danish.

'They'll only be four, Agnes,' Carmella said. 'I won't be joining them.'

Matt thought he detected a pout in her voice at the prospect. Agnes drew back a few steps as Carmella knocked once, motioned Matt and Agnes in, and left. Three men were waiting at the far end of a glossy mahogany table that had seating for twenty or so – Blaine LeBlanc, Robert Crook, and Armand Stevenson, the CEO of the entire company. Stevenson was five-seven if that, with thinning sandy hair and very quick, engaging blue eyes that remained fixed on Matt from the moment he stepped into the room. BC&C was one of the largest privately owned companies in the state, and Stevenson was something of a legend for the aggressive tactics he used to keep every component of the empire profitable.

After peering curiously at the gym bag, LeBlanc greeted Matt with a single pulse of a handshake, then released him as if trying to avoid a communicable disease. His tense expression had Matt wondering if whatever was about to transpire was not of his choosing. Crook avoided a handshake altogether, substituting instead a curt nod, a grunt that might have been Matt's name, and a momentary clash of his caterpillar brows. Armand Stevenson, on the other hand, was smiling, cordial, and very much in charge of the proceedings.

'Please sit down, Matthew, if I may call you that,' he said after his offer of something stronger than coffee was declined.

'Matt'll do.'

'And Armand for me. We appreciate your being able to come out at such short notice, Matt. I understand your father worked here?'

'He was a shift foreman.'

'And he died in an accident?'

'An explosion, yes.'

'Is that where your hard feelings toward the mine and our company stem from?'

Stevenson was firing straight from the hip. No wasted motion. Matt reminded himself that people like Stevenson didn't become gazillionaires by not knowing what they were doing.

'Perhaps that's true,' he replied. 'Some of the things I was told by my father's friends and co-workers led me to believe that the explosion and cave-in that killed him might have been preventable. Remember, I was only fifteen at the time.'

'Plenty of what I went through at age fifteen still influences my life,' Stevenson said, sipping at his Perrier. 'How long has it been since you returned home to practice?'

Matt wanted to demand he get to the point, but remembered his uncle's caveat. Besides, Stevenson hardly seemed like the sort one could push around.

'About six years,' he said, realizing that his inquisitor undoubtedly knew the answers to all the questions he was asking.

If the point of these preliminary questions was to put him at ease, they failed miserably. Stevenson opened his briefcase and set a thick file on the table.

'Matt, these correspondences are all from you to MSHA, the Department of Labor, the EPA, Senator Alexander, Senator Brooks, or Representative Delahanty.'

He slid the file across, but Matt held his palm out to indicate that wasn't necessary.

'I have copies myself,' he said, patting the gym bag.

'At one time or another without, to the best of my information, ever setting foot in the mine, you have accused us of substandard ventilation, antiquated and dangerous equipment, working hours in excess of the collective bargaining agreement with the UMW, toxic emissions from our processing plant, toxic waste dumping, illegal waste disposal, and just about every other violation imaginable short of not enough toilet paper in our rest rooms.'

'Actually, I think one of the miners I speak to from time to time did complain about that as well.'

Stevenson's laugh seemed genuine.

'And now you're posting notices and offering rewards,' he went on. 'Well, as I know better than anyone, your charges and allegations are groundless. And as you know better than anyone, all this paper you've generated hasn't amounted to more than a spit in the ocean.'

'Then why am I here?'

'Blaine?'

The head of mine safety and health's attempt at a

smile lacked any semblance of warmth. He cleared his throat and took a gulp of water. Whatever he was about to share wasn't coming easily.

'Well, Matt,' he managed finally, 'as Armand said, you haven't been the least bit successful in goading MSHA or the EPA or any of the others you've contacted to run an inspection on BC and C other than the routine ones they always do. But that doesn't mean you haven't been a pebble in our shoe. We have wasted a fair amount of time responding to your allegations, and in fact we have invited the MSHA people here two or three times just to prove we're on the up-and-up. But all that has taken up valuable time. So Doc Crook here made a suggestion.'

Matt glanced sideways at Crook and saw nothing other than disdain and maybe even a hint of despair. Whatever was about to be laid out was Armand Stevenson's doing, not Crook's or LeBlanc's.

'That's right,' Crook muttered.

'So,' LeBlanc went on, 'we're pleased to be able to offer you a position on our health advisory board. That way you can be right up close to the action here, and you can see for yourself how we do things. You'll be required to attend meetings every four months, and of course, to submit your concerns for the whole committee to evaluate rather than the vigilante way you've been doing it so far. The stipend for being on the committee is a nice round fifty thousand a year.'

Fifty thousand! Matt wasn't sure whether he had merely thought the words or shouted them out. Given the limitations imposed by managed care, and the socioeconomic status of his patients, he still wasn't earning much over that annually.

'Of course,' Stevenson added proudly, 'the money will be paid to you in such a way – absolutely legal, I assure you – that you will incur little or no tax burden.'

Matt was speechless. He knew a bribe when he heard one. But this was bribe with a capital 'B.' Money had never been a big deal for him. If it had, he would have been much more adept at generating it. As things stood, he was managing okay. But fifty thousand a year extra would enable him to start some sort of retirement fund, as well as enable him to give more to those causes he supported.

'I . . . thanks, but no thanks,' he suddenly heard himself saying. 'I appreciate your offer, really I do. But I find my hands are more useful when they're not tied down.'

'You're a fool, Rutledge,' Crook blurted out. 'I tried to tell them that, but they wouldn't listen. A troublemaker and a fool.'

Stevenson glowered at the cardiologist, then made one last attempt to save face.

'Perhaps you'd like to think over our offer for a few days,' he said, his smile now tight-lipped, his eyes darkened.

Matt shook his head.

'What I want is free rein to bring in a group of my choosing to inspect conditions in the plant and the mine, including a review of your records of how and where every drop of toxic waste is disposed of. What I want is for you to step back and stop paying off whoever you do at MSHA and EPA.'

'You're out of your mind!' LeBlanc shot out.

'No, you're out of *your* mind!' Matt could feel the blood rushing into his face. He usually had a fairly long fuse, but at the end of it was an explosive temper. 'You're out of your mind to think that any decent doctor' – he punctuated the words with a glare at Crook – 'would turn his back on cases like Darryl Teague and Teddy Rideout.'

'Tell me, Dr. Rutledge,' Stevenson asked, now clearly peeved, 'is it your wife's death that makes you so vindictive? Do you blame us for her as well?'

Matt went off like a Roman candle.

'As a matter of fact, I do!' he shouted. 'You're damn right I do! Lung cancer. You should try living with someone who's dying of it sometime! Yes, I blame you. I blame you for every single thing that's bad and sick around here! You're a sleazebag, LeBlanc! And you, Crook. Christ, how can you call yourself a doctor when you turn your back on death and pain? Screw you! Screw you all and your goddamn bribe!'

Armand Stevenson must have pressed a button beneath the table, because in seconds, two mammoth security men in BC&C-monogrammed sport coats and ties were in the room. Stevenson's order was a nod of the head. One of the behemoths took hold of Matt's arm.

'Let go of me, jerk!' Matt screamed. He wrenched away and grabbed his gym bag. 'Touch me again and you'd better have a spare set of nuts!'

In spite of himself, the guard checked out Matt's heavy motorcycle boots. Armand Stevenson saved him from having to find a way around them.

'Follow him outside and make sure he's off the property,' he said. 'You've made your choice, Doctor. Now you'll have to deal with the consequences. You're threatening to take jobs away from folks. That sort of thing isn't looked on very kindly around here. Not kindly at all. Now, get out!'

Chapter 6

Ellen Kroft knelt beside her granddaughter and held the girl tightly by her shoulders, trying to force even a moment of eye contact – of connection of any kind.

'Grandma loves you, Lucy,' she said, carefully enunciating every word as she would to a three-year-old. 'Have a wonderful day at school.'

The girl, now nearly eight, contorted her face into something of a grimace, then twisted her neck so that she was looking upward past Ellen, at the sky. Not a word. Nearly five years of expensive schooling at the best special-needs facility around, and there still were almost never any words.

'Lucy Goosey, are you ready for school?'

The teacher of Lucy's small class at the Remlinger Institute in Alexandria, Virginia, was named Gayle. She was in her twenties and new to the school, but she had the youthful exuberance, upbeat demeanor, and saintly patience required for a life of trying to reach and teach severely autistic children. Gayle held out her hand. Lucy's head kept swinging rhythmically from side to side like the switching of a horse's tail. She neither avoided the proffered hand nor reached for it. Only if it were something spinning, flashing, or brightly colored would she have reacted.

Eight years old.

It had been five years since the diagnosis of

profound autism was made on the girl and nearly four since Ellen began bringing her to school so that her daughter, Beth, could get to work.

'Come on, Lucy,' Gayle sang, leading her off. 'Say good-bye to Grandma.'

Say good-bye to Grandma. Ellen laughed to herself sardonically. There had been a time when Lucy Kroft-Garland could do just that. Well, not anymore. She turned and was opening the door of her six-year-old Taurus when Gayle cried out. Lucy, her back arched inward to an extent that seemed anatomically impossible, was on the lawn in the throes of a violent grand mal seizure.

Quickly, but with businesslike calm, Ellen reached in the glove compartment of her car, withdrew four wooden tongue depressors bound together at the end with adhesive tape, and then hurried over. Lucy's teeth were snapping together like a jackhammer, threatening damage to her lips and tongue. Saliva was frothing out of the corner of her mouth.

'What should I do?' Gayle asked. 'I've seen some of the children have seizures, but never Lucy.'

'Well, I have,' Ellen said, rolling her grandchild onto her side so that, should she vomit, she wouldn't aspirate her stomach contents. Next she squeezed her thumb and third finger forcefully into the angle of the child's jaw. Bit by bit, the pressure overcame the spasm in Lucy's muscles. A small gap opened up between her teeth, and Ellen expertly inserted the makeshift tongue blade device. With one hand holding the blades in place, and the other maintaining Lucy on her side, she nodded to Gayle that matters were under control.

'Should I have Mr. Donnegan call nine-one-one?' Gayle asked.

'No, dear. Lucy will be fine. We just need a little time here.'

'I'll go get Mr. Donnegan anyway.'

'Do that.'

The violent seizure had largely abated when the headmaster arrived. Ellen was sitting on the grass, Lucy's head cradled in her lap. The girl was unconscious now – 'post ictal,' the doctors called the condition. Ellen checked that Lucy hadn't soiled or wet herself, then looked up at the headmaster and shrugged.

'Should we send for an ambulance?' he asked.

'She'll be fine in twenty minutes. This hasn't happened for a while. Her medication may have to be tweaked. If it's okay with you, I'd just as soon she stay in school if possible. Just leave us right here for a bit. If she's not up and about in twenty minutes I'll take her home. But she's better off here with the other children. Much better.'

Donnegan looked for a moment as if he was going to object, but instead reached down and patted Ellen on the shoulder.

'Whatever you say, Mrs. Kroft,' he said. 'You know this kid best.'

Ellen sat on the newly mowed lawn, staring off at nothing in particular, rocking Lucy gently in her arms, and making no attempt to stem the steady flow of tears from her own eyes. Minutes later, the girl began to come around.

Ellen slid behind the wheel of the Taurus and headed north. In moments, in spite of herself, she was reliving the horrible sequence of phone calls that had signaled the start of it all.

'Mom, something's wrong with Lucy. I took her

to the pediatrician this morning. He said she was in terrific shape. Fiftieth percentile in height and weight, way ahead of most three-year-olds in speech and hand-eye coordination. Then he gave her two shots – a DPT and an MMR. That was about eight hours ago. Now she's screaming. Mom, her temperature is one-oh-three-and-a-half and she won't stop screaming no matter what. What should I do? . . .'

'. . . I called the doctor. He says not to worry. Lots of kids get irritable after their vaccinations. Just give her Tylenol. . . .'

'. . . Mom, I'm frightened, really frightened. She's not screaming anymore, but she's completely out of it. Her eyes keep rolling back into her head and she doesn't respond to anything I say. Nothing. She's, like, limp. Dick is getting the car right now. We're going to bring her to the emergency room. . . .'

'. . . They're going to keep Lucy in the hospital. They don't know what's wrong with her. Maybe a seizure of some sort, the doctor says. Mommy, it's bad. I'm so scared. It's bad. I know it is. Oh, Jesus, what am I going to do? My baby . . .'

What am I going to do?

Beth's panicked words echoed in Ellen's thoughts as they did almost every school day after drop-off. With effort, she forced them to the background. There were other things to focus on this day, most notably a strategy meeting across the Potomac at the headquarters of PAVE – Parents Advocating Vaccine Education.

Driving by rote, Ellen headed up the George Washington Parkway toward the Teddy Roosevelt Bridge and D.C. Now a trim, silver-haired sixty-three, she still recalled all too vividly the day just before her fifty-fifth birthday when she went, according to her husband at least, from being 'good-looking' to being 'a damn fine-looking woman for your age.' A year and a half later, Howard had left their twenty-nine-year marriage and run off to be with a thirty-something cocktail waitress he had met during an engineering convention in Vegas.

At the time, it was as if her life, on cruising speed, had hit a brick wall. She accepted an early retirement package from the middle school where she was teaching science, and then effectively pulled down the shades of her existence, shutting herself in and her friends out. Ironically, it was the tragedy surrounding Lucy that pulled her back into the world.

She had always been a positive, upbeat person, but Howard's hurtful and unexpected departure coupled with the end of Lucy's life as a vibrant, healthy child had been a one-two punch that threatened to send her spiraling to the bottom of a Valium bottle. With the help of unrelenting friends and a godsend of a therapist, she gradually opened the blinds again and began putting one foot in front of the other. Now, working out at the gym several times a week, intimately involved in her granddaughter's life, doing volunteer work at PAVE, and functioning as the lone consumer representative on the blue ribbon federal panel evaluating the experimental supervaccine Omnivax, she was running on all cylinders.

Ellen lucked into a parking space not half a block from PAVE headquarters. For a few years after its inception in the mid-eighties, PAVE had been a true grassroots organization, run from the kitchen tables of its two founders – Cheri Sanderson and Sally Lynch, both of whom were convinced that their children had been irreparably damaged by vaccinations. One family at a time, the two mothers discovered they were not alone. And now, through vision, patience, and hard work, PAVE had become a major force, with interest and even some support up to the highest levels of Congress, in addition to tens of thousands of supporting members. The words 'Research,' 'Education,' and 'Choice,' emblazoned on their logo, expressed the agency's goals.

'We are not a bunch of Carrie Nations charging into immunization centers with axes,' Cheri had explained during Ellen's first volunteer-orientation session. 'But we are tough when we have to be. We will not stop until the powers that be recognize the need for research on the immediate and long-term effects of vaccines, as well as the critical need for public education and ultimately parental choice when it comes to vaccinating our children.'

PAVE had its vehement detractors in the scientific, pediatric, infectious disease, and political arenas, but with each passing year, morbidity statistics; clinical disasters; well-attended, PAVE-sponsored scientific conferences; and parents who experienced what they felt certain was a cause-effect relationship between vaccinations and their children's disabilities added to the organization's influence, membership, and war chest.

In the early nineties, the now tax-exempt corporation moved its extensive library, dozens of drawers of case files, seven-person staff, and cadre of committed volunteers to the second floor of a brownstone on 18th Street between DuPont Circle and Adams-Morgan. Following the disaster with Lucy, Ellen had begun to send in modest donations. Later, she took the intensive workshop for volunteers conducted by Cheri and became qualified to man the phones. Then, a year or so after that, word was passed on to PAVE of the establishment of a consumer seat alongside the scientists and physicians on the federal commission evaluating Omnivax.

Ellen was told by Cheri and Sally that, as a retired middle school science teacher without a track record of militancy and confrontation on the vaccine issue, she would be the perfect person for the job. Ultimately, the powers at the FDA agreed. Ellen suspected that those who offered her the appointment were certain either that she would remain relatively silent, or that the scientists and physicians on the panel could easily preempt her views if they had to. Not that it mattered. She was only one vote out of twenty-three, and support for the megavaccine and its thirty components was overwhelming from the start. Even if she opposed the project, which in fact she did, it was clear from the first meeting of the committee that the final tally would stand at twenty-two to one.

The door to the PAVE offices opened into a crowded work area with half a dozen desks, all manned at the moment. As Ellen stepped into the room, the staff on hand rose as one and applauded. She did her best to wave them all back to their seats, then smiled good-naturedly and bowed. Over the past two-plus years, they had all received frequent briefings of the Omnivax sessions, and at times verbatim transcripts. They had all heard stories of how, armed with epidemiological and research data she had painstakingly accumulated, as well as affidavits from experts supporting the PAVE positions, she had stood up to some of the leading proponents of expanding the scope of immunizations. And as often as not, she seemed to have held her own.

'Please, please,' she said, 'that's almost enough applause. You there, a little louder, please. Much better. Now, those of you who desire to, and have washed themselves according to my protocol, may come forward, kneel, and kiss my ring.'

'Hey, where you been?' Sally Lynch called out from the doorway.

'A little trouble with Lucy at school,' Ellen replied. 'Nothing serious.'

'Well, Cheri's late, too, for a change. She'll be here in a few minutes unless she isn't. She says she has big news for us.'

In her mid-forties, Sally, tall, dark-haired, and businesslike, was more introspective and far less flamboyant than her co-director. It was a perfect match – one working behind the scenes, the other in front of the cameras, yet both possessing a high degree of intelligence, compassion, and drive. If Sally had a shortcoming, it was her extreme intensity, which sometimes clouded her judgment and at other times overwhelmed her patience. But that ferocious commitment was understandable. Within hours of receiving his routine vaccination shot, her six-month-old son, Ian, developed a temperature of over 106, had a seizure, and died. Just like that.

Sally's office was as well organized and neat as Cheri Sanderson's was cluttered. On one wall was a professionally made, three-foot-square, multi-colored graph showing that the number of autistic children seeking state services in California more than doubled in the eighties and nearly quadrupled in the nineties. The other walls were covered with dozens of framed photographs, most of them of autistic children, whose condition, their parents were certain, was caused by vaccinations. One of the photos, an eight-by-ten directly behind Sally's desk, was of Lucy. Tucked into the corner of the frame was a heartbreaking snapshot of the girl on a swing, taken a few weeks before her catastrophic transformation.

'Coffee?' Sally offered.

'No thanks. I'm already buzzed.'

'So, in a few more days it's over,' Sally said, referring to the impending commission vote on Omnivax – the subject of this morning's meeting of the three of them.

'So I hear.'

'Any headway?'

'You mean in changing votes? What do you think?'

Sally slammed her fist on the desk.

'Gosh, but this whole Omnivax business is frustrating,' she said. 'Look at this, Ellen, look. It's a research report put out by Congress. Congress! "Vaccine Controversies". Can you imagine? At last they're asking questions. All of a sudden, they care. Here, check this out. All the drug manufacturers are being required by the FDA and EPA to remove mercury from their childhood vaccines. Do you know how many millions of kids got shot up before anyone even thought to take a look at the mercury situation? Here, look, DPT and polio vaccines modified; rotavirus anti-diarrhea vaccine recalled because of infant bowel injury and deaths; hepatitis B vaccine being re-examined. Ellen, the Omnivax forces can't be allowed to win.'

Ellen sighed and stared out the window. Nothing

Sally was showing her now was news to her. Her small study at home was overflowing with notebooks, textbooks, Xeroxed articles, and computer printouts. Over the past two-plus years she had transformed herself from a concerned grandma to an expert on vaccinations and vaccines. True, there had been some victories, like the mercury removal and the rotavirus vaccine recall. But there was also an impressive regiment of respected and renowned scientists and pediatricians who were armed with data – valid or flawed, who could say? – showing the number of lives to be saved by each and every one of the vaccines slated for inclusion in Omnivax. Thousands upon thousands of lives.

'Sally,' Ellen said finally, 'you and I both know the power and influence of those pushing this thing, the deans of medical schools, professors of pediatrics, to say nothing of the President and his wife.'

'Hey, wazzapnin'?'

Cheri Sanderson bounced into the room, a cup of coffee in one hand, a bulging leather portfolio in the other.

Five-three, if that, Cheri was a kinetic ball of energy and optimism.

'Ellen tells me the vote's going to be twenty-two to one,' Sally said.

'What did you expect?' Cheri replied. 'These people were handpicked because they were going to vote yes. Hell, the pharmaceutical giants finance many of their labs. How would you expect them to vote? You've done great, Ellen. You stood your ground and presented our issues as well as anyone could have.'

'Thanks. I'm a little disappointed I haven't had more of an impact, but like you said, the deck was

78

stacked from the beginning. So, what's this news you have?'

Cheri paused dramatically.

'The news is, according to this press release from her office, the antichrist of sensible vaccine thought, Lynette Marquand herself, will be addressing the nation from the FDA on the day of the final panel debate on Omnivax.'

'Nice timing,' Ellen said. 'The final vote is scheduled for two days after that meeting.'

First Lady Lynette Marquand and Secretary of Health and Human Services Dr. Lara Bolton were the heavyweight champions of mass vaccinations. Four years ago, Lynette's husband, Jim, had narrowly won a bitter, hard-fought election. Now, with just a few months to go, he was in a dogfight again, neck and neck with the man he had beaten by only two points and just a dozen electoral votes.

One of his campaign promises – the one with the greatest likelihood of coming to fruition unscathed – was the development and distribution of a super-vaccine. The vaccine, Omnivax, was to be given to infants early in life, and eventually mandated for everyone. Containing up to thirty different antigens – killed or modified viruses and bacteria – it would be given as a shot for now, and orally as soon as research, already well under way, permitted it. The immune systems of the recipients would learn to make antibodies against the various germs so that, should they encounter any of them in the future, their defenses would be primed and ready to fight them off. Editorials had equated Jim Marquand's bold pronouncement with the John Kennedy promise to put a man on the moon. Now, in this arena at least, he was looking good.

'What subtle timing,' Ellen said. 'Lynette Marquand is out stumping for her husband, who is getting boatloads of PAC money from the pharmaceutical industry.'

'And like Cheri said, a lot of these doctors and professors on your panel owe their careers to vaccine research grants from various drug manufacturers,' Sally added.

'So,' Cheri asked, 'do we have any bombshell Ellen can explode at that session? If Lynette's media people do their jobs as well as they have so far, there should be a gaggle and a half of reporters covering the show.'

'I don't know what to say,' Ellen replied. 'Week after week, month after month, I've been searching for holes in what the committee is proposing, breaking down every component of Omnivax, looking for some kind of scientifically valid study that would confirm that one of the thirty vaccines was flawed – or even the opposite, if one of the components was flawless.' She gestured to the graph behind Sally's desk. 'I can't even find any hard data that prove vaccinations contribute to the increase in autism. Increased awareness, one expert tells me. Misdiagnosis, chimes in another. Environmental factors, pipes up someone else. Anecdotal, pooh-poohs a professor.'

She calmed herself before continuing.

'When I first joined the committee, my teeth were bared and I was ready to chew them all apart for what they have and have not done. I still want to do that, believe me, I do. But there're so few scientific studies, even on our side. Nothing about this whole vaccination business is clear-cut except that we need to know more – much more. In the meantime, the other side is going to win this particular battle, and Omnivax is about to leap into our culture. You and Cheri and everyone associated with PAVE, including me, have got to resolve to keep on fighting for the scientific truth, whatever that is.'

Sally looked clearly frustrated.

'All this time, all your studying, and you haven't turned up anything about any of the components of Omnivax?' she asked.

'I'm still working on it,' Ellen replied. 'Honest, I am.'

She felt the chill in Sally's expression and hoped the woman couldn't tell that, in fact, she was holding back some information. She believed that neither Sally nor Cheri could be trusted to remain silent until Rudy Peterson's work on their behalf was further along, especially with Omnivax about to be approved. Rudy had been sifting through information on the supervaccine components for well over a year now without turning up anything damning. There was, however, clinical data on one of the components that he felt was limited in scope and obtained by research that was a decade old and possibly shaky in design. That component was Lasaject, a vaccine against the virus responsible for causing deadly Lassa fever.

Rudy was steadfast in maintaining that the data might still support the conclusions that the vaccine was safe. He needed more time – time during which the vaccine's manufacturer was unaware of his investigation.

Ellen felt certain that this wasn't the moment to tell the aggressive directors of PAVE that while there was no immediate chance of defeating Omnivax, there was lingering hope at least of denting it.

Chapter 7

'Look, officer, I don't want to be a pest, but this woman is really ill and she's running around the city somewhere, certain that some people are trying to kill her. Are you sure word is out?'

'Ma'am, I promise you. This is the fourth day you've called. Everyone here knows about Kathy Wilson. We have every car and every officer on the street looking out for her. We'll call you as soon as we find her.'

Four days had passed since Kathy's call, and not another word from her until just now. When Nikki returned home from the office, there was a rambling message from her on their answering machine, but no hint on Caller ID as to the origin of the call. The disjointed, vitriolic message was terrifying as much for its tone as its content. Kathy Wilson was clearly insane.

Joe Keller continued to be as comforting as possible under the circumstances without being patronizing, as the police continued to be. He was, as Nikki would have expected, fascinated with the rapid development of what he assumed from her description were neurofibromas. Twice he began a tutorial teaching session with her on the differential diagnosis of the condition, but when it was apparent she was hearing only a fraction of what he was saying, he set his marker down.

Nikki paced restlessly about their two-bedroom flat, using a remote to change the five-disc CD player from Mahler to Carly Simon to Miles Davis to either of the two Bluegrass Ramblers CDs, and back. Every flat surface in the apartment seemed to hold a half-empty cup of tea or coffee. More than once she had to battle back the urge to go out and buy a pack of Merits – her brand when she quit smoking more than ten years ago. The living room was strewn with textbooks, each open to some aspect of either neurofibromas or acute paranoia. Outside, a steady rain had let up some, but the wind was howling.

Nikki flipped to the Mahler again – a powerful recording of his Symphony No. 7 – and then knelt down by one of her medical textbooks. Tuberous sclerosis, von Recklinghausen's disease, Sturge-Weber syndrome, von Hippel-Lindau Syndrome. The arcane collection of diseases that included neurofibromas were, for the most part, the result of genetic mutations on any one of several different chromosomes. All of them were accompanied by some sort of brain dysfunction, either by way of cancers or the actual growth of neurofibromas in the central nervous system. The best Nikki could come up with was that Kathy Wilson had some sort of variant of von Recklinghausen's disease, the most common of the conditions, reportedly occurring in one out of every 3,500 individuals. Von Recklinghausen's disease – outcome: fatal, sometimes within a few years from diagnosis. Treatment: none.

The jangle of the phone startled her.

'Kathy!' she exclaimed as she scrambled across her pathology text and snatched up the receiver.

'Nikki, Joe Keller here.'

'Oh, hi. Thanks for calling. No word yet. Every time the phone rings I jump out of my skin thinking it's her.'

For a few seconds there was an uncomfortable silence.

'Nikki, listen, dear,' Keller said finally, 'Kathy Wilson isn't going to be calling.'

Nikki sank back against the sofa, a veil of disbelief already descending over her mind.

'Oh, no,' she said.

'I'm sorry to have to tell you this over the phone. I couldn't think of a way to trick you into coming in so I could tell you in person. Nikki, Kathy's dead. She was run down by a truck on Washington Street about an hour ago. Her body's here now.'

No, no, no!

'Joe, I . . . she left a message here just a few hours ago. Oh, this is terrible.'

'Nikki, you tried your best.'

'I could have done something. I should have said something different when we last spoke.'

'Nikki, you've done everything you could do. I know you have. From the looks of her fibromas, I would say Kathy was in for a rapidly progressive illness, visits to doctors, and most likely premature death. If the reports on her behavior immediately before she died are true, this accident may actually have been a manifestation of her disease running its course.'

'What happened?'

'I don't know completely yet, but I will. The police will be by any minute. I heard that she was in a bar, disrupting the place. The security people escorted her out, and she suddenly broke away and raced directly into the street. The driver of the truck said he never even had a chance to put on his brakes.'

'Oh, God.'

'Nikki, I know this is hard, but can you come in to identify her?'

Nikki swiped at her tears with her sleeve. Off and on over the past week she had feared, even expected, the worst. Now it had happened.

'I'll be there in ten minutes,' she said.

Babies beaten and shaken to death, total body burns, shotgun blasts to the face, long-term submersions, accidents of almost every imaginable kind – over her years in the coroner's office, Nikki had encountered them all. But nothing prepared her for the horrible anguish of seeing Kathy Wilson's battered corpse, stretched out on the stainless-steel table right next to the one where Roger Belanger had been autopsied just days before.

From several feet away, it appeared from the unnatural angle of her head as if her neck had been broken. Above the sheet that covered her body, her pale face with its features already deformed by the multiple lumps was surprisingly spared. But there was a trickle of drying blood wending down from the corner of her mouth – a mouth that would never sing again. Feeling as if her chest were being compressed in a vise, Nikki stepped forward and gingerly pulled back the sheet. The police or the autopsy technician had stripped away Kathy's clothes. Like Nikki, Kathy was a runner, although she was broader across the shoulders than Nikki and more heavily muscled. In fact, the two of them ran together when their schedules permitted. Now Kathy's body looked frail and bony. It had clearly taken a high-speed, high-impact hit from the left. Her arm was ripped nearly off at the shoulder, and the entire chest wall on that side was caved in. It was a blessing of minuscule proportions, but given the angle of her head and the likelihood of her aorta being sheared by the blow to her chest, death had probably been instantaneous.

For a few moments, the sound of Kathy's mandolin filled Nikki's head. It was the soaring, looping, breathtaking solo from 'Nik the Quick,' a piece Kathy had written for her and recorded on the band's second album.

Thank God for the CDs. A part of Kathy Wilson would live on as long as her music did.

Nikki set the sheet back gently, then bent down and kissed her friend on the forehead.

'I'm done, Joe,' she managed.

She led Keller back to his office and sank down in the chair across from him.

'You should have heard her play and sing, Joe. People would be standing and cheering when she finished, screaming for more. Eighty-year-olds would be up in the aisle dancing. She was dazzling.'

'Thanks to the recording you gave me, I can truthfully say I agree with you. Hers is not music I am used to, but it is music I enjoy.'

'I'm pleased to hear that. Joe, if it's possible, could *you* do the post?'

Don't let Brad Cummings near her!

'I was intending to,' Keller replied. 'In fact, I will probably do it tonight.'

Over the years since the death of his wife, Keller had become married to his job. He could be found in the office at almost any hour, weekend or not, hunched over his microscope, asking questions of cells and their groupings, and far more often than not, receiving the answers. It was hardly unusual for him to spend the night in the on-call suite.

'And Joe?'

'Yes?'

'I have one other favor to ask of you. Even if it appears completely normal, will you do her brain?'

Keller looked at her quizzically.

'Even if I see no problem, you still want me to dissect, fix, and stain her brain?'

Unlike most other tissues, the brain required specialized, time-consuming, and expensive fixation and staining. The microscopic examination could not be performed for days, sometimes as long as two weeks. Because of the cost, unless there was specific evidence of an anatomic brain problem on gross examination, the microscopic part of the autopsy was never done.

'Please do it no matter what,' Nikki said. 'Do whatever special stains you can think of to look for toxins. She became insane, Joe. She kept talking about people trying to kill her. In just a few months she went from being one of the most creative, enchanting, centered women who ever lived, to being a paranoid lunatic, frightened that even I was out to get her.'

'How can I say no to you.'

'Thanks, Joe.'

'Um . . . I don't want to make this day any more difficult for you than it has already been, but nobody has notified her family yet.'

'I expected you would want me to do that. Both her parents are alive. Kathy hasn't been that close to them in recent years, but they were in touch, and when she could, she booked the band to play near there.'

'Where is she from?'

Nikki fished out her tattered address book from her bag.

'She's from a coal town in Appalachia. I have the number and address there. The place is called Belinda. Belinda, West Virginia.'

Chapter 8

The phone had rung several times before Matt snatched up the nearest of the four alarm clocks he had spaced progressively farther from the bed. With the clock disengaged and clutched to his chest, he was working his way back into a right-side-down fetal tuck when he realized the ringing was persisting.

'H'lo?'

'Dr. Rutledge, it's Jeannie Putnam in the ER.'

'That's nice.'

'Dr. Rutledge, are you awake?'

'I'm awake. I'm awake. How long have you been working at the hospital, Jeannie?'

'Three months, why?'

'Don't ever believe me when I say I'm awake.'

'But are you?'

'Yes.' Matt switched on the bedside lamp to be sure. 'Only I'm not on call.'

'I know, but a man just came into the ER and said his brother keeps passing out. He's outside in their truck but he won't come in unless you're here to see him. The one who came in said he didn't have to tell us his name, you'd know who they were. . . . Dr. Rutledge?'

Matt held the alarm clock beneath the light. Three-fifteen. He groaned and stretched. A dozen aching places on his body cried out in protest. He had finished sign-out rounds at seven in the evening, then raced over to the gym at the Y for his men's C&A basketball league – C&A, for contusions and abrasions. He had about a minute to warm up before he and a bunch of thirty-to-fifty-year-olds began two and a half hours of full-court battle. Matt had retained some skills from his days as captain of the high school team, but most of the combatants had lost whatever finesse they once had, and had replaced it with a mix of brute force and age-related clumsiness. If it weren't for the so-called referees they chipped in to hire, there was no way the ER wouldn't be flooded every Monday and Thursday.

'I'm awake, I'm awake,' he said again. 'Just stunned. Jeannie, the men who are there would probably be two of the Slocumb brothers.'

'Oh my.'

'It sounds like you've heard of them.'

'Some. I'm recently from Philadelphia. I thought maybe people were making up an Appalachia story just to shock me. How many brothers are there?'

'Four. The one who came into the ER, is he where you can see him?'

'No. He went back out to the truck. Dr. Rutledge, he smells something awful.'

'He may not think so. Do you remember if he has any teeth?'

'What?'

'Teeth. Does he have any?'

'Just a couple in the front, I think.'

'Well, that would be Lewis. Tell him to allow you to bring his brother into the ER and begin to take care of him or else I'm going to turn right around when I get there and go home. Be firm. Each of the Slocumb brothers is more stubborn than the next.

The only chance you have is to stand up to them. They respect anyone with guts.'

'Oh, I've got guts,' Jeannie said. 'It's permanently losing my sense of smell I'm concerned about.'

'Please get his BP and pulse lying, sitting, and if he looks like he can tolerate it, standing.'

'Okay.'

'EKG and routine labs if you can charm them into allowing it. Also, have the lab type and cross-match for three units and be ready to cross-match for three more.'

'You think he's bleeding?'

'No idea. But they would never come to the ER unless there was something very much the matter. They make their own moonshine in this hideous still behind their house. I wonder if maybe the whiskey has eaten away the lining of his stomach.'

'I'll get right on it. You're awake, right?'

'The odds favor it,' Matt replied, hauling himself out of bed. 'I'll be there in fifteen minutes.'

The pounding behind his eyes had him trying to remember how many beers he had downed with the guys after the game. Not that many, he decided, given how easily he had been awakened – certainly not too many to deal with whichever Slocumb was slumped on the front seat of the truck.

The Slocumb brothers, Kyle, Lyle, Lewis, and Frank, were all in their fifties or early sixties. They lived together as they had since birth on their combination junkyard and farm – a hundred acres or so located about eight rugged, densely wooded miles north of town. Their mother, who died decades ago, was perhaps the only woman who had ever set foot on the spread. Not once in Matt's long relationship with them had the Slocumbs mentioned their father.

Matt had heard of the 'Freak Brothers' from his early childhood. Rumors about the reclusive Slocumbs ranged from bizarre to perverse to downright frightening. Like most children in the area, Matt had been forbidden to go anywhere near their place. He was ten years old when some of the older boys dared him to try to get a Little League contribution from them.

None of the boys were willing to go any closer than the parallel dirt ruts to the farm that cut off from the narrow highway. One of them told Matt the place was just a little ways up the road. In fact, it was more than three miles. Matt alternately rode and walked his bike the whole way. At the door of the ramshackle house he hesitated, clutching the donation can so tightly he thought he might crush it. Then he took the sort of deep, calming breath he would one day use just before driving a large-bore needle into a young miner's chest, and knocked.

Twenty minutes later he was on the dirt road again. In his basket was a sausage sandwich on homemade bread. On his wrist was a bracelet forged out of bent horseshoe nails. And in the donation can were two crumpled, oil-stained dollar bills. Before a day had passed, the whole town had some version or other of the story. Matt's father docked him two weeks' allowance for disobedience and forbade him from going near the place again. From that time on, Matt kept his monthly visits to the farm a secret. Since returning to Belinda from his residency, he went out there every so often to do some doctoring or just to catch up. There was very little, if anything, he had learned about the four men over the years that he didn't like, although none of them would qualify as a prize-winning conversationalist. And he knew for a fact that there was a whole new generation of kids who were being forbidden by their parents from going near the Freak Brothers. The Slocumbs most definitely preferred it that way.

Matt threw on his favorite pair of denims and a plaid work shirt, and pulled on his boots. There was no chance he would be returning to the cabin before his workday began in earnest.

The envelope was lying on the floor by the front door. Matt had actually stepped on it before he noticed it. It was a plain white envelope, darkened in spots with grime and grease. 'Dr rutlege' was printed in pencil on the front, in a labored hand. Given the shape Matt was in after the rugged basketball games and the postmortem at Woody's Tavern, the envelope might have been there when he got home. He flipped on some lights in the living room and tore it open.

> Dr rutlege.
> you are Rite.
> Theres poyzon barryed in the Mountin.
> find it thru the Tunel in the Cleft.
> giv the Reward to them as needs it.
> signed
> a caring Frend.

The uneven scrawl was similar to the writing of many mountain people – mixed uppercase letters with lower, with phonetic spelling and no consistent attention to punctuation. Regardless of who wrote it, they were clearly on the right side – his side. His heart pounding, Matt put the note back in its envelope and stuffed it into his jeans. Quite possibly, this was the break he had been working for.

The tunnel in the cleft.

Matt had lived in the area much of his life, and still had no idea what the line referred to. But whoever wrote the note knew, and so, without a doubt, others did, too. Buoyed by the turn of events, Matt jumped on his Harley and raced down the hill toward the hospital.

He rolled his motorcycle to a stop next to the brightly lit Emergency entrance and dropped the kickstand. The Slocumbs' battered Ford pickup, parked nearby, was empty. For no particular reason, Matt guessed the one who had been passing out was Kyle – the most outgoing and obstinate of the eccentric Slocumb quartet.

Jeannie Putnam, wearing a set of maroon scrubs and a surgical mask, was waiting for him in the surprisingly busy ER. She was a tall woman in her late twenties, with a good grasp of emergency medicine and an obvious empathy for the patients.

'We're grateful for your coming in like this,' she said.

'Which brother is it?'

'Kyle. And you were right about the other one. It is Lewis.'

'Labs off?'

'Kyle drew the line at getting any tests until you were here to order them.'

'Lord.'

'But I changed his mind,' she added with a wink. 'I even got him to put on a johnny. He's really sort of cute.'

'You should see the room the four of them sleep in. "Cute" isn't the first adjective that would come to mind. But I am glad you appreciate some of his charm. What did you order?'

'The usual, CBC, Chem 12. Plus the cross-match. Tell me again why you ordered it?'

Matt shrugged and shook his head. 'I don't know. Kyle's never had any medical problem that I've had to deal with. Something you said about his passing out then waking up sounded like low blood pressure, so I thought maybe he was bleeding internally.'

'If you have made the correct diagnosis over the phone at three A.M., I would consider you very spooky.'

'You wouldn't be the first,' Matt said.

Looking absolutely ridiculous in a paisley-print johnny, grizzled Kyle Slocumb, the youngest of the brothers, nodded his approval as Matt walked through the door. Lewis Slocumb, who seldom spoke a word he didn't have to, was seated in the corner, half asleep. Matt went straight to the bedside and began his examination as he asked questions.

'So, Kyle, what's the deal?'

Skin pale, palm creases pale, nail beds pale. Jeannie might be right about his being spooky, he thought. Anemia of some sort was already at the head of the list of possibilities.

'Ah got up ta take me a piss an' got all dizzy, Doc. Lewis says Ah passed out, but he tends ta zaggeration.'

'Any pains?'

Pulse thin, rapid.

'Jes the usual.'

'You drinking much of that rotgut you guys make out there?'

Belly soft. Maybe a little protective muscle tightening over the stomach.

'A course Ah am. But so's the rest a the boys.'

95

'Your stool any unusual color?'

'My what?'

'Your stool. Your bowel movements.'

'My what?'

'Your shit, Kyle. Your shit.'

'Oh, that. How should Ah know? Nobody in their right mind 'ud ever look down thet outhouse hole.'

'Whazza story, Doc?' Lewis asked.

'I don't know, Lewis. Maybe low blood.'

'You'll fix him up.'

'I'll fix him up, Lewis.'

Matt did an efficient but detailed physical exam that showed a significant drop in blood pressure when Kyle sat up. Low blood volume, low blood count. Anemia. Now it was time to look for a source of blood loss, starting with the most likely. Matt pulled on a rubber glove.

'Whazzat fer?' Kyle asked.

'I think you can guess, Kyle. Roll over, face the wall, and pull your knees up toward your chest. I need to see if you're bleeding inside.'

Kyle did as he was asked, but the moment Matt's gloved finger touched his anus, he shrieked, stiffened his legs out, and began bellowing over and over again like a wounded beast. The staff – two nurses and the ER doc – came charging into the room.

'Ah din't think he 'uz gonna lak thet,' Lewis drawled.

'Well, why in the hell didn't you say something?' Matt replied, much louder than he had intended.

Jeannie Putnam and the two others stood at the doorway, transfixed. Matt, his gloved finger pointing skyward like a fan at some bizarre sporting event proclaiming his team was number one, smiled at them sheepishly.

'I . . . don't think I waited long enough for Kyle to agree to this procedure. Apparently it's a touchy area for him.'

'Apparently,' Jeannie said. 'Um, Dr. Rutledge, can we be of any help?'

'Well, actually, you can be sure that blood you sent is cross-matched for six units, and you can tell the lab we really need his hematocrit.'

'Is he bleeding internally?'

'That's my guess.'

'Guess?'

'I'd be a bit more certain if I could get some stool to test for blood. Kyle, how about if I go up there with a little Q-tip?'

'Nope.'

'Look, Kyle. It's three-thirty in the morning and you're sick and I have to know why. Now, either you let me do the procedure I want to do, or I promise you I'm going home and back to bed.'

'What?' Kyle and Jeannie exclaimed in unison.

'Ya wouldn't leave me, Doc,' Kyle said.

'Oh, but I would. Believe me, I would. Dr. Ellis here can take care of you for now, and in the morning they'll find you another doctor. That is, provided you're still alive in the morning. Now, what's it going to be?'

For half a minute, there was only silence. Then slowly, Kyle rolled back to face the wall and drew his knees up.

'Darn but yer an ornery summabitch doctor,' he said. 'Y'uz ornery as a kid an' ya jes got worse since then.'

'I'll be gentle, Kyle,' Matt replied.

*

By six-thirty, the impending crisis surrounding Kyle Slocumb was over. The hard-won rectal exam disclosed black stool that tested positive for blood. Perhaps cowed by the procedure, Kyle put up little resistance to swallowing a thin plastic tube, which Matt slid up one nostril and down the back of his throat into his stomach. Years of smoking potent homegrown cigarettes had done in his gag reflex, making the often difficult insertion a snap. The stomach contents aspirated through the tube were old blood (coffee grounds in appearance) and some streaks of fresh, bright red blood as well. Transfusions had quickly replaced the lost blood and circulating volume, so that by the time Kyle was wheeled into the GI Suite for an examination through gastroenterologist Ed Tanguay's scope, he had recovered his color and stabilized his blood pressure.

'So thet's it,' Lewis Slocumb said as he and Matt walked together out of the ER. The dewy morning air was fragrant.

'Just about,' Matt replied. 'We'll keep our fingers crossed that all Dr. Tanguay finds is some gastritis. That's like inflammation of the stomach lining. If it's a little ulcer, that'll probably be okay, too.'

'But if'n he got cancer he's finished.'

'Not necessarily. We can cure stomach cancer with surgery. But let's not go there until we hear what Dr. Tanguay finds. We're lucky he could do Kyle so quickly.'

'If'n thet doctor sez ol' Kyle has to stay overnight, Ah think he'd jes leave.'

'I was thinking he ought to stay anyway, just to get some medicine for his stomach and maybe another transfusion.'

'Ah tell ya, if'n he kin walk, they's no way he'll stay.'

'I got him to let me do that exam, Lewis. I can talk him into staying.'

Lewis Slocumb turned and looked up at Matt. The sharpness in his blue-green eyes was belied by the rest of his weathered, scruffy face.

'Wer different, Matthew,' he said. 'It's a way we done chose fer ourselves an' it don' mean nothin' ta us thet mos' folks think wer crazy or sick or evil. Thet is, 'til we cross the line inta their world. It ain't nothin' we enjoy doin', b'lieve me it ain't. Kyle an' me crossed thet line this mornin'. Now we want ta cross back as quick as possible. So yew make thet happen, Doc, an' we'll take our chances. Our kind, the mountain folk, unnerstand thet so long's ya don' hurt no one, ya kin be whoever ya want. Mos' people down here in town ain't none too pleasant ta us, an' thet goes fer yer hospital, too.'

Matt was so astonished, he could barely reply. Lewis Slocumb hadn't called him anything other than Doc since his return with his M.D. He had also just spoken more words than Matt could ever remember.

'Okay,' he managed. 'I'll do what I can to get Kyle out of here. But if I think he's in danger, you're going to have to sign him out against my advice.'

'We'll do thet. An' donchew worry none. We ain't gonna sue ya, no matter what.'

He guffawed, coughed, and spat.

Matt gazed east at the flush of morning sunlight brightening the sky from behind the hills. As he did so, he slipped his hands in his pockets and connected with the envelope.

'Hey, Lewis, tell me what you make of this,' he said, handing it over.

He felt pretty certain that all of the Slocumbs could read to some degree or another.

'Don' make nothin' of it,' Lewis said.

'You mean you don't know what the guy who wrote this note is talking about? You don't know where the cleft is?'

Lewis scuffed at the ground with the toe of his worn high-cuts.

'Ah mot know, then agin Ah mot not.'

'Lewis, I just saved your brother's life, and I've been coming out to the farm to check on you guys for years. This note is very important to me. It has to do with the mine.'

'Ah know what it has ta do with. Ya really got a burr up yer butt fer thet ol' mine.'

'I have good reasons,' Matt said, suddenly exasperated. 'My father and my wife, for two. A couple of dead miners, for two more ... Lewis?'

'Ah 'preciate what ya done fer Kyle in there, Ah surely do.'

'So?'

'It's really thet important ta ya?'

'It is. I put out notices offering a reward for information about illegal chemical waste dumping by the mine, and this note was slid under my door.'

Lewis scuffed thoughtfully, covering up the gouges he had made in the sand.

'So, whar's the big news?' he asked finally.

'What do you mean?'

'Ah mean, they's lotsa folks livin' in the woods what knows 'bout the cleft an' the tunnel and even 'bout the crap the mine people keep inside.'

Matt's pulse began to race.

'What do you mean "crap"?' he asked.

'Chemicals, jes like ya sed. Barrels of 'em.'

'Hot damn. Lewis, can you take me there?'

Lewis sighed.

'Inside the mountain? Ah s'pose Ah kin.'

'When?'

'When ya thinkin' ya'll be done with Kyle?'

'I don't know. Maybe late this afternoon.'

'Then we'll talk late this afternoon.'

'But you know about this poison the note talks about?'

'Ah know.'

'And you'll take me to see it firsthand?'

'Ah 'spect Ah will, but Ah cain't say rot now. It's sorta up ta m' brothers, too.'

'Lewis, surely you knew I've been trying to get something on BC and C. Why haven't you said something to me about this before?'

'We lak ya, Doc. But we lak eatin', too.'

'What's that supposed to mean?'

'It means Stevenson an' them people at the mine bin paying us ta keep quiet 'bout what we know.'

'I don't understand. What connection do they have with you?'

Lewis rubbed at his chin, then sighed again.

'Fer a time, we done hauled the stuff in thar fer 'em,' he said.

Chapter 9

For two and a half years, nearly all of the omnivax commission meetings had been held in one or the other of the two main conference rooms located on the third floor of the Parklawn Building, FDA headquarters in Rockville, Maryland. When Lynette Marquand made her speech later in the day, the sliding partition between the rooms would be open, allowing seating for the press, the Omnivax panel, the First Lady's staff, and those hundred or so dignitaries who had managed to procure invitations.

For the moment, though, the partition was closed so that the commission could hold its meeting in private. From what Ellen knew, this gathering was probably the last one before the session to vote formal approval for the distribution and general use of the supervaccine.

She scanned the first room as she passed by. Television camera crews were preparing to beam Marquand's message to the world, and several Secret Service agents were carefully inspecting the walls, podium, and beneath the chairs. Most of the Omnivax commission members were already in the other room, mingling in twos and threes. A few were settling down in front of their computer-generated cardboard place cards at the gleaming, football field-sized cherry conference table. Most of the members were men, and all of the members except for Ellen held either an M.D. degree, a Ph.D., or in a number of instances, both. Beneath their names were printed their titles, specialties, and agencies. Ellen's identified her simply as 'Ellen Kroft, M.S.; Consumer.'

Within weeks following Ellen's first meeting, Cheri and Sally gave her a detailed briefing on each and every one of the other members of the panel, including, where appropriate, the sources of their research funds, and any known stock holdings in the pharmaceutical industry. Ellen was stunned at how much information the two housewives had amassed. They were serious, big-time players in this game, and the worldwide impact they had made in a relatively short time reflected that. She was also astonished at the extent and complexity of the connections between the members of the committee and the drug industry. If Cheri and Sally's information was accurate, and nothing had come to light to make her think otherwise, too many of them had some sort of link.

Of those in the room, only a few took notice of Ellen with a smile or a nod. By and large, as usual, she was ignored. Moments after she took her place at what would have been about the ten-yard line, Dr. George Poulos, Director of the Institute for Vaccine Development, took his seat directly to her right. Poulos, one of those with dual degrees, was a darkly handsome man with classic Greek features. He was always elegantly dressed, and today, possibly in honor of the occasion, wore a crimson handkerchief tucked neatly in the breast pocket of his suit coat. Somewhere in a file folder in Ellen's study, the dossier Sally and Cheri had generated on him reported that he was a highly regarded clinician, researcher, and businessman, as well as a big-time supporter of President Jim Marquand. He could be swayed on some issues, but only if he thought making a concession would improve his position.

Unpredictable, and generally not to be trusted, it read. *Looked like a hero when he helped halt the experimental combined chicken pox and MMR vaccine testing in South America in the mid-1980s, after deaths and immune suppression in a number of female babies, but turned his back six months later when slightly altered versions of the vaccine were used.*

The last line in the report read simply, *Drives a red Porsche 911 Turbo.*

'So, Ellen,' he said, gesturing vaguely at those assembling in the elegant room, 'you have come a long way from teaching middle-school science.'

Ellen stifled a number of retorts, ranging from quick and very funny to downright nasty and offensive.

'It certainly has been an experience,' she settled on.

'And how does it feel to have worked hand in hand with such an accomplished group of scientists?'

'It . . . certainly has been an experience,' she said again, backing up her attempt at humor with what she hoped was a warm grin. 'Are you excited about the First Lady's visit?'

'Oh, very. Lynette and I are old friends. I consulted for her on the vaccination section of her book *Citizen Pioneers*. Omnivax is her baby, so to speak.'

'So it seems.'

'And after we vote, she will be sharing that baby with the nation and maybe the world.'

'Is that why the vote was moved up?'

'Perhaps. With the outcome foregone, many people in very high places would like this to be a done deal as soon as possible.'

Ellen felt her composure begin to shrivel.

'I wish I agreed with them,' she said. 'Have you seen how many letters from parents and grandparents have been written to congressmen protesting that Omnivax hasn't been studied long enough? Or how many op-ed pieces have been published warning against moving ahead with this project too prematurely? Why, even *I* have been getting letters and e-mail – five or ten a day for the past few months. There are very strong feelings about this project among the public.'

'Tree huggers,' Poulos said with undisguised scorn. 'This is only one of a dozen issues they write about and write about. I assure you, the vast majority of Americans are totally behind this project. They're just not the ones who write letters.'

Ellen had never felt too comfortable around Poulos, but now she was beginning to feel a legitimate dislike.

'I still think we're moving way too fast on this thing,' she replied. 'There are unanswered questions.'

'Specifically?'

Ellen cautioned herself not to be drawn into a discussion of Lasaject until Rudy had completed his research. She had purposely refrained from discussing with Sally and Cheri the work he was doing. Bringing it up now with a company man like Poulos would be reckless and dumb.

Lasaject, a vaccine against the horrible hemorrhagic disease Lassa fever, was one of the last components to be voted for inclusion in Omnivax. Endemic to the West African country of Sierra Leone, Lassa fever had been appearing in the U.S. with increasing frequency over the past few years.

'Specifically,' she replied, 'the question of why the current administration is putting pressure on us to approve this vaccine when there are so many unanswered questions and so many consumers who would like to see it scaled down or shelved altogether.'

There! I said it and I'm glad.

Ellen was continuing to research the disease even as Rudy was analyzing the clinical data accumulated for the vaccine. Lassa fever, caused by a virus similar to the deadly Ebola virus, showed up in Chicago and Milwaukee a decade ago, rapidly causing more than two dozen deaths. With the possibility of a major epidemic looming, Columbia Pharmaceuticals, a Maryland-based company, quickly developed and successfully tested a vaccine. But then, as suddenly as they began, the Lassa cases petered out. The potential for an epidemic vanished, and impending mandatory vaccination with Lasaject was tabled indefinitely by the FDA. For its hard work, Columbia was left holding a very expensive bag. Their subsequent attempts to market the vaccine in Sierra Leone were thwarted by political unrest and an economy that was one of the weakest in Africa. The World Health Organization simply refused to send its people into an area so volatile. So, for seven years the attenuated virus comprising the vaccine languished in the incubators of its creator.

Poulos eyed her disdainfully.

'You started out so well on this commission,' he said.

'I'm sorry to have become a disappointment to you.'

At that moment, the chairman of the committee, Rich Steinman, a professor at Georgetown, gaveled the committee meeting to order.

'Well,' Poulos said, turning his attention away from her and toward the professor, 'there are millions and millions of people out there who are going to sleep a whole lot better knowing Omnivax has rendered them and their children safe from a multitude of infectious diseases.'

'Well, George,' Ellen replied, 'it won't be because I voted for it.'

Professor Richard Steinman, looking as puffed as a pigeon, beamed out at the assembled crowd and, indeed, at the world. The partition between the two large conference rooms had been opened, and the conference table moved aside, allowing seating for 150 or so. Behind Steinman on a low stage sat various political and scientific dignitaries, as well as half a dozen of the more prominent members of the select federal commission on Omnivax, including George Poulos. Ellen was seated toward one side of the first row, sandwiched between the head of the Committee on Infectious Diseases of the American Academy of Pediatrics and the woman directing the Centers for Disease Control's Committee on Immunization Practices. Several rows behind her, politicking until the last possible moment, sat Cheri Sanderson.

As Ellen anticipated, the meeting of the select commission that preceded this session had been little more than a pep rally – scientists and physicians verbally patting one another on the back and celebrating that their work was almost done. Richard Steinman set the date for the closed ballot vote on the group's recommendation, and then went around the table for remarks. There was virtually nothing substantive brought up.

Ellen had no urge to add to the merriment by suggesting that there was still time for the entire gang to reconsider their votes. She gave passing thought to a simple 'Thank you for bearing with my incessant questions and for teaching me so much over the past almost three years,' but she knew her superego was too well developed to allow it. Instead, when her turn came, with a final internal warning to be brief, she took a sip of water, praying that no one noticed her hands were shaking, and rose to face the group.

'Everyone who has spoken thus far has expressed what a positive experience it has been serving on this panel,' she said. 'In fact, in many ways, it has been a positive experience for me, too. Please know that I have tried my best not to be too disruptive or contrary as we sifted through mountains of scientific and clinical data and reports. But I *am* the consumer representative on this panel, and despite knowing that our vote on Omnivax is a formality, I would feel remiss if I did not make one final plea on behalf of that group.

'It is far more difficult to stop a vaccination freight train once it has built a head of steam than it would be to keep it in the station until the clinical evidence supporting its safety and efficacy is overwhelming. Omnivax has only been followed in test subjects for six months or so, and many of its components have not been studied over an extended period, either.

'I know I have expressed my concerns in this area before, but I still remain uneasy about articles I have read – anecdotal, I grant you – hinting at an association between an increase in the number of vaccinations we give our children and an increase in immune-mediated diseases such as diabetes, asthma, and multiple sclerosis, to say nothing of the skyrocketing increase in conditions like ADD and autism. I can see a number of you itching to leap to your feet and refute my statement with your data. Well, if I have learned nothing else over the years we have worked together, I have learned how malleable statistics can be. The same data can be served up in any number of ways, sort of like chicken.'

There had been reasonably warm laughter from some around the table, but Ellen could tell by many expressions that she had already prattled on too long.

'So,' she had concluded, no longer at all nervous, 'while this will be our last meeting before we vote, I do intend to keep a close eye on Omnivax over the weeks, months, and years ahead. And perhaps sometime soon I can have all of you over to my place for dinner – chicken dinner, of course.'

Gradually, Ellen's attention drifted back from replaying her remarks in the final commission meeting to the business at hand. Steinman, flushed with the significance of the moment, finished introducing the most important of the luminaries. Then he paused, surveying the audience.

'And now, ladies and gentlemen,' he trumpeted finally, 'it gives me great pleasure to introduce the woman who has spearheaded this project with her caring and vision, the author of the landmark books *Prevention Is the Strongest Medicine* and *Citizen Pioneers*, the First Lady of the United States, Mrs. Lynette Lowry Marquand.'

The standing ovation lasted more than a minute. Marquand, dressed in a simple but stunning beige suit, motioned for all to be seated. Then, for fully fifteen silent seconds she stood there, surveying the audience and gazing into the cameras, emphasizing the significance of the occasion. She waited until the drama of silence was at its peak before she spoke.

'Ladies and gentlemen, distinguished scientists and healers, members of the press, citizens of this country and the world, it gives me great, great pleasure to introduce to you the real star of these proceedings.'

She hesitated just a beat, then whirled theatrically and tugged on a long, tasseled gold cord, releasing a three-foot-wide scroll that unraveled from the ceiling. Printed boldly on the scroll, beginning with DIPHTHERIA and proceeding down to JAPANESE ENCEPHALITIS, was a list of the thirty diseases that were about to be prevented if not eradicated by Omnivax. Third from the bottom of the list, just after CHOLERA and before SHIGELLOSIS, was LASSA FEVER.

Again, there was tumultuous applause.

In a dynamic, well-crafted speech, the First Lady went down the list one by one, saying just enough about each condition to personalize it for the audience and to have every parent across the country sighing in relief that their children would be spared its horrible consequences.

Ellen was impressed with the woman, even though she had voted against her husband in the last election and intended to do so again in this one. Still, with the end of almost three years of hard work at hand, and with Rudy still doing his research unaware that the vote had been moved up, she had trouble keeping her mind on the speech. In fact, she was so distracted that she very nearly missed the words from Lynette Marquand that would change her life forever.

'. . . The President, Secretary Bolton, and I,' Marquand was saying, 'are fully aware that there are those who are opposed to this project. Nothing of lasting value is ever accomplished without conflicting opinions and controversy. We are also aware of those who have tried to politicize this endeavor. Speaking for my husband and myself, I can say that is the last thing we wish to do. That is why the selection of the commission evaluating Omnivax was done with such care. In your programs is a list of the members of this commission and a few of the qualifications of each. I'm sure you'll agree that this is quite a remarkable, independent, and trustworthy team, and I want to take this opportunity to thank Dr. Steinman and each and every one of them for their hard work and devotion to this project.'

Marquand gestured to those commission members seated behind her, and also to those in the front row. Then she made them stand up as a group and led the audience in an enthusiastic round of applause. It was only as Ellen was settling back into her seat that her attention returned fully to the proceedings.

'For nearly three years,' Marquand went on, 'every single member of this august panel of world-renowned experts has studied Omnivax in detail from every angle. I have been briefed regularly on their progress. Soon they will be voting on whether or not to approve its distribution for general use. I promise you, the American public, that if even one, *just one*, of the twenty-three members of this commission votes against the release of Omnivax, we will hold up our inoculation program for as long as it takes to resolve any and all misgivings.'

The pronouncement, enunciated as energetically as any campaign rhetoric, was greeted with an immediate, boisterous standing ovation. Ellen sat dumbfounded, staring up at the First Lady until she realized that all the others in the hall were on their feet. Slowly, somewhat unsteadily, she rose and brought her hands together. It was then she noticed that, from his place just behind and to the right of Lynette Marquand, George Poulos was staring directly down at her.

Chapter 10

More keyed up than he had been in years, Matt rolled the Kawasaki out of his garage. His 250cc Honda was better in the woods and the Harley was without peer cruising the roads, but the Kawasaki had the power to carry two and the suspension to handle most of what the off-road trails had to offer. It was a 900cc Vulcan, ebony and silver, with a four-stroke, five-speed, V-twin engine, and it was to the Harley what a Corvette was to a Lexus sedan.

It was after one in the morning. There was a chill in the air dampened by a fine mist. The darkness was a good omen, Matt noted as he eased his bike down his gravel drive and onto the two-lane road. Somewhere beyond those dense clouds was a nearly full moon.

This would be his second trip today out to the Slocumbs' farm. The first was around four when he rode out to check on Kyle. After the youngest of the brothers had adamantly refused to allow the gastroenterologist to perform another rectal exam, it took some time for Matt to convince the specialist that it was still worth proceeding with a gastroscopy. The exam showed pretty much what Matt had expected, hemorrhagic gastritis, an erosive inflammation of the lining of Kyle's stomach. It was hardly the worst case of the condition he had ever seen, though, so when Kyle's vital signs and blood count had stabilized, he reluctantly agreed to discharge him on medication to block the production of acid, and antacids to soothe the damaged tissue. There was also a strict prohibition on alcohol of any kind, but especially the home-brewed, 150-proof rotgut produced by the brothers' still. Surprisingly, as far as Matt could tell, Kyle had followed every one of his orders, and was actually doing quite well.

Keeping his engine noise to a minimum, Matt slowly made his way along the last quarter mile of rutted road to the Slocumb farmhouse. Lewis was waiting on the porch. A grizzled, sinewy man in his early sixties, he was wearing denim overalls, a tattered black WVU sweatshirt, work boots, and a black watch cap. He had blackened his face and hands with some sort of greasepaint.

'Here,' he said, holding out a small jar of the stuff, 'lemme smear some a this on yer face.'

'What is it?'

'It's black,' Lewis said.

'Ugh! It smells like . . . Lewis?'

'Put some on yer hands, too.'

'I don't believe I let you do this,' Matt said. 'Are you expecting trouble? Is that why we're dressing up like farmer commandos?'

'Don' rotly know what ta expect. The people what run thet mine ain't survived the way they have by bein' stupid. Ya bring everthin' Ah ast ya to?'

Matt patted his backpack. 'Rope, hunting knife, camera, flashlights, flares, a compass, and some jars for bringing out samples.'

'If'n we get thet close,' Lewis muttered.

'You're a cheery one.'

Lewis just snorted and mounted the passenger seat of the Kawasaki.

'Go thet way,' he said, motioning to a muddy track that ran straight through the pitch-black field behind the house.

'This isn't really a dirt bike, you know,' Matt said. 'It's not built for driving through cow shit, either.'

'They's a path out there,' Lewis said. 'Good-size shortcut. Jes keep on goin' straight.'

Following the bike's slashing high beam, they jounced across the field and into the woods. For nearly twenty minutes they rode in silence, following what might have been an old logging road. It was difficult going with two, but Lewis was a surprisingly good passenger. He stayed centered and relaxed in his seat, and didn't try to help by leaning into turns.

The tar-black woods were eerie. Once a gigantic owl, probably a great horned, swooped through the high beam not ten feet ahead of them. The specter nearly stopped Matt's heart cold.

'A little chick,' Lewis chuckled.

As best Matt could guess, they were traveling due west, paralleling the tall hills that housed the mine on the other side. He expected the narrow track to vanish any moment, but it continued straight as a ruler through the dense forest. The mist was making it difficult to see through his Plexiglas visor, so he hooked his helmet to the handlebar.

'You sure you know where you're going?' he asked over his shoulder.

'Oh, Ah know.'

'How much longer?'

'Wer here. Cut the light.'

Matt did as he was told. Instantly, the ebony night enfolded them. Lewis held a finger to his lips.

For several minutes they sat in what seemed to be a small clearing, and listened.

'From here on out we whisper,' Lewis said. 'Ah don' know if'n the mine's got people out here'r not, but Ah wouldn' be supprised. Their security men are the nastiest summabitches ya'd ever wanna meet.'

'Tell me about it. How far is the cleft?'

'A ways. That motorbike a yourn ain't exactly sneaky quiet.'

Matt pulled the bike off into the woods and secured it to a tree. Then he took his compass out of his jeans pocket and checked it with a penlight.

'Which direction's your farm?'

'Back thar.'

Southeast, Matt noted, *maybe five miles.*

'We go thet way,' Lewis said, motioning along the track.

They walked for ten minutes – about half a mile. From somewhere to the right they had begun to hear running water. Overlaying it were the noises of insects and peepers, and the occasional call of an owl. The forest at night.

'Where's that stream go?' Matt asked.

'It cuts down inta the hill rot whar wer headed. Runs unnergroun' fer quite a ways, then comes out in the valley.'

'Where's it come from?'

'Runs past the farm. Thas all Ah know. Ready?'

'Ready.'

Lewis indicated a spot up ahead. Matt could make out a change in the darkness, but little else. Moments later he realized the change in shading was the steep side of a rocky hill. From their right, the stream, perhaps eight feet wide, raced into an opening in the rock.

'They's a bunch a ways inta the caves,' Lewis said. 'But this un's the cleft, an' that's what yer mystry man writ. It's also the one ain't likely ta be watched. Don' seem lak nobody's about, but we'd best keep it down jes the same.'

They stepped into the stream and ducked beneath a ledge to enter the hill through an opening that was about five feet high and three feet wide – the cleft. The water churned and deepened to their knees as it rolled through with them, then broke sharply to the right and over a foot-high drop to a long, dark pool.

'Lak Ah done said, this is jes one a the ways inta the hill,' Lewis whispered. 'They cain't brang the barrels in by this way, though. Too narrah with too many drop-offs.'

'Then how?'

'Some a t'other paths are wider, else they jes haul 'em back through the mine.'

'This tunnel goes all the way through the hill to the mine?'

'It does jes thet. Downhill all the way. The mine entrance is way below whar we are. The storage cave's plumb in the middle.'

'Lewis, how long has it been since you worked for the mine?'

'Well . . . we ain't done none for ten year or more.'

'I'm surprised they let you live, knowing what you do.'

'Oh, they considered sendin' men out, all rot, but then they got smart an' sent money instead.'

'They've been bribing you for ten years?'

'Ah s'pose ya could say that, yes.'

'Lewis, you know I'm going to close that dump down, if it takes the rest of my life.'

'Ah know.'

117

'Well, I don't know how much money you guys will lose when your payments stop, but I want to tell you how much I appreciate your doing this.'

'Ya bin good ta us,' Lewis said simply.

Matt panned his flash over the tunnel ahead. The walls, ceiling, and floor appeared to narrow like a corridor in *Alice in Wonderland*.

'How low and narrow does this get?' he whispered.

'Ya kin make it through,' Lewis said. 'Jes don't take no deep breaths.' He snickered.

'Lewis, I don't know how to tell you this, but I . . . I have trouble with tight, enclosed places. Always have. I get, like, panicky in them.'

'Now, whar in the hell did a Wes Verginny boy come up with thet? Ya gonna make it jes fine, Doc. They's only a few places whar yer gonna have ta crawl an' squeeze through.'

'Jesus,' Matt muttered.

'It's bin a while since Ah bin in here, so we'd best move slowly. Tain't the tight places ya got ta worry about. It's the drop-offs.'

Keeping their lights fixed on the damp stone floor, the two of them headed steadily downward into the mountain. The sound of running or falling water was a constant, at times seeming quite close, at times echoing through a side tunnel. Twice they had to press against a wall and walk sideways along the edge of a precipice. Once, Matt deliberately kicked some pebbles into the dark maw. The splash was barely audible.

'Ah don' thank y' wanna fall down thar,' Lewis said.

The narrow tunnel took a number of turns, and Matt began to wonder if they would have trouble making their way out again. But Lewis seemed to be moving with confidence through the stale, heavy air. Once, an especially low, tight passage forced him to his knees. Matt could not get down low enough and had to negotiate ten or twelve feet wriggling along on his belly, Marine style. His pulse instantly began pounding. He found himself thinking about cave hunters and wondering how they could possibly experience anything but terror traversing narrow slits in rock with no hope of being able to kneel, turn around, or even roll over, and no certainty that the way wouldn't suddenly end. The notion made him queasy and tightened the muscles between his shoulder blades.

Shortly after they were able to stand, the tunnel widened and began to receive broad tributaries from the left. The air became less oppressively heavy.

'Thar,' Lewis whispered, pointing down one such tunnel. 'Thet's one a the ways we brung the barrels in. Hauled 'em on dollies, we did.'

'Who does it now?' Matt asked.

'Beats me. Fer all Ah know, they done stopped.'

'I don't think so. . . . Wait. Do you smell that?'

'Ah do. The cave wer after ain't too far ahead.'

The odor was of chemicals – sweet, pungent, and slightly nauseating. Gasoline, toluene – Matt tried to pin it down, but couldn't with certainty. *Gotcha!* he thought. The frustrating years of trying to show the public what sort of morality was running Belinda Coal and Coke were about to bear fruit. In addition to the chemical smell, the sound of rushing water was again echoing off the damp stone walls. To their left, just beyond where Lewis was standing, Matt could make out a small river, bursting through a wide rent in the rock. His flashlight beam reflected off the dark water and lit the open space beyond. Overhead, the ceiling sloped upward. The organic odor was now intense. Whatever sorts of chemicals were up ahead certainly weren't well contained.

'Lewis,' he whispered, 'is this it?'

'Rot thar,' Lewis said, waving his light ahead, then cutting it off.

For nearly a minute, the two men stood together in the darkness. The sound of the rushing river filled the cavern, which Matt now sensed was quite vast.

'Go easy, an' move right,' Lewis ordered. 'No more light 'til wer sure we got no compny.'

'I can see them, Lewis,' Matt said excitedly. 'I can see the barrels!'

Looming ahead, filling only a fraction of the chamber, were two huge pyramids of oil drums, twenty feet across at the base and ten feet high. A third stack was just taking shape. Beyond the barrels, almost 180 degrees from the tunnel through which they had entered, was another, wider access, probably coming from the mine. A pale film of light, filtering in from somewhere deep in that tunnel, was what was backlighting the barrels.

They remained pressed against the chamber wall, still some distance from the barrels. Lewis switched on his flash, which was considerably more powerful than Matt's, and handed it over. The sight in front of them brought a knot of anger and sadness to Matt's chest. Many of the oil drums appeared to be in decent shape, but some of them were corroded. Several of those – six or seven that he could see from where they stood – had emptied onto the stone floor. Not ten yards behind the stacks, a broad stream was rippling through the cavern, headed in the general direction of the mine. It was impossible to believe the toxins weren't passing through major work areas, and from there into the environment.

'Son of a bitch,' he murmured. 'We'd best move quickly, Lewis, I have no idea what these fumes are doing to our lungs or brains.'

'Ain't nothin' that kin mess my brain up more'n it already is,' Lewis replied, punctuating the remark with a raspy laugh.

Matt slipped off his backpack, knelt down, and opened it. He removed his camera and took a half a dozen flash shots. Then he extracted a plastic bag with specimen collection bottles in it and took several tentative steps toward the barrels. He was about six feet away from them when floodlights mounted high on the walls snapped on, illuminating most of the cavern with midday brightness.

Matt caught a glimpse of gas masks and zip-up coveralls hanging from a rack nearby. Instinctively he dropped onto the damp floor just as two security men entered from the other tunnel. Their exact words were lost in the echoes of churning water, but he could tell they were laughing and joking. One of them keyed a security check box mounted on the rock wall.

Quickly, Matt scrambled on all fours toward Lewis, who was pressed back against the wall in a pocket of shadow.

'Hurry!' Lewis whispered urgently.

Moving as quickly as he dared, Matt was just a few feet from the shadows when one of the guards spotted him.

'Shit, Tommy, look! Over there!'

Matt could see the man drawing his gun.

'Run!' Lewis cried, already racing toward the tunnel.

Matt followed.

'Do you think we should just tell them who we are and that we don't want any trouble?' he asked as they ran.

'They ain't intrested in nothin' but makin' sure we don't leave this cave alive,' Lewis answered. 'Truss me on thet.'

At that instant, gunfire erupted from behind them, and bullets ricocheted off the rocks.

'Jesus!' Matt cried, hunching down.

He had left his backpack and camera behind, but by sheer providence still held on to Lewis's flashlight. He passed the light to Lewis and, following the beam, they plunged into the gloom of the passageway.

Initially, Lewis moved with surprising speed and agility. Quickly, though, his age and years of smoking took hold. By the time they reached the first narrowing of the tunnel, he was gasping. Matt knew he could have moved much faster alone, but even if he had known the tunnels, there was no way he would have left the man behind. He cursed himself for impetuously putting them in such a spot. He could have waited, maybe tried to go to the authorities with the mysterious note.

More gunshots. It seemed to Matt that there was no way they were going to outrun their pursuers, but Lewis had other ideas. They made a sharp right-hand turn, then dropped down into a series of back-scraping crawls that Matt didn't remember from the trip in. The pounding in his chest and tightness in his throat intensified as it always did when he was in a confined space. He forced himself to keep crawling ahead. Suddenly, he was thinking about his father. What had it been like for him those last seconds after the cave-in? Did he have time to be afraid? Would he have been afraid even if he did? Did the explosion kill him instantly, or was it the crush of rock?

Bullets continued to ping off the rock walls and crack into the stone beneath them. Then abruptly, the shooting stopped.

'This way!' Lewis called back, cutting his light. 'They cain't see us no more. Thas why they's stopped shootin'.'

He broke into a spasm of coughing, but hesitated only a few seconds and pushed on.

'You know where we are?' Matt asked.

'Les put it this way. Ah know whar *Ah* am.'

He laughed moistly and again began coughing.

'Lewis, are you okay?' Matt asked.

The older man didn't answer. Instead, he dropped to his belly and wriggled through a ragged ten-foot-long crevice not more than a foot and a half high and two feet wide. He was grunting loudly but moving ahead gamely. Matt closed his eyes and followed along the narrow passage, fearing that at any moment he was going to pass out, throw up, or simply get stuck and go insane. Two feet of extra headroom at the end of the crevice brought him the same sort of relief as the cessation of a dentist's drilling.

After what seemed like an eternity on their hands and knees or bellies, the ceiling sloped upward. The air began to taste fresher. Lewis rose to his feet rather shakily and his head and shoulders disappeared into the ceiling. Matt crawled over to him, tilted his head back, and felt a fine rain on his face. About eight feet past Lewis's shoulders, up a narrow chute, he could see the lighter shade of blackness that was the sky.

'Kin ya climb out thet?' Lewis asked, whispering again.

'If I don't get stuck, I believe I can.'

'Kin ya boos me up?'

'I think so. I'm going to put my head between your legs and stand up. Just don't punch me for getting fresh.'

Lewis missed Matt's tepid humor because he was coughing again.

'Ya sure 'bout this?' he asked when he had caught his breath. 'Ah ain't no flyweight, ya know.'

'If it means getting out of here, I could lift an elephant. Just rest your hands on the top of my head, and as soon as you can grab someplace to pull yourself up, go ahead. Once I'm standing, I'll push your feet up. Ready? Okay, one, two, three.'

Lewis couldn't have weighed more than 130, 140 tops. Matt had more than enough push in his legs to stand up, steadying Lewis by holding his sides, then his feet. Lewis groaned, cried out softly, and then pulled himself up the chute and out of the hole.

'Quick, an' be real quiet,' he whispered down.

Matt looked up and this time feared he might not have the strength or purchase on the wet rock to pull himself out. As he was scanning the walls, he became aware that his right hand was wet and sticky. He sniffed his palm and tried to see it, although he really didn't have to try too hard. He had been involved with enough severe crunches in the ER to know the feel and scent of blood.

He braced his back and shoulders against one side of the chute, reached overhead until his fingers curled over some rock, then brought his knees up until he could wedge himself in place. Inch by inch he worked his back up the rock until he could pull his knees up and repeat the maneuver. Finally, he felt the toe of his boot push down on a minute ledge of rock. A moment later, Lewis grabbed him by the collar and helped him out.

They were on a hillside, amidst dense trees. Twenty feet below them, two men with flashlights were searching along the base of the slope. The guards must have radioed for help.

'I'm telling you,' one of them was saying, 'if they make it out at all, it'll be through one of the places down that way. We ain't doing anyone any good looking around here.'

The second man scanned the side of the hill, missing their prostrate quarry by no more than a foot. Then the two of them moved on.

Matt, who had been holding his breath, moved over to Lewis, who lay quite still on the sodden, leaf-covered ground, breathing heavily.

'You're bleeding from someplace,' Matt said.

'Tell me somethin' Ah don' know,' Lewis replied, grunting the words and stifling a cough. 'If'n ya check m' left side, rot between m' ribs, Ah think yew'll find a bullet hole.'

Chapter 11

Ten minutes passed in absolute silence and darkness before Matt dared to switch on the flashlight. Lewis lay still, facedown, breathing shallowly, as Matt examined him. The left side of his overalls, sweatshirt, and the tattered T beneath it were soaked with blood. A bullet hole – the entry wound, Matt surmised – was next to Lewis's shoulder blade, at about the level of the sixth rib. Blood was still oozing from it, albeit slowly. Gingerly, careful to keep the flash shielded beneath the bloody shirts as much as possible, he rolled Lewis onto his right side.

Using his own shirtsleeve, Matt mopped some of the blood away. He sighed in relief when he spotted the exit wound, just to the left of the nipple. Mentally, he drew a line between the two holes. If the path of the bullet was true, it passed directly through the upper lobe of Lewis's left lung – the larger of the two lobes on that side. But he knew from experience with any number of shootings that, depending on the caliber of the bullet and many other factors, a straight path through the body was often not the case. He had seen a low-caliber shot to the chest where the bullet entered near the spine and exited next to the breastbone without ever passing through the chest at all. It had traveled instead halfway around the torso in the muscle just beneath the skin. In another case, the victim, an elderly shopkeeper shot while thwarting a holdup, had no symptoms except shoulder pain and numbness in his little finger. The entry wound was in the left upper arm, but there was no exit wound, and no bullet in the shoulder or arm on X ray. Eventually, the slug was found inside the man's stomach, having ricocheted down between ribs and lung, puncturing the lung four times before piercing the diaphragm and, finally, the stomach wall.

Matt set his hands on Lewis's back and tried unsuccessfully to determine if the left lung was expanded. Then he put his ear near the entry wound and listened for breath sounds. It was simply too awkward a situation to tell.

'Lewis, how's your breathing?' he asked, checking the pulses in Lewis's arms and neck, which were all strong and steady.

'Be better if'n Ah could have me one a them cigarettes in ma back pocket.'

Lewis grunted as he spoke, and stopped twice to cough.

'They'd be soaked. Everything's soaked,' Matt said, aching at what he had caused to happen to his old friend.

'Ah put 'em in a baggie. Matches, too.'

'Why am I not surprised. Listen, Lewis, as soon as we're away from here I'll give you one. Promise.' Matt cut the light. 'What do you think we should do right now?'

'Not stay here. Thet's fer certain.'

'Can you walk if I help?'

Matt guessed that fifteen minutes or more had passed since Lewis was hit by one of the wildly ricocheting bullets. Over that time, they had traveled quite a ways through narrow, low, winding tunnels. The man might be in his sixties and slight of frame, but he was an absolute bull.

'Ah kin try,' Lewis said.

Carefully, as silently as they could manage, they inched their way down the hill, sliding on their backsides. At the bottom they waited again, listening. Finally, Matt slipped his arm around Lewis's waist and helped him first to his feet, then across the narrow clearing between the hill and the woods. From somewhere in the distance they could hear voices, but the threat of discovery – at least imminent discovery – was gone.

By the time they had gone fifty yards into the forest, it was clear that Lewis was not going to be able to make it back to the motorcycle. Now, breathing more rapidly, he sank down against the base of a pine tree.

'Don' this jes friggin' beat all,' he said, punctuating the observation with an abbreviated burst of coughing. 'Ah spent two year in Nam without gettin' a scratch. Now this.'

'You look like you're having more trouble catching your breath.'

'Ah'll be okay.'

'Lewis, I've got to get you to the hospital.'

'Exceptin' Ah ain't goin'.'

Again, he was coughing, only this time he couldn't keep himself from crying out in pain. Matt checked his wounds, which were almost clotted, and his pulses, which still seemed fairly strong.

'Listen,' he said, 'you've got to stay here while I go and get my bike. Then I'll take you to the hospital myself.'

Lewis's eyes flashed.

'Zare somethin' wrong with yer hearin', boy? Ah

sayed Ah weren't goin' ta no hospital. They's a chance them mine guards don' know who they 'uz shootin' at. But havin' me show up ta the hospital with a damn bullet hole in me would be lak a death sentence – an' probly one fer you, too.'

He ran out of breath before he could say any more.

'Look,' Matt said, 'let me go and get the bike if I can find it. Then we'll talk.'

'Ah done all the talkin' Ah need to,' Lewis said, folding his arms across his chest.

As best he could manage, he gave directions to the path they had taken to get to the cleft. Matt took the flashlight and compass and prepared to set out. First, though, he knelt beside Slocumb.

'Lewis, I'm really, really sorry for what's happened to you,' he said. 'I wish it were me instead.'

'Well, Ah sure as shit don,' Lewis twanged. 'Ma brothers'd kill me in a lamb's heartbeat if'n they thunk Ah let ya get shot. Yer our doctor.'

'I'll be back soon,' Matt said. 'You stay put.'

'Ah 'uz plannin' on doin' that,' Lewis replied.

With his senses on red alert, Matt skirted the hill, giving it and the men searching its base a wide berth. He had never navigated by compass, and after a time, he abandoned the attempt as too difficult and uncertain. It was now after four. It seemed likely that the new day would bring an intensified search for them. In the dark it was impossible to appreciate whether or not Lewis was well concealed. Spurred by the thought that he might not be, Matt sped up, stumbling more than once on thick, exposed roots. Using the flashlight was still chancy, but after he tripped and lurched headfirst into a juniper bush, he decided it was a chance worth taking.

129

With a rough notion of where the hill was, he plunged on, searching for the small clearing where the Kawasaki Vulcan was chained. Getting to the motorcycle was requiring implicit faith in Lewis's directions and a hell of a lot of luck, but not nearly as much luck as he was going to need to get the five-hundred-pound bike back through the dense forest.

Locating the Vulcan turned out to be surprisingly easy. The key was maintaining a notion of where he was relative to the hills and keeping on until he hit the stream. Then he made a cautious right turn onto a narrow path and carefully inspected the woods until he spotted the bike.

Matt unlocked the machine and pushed it twenty feet or so over the uneven ground. Roots stopped him short, and even small rocks threw him off balance. He had estimated half a mile from the clearing where he had chained the motorcycle to the base of the hill. There was a chance that the damp, heavy air would swallow the noise of the engine, provided he didn't go too close to the men who were searching for them. But even if he managed to ride the bike through the forest to a spot equidistant to where Lewis was waiting, he would have to turn to the right and head back toward the hills where the guards were patrolling.

Were there any choices?

One possibility was to ignore Lewis's wishes and get the police and rescue squad involved immediately. Beyond trespassing in an area that wasn't even posted, they had really done nothing wrong, and whether their actions were lawful or not, their findings clearly showed the mine was guilty of storing and dumping toxic waste. Still, involving the Belinda police felt chancy at best.

There was little sympathy for any of the Slocumbs in the official quarters of town, and it was well known that Police Chief Bill Grimes was tightly connected with Armand Stevenson.

Perhaps it would be worth contacting his uncle, he thought now. Hal was tight with Grimes, as he was with most of those in town. Matt knew that if he didn't get help and something serious happened to Lewis, he would forever have trouble living with himself. But he would also have trouble living with himself if he betrayed the man's trust.

It was my clinical judgment, Lewis.

Well, screw yer clinical jedgment, boy. You jes signed our death warrant.

His stomach churning like a rock polisher, Matt checked the direction of the hill using his compass, started the engine, and swung the bike west into the dense forest. So much for clinical judgment.

Bushwhacking through heavy brush on a moonless night aboard a five-hundred-pound motorcycle built for the street was as challenging as running a disaster drill in the ER, and a hell of a lot more dangerous. Keeping his feet off the rests and his legs out straight for balance, Matt weaved between trees and under low-hanging branches, all the time trying desperately to keep from revving the engine too much. Brambles whipped across his visor and gouged his chin and lips. Once, the Vulcan skidded sideways on a thick root and fell over. Matt barely managed to keep his leg from being pinned underneath it or fried on the exhaust pipe. Five minutes . . . ten . . . Surely the engine noise had attracted attention by now. They probably had four-wheel ATVs and were already after the sound. Fifteen . . . It seemed like time to turn right toward the hill.

Hang on, Lewis.

Matt checked the compass, then cut the headlight and instead used the flashlight to illuminate the way. If they hadn't heard the growl of the 900cc engine by now, they would soon. Half a mile out, half a mile back. He checked the odometer every couple of minutes, as well as the compass. So far, so good. When he reached four-tenths of a mile, he stopped and cut the engine. Immediately, he was enfolded in a heavy silence. He waited a minute to let his senses adjust. Somewhere in the distance he thought he could hear voices. He had left Lewis about seventy-five yards from the hill – a bit less than a tenth of a mile. It was time to search on foot.

Matt leaned the bike against a tree and cautiously moved forward. The men's voices were clearer now, coming from somewhere to the right. He still couldn't make out any words, but the tone seemed urgent.

'Lewis,' he whispered loudly. 'Lewis, it's me.'

He moved another ten yards toward the hill. From somewhere far to his right, he heard a whining, high-pitched engine noise – probably an ATV.

'Lewis! Where are you?'

He felt as if he was the right distance from the base of the hill, but there was no way of knowing whether he had ridden too far before turning right, or not far enough. There was also the possibility that Lewis was either captured or, worse, beyond responding.

The whining engine seemed closer now, and Matt sensed himself beginning to panic. He cursed and called out to Lewis again, this time in a near-normal voice. Suddenly, he was grabbed from behind and hauled to the ground. He landed heavily, but keeping his wits he spun away from his assailant and whirled, preparing to be hit. Lewis knelt beside him, a finger to his lips.

'Fer a damn doctor ya ain't so bright sometimes,' he said, pausing every few words to catch his breath. 'They ain't so far away now thet they woun't hear ya if'n you bellered much louder 'n thet – even over the racket a thet damn Honda they're ridin'.'

'How do you know that?'

'They 'uz here. Two of 'em. Not twen'y feet thet way. Dang near run me over.'

'The bike's fifty yards from here. Can you make it?'

'Jes gimme a hand an' Ah kin. This sucker's startin' ta bother me.'

Lewis's bravado could not mask his obvious pain and shortness of breath. Again Matt slipped his arm around his waist. This time it seemed as if he was leaning on him more.

'Hospital?' Matt asked hopefully.

'Ah'd go ta hell first.'

By the time they reached the Vulcan, Lewis was coughing again.

'This isn't going to be easy,' Matt said, helping him to straddle the passenger seat. 'The bike didn't do that well navigating through these woods.'

'Then you'd best move quickly. Thet thang *they're* drivin's made fer these woods.'

'Can you handle it?'

'Jes crank 'er up an' go, brother,' Lewis said.

He set his right hand on Matt's shoulder and grasped his shirt, holding his left arm in tightly to splint his chest. Matt had constructed emergency kits in the saddlebags of both the Harley and the Vulcan. But this wasn't the time to play doctor. He hit the starter and began slowly retracing the route he had taken in from the path. Within seconds, they heard an increase in the engine noise behind them and to the left. There was no way they were going to sneak off.

'Bust it!' Lewis ordered. 'Don' worry none abot me. Ah'll manage. Head thet way. It'll be shorter.'

Matt switched on the high beams and set his foot on the gearshift. He had never tested the Kawasaki off road at any speed, but now was the time. With a slight twist of the accelerator, the Vulcan shot forward into the heavy brush. The next quarter mile was as terrifying as anything Matt had ever done on a motorcycle. He drove between twenty and thirty, paying attention only to the larger trees. The dense undergrowth he simply plowed through. The Vulcan bounced mercilessly over roots and rocks. Several times, he felt as if Lewis was about to be thrown, but somehow the man managed to regain his grasp and hold on. Branches snapped across Matt's visor and ripped at skin that was already lashed raw. More than once they went airborne, landing with just enough momentum to remain upright. Then, after a series of vicious jolts that had Matt close to laying the bike down, they broke free of the forest and onto the path, headed away from the hills. Matt decelerated momentarily. There was no sound other than the steady thrum of his engine.

'You okay?' he asked.

'Jes get me back to the farm,' Lewis grunted. 'An' A'll thank ya not ta take me fer no Sunday drives agin.'

*

Just minutes after their arrival at the farm, Lewis's brothers were in action. Kyle wheeled Matt's motorcycle back to the barn, removed the first-aid kit from the saddlebag, and then concealed the bike beneath a tarp. Frank helped Matt bring Lewis to a tattered couch in the large, cluttered living room. Above them, a balustrade ran along the second-floor hallway, fronting several doors. Matt watched as Lyle opened a closet there and began removing all manner of rifles, shotguns, and even two semi-automatic weapons.

'What's he doing?' Matt asked.

'Them mine people's pretty crafty bastards,' Frank said matter-of-factly, gesturing up at the arsenal. 'We don' lak ta tek no chances.'

Matt used a pair of shears to cut off Lewis's blood-soaked shirts. Kyle returned and set the first-aid kit down by the sofa. Then he went to the kitchen and brought out an unlabeled jar half filled with some sort of thick, pungent, beige-colored goo. He rubbed the paste over Lewis's face and wiped off the equally pungent black. Beneath his camouflage, Lewis was pale and tight-lipped. He looked at Matt and read his thoughts.

'No hospital,' he rasped.

Matt worked his stethoscope into place around his neck and knelt beside Lewis.

'Please get me a pan of fairly warm water,' he said. 'Put some soap in it if you have some – dishwashing soap would be best. A clean towel, too.'

The bullet holes, not at all helped by the jarring ride out of the forest, were nearly clotted now, although blood was oozing from the edge of the exit wound. Matt set his hands on Lewis's back and watched them as Lewis inhaled. The right side

135

definitely moved more than the left. Listening with the scope confirmed what he suspected. A large portion of Lewis's punctured lung had collapsed. He slipped a BP cuff around Lewis's right arm and inflated it to occlude the brachial artery that ran beneath the crook of his elbow. Listening over the artery with his scope, he slowly deflated the cuff until he heard blood begin pulsing through the vessel. The sound marked the top number of Lewis's blood pressure, which was 110, equivalent to the force needed to raise a column of mercury 110 millimeters. Could have been worse – much worse.

'Lewis,' he said, 'your lung has collapsed. The only way I can inflate it is by putting a tube into your chest. And the only place I can do that is the hospital.'

Lewis shook his head grimly and looked away.

'All right, all right,' Matt said. 'I'll do what I can. Frank, there's a small room upstairs with a bed in it. I want that room cleaned out and I want the cleanest sheets you have put on the bed and also two pillows with clean covers on them. Got that?'

'Gimme ten minutes,' Frank said.

'There's more. I'm going to need a pair of needle-nose pliers.'

'Got one.'

'And a plastic tube like the kind you use to siphon gas.'

'Got thet, too.'

'Good. And finally, I'm going to need a rubber glove from the first-aid kit.' He groaned. 'Darn it, never mind. I took the gloves out and put them in my backpack. Listen, for what I want to put together, a condom would be even better. You know, a rubber. Can one of you hurry into town and get me a pack of three?'

There was a momentary silence, then Lyle said simply, 'I got a couple here.'

Matt looked from brother to brother as Lyle went to their bedroom and returned with two Trojans. If the Slocumbs thought there was anything unusual about the revelation, their bland expressions hid it well. Smiling toothlessly, proudly, Lyle handed over the two condoms. The foil wrappers were crumpled but intact.

'I don't want to know,' Matt said to no one in particular. 'I *don't* want to know.'

While Matt waited, he allowed Kyle to swab goo on his back.

'Ouch, that stuff stings!'

'Looks lak ya may be needin' ta get ya a new razor, Doc,' Kyle said.

As soon as the upstairs room was ready, Lewis was moved there. His breathing was more labored now, and his color was clearly duskier. Matt had read about the emergency chest tube insertion in a manual of field emergency measures that he kept on the tank in his bathroom. Most of the methods described by the former Vietnam corpsman were imaginative. Some, like the emergency thoracotomy tube insertion he was about to perform, were downright spectacular. The key to the procedure was the condom. Once it was unraveled and the tip was cut off, he would use tape to attach the base of it to the end of the siphon tube that protruded from the chest. The collapsed latex tube would then function as a perfect one-way valve, allowing air to escape from the lung cavity without allowing any to get in. Cutting the fingers off a rubber glove might have worked, but probably not as well, and not nearly as colorfully.

The sheets on the upstairs bed – a faded floral print – were surprisingly clean and smelled that way. Ten minutes of boiling had removed the gasoline and any other contaminants from the six-foot-long, quarter-inch-wide siphon tube and the needle-nose pliers. The first-aid kit was a comprehensive one that included a magnifying visor, suture material, powerful injectable antibiotics, and the local anesthetic Xylocaine. Matt cleansed the bullet holes, packed them with antibiotic cream, and dressed them. Then he used Xylocaine to numb a spot just below and lateral to the exit wound.

'Lewis,' he said, 'I'm going to numb this the best I can, but it's still going to hurt.'

'More er less then bein' shot?'

'Good point.'

Matt used a scalpel blade to stab a hole in the numbed skin, then he cut the tip of the siphon tube to a point.

'Deep breath, Lewis, then hold it and get ready for me to push,' he said. 'Okay, now!'

Clamping the pointed end of the tube as tightly as he could in the needle-nose pliers, he jammed the pliers in until he felt them hit rib. Then he slid them beneath the rib, through the intercostal muscle, and drove them into the space created when the lung collapsed. Lewis, sweat dripping from his forehead, briefly cried out in pain, then lay still. Matt withdrew the pliers, leaving the tube in place. For several seconds all was quiet, then the condom began to flutter as air under some force rushed through it.

Eyes closed, Lewis lay there, breathing evenly,

utterly exhausted. Matt waited several silent minutes, then listened to his chest. The lung wasn't fully reinflated yet, but there were breath sounds where none had been a short while ago. He wondered how many others had ever actually used one of the techniques from the field manual. Someday, provided Lewis and he made it through this ordeal alive, he was going to write a letter to the author.

Once he had threaded ten inches of tubing into Lewis's chest, Matt sutured the tube in place and dressed the opening. He listened again. More breath sounds, more expanded lung.

'Well?' Frank asked.

Matt gave Lewis a high-dose injection of antibiotic.

'Well,' he replied, aware of the tinge of astonishment in his own voice, 'the doggone thing appears to have worked, at least for the moment. I'll sneak some oxygen and other stuff that I need out of the hospital and come back as soon as I can.'

'Ya done good, Doc,' Frank said.

Lewis's color improved almost instantly. He opened his eyes.

'Ah knowed we 'uz smart ta give ya thet money when ya come knockin' on our door fer yer baseball team.'

'We get you shot, we fix you up,' Matt said. 'That's our motto.'

He was still overwhelmed that a technique he learned reading in the john had quite possibly saved a man's life. What would the gang at Harvard have to say about this one?

'Hey, Doc?' Lyle said.

'Yes?'

'If'n you ain't gonna be usin' thet other rubber, kin I have it back?'

Lynette Marquand prided herself on being, as she phrased it, precise, punctual, and predictable. In the appropriate company, she would, with a wink, add passionate to the mix. Five days a week, when not on vacation, she was up at 4:30 A.M. and in her East Wing office at five. On Saturday, she slept until six, and on Sunday until seven unless her husband had need of her affection before breakfast and church. This predawn Wednesday morning, a rainy one in D.C., she had only one name written in her appointment book, Dr. Lara Bolton.

Lynette had, at best, lukewarm feelings toward almost every one of her husband's cabinet appointments, but Bolton was an exception. Six-foot-one and black, the Secretary of Health and Human Services had been depicted by more than one political cartoonist as a stork, and with her clipped Boston accent was an easy mark for the *Saturday Night Live* impressionists. But her brilliant mind and political savvy made her a frequent visitor to both Lynette's office and the Oval Office in the West Wing.

Bolton, as usual dressed in a crisp navy suit, knocked and entered Lynette's office at precisely five-fifteen.

'Well, Lara,' Lynette said after the Secretary had poured a cup of decaf from a carafe, 'my staff is lighter by one.'

'You did the right thing. Janine Brady has been in this game for a long time. She knows better than to assure you a vote will be unanimous without checking and rechecking.'

'So, where do we stand now?'

'Well, it appears Ellen Kroft does have serious misgivings about Omnivax.'

'Damn.'

'She's the consumer representative on the panel, so there's no way any of the pharmaceutical grant providers can put any pressure on her.'

'Was one of my people consulted before she was appointed?'

'I hate to say it, but it was Janine Brady. Wait, though, I was consulted, too, Lynette. Kroft seemed absolutely harmless – a token offered up by the people at PAVE. If she was more militant, we never would have approved her appointment. No one expected anything like this.'

'So?'

'Our man Poulos on the committee tells me he's dealing with the problem. He's optimistic something can be worked out.'

'Is it worth my meeting with her?'

'You can try, but I've learned that she contributed fifty dollars to Harrison's campaign last election and upped it to seventy-five this time.'

'Oh, that's just terrific. We're three points down in the latest polls. Jim is counting heavily on Omnivax to eliminate that. And here is a Harrison supporter threatening to screw up the whole thing.'

'If Kroft remains on this path, we're getting prepared to make the whole thing look political, being as she is a known Harrison backer.'

'That isn't going to give us back those three points.'

'I know.'

'What about our plans for the first inoculation?'

'I think we're there, Lynette. We have two

women here in D.C. due to deliver at the right time, so that their babies will be four days old when we're ready. Both attend the neighborhood health center in Anacostia, both are anxious to have their kids be the first to receive Omnivax.'

'Uneventful pregnancies?'

'No problems.'

'Do we know the sex of the babies?'

Bolton grinned. 'Mrs. First Lady, you said you wanted a girl; whichever mama we choose, we got you a girl.'

'It'll be great theater, Lara. There's three points in this, mark my words there are. Maybe more.'

'Maybe more,' the Secretary echoed.

Chapter 12

Nikki's drive from Boston to Belinda, West Virginia, was a somber, introspective one, filled with music – country-western, jazz, classical, and all manner of bluegrass. In addition to Kathy Wilson's two albums, there were a number where she played as a studio musician, backing up star performers, several of whom were singing songs she had written. Kathy's musicianship was transcendent on several instruments, but especially on mandolin, which she played as well as anyone Nikki had ever heard.

A chief selling point for Nikki's Saturn had been its sound system, which was surprisingly potent in all ranges. She drove most of the trip with the volume cranked up and the moon roof open. The backseat and trunk were packed with Kathy's books, clothes, stereo, personal belongings, and instruments, including her most prized possession, a Gibson F-5 mandolin, built, she was proud to tell anyone who would listen, whether or not they knew mandolins, by Lloyd Loar.

The day, like the one before, was sparkling and not too warm. Nikki had spent the night in a Best Western just outside of Harrisburg, Pennsylvania, and had left the motel early enough that morning to make Belinda with an hour or so to spare before the memorial service. Between the music and her reflections on the life and death of Kathy Wilson, hundreds of miles had passed virtually unnoticed.

The autopsy Joe Keller had performed on Kathy revealed disappointingly little. Her brain, at least on gross examination, appeared normal. No tumors, no old strokes, no vascular malformations or occlusions, no scars – in short, no explanation for the pervasive psychological transformation that had ultimately taken her life. The microscopic sections of her brain would be ready to be read as soon as today or tomorrow, but Nikki wasn't expecting anything from that or, in fact, from the detailed toxicology examination of her blood.

Tongue-in-cheek medical wisdom had it that internists knew everything but did nothing; surgeons knew nothing but did everything; and pathologists knew everything, but a day too late. In Kathy's case, the old saw couldn't have been further from fact. What they would be left with, even after a most exhausting postmortem examination, were questions – questions with precious few answers.

Even the striking neurofibromas had revealed little. Joe's initial impression of the lumps that covered Kathy's face and scalp was that they were fairly typical examples of the condition – cause unknown, except for the likelihood they were due to some sort of mutation or other genetic factor. He had assured Nikki that he wasn't giving up and would be calling some other pathologists for advice, as well as trying some special staining techniques. But for the moment at least, the questions that remained unanswered were like unfulfilled promises.

Nikki rolled the window down halfway and breathed in the fragrant Appalachian air. She had traveled some in the U.S. – a rafting trip down the

Colorado through the Grand Canyon, mountain-bike tours of Bryce, Zion, and Yosemite National Parks, plus a week here and there in places like New Orleans, San Francisco, and Chicago. But this was her first time in West Virginia. Even viewed from the highway, it was a stunningly wild and beautiful place. The forests were dense and lush, and largely unspoiled. Countless streams and broader rivers wound under the roadway, roiling off through prolonged stretches of whitewater or meandering through the intensely deep green canopy, toward distant, dusky mountains. Waterfalls that would have been a major attraction in many places were simply . . . there. Driving through this country, it was easy for her to understand the passion for the natural earth in much of Kathy's music.

The sign on Route 29 read BELINDA, 20 MILES. As planned, she would be there an hour or so before the service. She could have flown and rented a car as the band had done. But even though she would have to turn around and drive right back to Boston in order to avoid unnecessarily taking vacation time and, worse, being indebted to Brad Cummings for coverage, she wanted the extended time alone to listen to the music and reflect on the choices she had made in her own life.

Her decision to attend medical school, while it seemed to be proving the right one for her, was based on nothing more profound than the desire to emulate her father. Likewise, the decision to become a surgeon. If there was a single turning point in her life and her sense of herself, it was leaving surgery for pathology. At last she was no longer choosing paths merely because others were urging her to travel that way. Breaking her engagement to Joe DiMare – a man everyone, including her parents and many friends, deemed the perfect catch and perfect for her – underscored her evolution. It happened a year after completing her pathology residency. A year or so after that, she was dropping out of chamber-music groups and begging Kathy Wilson to teach her bluegrass.

At its most placid, her existence, like almost everyone else's, was unpredictable and frangible. Illness, accident, errors in judgment, errors in choices – they were all out there like boulders in a rapidly flowing river, along with the challenges of love, work, and relationships. The most she could do, she was finally learning, was to keep searching her own soul for who she was and what she wanted, to be fearless in making decisions, and to try to make every day matter.

The prim, white Baptist church was filling up when Nikki arrived. She was wearing a black linen pants suit with a sleeveless, silver silk blouse. But the day was already nearing eighty, and the crowd was dressed informally enough so that she carried the jacket over her arm.

Kathy's band greeted her warmly, as did Kathy's parents – Sam, a dairy farmer, and Kit, who made and sold quilts. They were severe, taciturn country people, their faces weary from the hardness of their lives, and even more so now from the death of their only child. Kathy had spoken of them with love and admiration, despite the differences in temperament and philosophy that had strained their relationship over the years.

Nikki was surprised when Kit asked her to walk with them along a dirt road that led past the church and through a broad, untended field. When she had

146

called them after the postmortem exam, beyond some indirect questions as to whether or not Kathy was drinking or taking drugs when she was killed, neither parent seemed interested in any of the details of her health or the findings of the autopsy. Maybe the shock was too much for any clear thinking, but Nikki still saw no reason to answer questions they hadn't asked. They quickly made up their minds in favor of cremation and a memorial service, and that was that.

Now Nikki shuffled along between them, unable to fully fathom their loss.

'We thank you for comin' down,' Kit said in a voice that was eerily like Kathy's.

'I miss her terribly,' Nikki said. 'She was a year younger than me, and I was the one who had spent my life in the big city, but she was so wise and so tuned in to life that I sometimes thought of her as an older sister.'

'I understand. Even when she was real young she was sometimes like that for me, too.'

'When I was first getting to know her, I played classical violin. I asked her if she could turn me into a bluegrass fiddle player. She said she would see. It wasn't that easy a decision. She picked me up the next evening and drove me way out into the country to this huge field. Then she set out a blanket, brought out some horrible-tasting apple whiskey in a flask, and a portable CD player. We stayed up way past dawn listening to one bluegrass performer after another and sipping that horrible stuff until it tasted like honey. In the morning, I was so badly bitten by mosquitoes that I could barely move. She didn't have a bite on her. Turns out she was swathed in bug repellent. She wanted to see if I got immersed enough in the music that I didn't notice I was being eaten alive. The next day she gave me my first lesson. Goodness, but she could play.'

'We know,' Kit said. 'We know. Sometimes the Lord's ways are hidden from us until we are ready to understand and accept them.' She guided her husband and Nikki back around toward the church, where Nikki could see the crowd continuing to build, then asked, 'Nikki, Sam and I want to know, Kathy had the most beautiful face – an angel's face. Did the accident . . . ? What I mean is . . .'

'Kit, she was beautiful at the end, too,' Nikki said, willing away countless unpleasant images. 'Two bones in her neck separated. That's why she died. Nothing else. Her face was completely spared.'

'Thank God,' Sam muttered. 'She always insisted on cremation if'n anything ever happened ta her, so we felt we had ta do it.'

Nikki accompanied Kathy's parents into the sanctuary and sat beside them during the service. They had asked her over the phone to speak at the service. Rather than deliver memories of her friend, which she simply wasn't sure she was strong enough to do, Nikki had chosen to read some of Kathy's poetry, along with the words to two songs whose melodies Kathy had not yet written. She had to stop several times to compose herself, but there was a strength and unabashed faith in the room that made anything she said or did feel right. The service lasted less than an hour and was so poignant, with hymns, readings, recollections, two cuts from Kathy's CDs, and a song by some friends and the band, that few eyes were dry by the time it was over.

The reception in the social hall adjacent to the

church was much more of a celebration of Kathy's life and music than a memorial. With her band at the core, musicians came, played for a time, went, and came back again. Most of them were amateurs, yet all of them amazingly talented. Someone would name a tune or simply start playing, and instantly the others would join in. Nikki changed into jeans and sneakers, and brought her fiddle in from the car. She was still pretty much of a greenhorn by comparison to most of the others, but she managed to sit in on the jam for half an hour or so without disgracing herself, and played a lick in 'Foggy Mountain Breakdown' that actually earned applause from the banjo player. Finally, mopping her brow with a handkerchief she kept in her case for just that purpose, she took a break and headed for the punch bowl.

'Here,' a man said from her right. 'Let me get you a cup. Alcohol-free or supercharged?'

He was somewhere in his forties and good-looking in a broad-shouldered, straitlaced sort of way, with razor-cut sandy hair, a muscular build, and dark gray eyes that were too small for Nikki's taste. He was wearing a white dress shirt and a black string tie with a large turquoise stone mounted on the slide. His mountain twang sounded far less pronounced than that of the others she had met, and his manner and speech had her guessing that he was college educated.

'Oh, no alcohol, please,' she said. 'I've got a long drive ahead of me this afternoon.'

'In that case, I must absolutely insist you stay away from the high-test stuff. For one thing, I think I know whose still it was brewed in, and for another, I'm chief of police here in Belinda. Bill Grimes.'

He extended his hand and Nikki took it. His grip was confident.

'Nikki Solari. Pleased to meet you.'

'That was a very moving reading you did.'

'Kathy was a wonderful writer. Her words are important to a lot of folks.'

'Kit told me you're a doctor.'

'I'm a pathologist by trade, but a musician by passion. Kathy was in the process of transforming me from a violinist into a fiddle player.'

'I was listening. She's done a fine job of that.'

'Thanks. I'm not in her class, but then again, not many are.'

'I didn't grow up in these parts, but I heard her daddy taught her music, and that since she was a child people flocked to wherever she was playing. Folks around here sort of took it personally when she left.'

Nikki smiled at the notion.

'I can believe that,' she said.

'Her death shocked us all. Dr. Solari, if the whole thing is still too raw for you to talk about, I certainly understand, but as a cop, and a friend of the family, I'm curious to know as much as I can about how it happened.'

'Talking about things helps me deal with them – even if they're very painful things like this. And it's fine to call me Nikki.'

'Bill for me. I get "Chief" so much it's like taken over as my name.'

The policeman had an easy, reassuring manner. Carrying their drinks they left the crowd and walked over to a solitary bench, set alongside a massive willow. The sun was beginning its move to the west, and off in the distance, the lush hills seemed phosphorescent. Nikki had never been much of a visual artist, but if she were, the colors of West Virginia would be Nirvana.

'So you're a pathologist,' Grimes said when they had settled down at either end of the bench.

'I work for the ME's office.'

'Interesting. Our ME was here at the service, but he left a while ago. Tall, thin, sort of dignified guy wearin' a grayish suit.'

'I'm afraid I haven't been noticing much of anything today,' Nikki said.

'That's understandable. Well, he's a pathologist just like you. Doc Sawyer's his name – *Hal* Sawyer. Nice guy. Real smart, too – not just concerning medical things, either. About Kathy?'

'Well, her death was actually handled by our office. My boss, Josef Keller, the chief medical examiner for the state, did the post.'

'He find anything out of the ordinary? Drugs? Alcohol?'

'Nothing like that. How much do you know about what was going on with Kathy before her accident?'

Grimes shook his head.

'All I know is that she was run over by a car.'

'It was a truck. She ran out of a bar and into the street. The poor driver never even had the chance to hit his brakes.'

'But you said she wasn't drinking.'

'Her blood alcohol level was zero. Toxic screen – at least the preliminary panel we've gotten back so far – was totally negative. She was insane, Bill. Absolutely insane. She had been slipping into a horrible paranoia for months before she died. Thought there were people out to kill her. I kept trying to get her help, but the more I tried, the further she withdrew from me.'

'Did you speak with her family?'

'I called them once, about four weeks before Kathy was killed, but they were just bewildered and also sounded angry at Kathy for having drifted away from them. They couldn't understand what they could do to help her if I was a doctor and I couldn't do anything.'

'The Wilsons are good people,' Grimes said, 'but simple and very set in their ways. Kathy was their only kid. They never thought she should have left.'

'I know.'

'So that was it? She just went crazy?'

'Just about. As I said, she was convinced at the end that men were after her, trying to kill her. I think she was trying to get away from them when she died.'

'Is it possible she was right?'

'Not that I could see.'

'So the autopsy your boss did didn't show anything else?'

'Nothing we weren't already aware of. There was one other thing that was pretty unusual about her, though. Something I didn't see any reason to share with her parents. Over a number of months before she died, coinciding to some extent with the development of her madness, her face was becoming disfigured by these lumps – neurofibromas, we call them.'

'Neu-ro-fi-bro-mas.' Grimes said the word slowly, as if committing it to his vocabulary. 'Cause?'

'Unknown, except maybe bad genetics or a mutation, that sort of thing. Possibly a virus. By any chance, did you ever see the movie *The Elephant Man*?'

''Fraid not. But I think I know what you're talking about.'

'Well, in its worst form, her condition would be like that. And it was getting there. She was pretty deformed at the end. No telling what she would have looked like had she lived.'

Nikki glanced up at the sun and then checked her watch.

'You really plannin' on leaving today?' Grimes asked.

'I'm on call for my office tomorrow night, so I have to be back by then. I'm one of the world's least reliable nighttime drivers, so I plan on going as far as New York, then the rest of the way in the morning. I'd like to play just a little bit longer, though, before I take off. There are a couple of Kathy's pieces I'd like to try with the gang.'

'I sure wish you could stay,' Grimes said, with invitation in his voice and expression.

'Thanks for the thought,' she said, not at all threatened by the police chief's tone, 'but I'm locked into getting home.' She stood. 'Why don't you come in and let us play something for you. Do you have any favorites you haven't heard?'

'I'm not much of a bluegrass expert,' Grimes replied, 'although I do enjoy the music. Tell me something,' he said, as he walked her back to the social hall, 'why did you decide not to tell the Wilsons about Kathy's neu-ro-fi-bromas?'

'I didn't see any reason to tell them over the phone. Then after I met them in person here, I still wasn't sure I wanted to. Then they told me . . . Kit asked if Kathy's face had been battered in the

153

accident. The poor dears had enough trouble getting their minds around her deranged mental state. It seemed cruel to tell them her face was deformed as well. Besides, the microscopic examination of her brain and the neurofibromas isn't done yet. If it shows anything to explain what happened, I plan to share that news with them. If it doesn't provide any explanation, I'll have to decide if it's worth telling them at all. As you know, Kathy's an only child, so there's no need to worry about some evil gene working its way through her family.'

'If I were in your position, I don't think I'd mention it to the Wilsons, either,' Grimes said. 'Nothing to gain.'

'Nothing to gain,' Nikki echoed.

'Well,' he said when they reached the social hall, 'I'm sorry to have met you under these circumstances, but I'm certainly glad to have met you.'

'Same here.'

'Who knows? Maybe we'll see each other again.'

'You never can tell. If I find myself headed back this way for any reason, I'll call you at the station.'

'Do that. And I'll call you at the coroner's office if I find myself in Boston.'

'I'd like that,' she said.

'And Nikki, if anything does turn up on those microscopic slides you spoke about, please let me know.'

Nikki picked up her fiddle and gently rubbed it down with a cloth.

'I'll do that, Bill,' she said, taking her seat among the musicians, who were currently between numbers. 'Since you don't have a request, I'll pick one. We've been playing some Alison Krauss. She was Kathy's idol. Mine, too.'

The smart, distinguished-looking medical examiner she had never gotten to meet might have left, but few others had. People were gathered around the buffet table and scattered across the dance floor, arm in arm, waiting for the next tune. Kathy would have approved and probably would have insisted on adding a keg of Bud to the celebration of her life.

Nikki closed her eyes and let the music fill her mind and her body. A few hours ago she was a total stranger in Belinda. Now, because of Kathy and the gift of bluegrass, she was connected to the town and the forests and the mountains and the water in ways that would endure as long as she did.

It was nearing three-thirty. Nikki helped transfer Kathy's things into the Wilsons' Dodge Ram pickup. After everything was set in place, she reached into the trunk of the Saturn and brought out the case containing Kathy's exquisite mandolin.

'Here,' she said, handing it over to Sam. 'Chief Grimes told me you taught Kathy to play.'

'Only fer a couple a weeks,' he replied, taking the instrument out and cradling it in his huge hands, a soft, wistful expression on his face. 'After thet she begun teachin' me.'

He ran his thick-jointed thumb over the strings, which Nikki had tuned before loading the instrument into the trunk. Then he took one of the picks from the case and played a brief riff of remarkable clarity and some technical difficulty.

'That was great,' Nikki said. 'No wonder Kathy was so good. It's in her blood.'

'Here,' Sam said, placing the instrument back in its case and passing it back to her. 'I want you ta have it.'

'But I –'

From beyond where Sam was standing, Kit stopped her short with a definitive shake of her head.

'Sam's got arthritis pretty good,' she said. 'We'd both be happy knowin' Kathy's instrument is with you.'

Nothing in either of Kathy's parents' faces encouraged debate.

'I may come back for a lesson on it,' she said.

'You'd be welcome if'n ya did,' Sam managed, his eyes moist.

Nikki set the instrument on the front seat, embraced the Wilsons, then headed down the arching church driveway toward the road north. At the outskirts of Belinda, she paused and gazed back through the rear window, down the length of Main Street. It really was a lovely town – gentle, earnest people; beautiful countryside; and an appealing pace of life. She ached to think she would never get to know the place with her friend.

She turned north, retracing her route onto the narrow, two-lane road that would bring her to Route 29. The road, snaking through dense forest, was deserted, just as it had been on the trip into town. Nikki pulled on a blue Red Sox cap to control her hair and opened the moon roof and her window. Sunlight filtered through the tops of the trees, dappling the pavement. As she rounded a tight turn, she saw a car pulled over at an angle on the narrow shoulder. A man in jeans and a yellow T lay face-down on the road. A heavyset man in a dark suit knelt beside him. Nikki's immediate assessment of the scene was that the man had struck a pedestrian. He looked up as she approached, then stood and waved to her. Nikki pulled over, scanning the ground around the victim for blood.

The man, in his thirties and obviously distressed, hurried to her window.

'I . . . I didn't see him. I came around the corner and there he was. Do you have a cell phone?'

'Is he breathing?'

'I . . . I think so.'

Nikki stepped from the car and hurried to the motionless man, expecting the worst. No blood, no obvious injuries. There was a slight rise and fall of his chest – he was most definitely breathing. She had no intention of rolling him over without stabilizing his neck. She knelt down next to him, peered at his face, and reached across to check his pulse. At that instant, he rolled over, and at the same moment, the large man standing behind her grabbed her roughly by the hair and clamped a cloth over her nose and mouth. It was soaked with a substance she knew well from the lab – chloroform.

'Beddy-bye, Doc,' he said.

Chapter 13

During her one year of surgical residency before the switch to pathology, Nikki had earned the nickname 'Cube' because of her absolute coolness and composure in the face of even the direst medical emergencies. She never could fully explain what seemed to be an inborn trait, but once she did check her pulse seconds after saving a patient by performing an emergency tracheotomy. Fifty-eight.

'I guess I'm just a very logical person,' she once told a medical friend by way of explanation. 'And a very positive one, too. Once a situation begins – critical or otherwise – all I focus on is what I have to do, almost never on what will happen if I screw up.'

The whiff of chloroform gave Nikki three seconds before the obese man in the business suit clamped the cloth over her mouth. As with emergencies in the hospital, her reactions over those precious seconds seemed reflex, but were, in fact, the product of a number of rapid-fire observations and deductions.

Chloroform – take in a sharp breath and hold it! . . . Quick, purposeful movements by the so-called victim – it's a trap! . . . Beddy-bye, Doc – he knows who I am! This is no random mugging. Trying to beg – to talk them out of whatever they're going to do – would be hopeless. . . .

Three times in her life Nikki had taken self-defense courses for women. She came away from each of them frustrated, embarrassed, and a little frightened by how much she had already forgotten. But there were three recurring rules the courses had permanently impressed on her brain: Do something quickly; go for the testicles, the nose, or the knee; and as soon as possible, run. Still on her knees, her back to the massive assailant, Nikki drew her fist up in front of her eyes and jackhammered her elbow back into the man's groin with all the force she could muster. Air exploded from his lungs. He grunted, released her, stumbled backward briefly, and dropped onto his butt like a sack of grain thrown from a truck. The chloroform-soaked washcloth flew off to one side. The rail-thin man in the yellow T-shirt was scrambling to his feet, but Nikki was quicker to hers. She kicked him viciously under the chin as he was coming up, snapping his teeth together and sending him sprawling backward. Then she whirled and sprinted across the road into the forest.

'Get her, Verne!' the larger man shouted, speaking without the mountain twang Nikki had become used to over the day. 'For chrissakes, just shoot the bitch!'

'Shit, Larry, she broke my tooth. She broke my fucking tooth in half!'

Nikki was several paces inside the trees when she dared checking over her shoulder. Larry, Mr. Business Suit, was wobbly, but upright. He had shed his jacket, revealing a torso the size of a Volkswagen. Sun sparkled off his expansive white dress shirt, highlighting a shoulder holster on the left and dark sweat stains beneath his ham-hock arms. Verne, also on his feet, seemed less dazed. He had pulled a snub-nosed pistol out of the front of his waistband and was starting across the road after her, still rubbing his jaw. He fired once, but Nikki was charging ahead into the brush and had no idea if the shot was even close.

These men know who I am and are trying to kill me! her mind screamed. *Move! Just move!*

Terrified and bewildered, she raced ahead, trying to get a sense of her situation and to formulate some sort of plan. On her side of the ledger, she was in far better shape than Larry and probably as fit as Verne. Also, she was running for her life.

Her disadvantages were obvious – two men with guns, knowing the area, angry as hornets, and determined to kill her. Not good. Still, she could feel herself maintaining some composure and continuing to fight the urge to panic.

'Cut in over there!' she heard Verne call out. 'If I don't get her first, she's going to run out of real estate in a hurry. Just don't let her backtrack.'

Nikki held her hands in front of her eyes to keep from being blinded by slashing branches. The town was several miles to her left. To her right, from what she could remember, was nothing until the main highway, maybe ten miles away. Verne sounded concerned about her doubling back between them, so that might be what she should do. She quickly rejected the notion. The chances of getting caught by one of them while heading back toward the road seemed too great, especially when there was no guarantee even if she made it that a car would come. It had to be straight ahead, searching for a place to hide until dark. Then she could make her way back into Belinda.

A plan, however thin, decided upon, she flattened

160

herself behind the thick trunk of a tree and listened. Verne wasn't that far behind. She could hear him speaking. It took a while before she realized that he wasn't speaking, he was singing – singing to her in a twisted, haunting child's voice.

'Come out, come out, wherever you are. All-ee, all-ee in free. Come on, little lady, there's no place to go.'

Her focus on Verne was interrupted by a gunshot from off to her left. The bullet slammed into the tree where she was hiding.

'What in the hell're you doing?' Verne called out.

'She's right there, jerk,' Larry responded. 'Right behind that tree. Give it up, Doc. There's no place you can go.'

There was a second shot, then a third, but Nikki was already sprinting ahead, weaving through trees and leaping over brush. The huge killer had moved much quicker than she would have imagined him capable of. Underestimating him was a mistake she wouldn't make again. The trees and dense undergrowth were both her ally and her enemy, concealing her to some degree, but at the same time tearing at her face and arms, threatening to trip her, or blind her, and always keeping her from getting up much of a head of steam.

Why are you doing this to me? Why?

Nikki wanted to stop and scream out the question. But these were men with orders, not answers. Instead, she plunged ahead, splashing into a shallow stream and trying, for a few dozen yards, to sprint down the center of it. There had to be somewhere to hide, or else a path where she could accelerate and put some distance between her and the men. She slipped on wet stones once, then again. Finally, she abandoned her efforts and scrambled up the muddy bank.

'She's in the brook,' Verne called out. 'No, there she is, on the other side. This way! This way!'

Two more gunshots cracked off. One of them snapped a branch right next to Nikki's face. Unless she could get some space to use her speed, she was going to be shot. She cut to her right, running low to make herself less of a target and to prevent the bushes from getting a straight-on whip at her eyes. It was late summer and the forest floor offered no collections of dead leaves large enough to hide her. She was gasping for air now, struggling to maintain her pace. But she knew she was slowing down. A voice inside began telling her to huddle on the ground behind a tree and simply pray they overlooked her. What other chance did she have?

She knelt on one knee and remained motionless as she tried to regain her wind. For ten seconds, fifteen, all was quiet. Could she possibly have outdistanced them that much in such a short time? The question was answered moments later by the breaking of a stick and some bushes rustling. At least one of them was near – very near. She was gripped by fear now, out of ideas. Again her internal voice warned her to stay put and take her chances. Her instincts urged otherwise. She sprang up and again began running, crashing through the dense brush.

'This way! Over here!' Verne cried out.

Nikki burst through some bushes and stopped short. She was standing in bright sunlight at the upper border of a rock ledge. Stretching out before her was a lake, nestled in a bowl of verdant forest. The ledge sloped slightly downward for about ten yards to a sheer drop-off fifteen feet above the water's surface. In the distance she could barely make out a couple of boats. This is what Verne had meant when he said she would soon run out of room. Her composure was completely gone now. 'Cube' no longer existed. She was trapped and going to die, and all she could think of to do was scream.

She sensed both killers pinching in on her. Running from them was no longer an option. The only move she could fix on was the lake – to dive in fully clothed and hope she wasn't a fish in a rain barrel. At the instant she turned to charge down the granite slope, there was a gunshot, then another. The second bullet grazed the side of her skull, just above her ear. Stunned, she spun and fell heavily. Her head struck the rock with dazing force. Helpless and barely conscious, she rolled down the incline and off the ledge.

She hit the surface of the lake face first, aware only of the cold water enveloping her and the fact that she couldn't seem to move in any purposeful way. The fall had driven most of the air from her lungs, and as soon as she entered the water, she began drifting downward. Within ten seconds, she had settled on the stony bottom. For a few moments she was aware, and consumed with the horror of her situation. Then, as blackness and peace closed in around her, she took a breath.

Chapter 14

It was after ten in the morning when Matt finally felt comfortable leaving Lewis with his brothers. Frank seemed naturally to assume the role of chief caregiver, and compared to Lyle and Kyle, he was Matt's odds-on choice for the job. Matt gave him a set of wound-care instructions and general observations to make, begged him to bring Lewis into the hospital if there was any change for the worse, and promised to return as soon as his workload permitted. Then he revved up the Vulcan and headed back toward his place to shower, change, and call Mae.

'Dr. Rutledge, I was just about to send the police out to your house,' she said.

'Sorry. I went for a long ride last night and ended up sleeping under the stars.'

'There were no stars last night, sir,' Mae replied in a syrupy drawl. 'No need to waste the truth on me. I'm your biggest fan, and I'm going to believe whatever you say.'

'That's just as well, Mae. Believe me. Everything okay?'

'No, everything is not okay. You are on backup for the ER today and they've been trying to reach you for an hour.'

'Lord.'

'Pardon?'

'I said, I'll call them right away.'

'The nurse said something about a fifty-year-old man from Hawleyville with diarrhea and a fever and no doctor.'

'He's in luck. I was voted the fever/diarrhea prize at Harvard. Is the office okay?'

'The office is fine. . . . Are you?'

'What are you, some kind of witch?'

'There are those who might say so. Anything I can do?'

'Not at the moment. Just keep the afternoon as light as possible.'

'I'll do my best.'

Matt called the ER and gave several holding orders – diagnostic and therapeutic – on a farmer who sounded as if he might have contracted a bacterial infection in his intestine, possibly salmonella or shigella. Then he stripped in his bedroom, kicked his filthy clothes under a chair, and basted himself in a shower as hot as he could stand. The scratches and nicks on his face weren't as bad as he'd anticipated, but it took several minutes of scrubbing before he realized that the blackness enveloping his eyes had nothing to do with Lewis's camouflage potion, and wasn't going to wash away.

As he was toweling off, he glanced over at the book on the toilet tank: *Manual of Medical and Surgical Field Emergencies*. It would probably be a lifetime before he ever needed to perform one of the procedures again. Still . . . He briefly flipped through the pages and then moved the book to the more prestigious location on his bedside table.

The farmer with fever and diarrhea was dehydrated and in moderate abdominal discomfort. Matt evaluated him, wrote a set of orders, and dictated his lengthy admission note. He was praying for an easy day, but that was simply not happening. Twenty minutes later, a ninety-year-old woman arrived by ambulance, sent in from one of the nursing homes with a dense stroke, unable to move her right side or speak. It was a medical and ethical nightmare, and of course her primary-care doc was on vacation. Matt wondered about the wisdom of treating her at all. He stood at her bedside, cradling her gnarled hand in his, looking into her glazed-over eyes, but receiving no definite message. His mother was much younger than this woman and wasn't nearly at this point yet, but her Alzheimer's was advancing steadily, and before too many more years, he would be facing constant questions of what was cruel treatment and what was not. But today was today for his mother, just as it was for this poor woman. Sighing, he picked up her chart and wrote orders for hydration, diagnostic studies, and a stat neurology consult. He would need more information about her, much more, before he put on his long white robes and began playing God.

By the time he had completed his second lengthy admission dictation of the day, seen several scheduled appointments in the office, and made rounds on his three other hospitalized patients, the afternoon was fading. Back in the ER, he consulted a list he had compiled of equipment and medications to be 'appropriated' from the hospital for Lewis. He had just put together a real chest tube and drainage system when an ambulance EMT, who had been drinking coffee in the lounge, hurried out to him. His name was Gary Lydon. He was earnest, baby-faced, and not much more than twenty.

'Dr. Rutledge,' he said breathlessly, 'dispatch just radioed. The police just got a call from a motorist on Wells Road. Apparently some kids just dove down and pulled a woman up from the bottom of Crystal Lake. They were fishing beneath Niles Ledge when she tumbled off it from right above them, and just sank.'

'She's alive?'

'So they say.'

Kirsten Langham, the second EMT, joined them. She had a bit more experience than Gary, but was still fairly green. It wasn't like Rescue to put together such a team. Matt accompanied the pair out to their ambulance.

'How long was she under?' he asked.

'Dispatch didn't say. There's a problem, though.'

'What?'

'Rick Wise is the paramedic on this shift and he's off on Harlan Road picking up a motorcyclist. If this woman needs to be intubated, neither me nor Kirsten is certified to do it.'

Crystal Lake near Wells Road. Matt estimated that by the time the two EMTs got the woman out of the woods, into the ambulance, and back to the hospital, a half an hour would have passed, maybe even more. If she needed a breathing tube – and unless she was wide-awake and talking sensibly, she did – it should be done as soon as they reached her.

'Hang on for just a minute,' he said. 'I'm going with you.'

'Bless you, Doc,' Gary said. 'I'll save you a seat up front.'

'No, I want to be in back to check the equipment.'

'Kirsten'll help you. I'll drive.'

Matt raced into the ER, told the nurses where

he'd be, and then hustled into the rear cabin of the ambulance. The return trip to the Slocumbs' farm was just going to have to wait. Hopefully, Lewis was still stable. If not, Frank Slocumb had better have the courage and good sense to bring him in.

Siren blaring, the ride to the spot on Wells Road took ten minutes. An empty Belinda PD black-and-white was parked on the soft shoulder, flashers on. Gary Lydon drove past the cruiser before pulling over beside a narrow trail that Matt knew led into Niles Ledge. He had prepared the large plastic crash case with all the equipment he might need to intubate. Hauling the case, he raced through the woods, sensing a powerful, unpleasant feeling of déjà vu. What Lewis and he had been through already seemed like a year ago. After a quarter of a mile, the winding track split – one path to the top of the ledge and one down to the water.

'Take the right fork,' he hollered, on the off chance that the EMTs hadn't grown up in the area.

'We hear you,' Gary called back.

The scene under the massive ledge was impressive. Several fishing skiffs had tied up along the shore, and their occupants had joined two uniformed policemen and two teenage boys. Crystal Lake was long and fairly large. The ledge, situated in a broad cove near the south end, was difficult to reach, but offered diving into fifteen feet of water, and around it, some decent fishing as well. The two boys, still wearing their waterlogged jeans but no shirts or shoes, stood off to the side. A policeman knelt beside a supine woman, alternately giving her a mouth-to-mouth breath and pausing to watch her take an occasional shallow breath on her own.

'These boys here are heroes, Doc,' the standing policeman said proudly. 'They saved her.'

But what's left? Matt wondered as he knelt beside the other cop.

'Officer Gibbons, sir,' the young policeman said. 'I think we've met before.'

'What's the story?' Matt asked, already into his examination.

The woman, thin, white, in her thirties, was unconscious and breathing ineffectually. Her dark hair was matted to her forehead. Her lips were purple. The officer was right to keep breathing for her, and Matt told him to continue. Her pupils were midposition, but did not react to a flash from his penlight – either the result of a technically limited exam, or a very grim sign. She wore jeans, sneakers, and a black T-shirt with a wavy musical scale on the front, and had a raw bruise and abrasion just above her left eye. There was also a long laceration, more of a gouge, along the hairline, just above her right temple.

The EMTs arrived and Matt instructed them to begin breathing her with a bag as soon as they could.

'These boys were fishin' here,' the standing officer said, 'when suddenly this lady came plungin' off the ledge from up above them. One of them, Percy Newley's boy Harris, swears he heard something like a gunshot just before she flew past him and into the water.'

'Did they get her up on the first try?' Matt asked, listening to her chest with his stethoscope as he was speaking.

'Excuse me?'

'Percy's boy and his friend, did they haul her up on the first dive?'

The officer's sheepish expression said that he had just grasped the significance of the question he clearly hadn't asked.

'Harris, how many tries did it take for you to pull this woman off the bottom?'

'Two. Michael tried first, then we did it together. We hauled her up by the hair.'

'Thank you,' Matt said, already preparing for an intubation.

He estimated the submersion time at two minutes and hoped he wasn't giving the boys too much credit. Meanwhile, Gary was setting the triangular cup of the breathing bag in place over the woman's mouth and nose while Kirsten was inserting an IV. After the breathing tube was in place, the cup would be set aside and the bag connected directly to the tube.

'Normal saline?' Kirsten asked.

'Exactly,' Matt said. 'You're all doing great. Thanks to these heroes and the good mouth-to-mouth technique they did, this lady's going to make it. But she still needs our help. I'm going to put a breathing tube in so we can get some concentrated oxygen into her lungs. Let's put her on the stretcher, Gary, and lift her up. I'd rather work with a little elevation than stretched out on my belly with her flat on the ground.'

In the hospital, the anesthesiologists were the royalty of intubation, having honed their skills hundreds of times in the operating room. During one of his residency electives, Matt had chosen anesthesia and 'tubed' dozens of cases under their guidance. Over the years that followed, he had multiple reasons to be grateful for every one of those opportunities. The main rule he had learned

170

was that if the caregiver performing the procedure wasn't absolutely comfortable, physically *and* mentally, the chances of a failed intubation were greatly increased. The most common disasters were intubating the esophagus instead of the trachea, thereby filling the stomach with air; tearing the tissues of the throat and causing bleeding, which made subsequent attempts that much more difficult; damaging the vocal cords by forcing the tube down without adequate visualization; and finally, inserting the tube too deeply and occluding one of the two main bronchial tubes.

Matt now did what had been taught to him and what subsequently he had taught to many students and paramedics – he took an extra few seconds to position his new patient and compose himself before proceeding. With the woman on her back on the stretcher, he tilted her head slightly downward, straightening her neck. Gary Lydon knelt beside him to hold her head steady in that position. Physically settled on one knee, and as confident as he could be given the circumstances, Matt slid a curved, lighted laryngoscope blade along the woman's tongue and pulled the blade straight up toward her chin. All he could see was lake water, welling up from her lungs. Trouble – maybe big trouble. In the ER there would have been suction to clear her airway. Not here. A blind thrust with the semi-rigid tube was possible, but treacherous. Doing so had to be a last resort.

Easy, now, easy.

The woman's color remained poor. Brain cells were being compromised every second. Soon, they would begin to die.

Come on, Rutledge. Stay cool and don't panic.

171

You can do this. . . . You . . . can . . . do . . . this.

Matt took a deep, calming breath, grasped the handle of the scope tighter, and pulled the blade upward another eighth of an inch. The move nudged the victim's tongue out of the way even more and lifted her epiglottis – the flap that protected the lungs from aspirating food or drink. The slight adjustment caused the pool of water to recede just enough to expose the two silvery half-moons of her vocal cords.

Yes!

Matt smoothly slid the tube between the cords.

'We're in,' he said, trying for some matter-of-factness but missing badly.

There was audible relief from both EMTs and the police.

'Nice going,' one of them said.

Matt used a large syringe to blow up the balloon fixed around the end of the tube, sealing it in place and preventing air from escaping around it. Kirsten Langham quickly attached the black latex bag to the tube and connected it to oxygen. In seconds, the mottled duskiness of the woman's complexion began to improve. She was almost certainly going to make it. How much of her brain would make it, too, remained to be seen.

Matt handled the breathing bag as the troupe awkwardly retraced their steps, pushing the stretcher along the path back to the ambulance. While the woman was being lifted into the back, Matt took the two teens aside.

'You guys did one heck of a job. In all likelihood, you saved this woman's life.'

'Lucky we was there,' one of them said.

'I'll say. You're Harris?'

'I'm Michael. *He's* Harris.'

'Got it. Two things. First, tell me again. You were fishing and she fell into the water right in front of you.'

'Yes.'

'And sank?'

'She might of stayed on the top for a second or two,' Michael said, 'but otherwise that's the way it happened. I got down ta her, but I couldn't get a grip afore I ran out of breath. Then we did it together an' brought her up by the hair.'

Two minutes, minimum, Matt estimated again. *Four maximum, depending on when they started breathing for her and how well they did it.*

'And you did mouth-to-mouth?'

'Harris did. I screamed for help.'

'Harris, did you hold her nose closed?'

'I did, sir. And I tipped her head back, too.'

'Where did you learn how to do mouth-to-mouth?'

'They taught us in Health, sir. We used a dummy to practice.'

'Well, we sure are glad you were paying attention in that class,' Matt said. 'Now, about those gunshots.'

'They weren't shots,' Michael said. 'They were too soft. They were branches cracking, probably. Maybe a car backfirin' out ta the road.'

'Were, too, gunshots,' Harris insisted. 'Michael, I'm telling you, pistols don't sound the same as backfirin'. There were two shots, maybe three.'

'Ready,' Gary called out from the rear of the ambulance. 'Kirsten's going to bag her with you. I'll drive.'

'You guys did great,' Matt said again. 'Lots of

people, doctors included, sometimes *think* they saved someone's life, when the truth is, they might not have. Take it from me, you two really did it.'

He jumped into the ambulance and waved to the boys as Gary closed the door. Then he took a seat on the bench opposite from the EMT and, for the first time, took a careful look at the woman who had come so close to dying beneath Niles Ledge.

She was still unconscious. The swelling above her left eye was pronounced and beginning to discolor. But to Matt's touch, there was no evidence for a depressed skull fracture beneath the bruise. The linear gouge above her right temple certainly could have been from a gunshot. There were also scratches on her cheeks and chin, similar to those Matt had sustained just half a day ago. It wasn't a stretch to imagine her terrified, charging through the dense woods with someone shooting at her.

He separated her eyelids and used his penlight to check her pupils' response to light again. This time the results were different.

'Pupils are both reacting,' he announced to the EMT.

'Great,' Kirsten said. 'Her oxygen sat is ninety-seven.'

'Decent enough. I can't say why, but she just doesn't seem that deep to me.'

'I know what you mean. She's sort of begun chewing on the tube a little.'

Matt brushed her sodden hair from her forehead. Her face, distorted some by the breathing tube, still had a peaceful, gentle quality to it – pale, unlined brow ... high cheekbones ... wide, almond-shaped eyes. He lifted her limp hand and set it on his. Her fingers were long and slender, nails cut short. If there was polish on them, it was clear. There was a gold claddagh friendship ring – two hands supporting a heart – on her right fourth finger, and a single gold bangle on her left wrist. No other jewelry. Her palms were soft without a hint of callus, but there was a fullness to the muscles. Matt imagined the hands playing piano or writing or throwing clay pots – something manual and artistic.

Come on, you, he urged silently, *wake up!*

The mobile MRI facility that served the region was currently in its two-month rotation at Hastings Hospital, twenty-five miles away. Montgomery County, though, did have a CT scanner, which for blunt head trauma was nearly as definitive. Matt radioed ahead and asked that the room be reserved in one hour. He also asked the nursing supervisor to call the Belinda Police Department and request that an officer come down to the ER to begin investigation of a possible shooting, and also to try and determine the identity of their patient. He wondered as he rang off whether or not the powers at BC&C had filed any complaint with the police against him.

Patient saved, doctor arrested.

The sort of news a small town loves.

The ER crew was waiting for them as they backed into the ambulance bay. For the next fifteen minutes, Matt was a secondary player. The nurses and respiratory technologist became the major caregivers while the phlebotomist from the lab and the tech from radiology spearheaded the gathering of diagnostic information. Their comatose Jane Doe was lifted from the stretcher to an ER bed, stripped down, and covered in a johnny and a sheet. Her IV and monitor lines were quickly transferred to hospital equipment. A catheter was placed in her bladder to keep close track of hydration and urinary output, and she was hooked up to a ventilator. Next, a portable chest X ray and skull film were taken.

Finally, the crew stepped aside and Matt resumed his position at the bedside. This time, his examination would be more detailed, including the critical visualization by ophthalmoscope of the retinas in the back of Jane Doe's eyes. He was relieved to see pulsation in the veins there, as well as a sharpness to the margins of the optic nerves. Loss of either would be a grave sign, indicating significant brain swelling from trauma and/or prolonged lack of oxygen.

'So, Dr. Rutledge, I understand you called?'

Grimes.

Matt turned slowly to face the Belinda police chief. The two of them had had some conflicts over the years, usually surrounding some action or other Matt was running against BC&C. Matt also complained more than once of being harassed with tickets – parking and speeding. Grimes was ex-military and kept the town on a pretty short leash. A displaced northerner with some sort of degree in criminal justice, he had adopted something of a mountain accent. He was divorced, with a kid in Florida someplace that Matt heard he never saw. Their contrast in styles alone would have strained their relationship, but Grimes's connection with Armand Stevenson and the other directors of the mine all but sealed their enmity.

Over the years, the police chief had appointed himself as a one-man watchdog committee to step in whenever Matt didn't have an appropriate permit or was posting notices against a town ordinance. Matt suspected Grimes or his lackeys were behind the disappearance of most if not all of the magenta fliers.

'I just asked for a policeman,' Matt said, 'not *the* policeman.'

'You're a very important person to us,' Grimes replied, smiling civilly. 'What do you have?'

Matt gestured to his patient. At the sight of her, Grimes's lips tightened noticeably.

'This woman plunged off Niles Ledge and into the lake,' Matt said. 'One of the two kids who rescued her said he heard several shots. The other kid doesn't think so. She's got a big bruise over her eye. That may be why she's unconscious, but she also has a scalp wound that could be from a gunshot. I'm legally required to report any possible shooting.'

'Thanks for telling me that, Doctor. From time to time I forget some of the laws. How long was she underwater?'

'I estimate two minutes minimum, four maximum. She had no ID, so in addition to reporting the possible bullet wound, I hoped maybe you could find out who she is.'

Grimes stepped forward, set his hands on the bed rail, and gazed down at the woman.

'Her name is Nikki Solari,' he said flatly. 'She drove down from Boston to attend Kathy Wilson's memorial service earlier today. I spent some time talking with her there. Wilson was her roommate. You know who she was?'

'I know about her, and I've heard some of her music, but I didn't know her personally.'

'Well, she was hit by a truck in Boston. Died instantly.'

'I heard something about it from Hal Sawyer. Apparently he knew the family and Kathy.'

'Yeah, he was at the service. Well, this woman played fiddle in Kathy Wilson's bluegrass band.'

Matt decided that playing fiddle was close enough to pianist. He was mentally patting himself on the back for astutely concluding that Nikki Solari's hands were those of an artist, when Grimes added, 'She only played music as a hobby. She's actually a pathologist – a coroner up in Boston. Spends her time working up to her elbows in gore and guts.'

Matt immediately stopped the patting.

'What do you think about that wound above her ear?' he asked.

Grimes studied it.

'I guess it could be from a bullet,' he said. 'But it could just as easily be from something else, like a broken branch.'

'Well, we'll find out for sure when she wakes up.'

Grimes suddenly whirled to face him.

'You just make sure that she does!' he snapped.

Chapter 15

Much of what I write here of my infection with the Lassa virus and my miraculous recovery I gleaned from conversations with those who cared for me during my thirty-day hospitalization. I use their accounts because I was delirious for much of the time, and remember almost nothing.

The words were those of Dr. Suzanne O'Connor, a missionary physician. She was working in the central Nigerian city of Jos in the spring of 1973 when a patient, Lila Gombazu, crazed with fever, clawed through her rubber gloves and broke the skin on the back of her hand.

Cloistered in one corner of the Library of Medicine at the NIH, Ellen Kroft read O'Connor's harrowing account with a dry mouth and an unpleasant fullness in her chest.

The poor woman who scratched through my glove went into convulsions the next day. In spite of the most heroic measures we could muster, she began hemorrhaging from her nose, womb, and rectum, and died horribly, crying out at the end for her children, two of whom, she had no way of knowing, were already showing symptoms of the disease. Twelve days after my encounter with Lila, my good health and the crush of work caring for our patients had driven the incident to the back of my mind. That day, a Monday, I mentioned to one of the nurses that I had a stuffy nose and scratchy throat, and thought I might be coming down with the flu. Tuesday was more of the same, although the discomfort in my throat was steadily worsening. I couldn't possibly take time off from my work, though. The hospital was filled to capacity and then some. I put myself on a high dose of penicillin and tried to force fluids past the inflammation and the raw, white sores that now dotted my palate and pharynx.

On Wednesday, I was making rounds on our patients when I was seized with uncontrollable shivering and profound weakness. Perspiration soaked my clothing as if I were standing in a thunderstorm. My temperature at that moment, as taken by one of the nurses, was 105 degrees Fahrenheit. Within an hour, I was a patient in my own hospital, moaning piteously from the pain in my muscles and joints, unable to take fluids because of the gaping, deep ulcers in my throat, and soiling myself and my bed with uncontrollable diarrhea. The next morning, I was delirious. My temperature had risen to 107 despite vigorous efforts to keep it down. For days, I am told, I lay unconscious, unable to take nourishment or fluids, oozing red blood from my rectum, and coughing up blood as well.

From the beginning, the diagnosis of Lassa fever was strongly suspected. My associate Dr. Janet Pickford made valiant efforts to fly experts from the CDC to Nigeria along with serum from a woman who had recovered from the disease and had circulating antibodies against it. Unfortunately, the government of Nigeria, angry about having the disease named for the village of Lassa, located along the Nigerian border with Cameroon, delayed issuing visas to anyone involved with my case. Finally, those State documents were approved, and on the tenth day of my illness I received an infusion of the woman's convalescent serum. By then I had required more than a dozen blood transfusions, and had been delirious or in a coma for almost the whole time. I had lost nearly thirty pounds from a frame that was slender to begin with, and was a mass of bruises and sores. My urine and stool were bloody, as was the mucus from my chest.

Incredibly, within just two days of receiving the serum, my condition began to improve. A miracle, everyone said. Gradually, the hideous ulcers in my mouth began to heal, and I was able to take nourishment. Over the next two weeks I regained much of my strength as well as my will to live. What I did not completely regain was my hearing, which was lost to the virus in both ears, and which has only returned slightly in my right. I would wish the illness of Lassa fever on no one, and pray that, with time, a cure or vaccine for this most terrible hemorrhagic virus might be found.

Ellen closed the book called *Closer Than You Think – Infectious Diseases in a Shrinking World*, and sank down in her chair, staring across the library at nothing in particular. Sixty-one. That was how many cases of Lassa fever had been reported in the U.S. over the past couple of years. Sixty-one and counting. Not that it mattered to Ellen whether the cases were here or in Africa, but for the time being at least, Omnivax was going to be administered here. And the Lasaject component of the super-vaccine was, she had come to believe, the weak link in the chain. Now, a day after a very sobering, highly charged meeting at the office of Dr. Richard Steinman, she wasn't so sure.

Lynette Marquand's startling pledge that if even one of the vaccine panel's twenty-three experts expressed misgivings, release of Omnivax would be put on hold until those problems could be satisfactorily addressed had hit her life like a wrecking ball. Following the pronouncement, Ellen had done her best to continue with business as usual, but that state of existence had proven highly elusive. Less than a day after Marquand's speech, Steinman had requested that she meet with him at his office at Georgetown. When she arrived, she found the renowned physician and scientist waiting for her, along with George Poulos. On the corner of Steinman's desk was a copy of the day's *Washington Post*. A headline on the front page proclaimed:

First Lady promises to rethink Omnivax if panel vote is not unanimous

The article, which Ellen had read, did not mention her by name, but did say that debate among members of the select commission on Omnivax would continue until the vote, to be held in just three days. Steinman, who had a certain amount of charm and warmth, was nevertheless extremely formal, and even after nearly three years addressed all of the commission members by their title.

'Well, Mrs. Kroft,' Steinman began, 'I appreciate your coming up here to meet with me. I hope you don't mind my having taken the liberty of inviting Dr. Poulos to join us.'

'No problem,' Ellen said, still smarting some from the exchange with Poulos at the final commission meeting.

'After Mrs. Marquand's speech, I, um, felt it was essential to review our conversation with Dr. Steinman,' Poulos said. 'I felt that in view of the

First Lady's promise to the nation, he should know that the final vote might not be unanimous.'

'I suppose I would have done the same thing in your position,' she said, somewhat coolly.

'Mrs. Kroft,' Steinman said, 'I confess I was somewhat taken aback to learn that, at least before Mrs. Marquand's speech, you were planning to vote against the implementation of Omnivax. Over the years we have been meeting together, I felt that you honored your mandate as a consumer on our committee quite admirably, by questioning issues until you understood them and always being prepared for our sessions. I wondered from time to time if you might vote against approval when yours was only one ballot of twenty-three. But now that your vote can effectively stop the entire Omnivax program, I thought, if it is all right with you, that we might review together what is at stake.'

Of all those on the Omnivax panel, Steinman was the one Ellen respected the most. He had guided every session evenhandedly, and had always been patient and encouraging when she began one of her 'Excuse me, but as a nonphysician, I was wondering if . . .' questions.

'I am open to any input or point of view,' she said. 'Despite what Dr. Poulos may have told you.'

Poulos tried unsuccessfully to inject some warmth into his grin.

'I admit that, right or wrong, I do recall your saying something to the effect that you didn't plan on voting in favor of approval.'

The man was right, but holding most of the high cards, Ellen didn't feel it necessary to respond.

Steinman passed two computer-generated pages to her.

'I know how you feel about statistics, Mrs. Kroft. As malleable as chicken, I believe you said. But you still must acknowledge that often in science, statistics are all we have.'

'I understand.'

'This is a distillation of material we have discussed in great detail in our meetings. It is, in short, our estimate of the lives that will be saved by Omnivax over one, five, and ten years, broken down disease by disease. Please believe me when I say that this summary was put together by statisticians who are as unbiased in their opinions as it is possible to be.'

Ellen scanned the list which was, as Steinman said, a summary of precisely what was at stake. Measles was included, as well as the other vaccines now legally a part of every child's immunizations. But with or without those vaccines, the number of lives to be saved was staggering. The one-year figure for Lassa fever was 240, which seemed in keeping with the statistics she knew. By five years, however, the death toll would be over eight thousand, and in ten, nearly fifty thousand. Ellen gazed out the window, thinking about Lucy and the hundreds of other tragedies represented in the files and photos of PAVE. Those were real flesh-and-blood lives, not statistics. Then there were the myriad cases of ADHD, learning disabilities, asthma, diabetes, multiple sclerosis, sudden death, Asperger's syndrome, and other forms of autism, whose possible link to their childhood shots still begged investigation.

'I'll think about this,' she said, slipping the data into her briefcase.

'Ellen, look at those numbers,' Poulos blurted out. 'Don't you see what these numbers mean?'

'Yes, I see, Doctor,' Ellen countered. 'I see perfectly. But do you see what it's like to have the life of a perfectly happy, healthy child suddenly ruined or snuffed out altogether by something that was done to her by her physician?'

'George, please,' Steinman said, discarding formality. 'Mrs. Kroft, we do understand that. Believe me, we do. Risk-benefit ratio is the bedrock on which all medical treatment is built. And not one of us would deny that there are some immediate adverse consequences of immunizations for some children. All we can ask of you is that you do exactly as you have said you would, think things over. But I feel I must underscore all that is at stake here.'

'And I do appreciate that, Dr. Steinman,' Ellen said, standing to indicate that she had heard enough – especially from George Poulos. 'I won't make any pronouncements about what I'm going to do, but I do promise to consider all the issues. I hope that's enough for the time being.'

'It will have to be,' Steinman had concluded.

Ellen had left Steinman's office in something of a daze. Why in the hell had Lynette Marquand done this to her? Things were fine when she believed that her vote would make a statement. Now that her vote could halt the project altogether, the pressure was immense.

She left Georgetown and spent much of the rest of that day in Bethesda at the NIH library. Now, after a second day of research, it was time to discuss matters with Cheri and Sally at PAVE, prior to making a final decision as to which way she was going to vote. Whatever that decision ultimately was, Suzanne O'Connor's gripping account of her battle with Lassa fever would be a strongly considered factor.

Lost in thought, she gathered up her things and headed out to her car. Following Marquand's speech, it was certainly expected that she would speak personally with Cheri and Sally. Yet she had kept putting off that meeting. Cheri Sanderson, however, hadn't waited too long before calling her. She was hardly a fool, and Ellen's uncertainty, however minimal, still resonated loud and clear.

'This is big stuff now, Ellen,' she had said over the phone. 'I'd be lying if I said that it wasn't important for us suddenly to be on center stage, and that you are in a position to put us there.'

A mile into the drive, Ellen used her cell phone to call Rudy.

'Peterson here.'

'Rudy, it's me,' she said, imagining him sitting at his desk on the second floor of his cabin.

'Well, greetings. Are you going to be famous?'

'You mean, am I going to vote against Omnivax?'

'That would certainly put you on the *Oprah* show.'

'I suppose it might. I met with the head of the committee yesterday, and now I'm on my way to speak with the moms at PAVE.'

'And?'

'I don't know anymore, Rudy. Do you have any information on Lasaject that might help me out?'

'I'm waiting for a call from a friend of mine at the CDC. All I can tell you at the moment is that the preliminary research on the vaccine was a bit sloppy in its design and severely limited in its scope. But as I said before, there are some other things that may be going on. That's what this call from Arnie Whitman at the CDC is all about.'

'So when will you know anything?'

'Maybe later today, maybe tomorrow. In the meantime, all I can tell you is that the vaccine seems okay, if not squeaky-clean. When's the vote?'

'The day after tomorrow.'

'I don't know. All I can say is, I'll keep in touch.'

'Thanks, Rudy.'

'Any plans to come by these parts?'

'As soon as this vote is over. I love it up there, and goodness knows I'll need the rest.'

'Good enough. I'll keep the kettle boilin' for ya.'

Ellen set the phone down. Rudy wasn't going to be the answer, at least not on this round he wasn't.

Unlike her last visit to the PAVE brownstone, this time Ellen could find no parking space. Reluctantly, she pulled into an $8 for the first half-hour lot three blocks away. There were problems with vaccines that the government and scientific community weren't addressing – pure and simple. She had absolutely no doubt that lives were being lost and destroyed because of the immediate and long-range complications of immunizations. But she also had no doubt that vaccines prevented a great deal of suffering and death.

There was no standing ovation this time when Ellen stepped into the offices of PAVE. No silliness. Suddenly, her valiant, quixotic stand on behalf of issues in which they all believed had turned serious. Ellen recalled the delightful book and movie *The Mouse That Roared*, in which a minuscule country with an army of two dozen or so archers wages war against America. Their plan is to quickly lose in order to reap the traditional harvest of postdefeat reparations from the American victors. Except that they win. Now what?

No one, but no one, had expected to be in a position to defeat Omnivax, even temporarily. All PAVE wanted was a platform on which to take one more baby step forward – to get concerns about vaccine safety presented to the world. And Ellen had certainly come through for them in that regard.

Now what?

'Hey, comes the conquering hero.'

Cheri Sanderson bounded from her office and exchanged hugs with Ellen.

'If I'm so conquering,' Ellen responded, 'how come I feel like there's a lemon lodged in my throat?'

'I understand John Kennedy got physically ill right before he called Khrushchev and told him to turn the missiles around or else. Come on in. Coffee? Tea?'

'No, thanks. Sally not here?'

Cheri's cluttered office featured framed articles chronicling the remarkable ascendance of PAVE, as well as mounting public recognition that vaccinations were not as warm, fuzzy, and uncontroversial as the powers that be would have everyone believe.

'She's spending the day with her husband. She's been getting a little emotional lately about this Omnivax business, and I think she's been a little hard on him.'

'I can understand. I know what she's been through with what happened to her son.'

'So today it's just going to be you and me. Quite a spot Lynette put you in, huh?'

Ellen stared down at her hands. This woman, no more than five-two or -three, was a giant, chosen perhaps by God to overcome massive odds in order to make a difference. Over the past decade and a half she had spent thousands of hours cajoling, writing, researching, debating, flattering, decrying, begging, consoling, sobbing in order to help the world right what she believed was a most serious wrong. She had fought beside mothers whose children were being hauled away from them because they refused to have them vaccinated. She had sat before specially appointed masters at the U.S. Court of Federal Claims, holding hands with parents who had just received a piddling sum to care for their vaccine-injured child – the legally declared maximum according to the National Childhood Vaccine Injury Act of 1986 – or worse, no compensation at all.

Ellen gazed up at one of the framed quotes. It was from a Wisconsin mother whose son, whose dream, was horribly, irreparably damaged: *The government forces us to give our children these vaccines,* it read, *and then when something goes wrong – too bad – you're on your own.*

'Look,' Ellen said finally, unable to couch the words, 'I'm sorry for seeming so reserved, but you have no idea what I've been listening to for the past three years and who's been saying it. These men and women are not monsters or criminals or killers. They're physicians and scientists and intellectuals. They really believe in what they are doing.' To Ellen's surprise, there was no knee-jerk rebuttal from Cheri. Her expression, which sometimes had the hardness of a diamond, was soft and sad.

'I know they are,' she said gently.

'I won't argue the fact,' Ellen went on, 'that many of them get research money from the pharmaceutical companies. But does that necessarily make

189

them wrong? For every graph I produced, they produced a dozen. For every question I asked, they offered incredibly logical, supported answers. For every expert I quoted, they brought in ten with qualifications just as sterling. When I thought my vote was going to be a token, a polite request for continued debate on the issue, that was one thing. I never wanted to be the epicenter of this controversy. I never wanted to be the linchpin.'

Cheri pushed back from her desk, then walked behind Ellen and embraced her, resting her cheek on Ellen's hair. There was nothing phony in the gesture, nothing patronizing.

'Look,' she said, returning to her seat, 'I'm not going to say this isn't important to us. But I will say it isn't everything. It's a battle, not the whole war. There were more than five hundred in attendance at the vaccine conference we ran this year. Five hundred from all over the world – professors, pediatricians, scientists, parents, philosophers. There will be more at the next one. The press and Congress are beginning to see that we are not hysterical radicals being led around by our bitterness, hormones, and emotions, devoid of logic, unwilling to listen to reason.

'Ellen, you've done a wonderful job – more so than any of us had the right to expect. You've made Sally and me and all the others out there proud. You've already helped thousands of parents know that their opinions matter. If you vote against Omnivax, you and I both know you're headed for a feeding frenzy in the media, and maybe even the cover of *Newsweek* and *Time*. We'd be naive to think otherwise. If you vote for it, life settles back down for you, and you'll still be welcome to resume your spot on the volunteer phone. But I promise you, either way, pro or con, nothing will change in our determination to have a true, long-term scientific evaluation of immunizations. Nothing will change in our crusade for informed parental choice. Nothing will change in our commitment to find the middle ground that is safest for all people.'

Ellen could tell by Cheri's expression that she wasn't playing any head games, even though she had the reputation in some quarters of being a master at it.

'My mind is nearly made up as to what I'm going to do,' Ellen said, 'but until I am absolutely certain, I'd like to keep things to myself.'

'That's okay,' Cheri replied. 'It would sure be nice to know as soon as you do, and I certainly hope you deliver a blow for us.'

'I intend to do what's right,' Ellen added, hoping Cheri might read that things were likely to go her way.

'That's all any of us have ever asked of you,' Cheri said.

As Ellen walked out past Sally's open office door, she peered in at the photos adorning the walls, and paused a moment to look at one in particular.

Ellen's home, an expanded seven-room Cape in Glenside, Maryland, southeast of D.C., was the one she and Howard had bought shortly after their marriage.

'If this is the only place we ever live, I'll be perfectly happy,' he had said at the time.

Sure.

On the way home, Ellen stopped at the local superette for some eggs and milk. She loved omelettes of all kinds, and with what there was in the crisper she would be able to create a gold-medal winner. Physically and mentally she was spent – as exhausted as she could ever remember being. As she was fishing out her wallet for the cashier, she glanced over at the magazine rack. Both *Time* and *Newsweek* were there. Imagine her face on the covers. Today buying eggs and milk at Kim's Korner, tomorrow her face around the world. Was she ready?

What do you think, Howie? Expect to see your new bride on a magazine cover anytime soon? Barmaid Monthly?

Ellen set her groceries on the front seat, chastising herself for her pettiness. Most of the time she managed to keep her anger and hurt in decent check. It didn't feel good at all when she had a slip. The supervaccine was too much, too fast. She thought of the horrible arithmetic Steinman had presented to her: lives lost or ruined if she voted for the drug versus lives lost or ruined if she voted against it. Based on the current level of knowledge of vaccines, it was really no contest. But that was precisely the main point for which Cheri and Sally and the others were crusading – an increase in our level of knowledge.

Ellen pulled into the garage and brought her bundle in through the kitchen door. Despite the unpleasant association with Howard, she really did love the place, from her window herb-garden, to the huge oak in the backyard, to the pesky squirrels, to the small balcony off her bedroom where she often sat and watched the first sunlight of the day filter through the trees. It was really a very lovely –

Ellen set down her package and sniffed the air.

Had someone been smoking in the house? One of Howard's pet peeves with her was her over-developed sense of smell, and one of *her* pet peeves was cigarette smoke in any form. Still sniffing curiously, she walked down the short hallway to the living room. Then she cried out and stumbled backward, clutching her chest to keep her heart from exploding.

Sitting calmly in the easy chair next to the fireplace was a large, powerfully built man. He was dressed expensively in a gray suit and black shirt – open collar, no tie – and ornately stitched cowboy boots. His head, square as a block of granite, was topped by thick, jet-black hair, combed straight back and held in place with some product that glistened. His hard, narrow eyes looked as black as his hair, and his wide mouth was accentuated by a short, thick scar that ran from the center of his upper lip to the base of his nose – possibly the result of surgery to repair a harelip.

'Golly, I'm sorry to have startled you, Mrs. Kroft,' he said, with a pleasant, gravelly voice and the cheerful, easygoing manner of a used-car salesman. 'Please have a seat, have a seat.'

Ellen remained fixed where she was. There was no evidence the huge intruder had smoked in her house, yet the reek of cigarettes was definitely coming from him. She debated running, but in truth, she didn't have the sense that she was in any immediate danger. The man had already gotten into her home. If he had wanted to harm her, he wouldn't have been waiting placidly in her living room.

'Who are you? What do you want?' she demanded.

The man smiled patiently.

'Who I am doesn't matter. What I want at the moment is for you to sit down . . . over here.' He motioned to the sofa next to his chair.

Ellen hesitated, then took a breath and did as he demanded. At close range, his eyes were more than dark, they were frighteningly cold. His thick, heavy-knuckled fingers rested in his lap, curled around a large manila envelope. The little finger of his left hand bore a gold ring with a square-cut diamond that must have been three carats or more.

'Now,' Ellen said, 'what are you doing here?'

'I represent a group that is very interested in getting Omnivax into circulation as soon as possible. That is all you need to know.'

'So? What has that got to do with me?'

His expression tightened. Ellen thought she saw a brief tic at the corner of his mouth. Still, he managed a patronizing grin.

'Mrs. Kroft,' he said, his tone still chillingly calm, 'I have neither the time nor the patience for games. Both you and I know the significance of the unfortunate promise Lynette Marquand made to the world.'

'And?'

'And I have it on good authority that you are the only person who might force her to honor that pledge.'

'Who do you work for? The President? The drug people? Who?'

The huge man sighed impatiently and ignored the questions.

'Mrs. Kroft, I am going to have to insist on your word not to block the planned release of Omnivax.'

'What do you have in that envelope,' she asked, 'bribe money?'

'Oh, I have no intention of trying to bribe you, Mrs. Kroft.'

There was something chilling in the way he said the words. He passed over the envelope. Ellen opened it, removed the photographs it contained, and gasped. Inside were half a dozen sharp, professional quality black-and-white eight-by-ten snapshots of Lucy. Lucy heading into school, hand in hand with Gayle; in the playground; at home in the yard; even asleep in her bedroom.

'You wouldn't dare harm this child,' Ellen rasped.

The man simply looked across at her placidly. She wanted to leap up and claw the smugness off his face.

'I will do whatever it is I have to do,' he replied firmly. 'Look at me and don't doubt me for a second. If you do, you and you alone will be responsible for the consequences. The people I work for have given this matter utmost priority. If you disappoint us in any way, I promise you that your granddaughter will simply disappear ... forever. What happens to her after she vanishes you don't even want to speculate about. And, depending on how angry my employers are, that may well only be the beginning.'

Her anger muted by the sheer arrogance of the monster next to her, Ellen could only glare at him.

'Do I make myself clear?' he asked. *'Do I?'* For the first time, he raised his voice.

'Y-yes,' Ellen managed.

'You can go to the police if you want, but I promise you two things. Number one, we will find out, and number two, they will be able to do nothing to prevent what I have promised you will happen. Clear?'

'Yes.'

'Good. We have an understanding, then?'

'Yes,' she said again, now perilously close to tears.

'Wonderful,' the man said, standing.

Stretched upward his full length, with his broad shoulders and massive head, the killer was daunting. As calmly as he might pick up the morning paper, he leaned down and retrieved the envelope and photographs. The cigarette stench of him at such close range had Ellen close to vomiting. He then took a cell phone from his pocket, flipped it open, and dialed a number with one button push.

'We're all set,' he said simply.

Seconds later a car pulled up outside.

'I thank you for your hospitality, Mrs. Kroft,' he said. 'And your family, I am sure, thanks you for your levelheaded decision making. There's no need to show me out.'

He closed the drapes to the picture window and, with a final grin, left. Ellen raced to the window, and stuck her head between the drapes, hoping to pick up the license plate number. But the car, a nondescript sedan, was already rolling off down the street.

Chapter 16

Matt seldom awoke remembering a dream and even less often was aware he was dreaming while one was still in progress. But this time, at some level of his mind he did know. He was at once a participant and observer, legitimately terrified, yet strangely detached and analytical.

It was a huge Gila monster, orange scales glinting in patchy sunlight. The venomous lizard, tall as a building, was swaying through a dense forest, its thick tail knocking over trees, its stubby legs crushing everything in its path. Its black tongue snapped out like a whip, shearing the tops off pine trees. Again and again it slammed itself against a rocky hillside, sending boulders hammering down close to where Matt was standing. All at once there were men with guns – indistinct shadows firing continuously, burying shot after shot into the lizard. The Gila reared up on its hind legs, balancing on its tail, searching for the source of its pain. More men . . . more guns . . . more shots . . . more flashes . . . more bellowing . . . and now blood, spewing from a hundred wounds along its flank. The massive orange and black head swayed from one side to the other, powerful jaws opening and closing on nothing but air.

'Noooo!' Matt heard himself scream. 'No more!'

Mortally injured, the beast toppled over, roaring

at its killers, flailing out with its front claws, ripping at Matt's arm again and again. It was then he sensed he had awakened. His eyes opened a slit. The clawing against his arm persisted. Then he became aware that it was nothing more malevolent than a hand, scratching at his elbow. He was in a chair in a glass-enclosed cubicle in the ICU – Dr. Nikki Solari's cubicle, he realized. Slumped to one side, he had been asleep, his head resting half on his shoulder, half on the bed. The touch that had awakened him from his bizarre nightmare was Solari's. Through the glass, Julie Bellet, one of the night nurses, waved to him, smiling. The wall clock behind her read five-thirty.

Matt's thoughts quickly cleared. The stiffness in his neck suggested he had not moved for some time. His patient, arms restrained with leather straps, was silently imploring him through the gloom. Her eyes were wide with fear and confusion. The polystyrene tube he had slid between her vocal cords was still in place. The bedside ventilator attached to it whirred and hissed as it forced air into her lungs with every breath. Julie Bellet stepped into the room.

'Hi, there,' she said. 'You've been out for almost three hours. But you looked so peaceful that none of us had the heart to wake you up.'

'I . . . um . . . was a little tired,' he managed. 'I guess it's time to ditch the decaf and go back to super.'

He grinned sheepishly and turned back to Solari. He knew from the accounts of many who had woken up on a ventilator that having a half-inch tube down the back of their throat and into their trachea was as unpleasant and frightening a sensation as any they had ever experienced, especially with their hands lashed down as well. He switched on the overhead fluorescents.

'Dr. Solari, sorry about falling asleep like that. It's been a tough couple of days. I'm Matt Rutledge, your doctor. Do you understand?' Nikki nodded, her eyes still fixed on his face. 'Good,' he said. 'You're in Montgomery County Regional Hospital in Belinda, West Virginia. The tube is in because you nearly drowned in a lake yesterday. You've been unconscious for more than twelve hours.'

Nikki, ignoring the throbbing in her temples, moved her hand as far as the restraint allowed, and pointed desperately back at her face.

The tube. Get it out! Please, get it out. It's choking me!

Nikki prayed her doctor understood.

Matt Rutledge was probably a few years older than she was, with a kind, rugged face. His dark hair was pulled back into a ponytail that came down just over the collar of his shirt.

'I know you want that tube out this instant,' he said. 'I know it's awful. But please, please try your best to relax and breathe easily. Do you think you need some medicine to help you do that? . . . Good. Give me a signal if you change your mind about that. The vent's on assist, so all you have to do is breathe. I promise I'll get the tube out as soon as I can. First, I need to get a film and check your blood gases. If I loosen the straps on your wrists, do you promise you'll keep them away from the tube?'

Nikki nodded. The nurse who was in the doorway came over, introduced herself, and undid the restraints.

'Nikki,' she said, 'the balloon on your tube is still

blown up. Please don't try and pull it out. It can damage your vocal cords if you do. Okay?'

Nikki forced herself to nod. The tube felt like a garden hose in her throat. Intellectually, she knew what it was and what it was doing for her, but at some uncontrollable, primal level, she was positive she was choking. She closed her eyes as her doctor listened to her heart and lungs, examined her belly, and checked the pulses in her arms and feet. Then he had her open her eyes and checked them with an ophthalmoscope. His manner was reassuring and his touch gentle. From what she could tell, he seemed to know what he was doing. She settled back into her pillow and forced herself to breathe more slowly. Piece by piece the events on the highway and in the woods floated into place.

Why? The question burned in her thoughts. *Why?*

'Things sound good,' Matt said. 'I'm going to write some orders and splash some water on my face. Then I'll be back.'

After he had gone, the nurse, Julie, straightened the sheets and wiped off Nikki's face and hands.

'You're going to be fine,' she said. 'Dr. Rutledge may not look like a med school professor, but trust me, he's a really great doctor – the best in this hospital. I understand you're from Boston. Well, he grew up here, but he trained at Harvard. He actually rode out to the lake with the ambulance and put that tube in you out there.'

Nikki nodded that she understood and made a weak thumbs-up sign.

Doctor. Just before the fat guy in the business suit had attacked her, he had called her 'Doc.' Who could have told him that? The two men weren't out to rob her or even to rape her. They were going to kill her.

Why?

Matt returned to Nikki Solari's bedside after washing, shaving, and gathering the things he had appropriated for Lewis Slocumb. The hours of sleep had served him well and, at least for the moment, he felt sharp and focused. Yesterday he had planned to return to the Slocumbs' farm to replace the jury-rigged chest tube after just a few hours of work in the hospital. Now nearly a full day had gone by. Well, he reminded himself, he could only do what he could do and hope that Frank Slocumb had the sense to drag his brother into the hospital if he was in trouble.

Solari looked alert and a bit more animated. Her X-ray had showed no pneumonia and her blood gases were excellent. It was time to keep his promise and remove the tube. Hopefully, then, the questions surrounding the events at Crystal Lake would be answered. One mystery that had already been answered was the bizarre dream in which Matt had been immersed. On the top of Solari's left foot was a tattoo, orange and black, of a Gila monster. Matt had noticed it during his initial exam, but was far too engrossed in trying to save her life to give it much thought.

The woman with the elegant, long-fingered hands, who he'd guessed might be a potter, had turned out to be a coroner. And the coroner, who played bluegrass music, had an orange and black Gila monster tattooed on her foot. As popular as tattoos had become in the general public, they were still not that common among middle-of-the-road med students and doctors. Was she offbeat enough to be into drugs in some way? he wondered. Maybe dealing? Is that why she was being chased through the woods near Niles Ledge?

Matt considered the possibility as he prepared to remove the breathing tube from her throat. He also pictured his own tattoo – injected into his arm as a constant, permanent reminder of love and loss. No, he decided, glancing up at Nikki Solari's expressive eyes, whatever the significance of the odd tattoo, it had nothing to do with drugs.

The technique for removing the endotracheal tube was as straightforward as the potential complications of the procedure were life-threatening. Suction out the trachea, deflate the balloon, have the patient attempt to cough, and pull out the tube. Simple. Lurking in the shadows, however, was the specter of a reactive spasm of the larynx severe enough to shut off the airway, and tight enough to make reinsertion of a breathing tube near impossible.

Matt had never actually performed an emergency tracheotomy, but he had the equipment to do so near at hand. At that moment, there was nothing in the world he wanted to do less.

'Dr. Solari, we're all set,' he said.

Nikki nodded and gave him a weak A-okay. The woman was tough, he was thinking. Whatever else she was, she was tough.

'Good,' he said. 'I know this next part isn't pleasant, but we've got to do it. Suction, please, Julie.'

The nurse snaked a small suction catheter down beyond the tip of the tube into Nikki's trachea.

Nikki reacted to the intrusion with violent coughing, tears overflowing her eyes and running down her cheeks.

'I'm really sorry,' Matt said, deflating the balloon on the tube. 'Let's get this part over with. Just take a breath and cough.'

Nikki did as he asked. A slight tug and just like that the tube was out. The nurse moved to suction out Nikki's mouth and throat, but Nikki pushed her hand away.

'Bless you,' Nikki croaked.

The nurse slipped a clear, polystyrene mask over Nikki's mouth and nose. For a minute, then another, no one spoke as Nikki took long, grateful draughts of humidified, oxygen-enriched air. Her blood oxygen level, as measured by the oximeter clipped around her fingertip, remained good, and her cardiac monitor pattern, steady. There was no significant laryngeal spasm.

'You all right?' Matt asked finally.

'Ugh, that was just awful,' Nikki said. 'Hardly the way to greet a new patient. Where I come from, doctors usually start by asking who their insurance company is.'

Lights in the ICU cubicle were dimmed once again. The nurses had gone off to prepare for another admission – an admission who would probably be given Nikki's room. Haltingly, dozing off every few minutes, Nikki shared the story of the faked accident on the roadway, the chloroform, the gunshots, and the subsequent chase through the forest. She had no recollection whatsoever of the events immediately surrounding her plunge into Crystal Lake.

The frightening account was totally engaging to

Matt, but no more so than the woman who was sharing it. Exhausted and clearly dealing with a headache, dizziness, and other effects of a concussion, Nikki (she insisted he call her that) had a spirit, intelligence, and wry humor that even her compromising condition could not diminish.

He had questions, dozens of them, and undoubtedly, Grimes would as well. But for the moment, he had no desire to deal with the man. Soon, after she was persistently awake, he would call the station. For now, he sat quietly and waited while she rested. He was actually surprised to realize he was studying her face. Why did it appeal to him so? There was little if anything about it that was reminiscent of the woman he had loved for so much of his life. If Ginny was beach sand and midday sun, Nikki was more moonlight and the still, dark water of a lake at night. Ginny's mouth was innocent and childlike, Nikki's full and sensual. Over the years since Ginny's death, he had, from time to time, been with one woman or another. But never had he been drawn to any of them this way. He felt awkward, strange, and a little disloyal. What was he doing contrasting and comparing this woman with Ginny?

. . . *Have those memories remind you of how wonderful life can be again.* Isn't that what Mae had said to him?

At that moment, the voice that bothered him with such things reminded him that he was her physician. Romantic involvement by a doctor with his or her patient was prohibited not only by the Hippocratic Oath, but by most states' legislatures as well. For too many docs, such involvement ended up being a shortcut to grocery clerkdom.

'Hey there, still here?' she asked dreamily.

'I . . . um . . . may have dozed off.'

'Again?'

'I aced nap one-oh-one in med school. Tops in my class.'

'Me, too. I was slated to be a surgeon, but they booted me out after I fell asleep at the operating table.'

'I can picture you toppling face first into an open abdomen. Nikki, tell me, why did all this happen to you?'

'I have no idea. But those men knew who I was. I'm sure of that.'

'Could they have been after drugs?'

'Anything's possible, I suppose. But from what I recall, I think they were after me, pure and simple. I think I heard them say each other's names, but I can't remember.'

Matt rose from his chair.

'I'll be back,' he said.

'Where are you going?'

'To call the police. Chief Grimes will want to know you're awake, and until we know what this is all about, I want a guard next to your door.'

Nikki rubbed at her eyes.

'I think I spent some time with the police chief.'

'You did. He told me.'

'From what I remember, he was very friendly.'

'That explains it,' Matt said, flashing on Grimes's totally inappropriate, thinly veiled threat in the ER.

'What?'

'Nothing. Nikki, we haven't contacted your family. Just give me the numbers and I'll call your husband or parents or anyone else you want.'

'My dad's recovering from a small stroke, my

mom gets hysterical at the sight of a robin eating a worm, and the candidates to be my husband are still out there fighting one another to the death for my favor. Since I'm probably going to make it, why don't we just not upset anyone? Oh, except my job. I was supposed to be at work.'

Matt wrote down the number.

'I'll be back,' he announced in a woeful Schwarzenegger accent.

'You're . . . very . . . nice,' she said.

He started to reply, then realized she was out again, breathing evenly and deeply.

When Matt explained what he wanted, the desk officer at the Belinda police station patched him through to Bill Grimes.

'Has she told you what happened?' Grimes asked.

'I haven't asked her much. I wanted to call you first.'

'Don't tell me you've gone sensible on me.'

'Very funny. She did say it was two men – one real fat, in a business suit. One athletic. Ring any bells?'

'Maybe.'

'She also said they were shooting at her.'

'So that *was* a bullet wound by her ear.'

'I would say so.'

'I'll have someone over there within the hour,' Grimes said. 'And I'll be by later to speak with her.'

'Just go easy,' Matt said, wanting instead to tell him to just stay the hell away from her. 'She's got a fairly severe concussion.'

'How long do you think she'll be in the hospital?'

'I don't know for sure. A couple of days, maybe.

I'm going to have the neurologist see her and maybe get an MRI if he thinks it might tell us anything more than the emergency CT scan we did.'

'Fair enough. One of the guys will be over there shortly.'

'Round the clock, okay?'

'Rutledge, how about you just do your business and let me do mine.'

'Nancy,' Matt said to the nursing supervisor, 'are you sure you can't keep Dr. Solari in the unit any longer?'

'Matt, you know I'd walk over hot coals for you,' Nancy Catlett said, 'but we have four criticals in the unit right now, and a post-op abdominal aneurysm repair due up soon. There's just no way I can justify keeping a patient who's awake and alert – even one of yours.'

'In that case, a private room.'

'That depends on her insurance.'

'Just find one for her. We're going to have a guard posted outside the door. I want only people essential to her care going in there. If she needs a specific order, I'll write it. If her plan still won't cover the private, I will.'

'Well now, I don't think we'll need to go that far,' Catlett said. 'But if that's the way you care for all your patients, I'm switching doctors to you. My HMO is terrible about paying for private rooms.'

Matt made quick rounds on the patients he had in the hospital, and then brought the chest tube insertion kit, drainage system, intravenous bags, antibiotics, and other purloined equipment to his motorcycle. Thoughts of Nikki Solari and questions surrounding the assault on her had now bivouacked in his mind, making it difficult to concentrate on much else. When he returned to the unit, the nurses reported that Nikki had been asleep since he left, drifting back out again immediately after each of the two neuro checks they had done. Still, the moment he stepped through the doorway, she moaned contentedly and opened her eyes.

'Welcome back,' she said, yawning.

'How did you know I was here?'

'Sometimes I just know things.'

'How's your headache?'

'Did you ever see *Riverdance*?'

'Ouch. I can have them give you some Tylenol, but I'd rather stay away from anything stronger.'

'Tylenol will be fine. I'm tough.'

'You don't have to convince me of that. The police guard is all set. You were right about Bill Grimes. He feels very protective toward you.'

'I hope he can get to the bottom of this,' she said.

'He's a pretty good cop.' *When he wants to be.* 'Listen, I've got a house call to make, but I'm going to wait around the ICU until the guard gets here. You just go ahead and sleep. Right now that's the most therapeutic thing you could do.'

'In a minute. Right now I'm wide awake. Can you sit for a little while? I sort of feel like Dorothy when she looked out the window and discovered she wasn't in Kansas anymore.'

'I'd much rather talk with you than write progress notes.'

'Thanks. The nurses tell me you trained at Harvard.'

'I did my residency in medicine at White Memorial.'

'I'm impressed. I wasn't accepted for their surgical program.'

'Surgery?'

'I did a year of surg at Metropolitan then switched to pathology. I wanted my patients to lie really, really still when I was operating on them. Where did you live when you were there?'

'Beacon Hill. The poorer part at the bottom. I liked Boston pretty much, but my heart has always been here in the mountains. I couldn't wait to get back.'

'That's not hard to understand. It's very beautiful here.'

'When you're not being chased by a pair of crazed killers it is. Can I ask you something?'

'Sure.'

'It's about your tattoo.'

'What about it?' she asked with a slightly defensive edge to her voice.

'Oh, nothing. I just wanted you to know that I run into Gila monster tattoos on the top of doctors' feet all the time around here.'

Nikki's eyes narrowed. *Are you making fun of me?* they asked.

Matt leapt in to save the situation.

'Uh-oh, I'm sorry,' he said. 'Sounding flip when I shouldn't is one of my less desirable talents. It gets me into more hot water than a boiled lobster. Mea culpa.' He pushed up his sleeve to reveal his own tattoo. 'I'm into hawthorn trees, myself.'

Nikki's expression softened.

'Sometime, *you're* going to owe *me* a story,' she said. 'Well, let's see. I had the tattoo put on a few years ago. Some of my musician friends were getting them and I decided I wanted one, too. I picked the dorsum of my foot so that I could see it whenever I wanted to, but I could also hide it whenever I wanted. I might have thought of some other location if I had known how much that one was going to kill. It's actually only half Gila monster. The front half is a salamander.'

'Many of our doctors choose that variation,' he commented in spite of himself.

Her eyes laughed. No problems this time.

'I once saw the combination on a clay pot at a Navajo reservation in Arizona,' she went on, 'and after the artist explained it to me, I ended up adopting the creation as sort of my totem. The salamander is shy, porous, vulnerable, weak, and secretive. The Gila is fearless, compact, warriorlike, determined, and so tenacious that when it grasps something with its thick jaws, one must often cut its head off to get it to let go.'

Matt flashed on the horrible death of the beast in his dream and shuddered. He had never been one to reject the mystical or supernatural, beginning with dreams, and this one was bothering him more every second. Was the unsettling scenario merely replaying a version of the events recently past, or was it a vision of things yet to be?

'I can see how those two men on the highway got more than they bargained for,' he said.

There was no response. Nikki's eyes were closed again, her brain muffled by exhaustion and the physiology of her concussion. The lingering effects of blunt head trauma were absolutely unpredictable and potentially devastating. Matt had seen professional athletes forced to the sidelines permanently, and others – intellectually sound initially with no visible changes on their MRIs –

become significantly impaired over just a few days.

Silently, he prayed for Nikki Solari and the music that she made – with and without her violin. He stood, and before he turned away, impulsively reached out to touch her hand. At the last moment, he pulled back. The gesture would be perfectly innocent and natural with nearly all of his patients. But not, he had to admit, with this one.

Chapter 17

With three quick raps, Dr. Richard Steinman gaveled to order the final meeting of the select commission on Omnivax. The scene outside the closed-door session was nothing like the throng of reporters and photographers that had covered Lynette Marquand's speech. But the media was still well represented. The drama of the First Lady's promise to go back to the drawing board with Omnivax if even one member of the august panel voted against it, coupled with the political and medical implications of the project, had kept interest high.

Around the elegant conference room, twenty-two physicians and scientists stopped their conversations and solemnly took their seats behind their name cards around the massive table. One place remained conspicuously empty – that of consumer representative Ellen Kroft.

'I would like to take this opportunity,' Steinman began, 'to thank each and every one of you for nearly three years of outstanding, deeply committed effort, which will culminate in this morning's vote. You have done a great service to your country, to the medical community, and ultimately to the people of the world. The agenda for this meeting is that you will individually be given the chance to make some final remarks on whatever subject you choose relative to the work we have been doing. After that, we will go around the table and each will vote Yea or Nay. For the purpose of the First Lady's promise to the American people, an abstention will not be viewed as a negative vote.'

He paused, looking as if he had just swallowed an underchewed chunk of meat.

'Before we go any further,' he said after clearing his throat and composing himself, 'there is a statement I have been asked to read to you. It was delivered to me earlier this morning with a note stating that copies of it are being sent to the *Washington Post* and the *New York Times*, as well as to all four major TV networks and CNN. It is from Mrs. Ellen Kroft, who will not be here today. I'm sorry there wasn't time to provide each of you a copy, but one will be distributed to you by the time our session is over. I have been asked by Mrs. Kroft to read her statement to you in its entirety.'

There was a stirring in the room and an exchange of glances. Some expressions were curious, some unabashedly disdainful. Seated next to Ellen Kroft's empty chair, George Poulos fixed his neutral gaze steadily on Steinman.

'There being no objections, then,' Steinman said, 'I shall proceed.' He again cleared his throat, then adjusted his glasses.

' "Esteemed colleagues, as the lone consumer representative on the Omnivax commission I have approached my responsibilities not as the scientist and/or physician that all of you are, but as a mother and grandmother. From the day of our first meeting, I established three mandates for myself. The first was to learn as much as I was able about the process by which vaccines are developed, tested, approved, and later on evaluated once they are in general use. The second was to acquaint myself in depth with the components of Omnivax – their production, individual characteristics, and interactions one with another. And finally, to speak with a cross section of fathers and mothers in a number of communities, recording their hopes and, yes, their fears about vaccinations in general and Omnivax in particular. I would like to address these tasks in that order.

' "There are many, including most of you, the First Family, and HHS Secretary Lara Bolton, who believe that one of the primary benchmarks of progress in a civilized society is how thoroughly its citizens are protected against infectious diseases. As you know, but others may not, since nineteen-forty the number of required vaccine doses for our children has risen from three doses of DPT to forty doses of twelve different vaccines. And now, with Omnivax, while the number of shots will drop impressively, the number of vaccines administered will more than double. Omnivax certainly seems like one giant leap for mankind. But will there be negative consequences?

' "The gold standard for any new drug investigation is the double blind study, in which the subject population is divided into two groups, equal in as many demographic and medical parameters as possible. The larger the study population, the better, so long as the characteristics of each group are equivalent. One of the groups then receives the drug being evaluated, and the other a placebo. The study becomes double blind when neither the patient nor the treating physician knows who is getting what. The longer the evaluation is

214

continued, the more reliable its results. In fact, many new drug studies have been conducted over a decade or more.

'"My research has shown that not once has a vaccine – any vaccine – been evaluated by a prolonged double blind study. The pharmaceutical houses are powerful, and fund much of the drug research done at our universities and medical centers. They also have polished, highly effective public relations offices that have, on a number of occasions, set out to convince the general public that we cannot afford to deprive the placebo group of the lifesaving benefits of a vaccine while waiting until a statistically meaningful double blind study can be completed.

'"Has this shortcut in scientific process hurt us in any concrete, medical way? That I cannot answer with any certainty. What I can say is that as vaccination rates have climbed, there has been an alarming increase in the incidence of a number of so-called immune-mediated diseases and conditions such as asthma, allergies, and juvenile diabetes, as well as others – autism, ADD, and other learning disabilities – whose classification as immune-mediated remains to be established. Is there a connection? Do vaccinations in some instances disrupt the normal development of the body's immune system? Until long-term, double blind studies are performed on those vaccines, we may never know."'

Here, Steinman paused for some water and to make eye contact with those on his committee. Several of them rolled their eyes in exasperation at being forced to listen to the shopworn, simplistic revelations of the one member of their panel with no research credentials.

215

'I can see what you're thinking,' Steinman said, 'but I am going to finish Mrs. Kroft's statement. She has done us all a great service by deciding to abstain from this vote. In our laboratories and clinics, we are powerful and influential. But in the court of public opinion, the consumer representative has more clout than almost any of us. When this meeting is over and our vote has been taken, we are each going to have to respond publicly to the issues she is raising. Any questions?'

'Just get it over and let's vote,' one of the pediatricians groused.

'Thank you, Mel,' Steinman said. 'That is just what I intend to do.' He straightened his glasses and took another drink.

'"And what about Omnivax?" Mrs. Kroft goes on. "First, let me say how impressed I am with the research and medical technology that has gone into the development of this amazing product. But once again, I must ask, Where is the double blind study? Where is the long-term evaluation? Once a drug or vaccine is released, the CDC and FDA rely on a post-marketing evaluation system of physician adverse reaction report forms. Studies have shown that only a small percentage of doctors have ever filled out such a form, despite knowing or sensing that many conditions they have encountered may be vaccine- or medication-related. Some are too busy or simply can't put their hands on a form at the moment they need one. Those who fill out such forms generally do so only when the suspected reaction occurs within a short time after the medication is taken and, more often than not, is spectacular. I would be remiss not to point out that there is no evidence at this juncture that Omnivax has caused problems in preliminary test subjects of a magnitude that even remotely approaches the mortality of the diseases it is preventing. But I would also be remiss not to point out that Omnivax is only as strong as its least extensively evaluated component.

'"Thirty vaccines, no double blind research. But also no obvious major adverse effects. For me those three facts make the decision on Omnivax a tough call.

'"That brings me to my final task, that of being a true consumer representative. Parents are frightened that government agencies and the pharmaceutical industry are keeping information on vaccine side effects from them. Those parents who wish to decline vaccinating their children are prosecuted sometimes even when they can show that doing so violates their basic religious beliefs. This shouldn't be happening in America. Wherever I go, parents are clamoring for three things: information, research, and choice.

'"So where does that leave us? We have a remarkable product that will unquestionably save lives. We have a basic, essential research design that has been skipped over just as it has for every other vaccine or vaccine combination we have ever used. We have parents wanting more information and more control over what is injected into their children's bodies.

'"After reviewing all these facets and issues, I have decided I can neither wholeheartedly endorse Omnivax nor vote to deprive the American public of its lifesaving gifts. I therefore have decided to abstain from the final vote on its approval. I wish my colleagues on the commission all the best and thank them for their forbearance and education over these past thirty-two months." '

Richard Steinman set his glasses aside. Around the room, expressions clearly said that none of the participants were the least bit moved by what Ellen had written. After several silent seconds, George Poulos raised his hand and spoke.

'I would like to move at this time that we dispense with the final comments and proceed right to a vote.'

'Second,' a weary voice called out.

'Objections?' Steinman asked. 'Okay, then. George, suppose we start with you.'

'I vote Yea.'

At the moment of the historic vote, Ellen was a hundred miles to the north of the FDA building, driving in no particular hurry through the lush landscape of Maryland's Catoctin Mountains, headed for the cabin of Rudy Peterson. Two hours before that, she had picked up Lucy at her home and driven the child to a small wooded park, bisected by a gently flowing stream. There she led her to a bench and sat beside her, holding her close, rocking in synchrony with her. Not far away, on a small playground, half a dozen children were playing on the swings and jungle gym. Lucy's gentle scent, scrubbed and clean, was no different from those kids', Ellen thought. Her hair, her skin, her beautiful eyes – all were perfectly normal. Yet here she was, as different from those children as if she had come from another planet.

Ellen scanned about, wondering if she and Lucy were being followed and observed. The notion made her queasy. There was no obvious candidate that she could see, but that meant nothing. The people up against her were professionals.

'I'm going to find that man, honey,' Ellen whispered softly. 'I'm going to find that man and I'm going to find out who hired him, and I'm going to hurt them. I'm going to hurt them like they have never been hurt in their lives.'

For fifteen minutes, they sat there, Ellen's tears dampening her granddaughter's hair. The children had all raced off to class. The playground was empty. Lucy, rocking less than usual, stared vaguely off in that direction.

'I love you, baby,' Ellen said finally, helping the girl to her feet and back toward the car. 'Come on, let's get going. Gayle is waiting for you at school.'

At eleven, Ellen was just a few miles from Rudy's cabin. She flipped on the radio and found a static-filled news broadcast just in time to catch the report from Rockville. In the unanimous vote promised by First Lady Lynette Marquand, general use of the Omnivax multivaccine had been approved. In just a few days, she would be present at a Washington, D.C., neighborhood health center as Secretary of Health and Human Services Dr. Lara Bolton administered the first injection of the drug. After that, inoculation with Omnivax would be required for all newborns and eventually for all older children as well.

Let the games begin, Ellen thought bitterly.

She felt anxious but keyed up as well. There really had been no choice for her. She had done what she had to do. If she had plowed forward with a negative vote on Omnivax, and something had happened to Lucy, she would simply have been unable to go on.

There was no mention in the news report that Ellen had abstained from voting. Rather, the focus of what she heard of the report was the political implications of the Marquand administration keeping a pledge made to the American public. Perhaps over the next day or so, she thought, her statement would get some press. Perhaps not. It really didn't matter.

Her hands tightened on the wheel as her mind's eye pictured the arrogant thug sitting so calmly in her living room, reeking of cigarette smoke. The bastard had done his job well. He had convinced her that, if he so wished it, none of her loved ones would be safe, and there really wasn't a damn thing she could do about it. What she hoped he did not know was that he had only won the first round. She had thrown a light jab in the form of her press release, but she felt certain her statement was nothing that would bring reprisals. Now she had to find a way to strike a more substantial blow – ideally a mortal one. In addition to protecting Lucy, by allowing the vote to proceed she had bought the time needed for Rudy Peterson to complete his work.

She cut off the main road onto an unmarked gravel drive that cut through a meadow festooned with wildflowers. Sunlight glinted off the colors. The sound of insects and scent of late summer filled the air. At the end of the drive, nestled in a young wood, was Rudy's rough-hewn cabin. Rudy had been Howard's college roommate and, later, best man at their wedding. He was for many years a bio-statistician at the FDA before he was prematurely nudged into retirement by reorganization. But that hardly told the story of the man. Despite his long-term friendship with her husband, Ellen had always thought of Rudy Peterson as the anti-Howard. Where Howard was handsome and dashing, Rudy was introspective, philosophical, and hardly the physical specimen women would chase after. Howard's humor was slapstick and ridicule; Rudy's, droll and subtle, with just a pinch of cynicism. Howard had turned out to be more flash than substance. Rudy continued to be a steady, loyal friend, who had never said a strongly negative word about his former roommate. In fact, he was the only one of their pre-divorce acquaintances who had managed to maintain a relationship with both of them.

Ellen parked behind Rudy's ancient pickup, surveyed the house, then walked around to the back. There was no sense looking for him inside on a day like this. A narrow, well-worn dirt path wound from the small backyard through the woods to Rudy's pond. It was a neat little pond, five acres he had said, fed by mountain streams, and stocked with trout and bass by a company who made a business of doing that. Rudy, in his rowboat, was out there in the middle, gazing up at the hills, pausing now and then for a cast. He was wearing his trademark Tom Sawyer–style straw hat. Even at this distance, Ellen could smell the cherry tobacco from his pipe. According to a well-run study from Scotland, he had told her, one pipeful a day of cherrywood tobacco added 3.2 healthy years of life, whereas two or more pipefuls were responsible for minus 5.

She sat down in the shade on the shore, but it wasn't long before he spotted her and waved.

'Ahoy,' he called out. 'Be right in.'

Ellen watched as he reeled in, shipped his rod, and rowed toward her. As soon as he had been let go by the FDA, Rudy had closed up his apartment in Rockville and moved out to the cabin full-time. Never married, he had a brother and a niece and nephew, some good friends, and passions for carpentry and classical piano, which he played better than most. Still, Ellen always worried that he spent too much time alone, and she made it a point to call once a week or so, and to drive out for an overnight every few months, bearing enough home-cooked food to last a few weeks. Since her appointment to the select commission on Omnivax, the calls and visits to her friend had been more frequent.

Rudy tied up on the trim little dock and then exchanged kisses on the cheek. He had a round, boyish face that looked as if it had yet to feel a razor. The hair on his head was completely gone, save for a silver monk's fringe. Ellen and others felt he bore enough resemblance to actor Gavin MacLeod to call him Captain. He had responded by painting 'The Love Boat' on the stern of his skiff.

'Where are the fish?' she asked.

'I throw them back. By this time of the season most of them know me by my first name. They bite on the hook just to come up and visit. Once in a while one of them will mess himself up enough that I'll have to bring him home and make a meal of him.'

'It's good to see you.'

She put her arm around his shoulders as they walked back to the cabin.

'So,' he asked after fixing two cups of tea, 'how did the vote go? Did you throw a monkey wrench into their machine?'

Ellen had spoken to him after Lynette Marquand's promise, but not since the visit from the man with the harelip scar.

'I didn't go in for the vote.'

Rudy's eyebrows arched just a bit.

'So,' he said, 'I assume our friendly neighborhood vaccine is now the law of the land.'

'Twenty-two to nothing.'

'With one abstention.'

'With one abstention. The first dose is scheduled to be given in a few days.'

'The first of millions.'

'Tens of millions, thank you,' she corrected glumly.

'It's not ready,' he said.

She brightened up.

'You have proof?'

'Not exactly. But as I told you before, we're closing in on something.'

'Tell me.'

Rudy looked at her kindly, then shook his head.

'You first,' he said. 'I'm a patient man, but there's a hole the size of Georgia in the middle of this conversation.'

'I'm sorry, Rudy. I know how worried you used to get about me after Howard left. I wanted to tell you what caused me to abstain without having you get too upset. I just couldn't figure out how.'

'Now, that's what I call one hell of an interest-piquer.'

Ellen smiled ironically.

'I suppose it is,' she said. 'I'm sorry. You know me, the queen of worrying about people worrying. Rudy, the day before yesterday a man broke into my house and was waiting for me when I got home.

223

He was huge and reeked of cigarette smoke, and had a thick scar right here above his lip. He sat there smiling while he produced pictures of Lucy, at school, in the yard, even one in her bedroom, and implied that she would be kidnapped and killed in a horrible way if I cast the vote that sent Omnivax back to the drawing board.'

Rudy exhaled, whistling softly. 'I'm sad to say I'm not that surprised. This big daddy vaccine means a lot of things and a lot of money to a lot of people. You can describe the bastard?'

'Of course, but what does that accomplish?'

'It's a start.'

'He was so damn sure of himself, Rudy. He just sat there smirking, knowing there wasn't a single thing I could do except listen. He said that if I went to the police, they would be able to do nothing, and he would find out.'

Ellen felt herself beginning to unravel. She bit on her lip and brushed some tears away with the back of her hand.

'He's probably right on both accounts,' Rudy said. 'I'm really sick that this happened to you.' He reached over and awkwardly patted her hand. 'Was there anything else you remember?'

'After he finished threatening Lucy, he made a call from his cell phone and a car pulled up. He walked out of the house as calmly as any door-to-door salesman and drove off, just like that. I tried to get the license number of the car, but it was gone too quickly.'

'Did he say anything at all that gave a hint as to who had hired him?'

Ellen shook her head. 'I don't think so. He said he was employed by someone who wished to get

Omnivax into circulation as soon as possible. I asked if he worked for President Marquand or the drug companies, but he brushed that off.'

'I wonder,' Rudy said. 'My money's on someone on the manufacturing end of all this. From what I know about Lynette Marquand, I doubt she's capable of hiring someone like this, but I can't speak for her staff – or her husband's, for that matter.'

'Wait, he said "employers". Plural. I remember that distinctly.'

'Well, here's some paper. I'd like you to write down every single thing you can remember about the man. His appearance, clothes, mannerisms, phrases he said, everything.'

'What good'll that do?'

'I don't really know yet, but as my granny used to say, it couldn't hurt. Maybe something you forgot will pop into your mind.'

'Maybe. I want to find him, Rudy. I want to find him and . . . and hurt him. I close my eyes at night and there's his hideous face leering at me. I wake up in the middle of dreams, soaked in sweat. Early this morning I actually got sick. I wanted so much to go to the police, but after what he said, I just couldn't.'

'Easy does it, El. I'll help you. If he's out there, we'll find him. But first, get the facts down on paper. You know me. I need data. Let me get you some more tea while you do that.'

'Then you'll tell me what's been going on with you?'

'Then I'll tell you,' Rudy said.

Rudy's study was the small second floor of the cabin, once an attic. The skylights, beamed cathedral ceiling, knotty pine paneling, and floor-to-ceiling

225

bookshelves helped make the room as comfortable as the man. Occupying much of the space was a large oak desk bearing a computer and other sophisticated electronics. A reading area with two worn leather easy chairs and a shared ottoman took up the rest. By the lone window, a telescope looked out across the yard toward the pond.

After she had finished writing down what she remembered of the well-dressed, well-spoken killer, Ellen kicked her shoes off and settled into one of the easy chairs. Rudy took the other. As he stretched his legs onto the ottoman, his bare foot brushed against hers. He quickly pulled it away and muttered an apology, his expression a strange mix of embarrassment and . . . *and what?* Ellen wondered. Then she noticed the heightened color in his cheeks.

'So?' she asked, as he replaced his foot on the ottoman a respectable distance from hers.

'Well, you know the problem I've been encountering trying to check up on this Omnivax. It isn't that there are any incriminating research data, there aren't. It's that, for a project this massive, there ain't that much data at all. And as a statistician, I like playing around with piles and piles of data almost as much as I like fishin'. The megavaccine has been field-tested, but not in any controlled way, and the components have all been tested individually and in some combinations, though not in any controlled way, either. Every piece of this lummox of a vaccine seems to work just fine, but only as far as it's been evaluated. I have no doubt that Omnivax protects people against every infection they say it does.'

'I hear a *but* coming on.'

'*But*, if this were a new arthritis medicine or birth-control pill, there is no way it would have been approved for general use on numbers this scant.'

'To the best of my knowledge there has never been a tightly controlled double blind study of a vaccine.'

'To the best of *my* knowledge, that is correct. Physicians and the pharmaceutical industry and some of my dear old friends at the CDC and FDA would rather take the chance there are no problems with a vaccine than risk depriving the public of protection against even one a them goldurn microbial buggers.'

'Go on.'

'Well, like I think I told you, I decided to focus what little time and resources we had on examining the weakest links in the Omnivax chain. So I weeded through the blocks of data available on each of the less common disorders – what I call the fringe players. And like I mentioned, this vaccine against Lassa fever heads that list. It's relatively new. So are the outbreaks of infection it was created to protect us against. It was approved for general use by the FDA about ten years ago. From a statistical point of view – *my* statistical point of view, at least – it was rushed into use too soon.'

'They were afraid a major epidemic was brewing here in the States.'

'I know, only it didn't happen – at least not then it didn't. Well, there are no major problems with the vaccine that I can tell, but it sure hasn't been tracked very thoroughly.'

'I already know about that,' Ellen said, hoping her tone didn't reflect her deep disappointment. 'That's what you have?'

Rudy took her reaction in, though, and for a few

seconds he just sat there. Then shook his head and grinned proudly.

'Nope,' he said. 'As a matter of fact it isn't what I have at all. I made some calls. One of them was to an old pal from the CDC I used to do projects with. His name's Arnold Whitman and he's an epidemiologist and a microbiologist. Arnie's been looking at these outbreaks of Lassa fever for us on the QT. If he gets caught mucking around in someone else's territory it could be his job. Anyhow, what he found may be nothing, but Arnie doesn't think so, and Arnie is very high on my list of very smart people who aren't wrong about science a hell of a lot.'

'You should be on that list,' Ellen said.

'Oh, I am. Seriously, listen to this. The incubation period for Lassa fever from exposure to symptoms is seven to fourteen days, twenty-one days tops. Eighteen of the cases in the U.S. appear to have brought the infection in with them from Africa. The rest of the cases are believed to have caught the virus from those eighteen. Given the known incubation period, it seems as if every one of the eighteen cases became infected on or about the very day they left Africa for the U.S.'

'Weird.'

'More than weird, my friend. This is the stuff my statistics were born to make sense of. And guess what?'

'They can't?'

'Precisely! They can't make sense of those eighteen cases all becoming infected as they are about to leave for the U.S., because something's wrong.'

'But what?'

228

'That is the conundrum. I can't say, at least not yet. But wait, there's more. In the countries where it occurs frequently, Lassa fever has a clear-cut seasonal predominance for the months of January and February. In fact, here's a little graph I put together with cases that occurred three years ago, which I got from a Sierra Leone health ministry report via my pal Arnie.'

'Impressive,' Ellen said.

'Not overwhelming, but the January/February pattern the textbooks write about is certainly there. Now look at our eighteen cases.'

Ellen held the second graph next to the first. There was only one case in January, none in February. Most of the rest were in the summer.

'And your statistics say?'

Rudy pressed an imaginary buzzer, adding the sound effect.

'Once again the numbers say that something's wrong. And need I remind you that these are my numbers, and my numbers never lie. From what I can tell, in the months of May, June, and July, you have a much greater chance of catching Lassa fever by flying to the U.S. than you do by staying in Africa.'

'What do we do with this information?'

'We try and turn it into a working hypothesis,' he replied, 'a scenario that fits and explains the data. We need to come up with some facts.'

'Starting where?'

'I would say starting at the Sierra Leone embassy in D.C. A friend of mine in the State Department tells me they have access to a passenger manifest of every flight out of their country. Plus, I'd be interested in how many Americans got Lassa fever

229

in Africa as opposed to after they came home. I believe you could get that information from the Sierra Leoneans as well. Data! I crave data!'

Ellen jumped up and threw her arms around Rudy's neck.

'I knew you'd come through. Rudy, you've been just the best friend in the world to me.'

'That's not exactly the hardest thing I've ever had to do,' he said, looking away.

Chapter 18

'Code blue, icu . . . code blue, icu . . .'

Matt was on Med/Surg 2, writing orders regarding Nikki's transfer to a private room, when the code call sounded. There was little doubt in his mind that the subject of the code was the sixty-something woodsman who had taken her bed. Matt had passed him in the corridor as he was being brought into the unit, and had noticed the pallor around his mouth and slight mottling of his skin, suggesting that his heart was not pumping effectively.

Matt raced to the unit, arriving simultaneously with two nurses and the respiratory therapist. Although he didn't regret the decision to switch from the one-patient-after-another approach in the ER to the more intense, in-depth relationships of primary care, he remained something of a hybrid, and the intense action surrounding a code blue or multiple trauma still brought a welcome rush.

He was in the room before he realized that the cardiologist at the man's bedside was Robert Crook. Matt hadn't seen his nemesis at all since the ill-fated meeting at BC&C. Crook greeted his arrival with a scowl and a derisive shake of his head.

'Need help?' Matt asked with accentuated cheeriness.

'I think I have enough,' Crook grumbled.

From behind him, nurse Julie Bellet vehemently shook her head and mouthed the word 'Stay!'

'Why don't I hang around just in case.'

'Suit yourself. Get ready to shock at four hundred joules, please.'

One twenty-five should be enough, Matt was thinking. Bellet looked over at him imploringly, but all he could do was shrug. The 400 was definitely overkill, but not a serious enough breach to go to war with Crook over.

The cardiologist plowed ahead, setting the defibrillator paddles against the man's chest.

'Clear! . . . Ready, shock!'

Julie Bellet depressed the button delivering 400 joules of electricity through the woodsman's chest. Almost immediately, the chaotic spikes of fibrillation were replaced by a rapid, regular rhythm.

'Okay,' Crook said in a purposefully matter-of-fact tone, 'he's now in a nice, supraventricular tachycardia. Let's give him a milligram of propranolol IV.'

No! Matt's mind screamed. *Wrong diagnosis, wrong treatment.* He moved forward next to Crook.

'Robert,' he said, softly enough so that most of those in the room weren't even aware he was speaking, 'that's V. tach. I'm certain of it. Xylocaine, not propranolol.'

Crook glared at him.

'A milligram of propranolol IV,' he ordered again. 'Make that two. Give it slowly.'

Damn! Matt thought, unsuccessfully trying to avoid Julie Bellet's desperate gaze as she and another nurse responded slowly, clearly stalling. War was about to break out.

'Robert,' he whispered again, 'get some Xylocaine in him and you might be able to keep him from fibrillating.'

Crook's sideways look was, if anything, more piercing than before.

'I'll thank you to –'

At that instant, with a flurry of ineffective beats, the woodsman's unstable ventricular tachycardia rhythm degenerated into immediately life-threatening ventricular fibrillation.

'Four hundred joules,' Crook ordered, pointedly looking away from Matt. 'Get a hundred of Xylocaine into him also. Let's hold off on the propranolol for now.'

At that moment, the resuscitation, which should have been straightforward and successful, could easily have gone either way. Fortunately, a power greater than any in the room decided it simply wasn't the old woodsman's time. The electrical countershock was followed by the Xylocaine he should have gotten in the first place, which was then followed by another shock, and suddenly there they were – a decent monitor pattern and a functional blood pressure.

'Nicely done,' Matt said.

There was no response from Robert Crook.

In minutes, the patient's cardiac situation had stabilized. His color had improved and his pressure rose and remained constant. Crook motioned Matt to one side of the cubicle, where he could whisper without being overheard.

'Take a word to the wise,' he said harshly, 'and think about finding another place to practice. Someplace far away from here.'

'But I like it here,' Matt said. 'I grew up here. I always thought I'd grow old here.'

'Well, you can damn well grow old someplace else. That is, if you *want* to grow old. You've stepped over the line, Rutledge.'

'I don't know what you're talking about.'

'People are going to get hurt, and I won't be a bit surprised if you're one of them.'

'Are you threatening m –'

'Dr. Crook?'

Julie Bellet was pointing to the monitor screen, where some irregular beats had appeared.

'Another fifty of Xylocaine IV,' Crook blustered. He turned back to Matt. 'You didn't fool anyone,' he said.

Matt suddenly reached out and grabbed the man by his tie and shirt in such a way that Crook's back screened the move from view of the nurses.

'Neither do you,' he rasped. 'Don't ever threaten me again.'

Stunned, his cheeks flushed with crimson, Crook pulled away and, adjusting his shirt and tie, returned to the bedside.

Matt couldn't remember physically assaulting anyone in his adult life. *Stupid! Absolutely stupid!* It was dumb luck that no one saw what he did. Fists clenched, he whirled and, without so much as a glance backward, left the ICU. Crook clearly knew about their penetration of the toxic dump, Matt was thinking. But was the warning from Armand Stevenson, or was the cardiologist overstepping the bounds of his position with BC&C? And exactly what did he mean by 'People are going to get hurt'? What people?

The Slocumbs!

Matt hurried to Nikki's room to see if the police guard had shown up. He had been away from Lewis Slocumb and his brothers way too long already. He arrived at the room just as Officer Tarvis Lyons came lumbering down the hall. Lyons had been Matt's classmate at Montgomery Regional High School. Tarvis's unofficial nickname, Tar Pits, referred to the speed with which he did just about everything. Matt's surprise that Tarvis had made it to graduation at all, let alone without a police record, was nothing compared to his shock when he returned home after his residency to find Lyons was on the force. It was hard to believe anyone would entrust the man with a pair of handcuffs, let alone a service revolver.

'Hey, Ledge, wazzapnin',' Lyons said, using Matt's high school nickname. His voice was an octave higher than one would have expected from his bulk.

'Grimes sent you?'

Matt hoped he hadn't emphasized the 'you' as much as he feared he had.

'I was off today. That means I'm available for overtime. The big O.T. The chief says there's a babe that needs watchin'.'

'Grimes called Dr. Solari a babe?'

'Um, I can't remember exactly.'

'She's a doctor, Tarvis. That's like twelve years of education after high school. I think she's earned something a little more respectful from you than "babe". Grimes coming over?'

'He said he'll be by soon to talk with her.'

'Do exactly what he says.'

'That's what he said.'

'What?'

'He said to wait and do exactly what he says.'

Matt sighed. 'Listen, post yourself out here. Make sure you or one of the nurses knows anyone who comes in to see her. I have to leave the hospital for a few hours. I'll be on my beeper. Just call the hospital operator if you have any questions and she'll find me.'

'I'm all over it, Ledge,' Lyons said. 'You still playin' hoops?'

'I still play at it. Not much left of the shot, though, or the legs, for that matter.'

'You always were a great shot, Ledge.'

'Thank you for remembering, Tarvis. Keep a close eye on Dr. Solari.'

Matt stood by the doorway and let his eyes adjust to the dimly lit room. Nikki was asleep, breathing sonorously through her oxygen mask. Concerned by what Crook had said, he was anxious to get out to the Slocumbs' farm. He hurried to the nurses' station and wrote an order for a neuro check every thirty minutes for two hours, then every hour after that for five hours. A final glance at Tarvis Lyons, who was pulling a chair out from a deserted room, and he raced off to his motorcycle.

The ride out to the farm seemed interminable. Once again, all the guilt Matt felt about putting Lewis Slocumb in harm's way welled to the surface. Crook was a jerk, but he was right. He had stepped over the line. Maybe it would be better just to let the whole thing drop – forget about the toxic dump and admit that he was no more of a match for Belinda Coal and Coke and their self-serving policies than his father had been. Then he pictured the horribly deformed faces of Darryl Teague and Teddy Rideout. How many others like them would there

236

be? How many were there already? No, he decided as he pulled up in front of the farmhouse, he wasn't going to back off no matter what. He would just be careful not to place anyone else in danger on the altar of his crusade.

Just as Lewis had been waiting for him on the porch for their trip to the mine, Frank was there now. He was leaning against a railing, a potent-looking shotgun cradled loosely in his arms. Matt wondered in passing if they somehow knew he was coming.

'How's he doing?' Matt asked.

'He's had a doggone mizrable time of it, mosly from the pain in 'is shoulder. But he's still alive an' cussin'.'

'That's a good sign. Frank, I'm really sorry it took me so long to get back here. The hospital got incredibly busy. I couldn't get away before now.'

'We knowed you'd be back soon's ya could.'

Not a hint of irritation or entitlement. These men, tough as nails, were used to taking life as it came and to giving their friends every benefit of the doubt. Lewis, wearing tattered jeans and nothing from the waist up, was in the upstairs room, propped by two pillows in a straight-backed oak armchair. His color was surprisingly good. The bandage around his upper chest was blood-soaked, but that was to be expected. The drainage system was intact, and the gauze he had wrapped loosely about the end of the condom was soaked with dried and drying blood. Clearly, the apparatus was functioning quite well.

Frank Slocumb and his brothers had proven to be quite capable nurses. The room was surprisingly clean, and the linens looked as if they might have been washed since he was last there. The three men stood proudly and respectfully to one side of the room as he worked.

'Your brothers have done well by you, Lewis,' Matt said, listening with his stethoscope and noting that breath sounds extended to all fields of both lungs.

'They knowed what'd happ'n to 'em if'n they din't. Am Ah gonna live?'

'Frank said you were too ornery to die, and he was right.'

Matt put an IV rig together and asked for a heavy wire to be hung from the rough-hewn ceiling as a hook. In less than two minutes Lyle had nailed in precisely what was needed. Matt hung up the small plastic sack filled with powerful antibiotic and started the medication running into Lewis's arm.

'This'll help make sure there's no infection,' he said.

'What 'bout this here contraption?' Lewis asked, motioning to the siphon tube.

'Well,' Matt replied, 'incredible as it may seem, it appears that this here contraption has saved your life.' No doubt about it, he was thinking, a letter to the author of *Field Emergencies* was definitely in order. 'Now, the way I see it, we've got three choices. Leave it in, pull it out, or change it.'

'You want us ta vote?' Frank asked.

The four brothers whooped at his humor, which had sailed over Matt's head.

'Fit's all the same ta ya, Doc,' Lewis said, 'Ah'd jes a soon ya din't go stickin' no more stuff in ma chest. Ah din't have the heart ta tell ya, but them pliers ya jammed in thar last time hurt lak hell.'

Out of respect for Matt, the three standing brothers kept their guffaws to a minimum.

'Okay, Lewis,' Matt said. 'I'm going to leave things as they are. The problem is, if I take the tube out too soon, the lung might collapse again, and if I leave it in too long, infection might set in. But listen, guys, if he starts to get sick with infection – fever, cough, pain, pus, redness spreading through the skin around the hole, anything like that, cut the stitch and just pull the tube out immediately. Got that?'

'Got it,' Frank said. 'Ya done a fine job, Doc.'

Matt took the bandages down, cleaned the wound, and then redressed it.

'Listen,' he said. 'I've got to talk to you all about something else. I think the people at the mine know it was me who was in that waste dump of theirs. I'm not sure they know that it was Lewis that was with me, but I wanted to warn you. This jerk at the hospital, Crook, is on the board. He made it sound like someone was going to be hurt or killed because of what I did, and that their blood was going to be on my hands.'

Lyle and Kyle exchanged sly looks.

'What?' Matt asked. 'What's with you two?'

This time it was Lewis who spoke.

'They knowed it 'uz me, Doc. We're sure a thet. Contrary ta what lots a folks round here thank, we got us some frands about – good uns, too. We hear thangs.'

'Well, what are you guys going to do to protect yourselves?'

Again the brothers exchanged knowing looks.

'We kin tak care a ourselves,' Lyle said. 'B'lieve me we can.'

Matt gathered his things and then motioned the three brothers out of the room.

'Lewis, you want me to help you back to bed?' he asked.

'Ah kin manage fahn maself. But if'n it's okay with the doctor, Ah'll stay in this here chair a bit longer.'

'I'm glad you're doing so well. I still feel really bad about what happened. I don't know what Frank and the boys keep smiling and smirking about, but I'm really worried that those bastards from the mine are going to come after you.'

'Ma brothers wuzn't zakly smirkin', Doc. It's jes that –'

A loud, repetitive warning buzzer cut him off. Immediately, there were heavy-booted footsteps across the wood floors downstairs and up the staircase as well.

' 'Scuse me, Doc,' Lewis said, standing, unhooking his IV from its makeshift hanger, and dragging his chair out to the hall. 'We got us some compny.'

Matt hurried along behind him, shutting off the flow valve to prevent blood from backing up into the IV tubing. The footsteps he had heard were the three brothers, moving through their house as if they had drilled for this moment many times. Someone had already shut the alarm off. Kyle raced up the stairs and slid a six-foot by three-foot sheet of metal between where Lewis had positioned himself and the railing. Then he opened the upstairs hall closet and again began unloading their weapons onto the hallway floor. This time Matt noted half a dozen shotguns, a number of handguns, several sophisticated rifles with high-powered sights, and two semiautomatic weapons. Kyle left two shotguns, a heavy pistol, and a rifle with Lewis, then set a black metal box with a keypad and several switches onto Lewis's lap. Next he began lowering weapons through the balustrade to Lyle.

Stunned at the size and scope of their arsenal, Matt could only stand behind Lewis and watch.

'How many?' Lewis called down.

'Ah thank four' was the reply from Frank. 'Looks lak ol' Lonnie Tuggle's one of 'em. Ah never did lak him much.'

Cameras! Matt thought, incredulous. Somewhere in the trees out there, the legendary backwoods hick Slocumb brothers had set up a warning system and surveillance cameras.

'Frank,' he said loudly, 'my Harley's outside. Do you want me to move it?'

'Doc, d'ya thank we'd let anythin' happ'n ta thet bee-yew-tee-ful machine a yourn? It's off safe inna barn.'

'Lewis, did you know these men were coming?'

'We heard they mot be.'

'Jesus,' Matt muttered. 'Some hermits you guys are. Hey, listen, be careful,' he cried out. 'I don't want any of you getting hurt. Or me, for that matter.'

'Ain't us ya got ta worry 'bout, Doc,' Lewis said firmly. 'Now ya go on inta thet room behind us an' keep yer nose down jes in case they's stupider than we thank.'

Matt did as he was ordered and dropped to his knees just inside the partially open door, a few feet behind Lewis. The eldest Slocumb, all sixty-two or -three years of him, just sat there with his makeshift chest tube still draining blood through the condom, his IV bag lying on the floor next to him, his right hand cradling the pistol, and his left resting on the black box.

'Here they be,' Frank said. 'Two still inna car. Two sneakin' round back on foot.'

'Jes stay cool, boys,' Lewis ordered. 'No happy fangers. No one says nothin' but Frank.'

At that moment there were three sharp raps on the front door.

'It's open,' Frank called out. 'Lemme see both yer hands as ya come in.'

From his vantage point, looking around the metal plate and through the railing, Matt could just see the door as it swung back. The large BC&C security guard who had escorted him from the meeting with Armand Stevenson took one step inside. He was maybe six-three, 260, with a shaved head that sat on his shoulders like a basketball. Matt couldn't see Frank, but imagined him across the living room, his shotgun resting lazily in the crook of his arm.

'Lonnie,' Frank said.

'Frank. Listen, we don't want any trouble, but we been sent out here to do a job. You know how it is.'

'An' whut job'd thet be?'

'Two men trespassed onto mine property the other night. We think one of them was Dr. Rutledge from in town.'

'So?'

'An' we think the other was one of you brothers.'

'Now, whut meks ya thank that?'

'Look, Frank, we've known each other a long time. Don't bullshit me and I won't bullshit you. Mr. LeBlanc from the mine wants to meet with whichever one of you it was, and also with that doctor. He says they may have been exposed to a dangerous chemical, and that they'll be in some kind of danger if they don't do the right thing.'

'Lonnie, you go tell Mr. LeBlanc thet ya tried yer

best, but no one here even knowed whut y'uz talkin' 'bout.'

'Frank, where're Lewis and the others?'

'Ain't ma word good nuff?'

Matt risked peeking through the railing again just as Lonnie Tuggle pulled a gun from his waistband.

'Frank, one of the two men who trespassed got hisself shot. There was blood on the stones inside the mine. It wasn't the doctor. Now, where is Lewis?'

'Lewis is rot here,' Lewis said, moving forward and resting his gun hand on the railing. 'Now it's time fer ya ta go.'

'You look a bit under the weather, Lewis,' Tuggle said. 'You wouldn't by any chance have taken a bullet recently?'

Every muscle in Matt's body was tensed. There was going to be a firefight. He just knew it. He started inching through the doorway toward the shotguns on the floor beside Lewis. If things opened up, there was no way he wouldn't be fighting on the Slocumbs' side.

'Stay there!' Lewis whispered harshly over his shoulder.

Matt sank down to the floor.

'I was told to bring you back with me, Lewis. I can't leave without you.'

'Ya can an' ya will, less'n ya want ta leave here feet first.'

'I have men with me. One of them's got a gun on Frank right now.'

'Ah see 'im,' Lyle said from down below. 'He best be a darn fast shot ta get Frank an' 'void takin' one a these here bullets in the haid.'

'Same goes fer you,' Kyle said, stepping onto the

243

balcony from the room at the end of the hall, ten feet down from Lewis.

Lewis quickly punched in some numbers on the keypad of the black box.

'This is a warning, Lonnie,' he said, pressing the firing button.

The window-rattling explosion from the broad dirt courtyard outside was enough to cause Tuggle to whirl. In that instant, Frank was across the room, his shotgun against the back of the huge man's head.

'Drop the gun! Drop it now, Lonnie.'

Reluctantly, Tuggle did as he was ordered.

'Thet bang were 'bout ten feet behind yer car,' Lewis called down. 'The nex one'll be unner it.'

'An' the nex buckshot from this gun'll be in yer brain,' Frank added. 'Now, yev got ten seconds ta git yer boys an' git outta here. Tell 'im ta set his revolver down afore he moves.'

'Do it, Cork,' Tuggle ordered.

Tuggle motioned to the man behind Frank, and in a moment, he came into Matt's view, cowed and weaponless. The two of them backed out of the front door and called to the other pair.

'You're going to regret this, Frank,' Tuggle said. 'You ain't the only one who can blow things up.'

'You gotta git t'us ferce, Lonnie. An' you ain't done so good at thet. Do us all a favor an' don' tra it. We don' git much pleasure outta killin' helpless critters. Tell ol' LeClair t'weren' none a us out at the mine. The doctor neither. If'n anythin' happ'ns ta him, yer the one we're gonna blame. Got thet? Ah said, Got thet?'

'Yeah, yeah. I got it.'

Matt listened to the car depart and then straightened up and crossed over to Lewis.

'I can't believe you have this place mined,' he said.

'Ah had me an adventrous spell back in the lat sixties, an' joined the army,' Lewis replied.

'I remember you telling me about that.'

'Well, what Ah may not a tole ya was Ah signed up mostly 'cause Ah wanted ta learn how ta blow thangs up. I'z in demolitions in Nam. Come in handy from time to time, blowin' up stumps an' such. Plus nobody gits near to this here place less'n we want 'em to.'

'Or away from it, either, it seems. You guys never cease to amaze me.'

'Gimme a hand back ta bed, Doc,' Lewis said, picking up his intravenous bag and chest tube. 'Allis excitement has me a mot tuckered.'

Any benefit Matt had accrued from his nap at Nikki's bedside was gone. His eyes burning with fatigue, he gazed up wistfully at the turnoff to his house as he pointed the Harley back toward the hospital. He would make rounds and then sign out to whoever was taking over coverage. After that, bed.

It was still possible the BC&C thugs might come after him, but besides being careful, there wasn't anything he could do about it except run, which he wasn't going to do. The Slocumbs had made their point and made it well. *Come after us again only if trying to get us is worth dying for.* As for the toxic dump, there was no way to predict what Armand Stevenson and the other powers at the mine were going to do. The only thing that was certain at the moment was that because of an anonymous note from a barely educated local who didn't want acknowledgment or even a

245

reward, his long struggle against BC&C had been vindicated.

The doctors' parking lot was nearly filled. Just fifteen years old, the hospital now boasted specialists in every area of internal medicine, and most of the surgical specialties as well. It pained him to give BC&C kudos for anything, but in fact the company was largely responsible for the continued growth of the place.

He found a space close to the ambulance bay and locked the Harley. Then he crossed the ER and headed up the stairs to Med/Surg 2. Not too surprisingly, Tarvis Lyons was dozing in his seat by the door to Nikki's room, his chin resting on his chest. Something – Matt's footsteps on the tile or perhaps a breeze down the hallway – roused the policeman just before Matt reached him.

'Hey, Ledge, wazzapnin'?' he said.

'Everything okay?'

'Yep. Your lady got off just like clockwork.'

'Got off where?' Matt asked, feeling a sudden chill.

'For the MRI you ordered,' Lyons said, clearly bewildered.

Matt raced to the doorway. Nikki's bed was empty and had been made, awaiting a return Matt doubted would be happening.

'Tarvis,' he said, his pulse hammering, 'I didn't order an MRI.'

Chapter 19

It was right there in the physician's orders section of Nikki's chart, right below the order Matt had written for neuro checks.

MRI at Hastings Hospital. Ptnt to go by ambulance.
T.O. Dr. Rutledge.

T.O. – telephone order. Someone had called the ward secretary using Matt's name and had ordered that Nikki be transported by ambulance for an MRI at Hastings Hospital. Quickly, Matt called the radiologist there. He was not at all surprised to learn that, at his request, Nikki had been inserted into their MRI schedule as an emergency. Her appointment was for thirty minutes ago, but as of yet she hadn't shown up.

Tarvis Lyons, looking nonplussed and bereft, was waiting by the doorway to Nikki's room.

'I screwed up, didn't I,' he said.

'Just tell me what happened.'

'You and Chief Grimes both said not to let no one into the room unless I knew who they were. Well, if I don't know the Stith brothers, I don't know anyone.'

'The Stith brothers?'

'Marty and Gerald. They drive for Gold Cross

Ambulance. Marty's part-time with the fire department, too. They're regulars on Saturdays at Snooky's, just like me. So, first the nurse came and told me you had ordered an MRI and the ambulance was coming. Then a little while later the Stiths showed up and took her. I had no idea I wasn't supposed to let her go.'

Matt rubbed at his eyes. *Who in the hell could have engineered this?* It had to be someone who knew the hospital and how things were done. A doctor? A nurse? He snatched up the phone and called the operator.

'Hi, it's Dr. Rutledge. Could you please get me Gold Cross Ambulance?'

'Right away, Doctor.'

'Gold Cross, Mary speaking.'

'Mary, it's Dr. Matt Rutledge at the hospital. Would you please radio the ambulance that's taking Nikki Solari from Montgomery County to Hastings Hospital?'

'What do you want me to tell them?'

'Tell them to turn around and get back here as soon as possible. Don't take the patient to Hastings.'

Matt tapped his foot and fidgeted with the light cord, but he knew what was coming.

'Dr. Rutledge,' the dispatcher said, 'this is very strange. I can't seem to raise them.'

'Maybe they're in the hospital already.'

'They each have portable units that kick in as soon as they leave the ambulance. I'll check on the trouble. Do you want me to keep trying the radio?'

'Yeah, sure,' Matt said. 'Keep trying.'

At that instant, Tarvis Lyons's radio crackled to life.

'Lyons.'

'Tarvis, it's Chief Grimes.'

'Shit,' Lyons whispered. 'Yes, Chief.'

'I told you not to let that woman out of your sight.'

'I don't remember you sayin' –'

'Tarvis, give me that,' Matt snapped, snatching the radio away. 'Chief, it's Matt Rutledge. Someone using my name called in an order to have Nikki taken to Hastings for an MRI. She never arrived and the Gold Cross people can't raise the ambulance on the radio.'

'That's because the drivers have been duct-taped to a tree in the woods off Highway 29. They just got brought in here. Nikki Solari's not with them.'

'Damn. I'm coming right over.'

'Listen, don't bother. I'll be over to –'

Matt handed the radio back to Lyons.

'Tarvis,' he said, 'if the chief calls back, tell him I didn't hear what he said and I'm on my way over.'

The police station, standard redbrick issue with an attached garage and jail in back, was situated as far on the east end of town as the hospital was on the west. Matt rode the Harley over, searching his mind for a hint as to who could have engineered Nikki's abduction, and why. Whoever it was had to have been watching him to know he had left the hospital. If only Nikki had shared a theory – any theory – as to why the two men were waiting for her in the first place.

The patrolman on the station desk phoned Grimes and then, with a shake of his head, motioned Matt toward a bank of folding chairs. Through the open blinds on the interior picture window in Grimes's spacious office, Matt could see the chief talking to the two ambulance drivers. The Stith brothers, both freckled and red-haired, seemed to be talking at once. Matt had never spoken more than a few words to either of them, but that contact was enough for him to know that neither man was going to win the Nobel prize for rocket science. Grimes's right-hand man, a hard-nosed sergeant named Steve Valenti, faced the drivers from a seat beside the desk, his eyes narrowed as if probing their account for inconsistencies. As Matt approached the office door, Grimes caught his eye and held up a hand for him to wait a moment. Then, after a few words with Valenti, he motioned him in. Even before Grimes spoke, it was clear from his expression that he held Matt somehow responsible for what had happened.

'Rutledge, I warned you to be careful with that woman.'

'I didn't do anything except go on a house call,' Matt replied flatly.

'I also told you to stay at the hospital.'

'Well, I don't handle being told what to do. That's why I went to med school. What's with you, anyway? Did Solari say something kind to you at the funeral? Is that what's going on?'

'Don't push me, Rutledge.'

'Don't go ordering me around, Grimes. Hey, hi, guys.'

'Hi, Dr. Rutledge,' the Stiths said in unison. 'We're sorry about this.'

'I'm sure there was nothing you could have done about it.'

'No, there wasn't. We got a flat on 29. One of the bastards drove up and –'

'Gerald,' Grimes snapped, 'we've already covered all this. It's Dr. Rutledge's turn to answer some questions. Listen, why don't you two wait outside. I'll call you back when I need you again.'

Heads down, the brothers shuffled from the office. Valenti closed the door behind them and took his seat again. This time, the probing, eyes-narrowed stare was fixed on Matt.

'So,' Grimes began, 'you say you never ordered any MRI on Nikki Solari, but the ambulance people say they saw the order.'

'It was a telephone order, called in by someone other than me.'

'Not you, but using your name.'

'That's right.'

Matt felt the warmth building in his face – historically the first sign that some sort of eruption was imminent. Grimes's snide, supercilious tone was pushing a number of hard-to-reach buttons.

'So, where were you while all this was going on?'

'I was making a house call.'

'To who?'

'I don't talk about my patients to anyone. It's unethical.'

'And you, of course, are Mr. Ethics. So while you were caring for a victim of a brutal attempted murder, you decided it was the perfect time to make a house call.'

'Back off, Grimes,' Matt warned, the red warmth creeping up a few degrees. 'I had been with her for more than twelve hours when I left the hospital. She was reasonably stable, and I had other people to attend to. Besides, if you had sent someone else out other than that lump Tarvis Lyons, they might have thought to have me paged to check on what was

251

going on, since I didn't say anything about ordering an MRI.'

'I don't know what in the hell is going on, Rutledge, but I can't shake the sense that you're right in the middle of it.'

Matt pointedly ignored the remark. 'What happened, anyway?' he asked.

'Sounds like the same two men who went after her before.'

'If at first . . .' Valenti interjected, sounding like Ed McMahon.

'One of them probably shot out a tire on the ambulance, then both of them pulled silenced revolvers on the drivers. The whole thing took two minutes at the most. Dark sedan is all we can get out of the Stiths.'

'You know who the men are?'

'Do you? Jesus, Rutledge, how could you go and let this happen to that woman?'

'Grimes, instead of trying your best to connect me to what happened, why don't you have every man on your so-called force out there looking for her.'

'You tend to your friggin' business, Rutledge, and I'll tend –'

'I know, I know. You did that one before.'

'Just don't go on any more house calls until we have this business cleared up. Got that?'

'Okay, okay, I got it.'

'Good. Now scram. Tell Lyons to get on over here.' Grimes turned his back on Matt. 'Steve, let's get an APB out on Dr. Nikki Solari.'

Valenti picked up a clipboard.

'Out,' Grimes said.

Matt slowly gathered up his denim jacket and keys and headed for the door.

'White female, thirty-six years old,' Grimes dictated to Valenti.

'Thirty-four,' Matt said over his shoulder.

'Out! Make that thirty-four. Medium-length dark hair, five-seven, slender build, may be wearing surgical scrubs.'

'Green.'

'Dammit, Rutledge. Okay, *green* surgical scrubs. Now get out of here. What a dick,' Grimes muttered, loud enough to be easily heard from where Matt was.

Matt left the office. The door swung nearly closed, but remained slightly ajar. He turned to finish the job, then realized that neither policeman had noticed. Instead he lingered off to one side, where it was easy for him to overhear the ongoing conversation.

'So,' Valenti asked, 'is the jerk right? Did she come on to you?'

'None of your business,' Grimes replied with a sly smile.

'Rollins was at the funeral service. Said the girl was looking pretty interested in you.'

'So, maybe she was. I got enough goin' on around here, believe me I do. Come on, now, let's get this over with.'

'Marks or scars?' Valenti asked.

'How should I know?' Grimes replied. 'Wait, I do know one. Get this. She's got this weird tattoo on the top of her foot. Some sort of lizard. Can you believe that?'

'Top of her foot, huh? Women don't go around showin' me the top of their feet.'

'They wouldn't show you their face, either, if they didn't have to.'

'What kind of lizard?'

'An orange one. How in the hell am I supposed to know what kind?'

Matt, who had turned toward the exit, stopped still. Nikki had been wearing sneakers when he intubated her at Crystal Lake. *How did Grimes know about the tattoo?* He had been there at the ER, but as far as Matt could remember, Nikki was covered up by the time he arrived, and stayed that way. *Could someone on the staff have mentioned it to him?* Possible, but doubtful. He had no trouble believing that Grimes had come on to Nikki in some way, but he hadn't even considered that she might have flirted with him. Immediately, he discarded the notion. The reason Grimes knew about the Gila monster wasn't because Nikki had shown him.

Bewildered, Matt headed out to his bike. The only logical explanation he could come up with was that Nikki was wearing some sort of strapped shoe at the memorial service. As he approached the hospital, still another explanation occurred to him – the possibility that Grimes was with Nikki after she had been abducted.

Tarvis Lyons, looking balefully about, was still at his post by the doorway to Nikki's empty room.

'Any word?' he asked.

'Nope. She's gone.'

'Shit. Is the chief pissed at me?'

'He wants to see you over at the station.'

'Shit. Ledge, you gotta tell Grimes I didn't do anything wrong.'

Without responding, Matt went to the small closet in the room. Nikki's clothes were hanging up to dry rather than being stuffed in the usual plastic bag. Her sneakers were there, too – New Balance, a fairly new pair, still damp. She must have been wearing hospital slippers when the Stith brothers wheeled her away. They could have easily fallen off or been removed during or after her abduction. If Grimes was involved in the kidnapping, that would certainly explain his choosing Tarvis to guard the room.

Nikki had jeans, sneakers, and a T-shirt on when she went into the lake, but it was unlikely they were the clothes she wore to the service. Her car had probably been towed or driven to the station. More than likely, her clothing and possessions had been catalogued and examined. They had to be in the evidence room. If her shoes were closed on top, he could rule out the possibility that Grimes had seen the tattoo beneath any straps.

He returned to the policeman.

'Tarvis,' he said, 'you want me to tell Grimes this wasn't your fault?'

'I need you to, Ledge. I've had some trouble lately and –'

'In that case, I need a favor from you.'

Lyons brightened. 'Name it, Ledge.'

'When she was loony from her concussion, Dr. Solari started babbling on about what she was really doing down here. It seems she runs a business up north where lady doctors provide, you know, services, to high-roller men who have big bucks to spend.'

'Services?'

'Sex, Tarvis. She runs a prostitution ring where the women are all doctors.'

'Holy –'

'And she has a book – a black book with the names of all her clients and all the women doctors in

Boston, New York, and around here who work for her.'

'She really is a babe,' Lyons said wistfully, his imagination clearly running as far amuck as it was capable of. 'That's what they were after her for? That book?'

'Exactly. Grimes didn't mention it, so I don't think he has it yet. If we can find it, you'll be a hero.' He bent over and spoke man-to-man. 'Plus, you'll know which lady doctors in these parts give . . . the best exams.'

He punctuated the remark with a nudge.

'What do you want me to do?'

'Can you get me into the evidence room?'

'I have a card. We all do. I just have to swipe it.'

'Well then, what are we waiting for?'

Lyons had driven his battered, grease-stained Wrangler to the hospital. Matt followed him back toward the station, but cut off a block from the building, parked the Harley, and met him by the basement door in back.

'So how many lady doctors are in this book?' Lyons asked.

'Don't know. Dozens, I'll bet. When it comes to admitting women students, the med schools often insist on brains *and* looks.'

'Ooee,' Lyons said, swiping the electronic lock and opening the solid oak door. 'There's an electronic record of whoever swipes in, so I gotta sign the ledger.'

There were ten large plastic baskets, but only two of them held evidence. Both were labeled SOLARI.

'The book is small,' Matt said, rummaging through the first basket. 'It may be able to fit in the heel of a shoe.'

'Not these shoes.'

Lyons was holding up a pair of black flats – plain, closed top, no straps.

So much for an accidental sighting of the tattoo.

'So, these are the little mice who set off the evidence room warning light.'

Grimes and Steve Valenti stood shoulder to shoulder in the doorway.

Matt felt his heart freeze.

Tarvis, you jerk!

'Oh, hi,' Matt said, too brightly. 'I asked Tarvis here to show me Nikki's things. We thought we might find something that would suggest who might have done this or why. I guess he forgot there was a warning light.'

'And did you?' Grimes asked.

'Did I what?'

'Did you find any undiscovered clues?'

Matt's pulse now had gone from standstill to jackhammer. Never an adept liar, he was having great difficulty maintaining eye contact with the policeman. It was clear from the man's tone that he didn't believe a word of what Matt was saying. Off to one side, Valenti appraised the situation, his face an unfathomable mask.

'Oh, no,' Matt stammered. 'No, actually, we didn't find anything. At least I didn't. How about you, Tarvis?'

Lyons looked as if he had been shot with a blowgun.

'Nothing, Chief,' he managed finally. 'I, um, hope you don't mind my bringing the doctor down here.'

'Why would I ever mind that, Tarvis? I always thought it was stupid for us to take all these precautions just to lock up a bunch of evidence.'

Matt could feel the wheels spinning in Grimes's head, searching for an explanation – any explanation – as to what he and Lyons were doing in the evidence room. Finally, he exchanged glances with Valenti, who merely shook his head.

'Okay, Rutledge,' Grimes said, 'I don't know what in the hell you're doing here, but I don't think I'm going to find out from you. Mark me well, though. This is the last time I'm kicking you out of my station house. Next time you'll be begging us to let you go.'

'Go easy on Tarvis,' Matt said. 'I asked him to let me in here so I could look at Dr. Solari's things.'

Ramrod straight, chin up, he strode past Grimes and Valenti and down the corridor to the stairs, half expecting to hear a shot and feel a bullet smack into his spine.

What he heard instead was Grimes saying, 'Tarvis, get the fuck upstairs to my office.'

And Lyons replying, 'I can explain everything, Chief.'

Chapter 20

Matt spent the hours following his clash with Bill Grimes consumed by dread for the life of Nikki Solari. He was bone weary from a dearth of any healthy sleep, but over his years of training and medical practice, he had developed internal techniques for coping with that sort of exhaustion. What he was much less adept at dealing with than the lack of sleep was the lack of answers. He felt like a marionette, dancing to the commands of some deranged puppeteer. But who? Right now, the only viable candidate was Grimes. But why him? And how was he able to pull together the elements of Nikki's abduction from the hospital so quickly and smoothly?

This is Dr. Rutledge calling. I've scheduled Dr. Solari for an emergency MRI and arranged for immediate ambulance transport.

Smooth.

Matt had two patients in the hospital. One of them, an elderly diabetic recovering from an arterial bypass to her leg, was in the room across the hall from Nikki's. He was on the way in to see her when he stopped and, using the phone at Nikki's bedside, called information and got the number for Kit and Samuel Wilson. Kit answered on the first ring.

'First of all,' Matt said after establishing that she

knew who he was, 'I want to tell you how sorry I am about your daughter.'

'Thank you. The service yestiddy made everyone that knew Kathy feel jes a little better.'

'I'm glad. Mrs. Wilson, I'm calling about Nikki Solari.'

'Nikki? What about her?'

'I guess you haven't heard. I hate to be the bearer of bad news with all you have been going through.'

'Please, what about Nikki?'

'Shortly after she left the church yesterday, two men ambushed her on Wells Road. She got away from them, but nearly drowned in Crystal Lake in the process.'

'Oh, my God. Where's she now? She all right?'

'I'm afraid we don't know where she is right now, Mrs. Wilson. Someone – not me – called in an order in my name, sending her to Hastings Hospital for an MRI. Then they kidnapped her from the ambulance on the way.'

'Oh, my God. How awful. Why'd anyone do such a thing?'

'That's what I'm trying to find out. Can you remember anything from yesterday that might help us figure out what happened? Anyone she spoke to?'

'Not that I kin recall. She read at the service, then played music most a the afternoon. She never left the churchyard 'cept ta walk a spell with Sam an' me. She did speak with Chief Grimes for a time on the bench under the big willa 'cross the churchyard. Oh dear, this is jes terrible news. Nikki and our daughter were very close. Kathy was teachin' her ta play the fiddle.'

Matt had heard what he needed to.

'Mrs. Wilson,' he said, now anxious to go, 'please call me if you or your husband think of anything, anything at all, that might help us figure this out. I promise to keep you posted.'

'I begged her ta stay with us,' Kit Wilson said.

Matt wandered out to his bike, lost in thought over the significance of what he had just learned. Kit Wilson's information certainly suggested that, although they might have spoken at some length, Nikki and Grimes were never in a place where she would have taken off her shoes. Assuming that, and knowing her feet remained covered when Grimes came to the ER, what was left? He must have seen the distinctive tattoo after she was abducted from the ambulance. No other conclusion fit the facts.

Also supporting that theory was something Kit Wilson did not say – specifically, that she already knew about Nikki. The news took her completely by surprise. Twenty-four hours had passed since the woman was nearly killed, and Grimes hadn't bothered questioning the Wilsons. True, he had been at the service and could have made his own observations there, but he should certainly have wanted to know if Nikki had said anything to Kit or her husband, or if they knew of any reason why someone might have wanted to harm her. The man was smarmy, but he was hardly dumb. The only explanation Matt could think of for him not bothering to call the Wilsons was that he already knew what had happened.

At an unobtrusive pace, Matt cruised through the lengthening shadows along Oak Street parallel to Main, heading across town toward the police station. Bill Grimes's love of flashy cars was commonly known, as was his latest trophy, a fire-engine-red Dodge Viper. Earlier in the afternoon, Matt had noticed it parked in the staff lot behind the station. From the corner of Oak and Waverly, Matt could see that it was still there. He backed up his bike until he could just see the car, then rested it on its stand and took out his tool kit, just for appearances. Twice over the next hour, while he was puttering around the engine, patients of his stopped to offer him a hand. Two cruisers left the lot, and later a minivan. Dusk settled in. The strain of staying fixed on the Viper only added to Matt's burgeoning fatigue.

Finally, just as he was considering packing it in for the night, Grimes came striding through the gloom to his car. Matt stowed the tool kit, mounted the Harley, and waited until the door of the Viper had closed before punching the electric starter. The powerful engine rumbled to life. His pulse racing, he felt instantly energized and alert. Grimes was single and could have been headed home or on a date or out for dinner. But without any better options, Matt was determined to play this one out.

Instead of turning left toward Main, the Viper, lights on, swung right, directly toward the corner where Matt was waiting. He had only time to pull on his helmet and lower his face before the car sped past no more than thirty feet away. His Harley was as well-known around town as the Viper, and Grimes was certainly a keen enough policeman to have noticed him. Clearly he was distracted. Matt's tension increased a notch. Grimes lived south of town, on the banks of the Belinda River. Now, in addition to being preoccupied, he was driving north, into the hills. This wasn't a purposeless evening jaunt.

Matt stayed as far back as he dared. The waning evening initially provided enough light for him to see, but with his headlight off, he had serious doubts any oncoming drivers could see him. Fortunately, for nearly ten minutes, there were none. The roughly paved road angled steeply upward. It was one Matt had ridden when he was much younger, but rarely since then. To the best of his recollection, it turned into gravel, then dirt, and eventually petered out in the forest. Its final incarnation was as a narrow, heavily rooted trail favored by dirt bikers.

Shadows from the dense woods brought the night on prematurely. The lights of the Viper were still fairly easy to spot in the distance, but the soft shoulders were invisible and posed a constant threat. Matt didn't dare flick on his lights or take his eyes off his quarry.

From time to time, on one side or the other, a rusted mailbox or a rutted dual path marked the entrance to a dwelling that could have been fifty feet into the forest or five miles. It was into one of those driveways that Grimes suddenly turned. Had Matt been looking down at the road, he would have missed the move completely, but as it was, there was a brief jounce of the taillights just before they began moving at right angles to the road. By the time Matt reached the drive where he thought Grimes had turned, the lights were gone.

Helmet off, he rolled cautiously through the ebony forest. Though he was keeping the RPMs down, his engine noise still reverberated like heavy equipment. Had Grimes stopped? Had he set up an ambush somewhere up ahead? Matt cut the engine and listened. Nothing. For a time, he tried pushing the heavy bike ahead. Finally, realizing he really had no choice, he hit the starter and rumbled forward, his legs stretched out off the pegs for balance. The Kawasaki would have been a little quieter and easier to maneuver at slow speed, but he had needed the storage capacity of the hog for all the drugs and equipment he had brought out to the Slocumbs.

For five minutes he rolled on, every fiber tensed against a voice, an attack, or a gunshot. Then, flickering through the trees up ahead, he saw light. He turned the Harley around and with some difficulty backed it into the woods, far enough so it seemed undetectable from the road. Then he cut off some pine boughs with his Swiss Army knife and laid them across the chrome of the handlebars, gas cap, wheels, and engine. Cautiously, he advanced up the road.

The Viper was parked alongside a Land Rover in front of a dilapidated cabin. The cabin, rough-hewn with a small porch and chimney, occupied the center of a clearing that was surprisingly large – maybe four or five times the footprint of the structure itself. Two windows, both illuminated, faced the driveway, and there were more on the side.

Staying within the tree line, Matt made his way around to the side of the cabin. A shredded screen hung off one of the two windows, and several panes of the other appeared to be missing. He held his breath and tried unsuccessfully to make out the voices from inside. Then, on his hands and knees, he ventured out from his cover and across forty feet of dirt and pine needles, flattening his back against the wall of cabin. Painstakingly, he rolled over onto his knees again and pushed himself up so that he could just peer inside. Initially, he could see nothing other than the denim-shirted back of a massive man. From beyond the man he could hear Bill Grimes's distinctive pseudo-twang.

'I know what you're telling me, dear doctor,' he was saying, 'but I don't know if you're telling me the truth.'

'I've told you all I know,' Nikki said, her voice weary and hoarse. 'If you don't believe me, that's your problem.'

'Correction, my friend. That's *your* problem.'

The huge man moved aside, and Matt dropped beneath the window. When he inched up again, he was looking into a grungy bedroom, no more than ten feet square. The ceiling was unfinished pine, and the walls unadorned. The gargantuan was still obstructing the view of the doorway where the chief was standing, but now Matt could see Nikki. She was unbound, dressed in green hospital scrubs, lying supine, eyes closed, on the bare mattress of a metal-frame bed. Two pillows without covers were bunched under her head, and a grimy sheet was thrown over her legs. She looked gray and uncomfortable and absolutely spent, but he could see no evidence she had been beaten.

'I want to go over this one more time,' Grimes was saying, 'starting with the funeral. Who did you talk to there besides me? Well?'

Matt heard a scraping to his right moments before a man appeared. He was tall and wiry, wearing a cowboy hat and boots. A pistol was jammed beneath his broad belt at the small of his back. Matt dropped to his belly and forced himself against the cement foundation of the house. He was still in plain sight, though, no more than twenty feet away. The man tapped out a cigarette and lit it with a kitchen match he struck on his zipper. The smoke instantly wafted to where Matt lay in the shadow of the house. Desperately, his mind sorted through possible responses should he be spotted. None of them made any sense.

The smoker took a few paces away from the house, tilted his head back, and blew a cloud up toward the dark sky above the clearing. Matt steeled himself. The angle between them had changed. Now, as soon as the man turned back toward the cabin door, it would be over. Matt prepared to bolt into the trees as soon as he was spotted. At that moment, from the woods beyond the cowboy and to his right, there was the crunching of brush and rustling of branches. Seconds later, a small, white-tailed doe burst through the undergrowth and loped across the clearing, not fifteen feet away. The man took several steps in pursuit, at the same time fumbling for his gun.

'Larry,' the cowboy hollered. 'Larry, get out here, quick!'

Matt could hear the huge man thump onto the porch.

'What? What?'

'Biggest fuckin' deer yew ever saw jes ran by close enough to lick the snot offa my nose. If my gun hadn't got stuck in my belt, we'd be eatin' venison right now.'

'Verne, you are just a total jerk,' Larry said, with essentially no mountain accent. 'Get on in here. The chief wants you to drive him to town an' back. You an' me are gonna stay here tonight with the bitch. We need some coffee an' toilet paper an' shit to eat. The chief has some stuff he wants to get from the station, too – stuff that'll make her sing like a canary. Now get in here.'

Matt held his breath until the two had disappeared into the cabin, then scrambled back to the safety of the forest. Grimes and Verne-the-Cowboy would be taking a ride to town and back. The trip would be twenty minutes each way, maybe twenty-five, allowing for time in the store. During those forty or so minutes, he had to find a way to overpower a man the size of a bus and get a barely conscious woman onto her feet, secured on the Harley, and away to safety. He regretted now that he had rejected the notion of stashing one of the Slocumbs' many pistols in his saddlebag. But in truth, he had never felt comfortable around guns of any kind, and he feared that this ineptness, coupled with his unpredictable temper, was a recipe for disaster.

He tried playing out a scenario wherein he somehow drew Larry outside, then knocked him out with a piece of wood or a wrench from his tool kit. The chances of actually disabling the beast with anything less potent than a hammer seemed slim, and there wasn't one in his tool kit.

What, then?

Grimes and Verne were crossing the porch, headed toward the Land Rover, when Matt began considering the saddlebags on his bike. The two large side bags and the carryall mounted behind the passenger seat were loaded with, among other things, drugs – his well-stocked house-call and emergency pharmacy, hastily augmented by a variety of medications purloined for possible use on Lewis Slocumb.

Matt suspected that he wasn't beyond killing a person to save his own life or that of someone close to him. But he also knew it wouldn't happen easily,

267

and the internal consequences would be severe. Besides, the only drug he could count on to kill Larry was a muscle paralyzer like curare or Anectine, and he wasn't at all sure he had packed any. He needed something with a rapid onset that could be given intramuscularly and would disable Larry without killing him. Then he had to find a way to get it into the brute without being torn apart.

Verne started up the Rover and flicked on the headlights. As soon as they were headed down the drive, Matt switched his Timex to timer mode and began the countdown.

Forty minutes.

Ticking off the features of the drug he needed, he raced back to the bike, located his penlight, and rummaged furiously through the medications in the carryall, discarding one after another into the woods.

Thirty-eight minutes.

Calm down! he shrieked to himself. *Just cool it.* He stared down at the vial he had actually been about to throw away, and caught his breath.

Ketamine – 100mg/cc!

Ketamine, a first cousin of PCP and nitrous oxide, was used preoperatively to induce a state called dissociative anesthesia – dreamy helplessness. Matt had tossed it in with the other meds just in case Lewis required any kind of minor surgical procedure. From what he remembered, given intramuscularly, the drug had a very rapid onset. The usual dose was 100mg, but of course, Larry was no usual specimen. The vial held 10ccs – a total of 1,000 mg. Was a thousand enough to bring down such a beast, or was it enough to do even more than that? There was only one way to find out. Matt fished out a 10cc syringe; twisted a large-bore, inch-and-a-half-long needle onto the end; and drew up every drop in the vial. If there was any chance for the drug to work, it would have to be injected into muscle, not into fat, where the circulation was minimal and absorption would be ineffectively slow. Larry was like a planet that was covered 90 percent with fat. Matt selected the occipital muscle at the base of the skull, and mentally played through how he was going to get the needle in and the plunger depressed without getting himself killed. He checked the time again. Thirty-four minutes before Verne and Grimes would be back. The issue now was how to get Larry outside without having him on red alert with a gun in his hand.

Fire!

Verne had carelessly tossed his butt aside when the deer dashed past him. Larry's first thought upon smelling smoke now would be to blame the man he had just called a jerk. At least that was what Matt was counting on. He took a book of matches from the carryall, then reached deeper down and removed one of the two flares he carried, and a box of gauze pads to use for kindling. Next he made his way back to the woods opposite the cabin. Cautiously, with agonizing slowness, he hauled several armfuls of brush across to the corner of the porch. Pausing for a few seconds, he chanced looking through the window. Larry, a holstered revolver tucked under his massive left arm, had settled onto a slat-backed chair at the foot of the bed. Nikki lay on her back, sleeping deeply, her right hand twitching rhythmically every few seconds.

Another time check showed nineteen minutes.

Matt chose the Viper for cover. With any luck, Larry's back would be to him when he made his move. If not, Matt had reason to believe he'd be dead before he had injected even a drop of the Ketamine. He knelt by the brush and jammed the paper-wrapped gauze pads into place. Next he lit the paper in several places and made certain it was blazing. Just in case, he inserted the flare unlit. Setting it off at this point might be too much noise.

Keeping low, the syringe tucked in his right hand, Matt raced around to the far side of the Viper, flattened out, and watched underneath the car as the brush pile began, ever so slowly, to burn.

Come on, baby. Burn, for crying out loud! Burn!

One twig caught, then another. He should have chanced the noise of packing the brush down a little, or maybe even set the flare off. The twigs were taking way too long to catch.

Fourteen minutes.

He hoped the odor and sound of the fire would be enough to get Larry outside. Failing that, plan B was simply to make some sort of nonspecific noise and hope for the best. It was a plan with little chance of success and a potentially lethal downside, but time was running out. He was preparing to make some sound when he smelled smoke. Risking a peek over the hood of the Viper, he saw that the cardboard box from the gauze pads had caught, and branches all around it were going up. There was crackling from the pile now, too.

Okay, Tubby. Wake up and smell the bonfire.

'What the – ?'

Larry clomped across the porch, down the single step to the fire, and began kicking at it with the toe of his shoe.

270

'Fucking Verne,' Matt heard him say.

Holding the syringe like a dagger, with his thumb on the plunger, Matt got some purchase for his back leg against a root and sprang ahead. At that instant, the flare ignited with a burst of light and heat that sent Larry stumbling backward several steps, holding one arm up to shield his eyes. He was two or three inches taller, but Matt had his move planned. He leapt from several feet away, slamming against Larry's back and hooking his left arm around his throat. Simultaneously, he jammed the needle to the hilt at the base of the giant's skull, and an instant after that pressed down the plunger. Larry, who had staggered forward only a step from the force of Matt's assault, bellowed and swung around with the power of a steam shovel. Before the Ketamine load could be fully delivered, Matt and the syringe were sent flying.

Nostrils flared, eyes wide with surprise and fury, Larry charged. Matt rolled over once, then again, but he wasn't quick enough to avoid being kicked in the belly. The hulk was winding up again when Matt made an awkward half somersault and scrambled to his feet. Larry lunged for him, but missed short. He was fumbling for his gun when Matt took off, zigzagging down the drive in an effort to make himself less of a target. There was a shot, then another, but they sounded strangely far away. Matt kept pounding ahead, into the protection of the darkness, but he was reluctant to get too far from the cabin. He checked over his shoulder. Larry had broken off his pursuit and was standing at least fifty yards back, hollering something Matt couldn't make out, but probably could have guessed.

The stopwatch was at thirty-five minutes now.

Only five minutes or so remained before Grimes was expected back.

The Harley was just a few yards away. If Larry decided to come after him again, he might not get the bike uncovered and started before he was in range. Still, it seemed worth a try. He had blown things big-time. There was little chance now to get past Goliath to Nikki. The only option that made any sense was to race into town and try to get help. But by the time he returned – if he returned – she would certainly be gone, and Grimes, Larry, and Cowboy Verne would have bullets marked for him.

What a screwup!

He threw aside enough branches to expose the ignition, then jumped aboard and burst through the brush onto the driveway, prepared to dodge gunfire. Instead, he saw Larry standing motionless right where he had been, a hot-air balloon silhouetted against the light from the cabin. Matt stopped the bike and watched as in slow motion the behemoth cross-stepped gracelessly from one side to the other, then flapped his arms in the air once and collapsed. Wary of a trap, but feeling there was room to speed past the man and around the cabin, Matt rolled up to where he lay. The whale was beached, his head lolling impotently from side to side. The snub-nosed revolver lay a few feet away. His eyes fixed on Larry, Matt bent over, picked it up, and dropped it into the carryall.

'Sweet dreams,' he said, knowing that fearsome nightmares often accompanied the awakening from Ketamine sleep. *Sweet dreams.*

He slipped the clutch and spewed a rooster tail of dirt as he sped to the cabin. The brush was still burning. In fact, a corner of the structure was smoldering and beginning to flame. His stopwatch was passing forty-four minutes as he raced inside.

'Hey, you, time to wake up,' he said, taking Nikki's hand in his and gently cradling her head.

Nikki blinked dreamily and actually smiled up at him before suddenly remembering where she was.

'Matt, it's Grimes, he –'

'I know. Listen, we've got to get out of here. Grimes'll be back any moment. Can you walk okay?'

'I'm a little wobbly and my head is still pounding, but I think I can walk.'

'Hurry, then. I'll help. My bike is outside.'

'Bike?'

'Motorcycle. Please.'

She let him pull her upright, then used his arm for balance.

'Sit up in front of me until I'm sure you can hold on,' he said. 'Just keep your feet right here, away from the engine, or you'll be burned. Hold on to my arms or the handlebars. Ready?'

'Ready. How did you – ?'

'I'll explain everything after we're out of here.'

Headlight off, Matt accelerated. He slowed briefly as they passed Larry.

'Is he dead?' Nikki asked.

'I don't think so. He's taking a voyage on the good ship Ketamine.'

'Matt!'

'It's them.'

Ahead, the dirt drive swung sharply to their right. Through the trees, they could see headlights bobbing toward them. Matt waited until the approaching high beams were just about to reach them, then he threw on his own high beam and

273

accelerated. Before a startled Verne could react, the motorcycle had sped past. Matt caught enough of a glimpse of Bill Grimes in the passenger seat to see his recognition. Through the rearview of the bike he saw the Land Rover make a rapid two-part U-turn.

'Hold on tight, Nikki,' he said. 'This isn't going to be easy.'

Chapter 21

Matt sped down the dirt drive with some confidence. The Land Rover was far better on the ruts than his street bike, but at the end of the drive, he could make a right turn and head to the wooded trail at the end of the road. The Harley certainly wasn't equipped for off-road riding, but from what he remembered, the trail was too rugged and narrow for a car of any kind, even the one pursuing them.

'Duck down a little bit and the windshield will keep things out of your eyes,' he cried out.

The small windscreen was sloped to deflect air – and bugs – up and over the head of the driver and anyone on the passenger seat. Their arrangement, though, with Nikki in front, placed her face directly in the jet stream. She hunched over as he suggested and continued to be a perfect passenger, flowing with the turns of the bike rather than trying to help Matt make them happen, and keeping her exposed feet and ankles away from the scalding exhaust system.

As they neared the end of the drive, Matt risked a peek over his shoulder. Verne and Grimes were still a ways back, but it appeared as if they had made up some ground.

'Hang on tight!' he yelled as the end of the long driveway suddenly appeared.

He downshifted and just managed to lean

through the ninety-degree right turn without sending the bike skidding out from under them. When he was a teen he had done some dirt-bike racing and even a little motocross, but the kids he topped in Geometry and English at school consistently trounced him on the track. Now what skills he did have were about to be sorely put to the test. They were on a six-hundred-pound touring machine headed toward the woods. He added just a bit of throttle and, engine screaming, they shot forward. Moments later he saw the high beams of the Land Rover dance against the trees as it, too, turned onto the road. After half a mile or so, the pavement turned to gravel, then to uneven, rocky dirt. The shocks on the Harley were more sluggish than those of an off-road machine and Matt had to slow a bit to keep the two of them from being bucked off.

'You okay?' he hollered.

Nikki nodded and ducked her head even farther down beneath the windscreen. The night was too cool and breezy for her to be comfortable in a set of scrubs. Her hands clutched his forearms with some strength, but he doubted she would be able to hang on tightly enough to remain aboard the passenger seat.

You bastard, Grimes, Matt was thinking, holding her in place. *If it's the last thing I do, you're going to pay for this.*

He scanned ahead, looking for the expected trail. They had already gone farther than he remembered. Instead of narrowing, though, the roadway actually seemed to widen and become more smoothly graded. Just then his high beam reflected brightly off the white of a billboard-sized sign up ahead, featuring artwork depicting happy boaters, fishermen, swimmers, tennis players, golfers, and barbecuers.

**COMING SOON
SHADY LAKE MANOR ESTATES
A GATED PLANNED COMMUNITY
WASHAW, WEST VIRGINIA
THE PLACE TO BE IN THE EASTERN
MOUNTAINS
BUILDING LOTS GOING FAST
RESERVE YOURS NOW**

Planned community! So much for the narrow dirt-bike trails. They had just cruised through the forest that Matt had anticipated would separate them from Grimes and his henchman. In fact, they were out of Belinda entirely and into the next town. Trouble.

The lots of Shady Lake Manor Estates might have been going fast, but the landscaping and construction still had a long way to go. The land had been clear-cut, but at the moment, the place to be in the eastern mountains consisted of a maze of interconnected dirt streets demarcating large dirt lots. There was no lighting, and very little in the way of heavy equipment, and Matt wondered if the project might have gone under. He hoped so. To his way of thinking, such 'communities' gouged the landscape as much as any strip mine. But while there was little in the way of construction paraphernalia throughout Shady Lake Manor, what there was, everywhere, were signs. Street signs, directional arrow signs; future-home-of signs, lot-number signs; a sign by a broad, shallow foundation hole that read:

CLUBHOUSE; another nearby that boasted: CENTRAL POOL.

Well, Mr. and Mrs. Jones, that number 281 stuck in the mud over there may not look like much at the moment, but . . .

There was no question Verne was gaining on them now. Less than fifty yards separated them. There was virtually no terrain over which the Land Rover didn't have a heavy advantage. In fact, the situation at the moment was so one-sided that Matt actually had a vivid image of Grimes laughing at them.

Matt scanned ahead for some way to put more distance between them. The Land Rover was way too close to consider trying to search out a place to hide. The only hope he could see was to work toward the far side of Shady Lake Manor by making sharp, unpredictable turns, and hope that they could find the opening to a narrow track and escape into the woods. He tried cutting across some lots and hit a steep slope of firm, packed dirt that sent the Harley airborne. The landing was anything but smooth. Nikki cried out as her head snapped forward against the windshield. Behind them, Verne took the same jump with ease.

Back on one of the streets, Matt sped onto rolling, sparsely treed land that was probably a golf course in the making. They were bouncing viciously now. Matt did his best to avoid the major pits and rises, but they were moving too fast for him to do much in the way of prevention. Then, up ahead, his headlight glinted off a vast, uniform darkness. Before he could completely analyze the situation, they were airborne again, sailing over the edge of what was one day to be Shady Lake.

'Sit up straight and hang on!' he screamed.

Just as Nikki did so, the bike landed with surprising gentleness on the side of a steep embankment, maybe twenty-five feet high. At the bottom of the slope, as far as Matt could see, was water. What there was of the lake could have been six inches deep or six feet. There was no way to tell. They were out of control, speeding and skidding downward toward the smooth blackness. But Matt had been riding motorcycles of one kind or another for most of his life. By staying upright, using his outstretched feet, and delicately playing the front and rear brakes, he was able to skid the Harley into a right-hand turn and onto a stony rim just a foot or so from the water.

Nicely done, he thought.

He cut the lights and braked to a stop. Nikki sighed loudly, straightened up, and sank back against him. He quickly stripped his jacket off and helped her get it on.

'I knew I'd hate this,' she groaned.

'What are you talking about?'

'This is my first time on a motorcycle. Now I know why I said no thanks so many times.'

'But this isn't exactly –'

'Rutledge!'

High up and behind them, Verne had pulled to a stop at the rim. The twin beams of the Land Rover knifed out over the huge crater. Against the bright night sky, Matt could make out Grimes's silhouette, standing hands on hips on the edge of the embankment.

'What?' Matt yelled up, using the light from the Rover to scan the nearly empty lake. The sides, as far as he could see, were too steep to ride back up, but he sensed he was viewing only a small portion of the excavation. The lake bed itself was lined with three- or four-inch stones, extending up a foot or so beyond where they were standing. If the water wasn't too deep, and if the stones covered the entire bottom, it was possible they could ride across. *Big ifs*. And ride across to what?

'There's no way out of there except on foot, Matt. Come up and let's talk.'

'Sounds good to me. You've always been an upstanding, trustworthy guy. Just turn off those lights and we'll be right up.'

'Rutledge, my man has a rifle and he's a damn good shot. Come out of there now and I can keep you from getting killed.'

'Just how do you plan on doing that?' he asked, buying a little time. 'Nikki,' he whispered, 'how're you holding up?'

'My kidneys are still bouncing, and my heart hasn't slowed down from that little ride down the cliff, but at least I'm not thinking about my headache anymore. Where are we?'

Matt was pleased to hear her humor, and if anything, her voice sounded stronger.

'We're in Disneyland a year or two before Mickey arrives,' he replied. 'Listen, if you can handle it, I'm going to try and motor around the lake just in case the slope gets any less someplace and we can drive out. Can you hang on?'

'Would it be easier if I was on the back?'

'Not if you fall off.'

'I can do it.'

'Keep your feet on those rests at all times. If you hit the exhaust with your bare tootsies, you're going to need smaller shoes.'

'Rutledge, this is your last chance!'

'Okay, we're coming, we're coming,' Matt called out, buying time. 'Nikki, you all set?'

'Is there something I should be holding on to?'

'Those railings beside your seat, or else me.'

She slipped her arms around his waist, squeezed tightly, and pressed her cheek against his back.

'Go,' she said.

Matt squinted through the darkness to gauge how far ahead he could see in order to skirt the water's edge without turning on his headlight. Then he picked up a stone and threw it across the water as far as he could. Along with a splash, he heard the distinct click of rock hitting rock. That far out at least the water was very shallow.

'Rutledge!'

Matt shifted into first and gunned the Harley ahead. If there was a rifle crack from overhead, he didn't hear it. Ten, twenty, thirty mph. The magnificent bike surged forward over the stones. Over his shoulder he could see that the Rover had backed up and was now paralleling them overhead, a short distance back. The darkness made speed difficult, and Matt finally gave in and switched on his light for a short while. The lake, while not quite as vast as he had thought, was an oval, maybe half a mile long and a quarter mile across. If, in fact, it had actually been a shady lake, there might have been some trees overhead to slow up or even detour Verne and Grimes. But as things stood, they were having no trouble racing along twenty or thirty feet above them. The engine noise from the Harley reverberated off the water and the steep walls, making it impossible to tell if they were being fired on or not.

It was then that Matt spotted the opening up ahead. It was a massive, corrugated steel tunnel built through the embankment on their right. The opening was about six feet across, and the floor was three feet or so above the stony track where they were riding. From the way it was positioned, it had to have been constructed to empty the lake. He judged that there was enough of a slope up to the floor so that they could make it over the edge and inside – provided they came at it head-on, through the water. If the depth at the center of the lake was greater than a foot, though, they probably wouldn't make it across on the Harley. Matt thought about looping out into the lake and then back toward the tunnel, but that would still leave Grimes and Verne directly above them. Riding across from the other side made more sense – provided, of course, they made it.

He switched on the high beam of the Harley, checked the odometer as they passed the tunnel, and accelerated again. The shifting stones made it challenging to keep the bike upright. Thirty felt barely controllable, but he pushed the bike to thirty-five. Overhead, the Land Rover kept pace.

Nikki continued to be the perfect passenger, holding on tightly, yet staying relaxed enough not to affect Matt's delicate balancing act. The woman was tough.

To their right, the embankment continued steep and high. The slim hope that there would be a gentler slope at the end of the lake vanished. If anything, the grade was even sharper. As they passed the hairpin end and sped down the other side, Matt watched the odometer until he was at the point directly across the lake from the tunnel. Then he cut off his headlight and made a sharp left-hand turn into the water. If Nikki was startled at the move, she hid it well. Matt plowed ahead as fast as he dared. The water – probably from recent heavy rains – was six or so inches deep, and the stony bottom was identical to the track on which they had been riding. If the depth increased much, passage would probably be impossible. If they stalled and couldn't get restarted, Matt had decided to leave the bike where it was and try to make it to the tunnel on foot.

'Come on, baby,' he urged. 'You can do this.'

Through his rearview, he could see the lights of the Rover shining directly out over the lake. *Confusion at last*, he thought, smiling.

Come on, bike!

They were at least at the center of the lake now and the depth was holding. If he could keep the Harley upright while maintaining his speed slow enough to prevent water from splashing up into the electrical system, they were going to make it across. His fear now was that even though he entered the water at the right spot, he hadn't held a straight enough line during the crossing. Behind them, the Land Rover was on the move again, continuing around the lake toward the spot where they had started. With luck, neither Verne nor Grimes knew anything about the tunnel. If that was the case, in Matt's perfect scenario, he, Nikki, and the Harley would vanish like something straight out of Siegfried and Roy.

He waited as long as he dared, then flicked on the headlight. They were no more than fifty yards from shore, and the tunnel was there, just twenty feet or so to the right.

'Hang on tight!' he hollered over his shoulder.

The arms around him tightened a notch. He swung right, straightening the path to the opening, and called on the Harley for some more speed. Engine screaming, they exploded out of the water, up the low bank, and hurtled into the tunnel. The corrugated steel ceiling flashed past less than a foot above their heads. The bike jounced viciously over the floor. Ahead, there was only darkness. Ten yards, twenty, fifty. Matt slowed. The end of the tunnel was just ahead. He cut the light and rolled out into a dry streambed that sloped gently downhill. Braking to a stop, he checked behind them. The metal tunnel was built into concrete, with a massive metal door that was, gratefully, open all the way. It seemed that Shady Lake was something of an engineering marvel – a reservoir that provided recreation and a source of water for the pools and golf course. It wasn't clear where the water to fill the lake would be diverted from. Maybe that's why the construction had stalled, Matt mused, smiling.

Lights off, they cautiously followed the streambed through the rolling outline of what one day was to have been the golf course. Behind them, toward the lake, there was only darkness.

'How are we doing?' Nikki asked softly, her cheek still pressed against Matt's back.

'Well, I think we're going to make it out of this place,' he said, mopping sweat from his forehead with his sleeve. 'The question now is: Where to from here?'

'Boston,' she said firmly. 'Take us to Boston.'

Chapter 22

With one eye on the rearview mirror, Matt rode the nearly dry streambed into the forest, where it merged with a running brook. He paralleled the brook for nearly a mile before they heard traffic noises. The two-lane road was one Matt didn't know well, and in fact, they headed south for several minutes before he realized his misjudgment and turned around. By then, despite wearing Matt's jacket, Nikki's teeth were chattering. He offered his socks to cover her bare feet, but she insisted he push on until he was certain they were out of danger.

She was absolutely beat, but hung on gamely for almost twenty miles more until Matt felt it was reasonably safe to stop. At a Target store they picked up a hairbrush, some toiletries and clothes for both of them, and sneakers for Nikki, and at the Sunoco station next door they got gas and a road map. From there they found a back road that paralleled the highway, and headed north.

A few miles past the Target store they spotted a railroad car diner dropped, it seemed, in the middle of no place. Nikki had changed at the store into jeans and a flannel hunting shirt, with a red bandanna tied loosely around her neck. Her lips were dry and cracked, and there was a lattice of healing scratches across her face. Dark shadows enveloped her eyes. Still, there was a gentle beauty and intelligence about her that Matt found totally appealing. The few occasions over the past years that he had been with a woman he had been so totally disinterested and distracted that at times he was actually embarrassed to the point of apologizing. The fullness in his throat and his keenness to learn more about Nikki Solari were as threatening as they were exciting, as bewildering as they were pleasant. His memories of Ginny were no less vivid than they ever had been. But over just two days, he knew that something inside him had changed.

Is it that enough time has passed? he wondered. *Or is it this one woman?*

'You all right?' he asked.

'I'm not ready for the obits, if that's what you mean, but I might be a candidate for the comics. This is totally unreal. Matt, we've got to go to the police or . . . or the FBI. Isn't kidnapping a federal offense?'

'It is, yes,' he replied. 'I have no idea what it would be like trying to bring charges against a police chief, even as two physicians sharing the same story. Despite losing to us tonight, Grimes is far from dumb. He's a killer, and now he's desperate. I'm sure he'll come up with some sort of countercharges, like maybe I kidnapped you and then brainwashed you with drugs or something. Weirder things have happened.'

'What else can we do?'

'I don't know. For the moment I really want to move against the mine before they have a chance to empty that dump. Now that they've lost both of us, that might be the direction they go in. If we suddenly get embroiled in charges and countercharges with Grimes and some police department or FBI office, I think we might end up losing. Besides, once we come out into the open, Grimes has another shot at us both.'

'I guess I understand. So, then, now what?'

'I don't know. Connect with some family or friends or . . . or maybe a lawyer. Tell them what happened. Form some kind of strategy. Then maybe go see the police. I'd really like to come up with some approach to dealing with the mine people before we make any other move.'

'Okay. I'm not sure I agree, but I am sure you just saved my life. For now we do it your way, starting with my boss.'

'Great, and then maybe my uncle, Hal Sawyer, the pathologist. Some way, somehow, we'll get to the police. I promise.'

Nikki ordered black coffee and anything that was greasy and hot. Matt went for the chili. After the waitress had left, Nikki shared the stunning details of Kathy Wilson's illness and death.

'Her condition was all Grimes wanted to know about,' she said. 'He never explained why. All he kept asking was, "Who else knows about her? Who else knows about her?"'

It was astonishing for Matt to hear the description of Kathy's facial nodules and mental deterioration. Nikki could just as easily have been speaking of Darryl Teague or Teddy Rideout. But there was a problem. Kathy Wilson had never worked at or near any facility of the Belinda Coal and Coke Company, and had left home to follow her destiny in music nearly nine years ago.

'Are you sure she hasn't been back to Belinda since she left?' Matt asked.

'Maybe before she and I met she had, or maybe for a day or two here and there when she and the band were on the road.'

'But nothing extended.'

'I don't believe so.'

'And what did you tell Grimes at the church?'

'I can't seem to remember the details of anything he and I spoke about.'

'That's understandable. With the sort of concussion you suffered it could be weeks or months before you recall some recent things – or even never.'

'Up at that ... that cabin, he just kept hammering away at the same thing, asking who else knew about Kathy's condition besides me. He seemed especially interested in what I had told you.'

'I'll bet he was.'

It was Matt's turn to share what he knew, including his ill-fated trip into the mountain with Lewis and his subsequent treatment of Lewis's collapsed lung. When he finished, Nikki merely shook her head and shrugged.

'It doesn't sound like any toxic syndrome I know of,' she said. 'But I suppose it's possible.'

'What could it be, then? Three people from the same town with such a bizarre syndrome, coupled with a nearby toxic waste dump that has a river running right through it.'

'Maybe you're right,' Nikki said pensively, 'maybe the groundwater is contaminated from the dump, and maybe Kathy somehow did get exposed. The gun on the wall is certainly smoking. But it all still sounds a little shaky to me.'

'If she really never worked at the mine, ground-water contamination's got to be it.'

'I'm curious. What did the pathology of those two miners' brains show?'

'My uncle, Hal Sawyer, is the ME and actually did the posts. He reported that the lumps were standard issue neurofibromas, and that both men's brains were grossly normal, so he didn't bother doing a microscopic.'

'I don't blame him,' she said, 'but a number of devastating central-nervous-system conditions have brains that look fairly or totally normal on gross inspection. Maybe we'll learn something from Kathy's microscopic.'

'You did one?'

'My boss, Joe Keller, did. I insisted on it. I've never done well with loose ends, even tiny ones.'

'I'll be anxious to hear what he found. Maybe he can order some sort of toxicology on the tissue. I'm still certain the mine is at the bottom of all this.'

'You'll get no argument from me,' Nikki said, draining the last of her second cup. 'Besides, who am I to question the clinical acumen of a doctor who saves his patients' lives with unrolled condoms?'

The Starlight Motel in Red Wolf, Pennsylvania, was just the sort of place Matt hoped to find. It was a mom-and-pop operation, far from any main drag. Room 212 was on the second floor in the rear, overlooking a small pond. He gathered their things and helped Nikki up the stairs. The room held the must of years of service, plus a hint of smoke. Nikki went into the bathroom and emerged wearing a pair of thin sweats and a Champion-logo T. Bracing herself against the wall, she pulled down one side of

289

the bedcovers and crumpled onto her side, breathing heavily.

'Here, lift up your tongue,' Matt said. 'I want to check your temperature.'

'Sleep. I need to sleep.'

'I know. One more minute.'

Matt slipped the digital thermometer beneath her tongue – 100.5. He brought up his stethoscope and listened to her chest and back – a few crackles suggesting some low-grade pneumonia, but nothing that needed immediate attention.

'Hop in,' she said weakly. 'You saved my life twice in two days. That means you don't have to sleep on the floor.'

'I'll try not to kick too much.' He shut off the lamp, but some light filtered through the gauzy curtains. He rolled onto his back next to her and pulled the sheet and thin blanket over both of them. 'You know,' he went on, 'I've been trying to figure out how Kathy might have gotten exposed to the toxins from the mine. It seems possible that she might have been in the wrong place at the time of a particularly dense spill. Maybe the two other cases were there at exactly that time, too. Do you think that's possible? . . . Nikki?'

Her eyes were closed, her respirations raspy, but even. She had hung on as long and as hard as she could.

Matt turned onto his side, facing her. For a time, he studied her face in the dim glow, breathing in the scent of her.

'Good night, pal,' he whispered finally. 'I promise, next time we go to a nice quiet museum.'

*

'Here comes another contraction.'

'Okay, hon, you know what to do.'

'I'm okay. . . . I'm okay, Donny. . . . I got this one. No sweat . . . No sweat . . . I got it.'

Her friends and family had told her how hard it was going to be. How painful. The nurse in charge of the birthing class had begun the class on labor and delivery by saying, 'Whoever named labor had clearly been through it.'

Sherrie Cleary, now in her ninth hour of serious labor, just focused her thoughts on all the doom-sayers and naysayers and smiled. Sure, the contractions hurt. Sometimes they hurt like hell. But pain was just that, she told herself over and over again, nothing more, and she was still hanging in there. At twenty-six, this was her first baby, and she was most definitely not going to be her last. Her husband, Don, had gotten a nice raise at the body shop, and thanks to an uneventful preg-nancy, she had been able to waitress until just three weeks ago. They were still living in the Anacostia projects, but the people from Fannie Mae were optimistic that before long they would qualify for a mortgage. Could anyone blame her for wanting more kids?

Margie Briscoe, the midwife, breezed into the birthing room, checked the baby monitor, and then came to the bedside.

'Looks great,' she said. 'How you doing, Sher?'

'I can handle the contractions, at least so far, but I am getting a little impatient.'

'You wouldn't be normal if you weren't. Here, let me check you. Just relax and let your knees flop apart. . . . Perfect . . . You're stretched out nicely, too. Because of all that preparation you did, I don't believe we're going to have to make that episiotomy cut.'

'That's great.'

'Not much longer, my friend. Not much longer at all.'

'Wonderful.'

'You still going with Donelle?'

'Donelle Elizabeth Cleary. She was going to be Donald Junior if she was a boy. Elizabeth was my grandmother's name.'

'It's a beautiful name.'

'She's going to be a beautiful baby. Oh, Donny, here comes another one. . . . Goodness . . . Oh, my, this is a little worse than the others. . . . No, wait . . . Oh, Lord, make that a lot worse. . . . Oh!'

Margie set her hands on the volleyball-sized rock that was Sherrie's contracting uterus and watched as the monitor screen showed nothing more than the expected slowing of the fetal heart rate. One minute, two, three. Sherrie groaned and gasped continuously.

'I . . . don't . . . know . . . if . . . I . . . can . . . Wait, wait, it's getting a little better. It's going away. Oh, gosh . . .'

'The contraction will be right back,' Margie exclaimed, 'because it's happening! Little Donelle is on her way. Don, will you poke your head out the door, please, and tell Sue it's time. Sherrie, I'm just going to do a little more stretching of your skin to help your baby get on out here. . . . Great. You've made it, Sher. You've made it all the way without any medication. Now, just continue your rapid breathing and get ready to push. Everyone set? Pediatrician on his way, Sue? . . . Terrific. Don, get those gloves on and get over here and take my place.

I'll be right next to you. You're going to bring this daughter of yours into the world. Ready?'

'I . . . I think so.'

'You'll do fine. Sherrie, get ready to push. Get set. Okay, here comes her head. Push, Sherrie, push! . . . Here she is, Don. First her head, now I'm going to bring her little shoulder out. You got her? . . . Great! Now the other shoulder, and here she is. Beautiful. Just beautiful. Nine-fifteen P.M. Sue, suction, please.'

The bleating cries of Donelle Elizabeth Cleary filled the birthing room. Don Cleary, who had the muscled physique and stoicism of a longshoreman, was openly weeping as the nurse took his daughter, wrapped her, and brought her up to rest on Sherrie, who was beaming like the midday sun, tears streaming down her cheeks.

'I told you,' she said to everyone and no one in particular. 'I told you it was going to be incredible.'

Three hours later, when the nurse Sue came into her room, Sherrie was dozing but still smiling. Her husband, sitting off to her right, was gazing in awe into the bassinet at the perfection that was their child.

'Sherrie, hon, wake up,' Sue gushed. 'You have a visitor, a very special visitor. Here, I'm going to wipe your face with a cool cloth. Good. Are you awake?'

'I'm awake. What's going on?'

'Mr. Cleary, how about you? Are you awake?'

'Sure. Who's here?'

'I'd tell you, but I think you're going to have to see for yourself.' She went quickly to the door and called out into the hallway. 'They're ready for you now.'

The wife of the President of the United States, unaccompanied, strode calmly into the room and crossed directly to Sherrie's side. Sherrie's and Don's expressions made it clear no introduction was necessary.

'Mrs. Cleary,' she said just the same, 'I'm Lynette Marquand. Congratulations on your beautiful daughter. You, too, Mr. Cleary.'

'Thank you,' Sherrie managed. 'Thank you. This is such a surprise.'

'Well, it's a pleasure for me to be here on such a joyous occasion,' Lynette said. 'Mr. Cleary, Mrs. Cleary, I have some wonderful news for you.'

Chapter 23

The Sierra Leone Embassy in D.C. was on 19th Street, not far from the PAVE offices. Once a stately town house, it had fallen into fairly impressive disrepair. The drapes and carpeting were tawdry, and the air-conditioning consisted of scattered window units, some of which did not appear to be working. Ellen had been in embassies before – Canada, Mexico, and France. There was absolutely nothing in any of those facilities that was as outdated as anything in this one.

She had arrived on time, but it was clear from the torpor of the young man behind the reception desk that she would be seen by His Excellency Andrew Strawbridge when it happened. The waiting area – six nondescript, straight-back wooden chairs and three end tables – was devoid of any reading material save several copies of an ancient propaganda pamphlet extolling the virtues of Sierra Leone, and a dog-eared copy of *Time*. It was just as well the ambassador wasn't ready to see her, Ellen thought. She needed time to compose herself and regain her focus. At the moment, there was someone displacing both Lassa fever and Omnivax from her mind, namely Rudy Peterson.

As she had done any number of times, Ellen had slept over in the guest room of Rudy's cabin. She was anxious about the Lassa fever revelations he had shared with her and also the meeting with Strawbridge. After a few hours of fitful sleep, she climbed out of bed, pulled on the terry-cloth robe Rudy had put out for her, brewed some coffee, and brought her notes up to his second-floor study. It was not yet four-thirty in the morning. She was searching for a pen in the top right-hand drawer of his desk when she spied the envelope. It was on the very bottom of a pile of papers and would have escaped her notice except that her name and address were on it, written in Rudy's precise hand. There was also a stamp pasted in the upper right corner, but not postage enough to get the envelope mailed. Ellen wondered, correctly as it turned out, if perhaps the letter had been written some time ago, when rates were less.

She slipped the envelope back in the drawer and for the next half hour tried to convince herself not to retrieve it. She had always been a curious sort – probably more so than most – and she had an affinity for gossip that often embarrassed her. Given her makeup, this discovery was a tough one to resist. And at nearly five in the morning, she wasn't as detached and analytical as she was capable of being. Over those thirty minutes, her rationalizations became increasingly lame. If Rudy hadn't meant for her to see it, why had he left it in his desk where she might well come across it? If he was agonizing over whether or not to mail it, wouldn't she be saving him anguish? As absurd and flawed as her reasoning was, she still managed, bit by bit, to bury her common sense beneath it. Almost before she realized she had actually done it, the envelope was open in her hands. Her resolve not to read the contents lasted only seconds.

Dear Ellen,

I suppose the best thing I can do is just get this part out of the way first. I love you. I have since the day Howie first brought you into our dorm room and introduced us. It's been four years now since he left your home, and here I am as much in love with you as ever, knowing you have never felt that way about me. What to do?

As you know, I dated a fair amount over the years following our first meeting. I slept with some of those women, and even tried to get serious with a couple of them. But I always knew I wasn't being fair to them. Then, a few years before he broke up your marriage, Howie started telling me in our man-to-man talks that he wasn't being faithful to you. I wanted to tell you then what he was doing and how I had always felt about you. But it just seemed, I don't know, wrong. With that painful knowledge and my feelings for you, I still couldn't stop being his best friend. For that I'm ashamed.

Well, now Howie's been gone for quite a while and I see the way you've bounced back. You tell me about all you've been doing, and even about dates you've been on. That has hurt. 'I'm right here!' I want to shout. 'Right under your nose! And I've loved you for thirty-five years.'

I probably won't send this letter, but maybe I will. Either way, I think it's great that you have accepted the position on that vaccine commission, and that you have asked me to assist with some research. I promise to do everything in my power to help you become an expert in the field. I wish I were a little more colorful and charismatic and a little less shy, but hey, I am who I am. And I don't regret the path my life has taken one bit.

I just thought maybe it was time that you knew.

Your devoted friend,
Rudy

Ellen looked up from the frayed patch she had been studying on the Oriental rug in the embassy's waiting area, and realized that Andrew Strawbridge's attaché was smiling over at her.

'Soon,' he said in a velvety English accent. 'Ambassador Strawbridge will be with you shortly.'

'Thank you. I'm fine to wait.'

The letter was still in her purse. Rudy had gotten up around six and, without realizing she was upstairs in the study, went out to the backyard where he did twenty minutes of tai chi – fairly advanced tai chi from what she could tell. She knew he practiced the beautifully controlled martial art, and from time to time had watched him work out alone in his yard. She had never thought of asking to join him, and true to his reserved nature, he had never pushed the possibility on her. This morning, though, she studied him as he practiced. Later on, during a breakfast of mushroom and Brie crepes that he had cooked to perfection, she learned that he taught tai chi classes in a nearby community hall.

Several times she came close to bringing up the letter and admitting what she had done, but each time she pulled back. When they embraced as she was preparing to leave for D.C., as they had done hundreds of times over the years, it was as if they were touching for the first time.

Why didn't you just put the darn thing in the mail when you were supposed to? she was thinking as she drove off.

'Mrs. Kroft? Mrs. Kroft, I'm Andrew Straw-bridge,' the ambassador said, his voice rich and melodic.

Startled out of her reverie a second time, Ellen leapt awkwardly to her feet, mumbled an apology, and took the ambassador's hand. He was a short, slight, dapper man, with warm, deep-brown eyes and rich black skin. His face was slightly pocked from what she assumed was a childhood infection.

'Thank you for coming out to greet me personally,' she said.

'Leighton's already gotten out of his chair once,' he replied, winking, 'I didn't want to tax him. The truth is, I came out myself because your call yesterday intrigued me and I was anxious to meet you.'

'Thank you.'

'You said you were on the commission that recently approved the supervaccine?'

'I was. Only I didn't end up voting for or against its approval. I abstained.'

'Sometimes, abstention is a very powerful statement,' he said.

He led her into a spacious, mahogany-paneled office, with a conference table and a wall of well-stocked bookshelves. A framed green-, white-, and blue-striped flag hung behind the expansive desk. The other two walls featured the usual photos of diplomats and dignitaries shaking hands with each other, as well as a large, framed map of Sierra Leone.

'Coffee? Tea?' he asked. 'I joke about Leighton, but he is excellent help for me, and he brews a superb cup of coffee.'

Ellen pictured the small armies of employees manning the other embassies she had visited.

'In that case, I'll have mine black,' she said.

'Leighton, black coffee for Mrs. Kroft, please. The usual for me.' He left the door ajar and motioned her to a seat across the desk. 'So, now, you have come to talk with me about a vaccine.'

'Yes, against Lassa fever.'

Strawbridge sighed.

'A touchy subject with us, I'm afraid, Mrs. Kroft.'

'I don't understand.'

'The company that developed Lasaject about ten years ago is Columbia Pharmaceuticals, located not far from here.'

'I know that.'

'From all we can tell, the vaccine is very effective. Do you agree?'

'Yes and no,' Ellen said. 'The vaccine was tested in a very small group of people in your country, and did seem to be protective. But for some reason, the testing was stopped. The vaccine was evaluated later on in a larger group here in the States.'

Strawbridge nodded knowingly and chewed on his lower lip. Ellen sensed he was debating how much of the truth to tell her.

'Unfortunately,' he said finally, 'at the time Columbia was trying to evaluate Lasaject, our country was in a certain amount of, how should I say, turmoil. They chose to pull their people out and test their vaccine elsewhere.'

'That's the testing I mentioned that was done

here. But instead of measuring protection against Lassa fever, they measured protective antibody levels stimulated by the vaccine. Columbia's report to our Food and Drug Administration states that the inoculations did very well in that regard.'

'I'm very happy for them,' Strawbridge said sarcastically. 'Alas, not one person in my country has benefited from their research. I'm sure it comes as no surprise for you to hear that Sierra Leone is hardly a wealthy country. The two people at the head of Columbia, a woman virologist and another doctor, came to Freetown and met with our health ministry. Regrettably, they could not find, how should I say, common financial ground to initiate a mass vaccination program.'

'I'm sorry. I read that the World Health Organization was reluctant to get involved until the political unrest was resolved.'

Strawbridge's dark eyes blazed, then just as quickly softened.

'Unfortunately, there has been some discord in our country,' he said, 'but not enough to deprive millions of a medical breakthrough.'

'I'm sorry.'

Ellen was embarrassed to find herself at that moment thinking about Rudy – how much more comfortable she would be feeling if he were there with her, how foolish she had been to open his letter to her. Why in the hell hadn't he ever spoken up?

'So,' the ambassador was saying, 'when you called, you presented me with two tasks.'

'I know what I was asking might be difficult.'

Strawbridge smiled patiently.

'We may not be able to afford Columbia Pharmaceuticals' exorbitant rates for their vaccine,' he said, 'but gratefully, we can afford computers. Your first question had to do with the number of cases of Lassa fever that have occurred in Americans.'

'Over the last three years, yes.'

'Well, I am not allowed to give you the names because of my nation's rules on medical confidentiality. But I can tell you that over the past three years there have been six cases of Lassa fever in Americans in Sierra Leone, two of whom died.'

'That's all? Six?'

'Three of those were hospital workers.'

Six cases in Americans in three years in a country where Lassa fever was endemic. Eighteen cases in three years in Americans flying back from West Africa.

'Curiouser and curiouser,' Ellen said.

'*Alice's Adventures in Wonderland* by Lewis Carroll,' Strawbridge exclaimed. 'It is one of my favorite books.'

'Mine, too. Well, Your Excellency, for the past week or so, that's precisely where I feel like I've been – Wonderland.'

'Mrs. Kroft, are you at some point going to tell me what this is all about?'

Ellen felt herself blush.

'Ambassador Strawbridge, I'm truly sorry for seeming so oblique. I beg you to be patient with me. I'm investigating some loose ends surrounding the Lasaject vaccine. That's as much as I feel comfortable sharing right now.'

'Is there something wrong with the vaccine?'

'No. I have no reason to think so.'

'You will keep me posted?'

'As soon as I have any firm information.'

Ellen held her breath as the diplomat pondered his situation.

'In that case,' he said finally, 'let us move on to your second request.'

'The passenger manifests.'

Rudy's contact at the CDC had obtained the flight each American Lassa fever victim had taken getting back to the States. Ten of them had flown from Freetown to London on Sierra National Air, and from London to various cities in the U.S. The other eight had flown Ghana Air from Freetown to Accra, Ghana, and then directly to Baltimore. Their hope was that the passenger manifests might provide a recurring name – maybe indicating a carrier of the disease.

'You know,' Strawbridge said, 'we diplomats are taught never to give away something for nothing. If I hand over these documents, I do have a request of my own.'

'Yes?'

'Ever since they chose to hang on to their vaccine until we could meet their price demands, my government has been very disappointed with the people at Columbia Pharmaceuticals. If there is any way you uncover that we might, how should I say, make life more difficult for them, I would like your word that you will let me know.'

Ellen sat on a sunlit bench in DuPont Circle, cradling her cell phone in her lap and following one passing couple after another. Andrew Strawbridge had come through not only with the passenger manifests of the Sierra National flights, but with those of Ghana Air as well. The next logical step would be to interview some of the few surviving

Lassa fever victims. She had enough of a credit line on her VISA to make any necessary flights.

Since the confrontation in her living room with the monster who threatened her grandchild, she had been consumed with finding a way to bring the production and distribution of Omnivax to a halt without endangering Lucy or anyone else in her family. The man's huge head, soulless eyes, and hallmark scar burned in her mind. Somehow she was going to find him. She was going to find him, and when she did, she would also find the means to destroy him in as painful a way as possible. Surprisingly to her, over the days since he appeared in her living room with his smugness and his threats, she had realized in her heart that she was perfectly capable of killing such a man. But in the meantime, she would take whatever chances were necessary to bring down those who had hired him. The problem was that, suddenly, she didn't want to do it alone.

Over the years since Howard's departure she had managed to hold her vulnerability and loneliness in check. Reading Rudy's letter had changed things. Suddenly she felt uncertain and frightened. The last thing she needed at this point was to lose her incisiveness – to dilute in any way the hatred that was driving her. But that was exactly what appeared to be happening.

The first of the cases on the list Rudy had obtained did not answer the phone and had no machine or service. A man answered Ellen's second call and assured her that, yes, his wife had survived her terrible illness, and yes, they would be happy to meet with Ellen after his wife returned home from work.

Next Ellen called information and jotted down the number of United Airlines. Then, barely realizing what she was doing, she dialed Rudy's cabin.

'Hello?'

'Rudy, hi, it's me.'

'Calling from the big city?' he asked with a make-believe twang.

'DuPont Circle.'

'How'd ya make out?'

'Six cases in three years, Rudy. That's the sum total of all the Americans infected with Lassa in Sierra Leone. Six. Three were hospital workers.'

Rudy whistled.

'I don't think I need my degree in statistics to know that ain't very many compared with those who got infected on those airplane flights,' he said.

'I think not. Strawbridge gave me the manifests, too. All eighteen of them. I've already contacted one of the patients from your list. She lives outside of Chicago.'

'Going to go see her?'

'I want to.'

'Well, I say go for it.'

'Rudy?'

'Yes?'

'I . . . I want you to come with me.'

'Hey, that's very nice of you. When are you going?'

'Today. This afternoon.'

'Oh, shoot. I'm really sorry, El, but I have a class to teach and a private lesson. I'm afraid tomorrow's tight, too. I have this family of Russian immigrants that I teach English grammar and reading to. I might be able to change them to another day if I can get ahold of them, but they don't have a phone and –'

Ellen watched a couple snuggling on a bench across from hers, and felt a knot in her chest.

'No, no. Please don't change your plans,' she managed. 'I'll be fine. I'll fly in and back, and drive out to the cabin late tonight or first thing in the morning.'

'You're right,' Rudy said. 'You *will* do fine. Who's the woman? Where does she live?'

'She lives in Evanston. Her name's Serwanga. Nattie Serwanga.'

Chapter 24

The massive killer moved across the floor with surprising stealth and closed in on Nikki as she slept. Her eyes opened a slit, but it was too late. Before she could make a sound, his huge, fleshy palm clamped over her mouth. His knee ground into the small of her back, increasing pressure on her spine until she knew it was going to crack in two.

Please, no! Please stop! her mind screamed. *I don't want to be paralyzed!*

Paralyzing her was clearly only part of what the man had in mind. He had tried to kill her before and botched it. He was not going to miss again. His moon face puffed into a lurid smile as he hooked his fingers beneath her chin and pulled her head back. His knee was pressing straight through her body.

Nikki awoke lost and totally disoriented, clawing at her pillow. The air in the strange room felt thick and stagnant. Then, as she was forcing herself to calm down, she heard the steady breathing of the man lying next to her. Startled, she sat up on the side of the bed, trying to ignore the land mines exploding behind her eyes. The sight of Matt Rutledge, sleeping deeply, his face peaceful and unlined, brushed aside the last of what had been a series of exquisitely vivid and frightening nightmares. A piece at a time, some of the events of the night just past drifted into place. The man lying there, her doctor, had saved her from certain torture and probable death – just rode in on his motorcycle and saved her life. She wondered how much her managed-care insurance carrier allowed for that service.

The postage-stamp room featured a bed that was probably rented out as a queen, but looked smaller, and a fan-back, white wicker chair. In addition, there was a small, three-drawer bureau with some clothes neatly folded on top. Nikki padded to the tiny bathroom, washed her face with cold water, then brushed her teeth and hair with brand-new supplies that seemed to be waiting there for her. Her arms were a mass of bruises from IVs, blood drawing, and God only knew what else. There was a thick, tender scab, an inch or two long, just above her right ear. She felt certain she knew what had caused it, but with her thoughts careening about like bumper cars, she just couldn't seem to get her mind around anything specific.

She returned to the bedroom, settled onto the wicker chair, and dropped her feet heavily onto the bed. The impact was enough to visibly jar Matt, but he lay there undisturbed, his half smile suggesting that whatever *his* current dream, it was far removed from those that had been tormenting her. He had kicked the sheet aside, and lay there in a pair of sweat pants, naked from the hips up. He had the full waist and broad shoulders of an athlete past his prime, but managing to keep up. She had never been particularly drawn to men who wore their hair in a ponytail, but his seemed to fit his rugged features well. All in all, he was not Hollywood handsome, but he was damn attractive in most of the physical ways that mattered to her –

and he had just saved her life. She knelt by the bed and studied the tattoo on his deltoid. It was – what had he said? – a hawthorn tree, about two inches high – beautifully rendered as far as she could tell. Because of her own unusual tattoo, she always paid attention to them on others. A tree was a first. There was a story there, she was certain of that. She brought her face up so that her eyes were just a few inches from his. She felt his breath and expected him to react in some way to her closeness. Nothing. He continued his sleep and, judging from his peaceful expression, his dream as well.

The clock radio on the bureau read seven-thirty, which more or less corresponded to the light filtering through the curtains. It seemed like waking her new roommate was going to take nothing short of a frontal assault, but not just yet. She shifted back onto the chair and sorted through what she could remember of the strange and deadly events since her departure from Boston. One thing, and maybe only one, was clear – Kathy Wilson was at the center of whatever was going on. She was one of at least three people from Belinda with a bizarre, terrifying, inexorably lethal syndrome. Matt was certain that a toxic exposure was responsible for the unusual constellation of signs and symptoms. His theory made as much sense as anything did, especially backed up by his discovery of large-scale toxic waste storage in a cave near the Belinda mine. But what was Kathy's connection with the mine? And why did the chief of police send men to kill Nikki and subsequently become obsessed with finding out whom she had spoken to about Kathy's condition?

At the moment, she didn't have the wisp of an answer to any of her own questions. But knowing

Joe Keller as she did, if there was a clue in the anatomy of Kathy's nervous system, he would find it. There was a phone on the bureau with a note taped to it that local calls were free and long-distance calls had to be collect or credit card. Holding her breath, she dialed 1-800-COLLECT and placed a call to what she hoped her disrupted memory had held on to as Joe Keller's direct line. If the clock radio was correct, her boss would have been at the office for an hour already – possibly two – sipping his thick black coffee and working out anatomic and biochemical puzzles.

'Bless you,' she muttered when his voice came on the line and accepted the prompt to say 'yes.'

'Joe, I'm all right,' she said quickly.

'Thank God. People have been very worried about you. We even called the police.'

Nikki started to explain that a chief of police was, in fact, responsible for her trouble, but quickly stopped herself. There would be time.

'I'm on my way home right now. I should be there by late tonight.'

'Excellent.'

'Joe, I've had some trouble in West Virginia related to my friend Kathy – the one you autopsied.'

'What sort of trouble?'

'There are two other cases down here that looked and acted exactly like hers – neurofibromas and progressive paranoid insanity.'

'Well, now, that *is* something,' Keller said. 'You see, your instincts were absolutely correct in this case. I am looking at the slides of Miss Wilson's brain right now. She has unmistakable spongiform encephalopathy.'

Spongiform encephalopathy. Nikki caught her

breath. The degenerative, transmittable, ultimately fatal nervous-system disease had a number of forms, including a syndrome called Creutzfeldt-Jakob disease; kuru, once found in the brain-eating cannibals of New Guinea; fatal familial insomnia; and bovine spongiform encephalopathy, also known as BSE, or more commonly, Mad Cow disease.

Excitedly, Nikki stretched out and kicked Matt firmly on the sole of his foot. He bunched his pillow beneath his head and pulled his foot away. She kicked him again, even more forcefully, this time with her heel against his calf. He moaned and began to stir.

'Go on, Joe,' she said, knowing better than to ask if he was sure. 'This is quite incredible.'

'You say there are two other cases where you are?'

'In the town where Kathy grew up, yes.'

One final kick and it was clear Matt had at last ascended to a higher plane of wakefulness. If he hadn't taken some sort of drug, he was a candidate for the *Guinness Book of Records*. Her clients in the coroner's office were easier to rouse.

'And these other cases,' Keller asked, 'they had spongiform encephalopathy also?'

'I don't know. Their brains appeared normal on gross exam, so the microscopic wasn't done.'

SE was caused by germs known as prions – infectious protein particles capable of reproducing themselves without DNA or RNA. One of the characteristics of SE was that despite an often spectacular clinical picture, the brain looked grossly normal until sections of it were examined under the microscope, where diffuse, spongelike holes could be seen. Another characteristic was that the incubation period of the disease was often a decade or more, during which time the victim might well be infectious to others.

'Did these cases of yours also have neuro-fibromas?' Keller asked.

Matt was awake now, pawing sleep from his eyes and looking over at her quizzically. She put a finger to her lips and motioned that she would fill him in momentarily.

'Yes, both of them. From what I have been told, there was nothing unusual about them on micro-scopic.'

'Well, maybe and maybe not,' Keller said. 'I tried a number of stains and stain combinations on them, and found an approach that clearly distinguishes these lesions from the reference neurofibromas in my library.'

Keller the ever-curious, Keller the intellectual. Nikki smiled just picturing her boss. He was forever playing with stains and with his department's powerful electron microscope. His library, in addition to the hundreds of texts, included hundreds, probably even thousands, of unstained specimens from every organ and countless disease states, each carefully catalogued. Evidently, among those unstained tissues were some run-of-the-mill neuro-fibromas – the reference specimens.

Spongiform encephalopathy with unusual neuro-fibromas. *The Belinda syndrome*, Nikki speculated. . . . *Or maybe Rutledge-Solari disease.*

'Joe, listen, we'll be home between ten and twelve tonight.'

'I should be here then.'

'If you are, great. But if not, we'll see you tomorrow morning.'

'We?'

'A doctor from down here saved my life two or three times recently. He's got more than a passing interest in this syndrome. He thinks it's due to a secret industrial dump spilling toxic waste into his town's groundwater.'

'Given what we know about prion infections,' Keller said, 'I really don't see how.'

'Well, we'll talk about it when we get there. Thanks, Joe.'

'I'm so relieved you are okay,' Keller said. 'Oh, by the way, the police had no trouble finding the man who killed your drowning victim, Roger Belanger. His name was Halliday. That was what the "H" was for. They were friends and business associates. The police believe they fought about money. Halliday invited him over to his place to make up. He wrote a check and the two of them had a few drinks. Once Halliday got him into his pool, he got his hands around Belanger's throat and dragged him to the bottom.'

'Process,' Nikki said.

'Exactly,' Keller concurred.

By the time Nikki set the receiver down, Matt had pulled on a new, blue sweatshirt with YALE block-printed on the front.

'Mornin',' she said.

'Mornin', yourself.'

She motioned at the sweatshirt.

'Did you go there?'

'No, but while you were trying on things in that Target store last night, I bought some stuff for me. This was one they had in my size.'

'Believe it or not, I remember. Well, sort of. Where *did* you go to school?'

'Good ol' WVU. The Mountaineers. That was the only college we could afford. Turned out to be a great place.'

Nikki felt certain she recalled a nurse telling her that Matt had gone to Harvard Med, yet he didn't feel that minor factoid was worth tossing in. She gave him high marks for modesty, as if he needed any more high marks after what he had done for her.

'You sleep soundly,' she said.

'People have noticed that from time to time, yes.'

'If you have trouble walking today, it's from me kicking you to wake you up.'

'The nurses at the hospital quiz me when they call, to be certain I'm awake. They don't know that I've mutated so that I can now answer most of their questions, even the complex mathematical ones, in my sleep. Do you remember much of last night?'

'Unfortunately, I think I do. I hope I thanked you enough for rescuing me the way you did.'

'I have a thing against losing patients. So, what was that call all about?'

'I phoned my boss, Joe Keller, to tell him I was alive and well, and to see if anything had turned up in Kathy's microscopic.'

'And?'

'You're not going to believe this, Matt. Kathy had spongiform encephalopathy. Joe's absolutely certain of that, and believe me, he's, like, never wrong.'

Matt sank back onto the bed, incredulous. He was hardly an expert on the various versions, but he was keeping up on the condition in the medical literature – at least as much as his cramped schedule would allow.

'Prion disease?'

314

'Yes,' Nikki said. 'Quick point of interest – most people pronounce it *pry-on,* the way you do, but Stanley Prusiner, who won the Nobel prize for describing the beasties, pronounces it *pree-on.* I heard him speak a year or so ago.'

'Pree-on it is. This is incredible. Do you think my two cases had SE as well?'

'How can I not?'

'Well, what in the hell? . . . What about the neurofibromas? Anything special about those?'

'Apparently there was. Joe Keller is sort of a stain freak. He might try a dozen different staining techniques on a piece of tissue just to see what shows up. He tells me Kathy's facial lesions take up this one obscure stain differently from the usual Elephant Man type of fibromas.'

'I just don't get it.'

'Neither do I. But listen, Matt, the way I see it, maybe you're still on the right track. Before we jump to any conclusions, let's go up to Boston and see what Joe has to show us.'

'Give me a few minutes to get put together and we're off.'

'Only as far as the nearest IHOP, though. I have this sudden, insatiable craving for pancakes drenched with maple syrup.'

'IHOP, she wants,' Matt mumbled as he headed to the bathroom. 'First she lays prions on me, then she wants IHOP. What kind of a woman is this, anyway?'

Nikki was impressed with his attempt at cheeriness, but she knew Joe Keller's revelation had stung. From what Matt had told her last night, he was determined to expose the directors of the Belinda mining corporation for all the shortcuts they had taken over the years, and all the people they had harmed along the way. The bizarre cases were just the catalyst he had been looking for to bring them down – proof that mishandling of organic toxins was causing serious biologic injury. But it was going to be hard connecting the mine with prion infection. Well, she reminded herself, nothing was decided yet.

If there were answers, though, Joe Keller would have them.

Matt returned to the room scrubbed and shaved and looking very good. He had stripped off the Yale sweatshirt and replaced it with a black T and the denim jacket he had been wearing when he rode to the cabin in the woods and rescued her. Nikki liked the change. He was much more denim than Ivy League.

'Ready to go?' he asked.

She stood and set her hands on his shoulders. His eyes immediately found hers.

'You were very cool and very brave last night,' she said.

'If I had thought about what I was doing, I probably would have fainted.'

'I doubt it.'

There was much more that she had planned to say, much more she wanted to know about him, but suddenly she was on her tiptoes, her arms around his neck.

'Thank you, Matthew Rutledge,' she whispered. 'Thank you for saving my life.'

Maybe she had known all along that she was going to kiss him. Maybe she had promised herself, clinging to him on that motorcycle, that if they survived and somehow escaped, she would kiss him whether he wanted her to or not. Still, the actual act of placing her lips against his, briefly and tenderly, was as surprising to her as it was exciting. She drew away just far enough to read his eyes, and saw no doubt in them. Their second kiss was deeper, more prolonged, and more passionate. His muscular arms enfolded her as his lips and tongue explored hers. She set her hands against the sides of his face and ran her fingertips over his cheeks and jaw. When at last they broke apart, she could barely stand.

'I don't remember the last time I wanted to kiss a woman so much,' he said.

'In that case, I'm glad I came along when I did.'

'Very funny. Actually, that *was* very funny. You know, I have no recollection of the exact words, but doesn't kissing my patient violate some paragraph or other of that Hippocratic Oath we took?'

She kissed him again, this time playfully.

'Call it mouth-to-mouth resuscitation,' she said. 'I think my HMO might even cover it.'

He looked over longingly at the bed, but made no move to lead her there.

'There'll be time,' she whispered gently. 'I promise you that. But right now we have work to do.'

'Work to do, pancakes to eat. God, but you kiss splendidly.'

'As do you. Tell you what, we'll practice every hundred miles or so, just in case we can perfect the art a little more.'

'That certainly would do wonders for my road rage. Oh,' he added, 'here.' He handed over the Yale sweatshirt. 'I actually bought this for you. It's a large, but that's the only size they had.'

'And why Yale?'

'Because that's the only one I could find that

317

didn't have some silly foreign version of an English phrase on it, like Sport Tough or Big Run.'

'Well, you're much more West Virginia than Yale anyway, and coming from me that's a high compliment.'

'How so?'

She pulled on the sweatshirt, then kissed him on the cheek.

'Because,' she said, underscoring the four block letters with her palm, 'I graduated from here.'

Nattie and Eli Serwanga lived in a modest Cape in an integrated neighborhood of Evanston, just up the Lake Michigan coast from Chicago. Ellen sat at the dining room table, sipping tea with honey and trying to remember the last time she had felt this sad. There was the situation with Rudy, and the incredible guilt and humiliation she was feeling over having opened his letter. But that situation paled in light of what these two had been through. As they talked, she flashed over and over again to Dr. Suzanne O'Connor's incredible account of the horrors of her battle with Lassa fever.

In their early forties, Ellen guessed, the Serwangas were kind and generous toward her, and clearly in love with each other – the perfect couple to have and raise children. Only they had none and weren't ever again going to get the chance. Deepening their tragedy was irrefutable evidence that Nattie was responsible, albeit inadvertently, for the deaths of two eight-year-old children who attended the day-care center at the hospital where she worked. Nice stuff.

'Tell me again, Nattie,' Ellen asked, 'when did you know you were sick?'

Nattie pulled a tissue from a half-empty box and dabbed at some embryonic tears. She was a beautiful woman – large and expansive, with huge, expressive eyes, and ebony skin.

'It was nearly two weeks after we got back from Africa,' she said. 'We came back on a Tuesday, and I first felt the sore throat two Mondays after that. Ten days later I was in the operating room. They delivered the baby, but he was stillborn. Then they tried to save my womb, but there was just too much bleeding.'

Eli, who was still wearing his suit and tie from work, rose and moved behind her to comfort her. It was his relatives they had been visiting in Sierra Leone, and he expressed some guilt at having talked her into staying for an extra week while he straightened out some family business – the week in which the doctors believed she became infected. Ellen sipped at her tea and reflected on the impact of her own newly acquired guilt.

'If my questions upset you too much,' she said, 'you must tell me.'

'We're doing okay,' Eli replied. 'But it would be good if you could tell us where all this is leading.'

Ellen set the passenger manifest on the table. During the flight from D.C. to Chicago, she had managed to curtail the attempts at conversation by the recently divorced, totally self-absorbed appliance salesman seated next to her long enough to scan all the flights, searching for matches – passengers who had been on more than one flight with a soon-to-be-victim of Lassa fever. There were at least six.

'I have reason to be suspicious that Nattie may have gotten infected with the Lassa virus either just before or just after leaving Sierra Leone, or else on the plane ride home.'

'But how?' Nattie asked.

'I don't know.'

'Do you mean,' Eli said, 'that you think somebody deliberately infected her?'

'That's the possibility I'm looking into. Please, both of you, I beg you not to say anything to anyone about my suspicions until I can finish my search. It's a matter of life and death. Can you give me your word on that?'

'Yes,' they said in unison. 'Of course,' Nattie added.

'Thank you. I'm looking into the possibility that someone on the flight home transmitted the virus to you. Nattie, this is a list of the people who were on your flight from Freetown to Ghana, and then from Ghana to the States. Do any of these names ring any bells? As you can see, there were forty-six on the first leg, including the two of you, and thirty-seven of those among the hundred and sixty on the flight to Baltimore. Do any of these names stand out as someone you remember?'

Nattie shook her head.

'It's been three years,' she said. 'Plus I think I lost some of my memory when I was sick. I'm afraid I can't help you. I'm sorry.'

'Your memory is just fine,' Eli countered. 'These names mean nothing to me, either. Tell me, do you think this infection was random, or do you think my wife was singled out?'

Ellen considered the question for a while.

'You know, I never thought of that.'

She searched for the words to speak about the ten cases of Lassa fever that Nattie was believed to have caused through her job as a dietary worker – including two that died. Nattie saved her the trouble.

'If someone did want to spread the infection, someone with a job like mine would be perfect, provided they somehow knew what I did for a –'

'What is it?' Ellen asked, noting the odd expression on the woman's face.

'Eli, remember that man on the flight from Sierra Leone? The big man who talked to me outside the rest room. He was on the other plane, too.'

'The white man?'

'Exactly. He sold something. Insurance, I think. You mentioned how scary-looking he was.'

'I do remember him, yes.'

'He was a smiler and a talker, that one – asked me all sorts of questions about myself. Made it a game, like he was such an experienced insurance salesman that he could guess things about me.'

Ellen felt a little burst of adrenaline.

'Anyone else?' she asked just in case.

'No one that I can think of.'

She remembered the memory exercise Rudy had done with her.

'Okay,' she asked, 'can you bring me a paper and pen?'

'Certainly.'

Eli brought in several sheets of typing paper.

'Okay,' Ellen said, 'I'm going to go and sit in the living room. I'd like you to put your heads together and write down every descriptive word you can remember about this man – what he looked like, what he acted like, even the things you've already told me. Just relax your minds and free-associate. I know it's been a long while, but just do your best.

Take as much time as you need, and if you disagree on something, write down both opinions.'

'We'll try our best,' Nattie said.

Fifteen minutes later, the Serwangas were out of recollections. They called Ellen back to the dining room and apologetically handed her their description.

Big
Tall
Strong
Slick
Smooth
Smiling
Glad-hander
Thick hair
Flat face . . . like a cartoon character hit with a frying pan
Deep voice
Maybe a Texas-type accent
Scar on face

Ellen felt her heart stop.

'The scar,' she asked, her voice trembling. 'Can you tell me about the scar?'

'That's Nattie's,' Eli said. 'I don't remember any scar.'

'Well, there was one. I'm sure of it. Right here.'

She pointed to the space between her nose and upper lip.

'That's him,' Ellen said.

'Who?'

'A very bad man. I think we're onto something.'

'Well, I just thought of another word we should have put on the list – clumsy.'

322

'What do you mean?'

'I was standing waiting for the rest room. He came up the aisle, tripped, and slammed into me. The man nearly knocked me out of the plane.'

Chapter 25

Matt and Nikki had breakfast at pancakes on Parade on the banks of the Susquehanna. If it was possible for a family restaurant to be romantic, this one, with a broad porch set on tall stilts out over the river, surely was. But then again, on this particular morning, the two of them would have found any McDonald's or Burger King atmospheric. For over an hour, not a word was spoken about Bill Grimes or spongiform encephalopathy or Belinda Coal and Coke. Instead, they touched fingertips and thumb wrestled, laughed to tears at the silly or embarrassing stories of each other's lives, and commiserated with the sad ones. Grace, their husky, gum-chewing waitress, called Matt 'Slugger' and Nikki 'Dearie.' After the third time she found they weren't ready to order because they hadn't looked at the menu, she brought them heart-shaped lollypops and a bill for two dollars for mooning at each other in public.

'It's been a long, long time since I mooned,' Matt said. ''Cept maybe for the time a couple of years ago when my shorts ripped while I was playing basketball.'

'Boston men are too sophisticated to moon,' Nikki said. 'Instead, they discuss lunar landings and the Hubble telescope.'

There was a pay phone in an alcove by the rest rooms. Before their order arrived, Matt called his uncle at the hospital.

'Hey, Unk, it's Matt.'

'Hey,' Hal said, 'how goes it? Any word about that patient of yours?'

'It goes not too well, actually. And yes, Nikki Solari is safe. She's with me in Pennsylvania. Hal, something really weird and really dangerous is going on. It has to do with those odd cases.'

'The miners?'

'Them and the girl who died, Kathy Wilson. And Bill Grimes is right in the middle of it.'

'My read on Grimes is that he's slick and power hungry,' Hal said, 'but he's not evil.'

'Unk, he's evil. Believe me, he is.'

Hal Sawyer listened patiently as Matt recounted the story of Nikki's abduction and subsequent rescue, and this morning's revelation regarding the microscopic findings in Kathy Wilson's brain.

'Spongiform encephalopathy,' Hal said when Matt had finished. 'Now, doesn't missing something like that make *me* feel a bit sheepish.'

'There's no reason. The Wilson woman's brain looked normal, just as I'm sure our two cases' did. You wouldn't be expected to do a microscopic on their brains. This guy in Boston only did it because Nikki Solari insisted.'

'You still think the mine's at fault?'

'I'm sure of it. I don't know the precise connection between what they've done and spongiform disease, but I do know that somehow they're the cause of this, and Grimes is on the take from them. Any ideas what we should do?'

Hal thought for a time.

'It seems showing someone in authority that toxic dump you found is the place to start.'

'I agree.'

'There is a man, Fred Carabetta, at the Occupational Safety and Health Administration in Washington, who owes me a favor for some expert witness work I did for him a few years back. Maybe the way to go is to see if I can call in my marker and get him to come with us and view that dump. Once we've got an OSHA official believing, we can bring some legitimate pressure to bear against BC and C.'

'If the dump is still there.'

'Now, nephew, you know we can't control that. That's rule number two in your Godfather's Lexicon –'

' – of Youth. I know, I know. Rule number one: There's no such word as "can't". Rule number two: If you can't control it, don't let it control you.'

'Excellent. I'm proud that you haven't forgotten the Lexicon rules after all these years.'

'That's 'cause you still spout them at me every chance you get.'

'In that case, I'm glad you've been paying attention. Listen, Matt, I'll see what I can do with Fred Carabetta. How can I get ahold of you?'

'Just call the house and leave a message on my machine. I'll check it frequently and get back to you.'

'And I'll call that coroner in Boston, too. See if he can tell me about that special stain he used.'

'Do you have any tissue left from those two miners?'

'I suspect I do.'

'Please don't speak with anyone about Grimes until you and I have a chance to talk, okay? He's more dangerous than you think.'

'If you're that certain about him, why don't you just go to the police somewhere and file a complaint?'

'Nikki wants to, but I've talked her out of it for now. From what I've heard, the police are a pretty tight fraternity. There's no cop who's going to listen to us and run right down to Belinda to make Grimes assume the pat-down position. And once we come out into the open, he'll have us between his crosshairs regardless of what we allege he did. For the time being, I'd rather wait.'

'Okay, whatever you say. Just be careful. I'll call you later today. By the way, I visited with your mother this morning. She's really slipping.'

'I know. I saw her for a few minutes yesterday. It won't be long now before she'll need some sort of comprehensive care. I'll look into it when I get this business settled. Listen, Hal, thanks for your help – with her and with this.'

'You're on the right track, Matt. I'm certain of it.'

'Me, too, Unk,' Matt said. 'Me, too.'

Nikki gave the pancakes a solid eight. Matt claimed to have wolfed down his Spanish omelette too rapidly to grade it for taste. He left Grace a tip that was twice the cost of their meal, along with a note that thanked her for presiding over their morning mooning.

'You know what I'm really relieved about?' he asked as they headed out to the Harley. 'I'm really relieved those guys didn't kill you.'

'Aw, gee. You certainly know just what to say to a girl, you romantic devil you. It's good to know we actually have something in common. I'm relieved they didn't kill me, too.'

She reached across the bike and kissed him

intensely enough to get a honk from a passing trucker. She had just let up when they felt some tentative raindrops. Fifteen minutes later, it was drizzling steadily. Matt found a Wal-Mart outside of York and VISAed some rain gear for each of them, but for the next five hours the going was slow and not pleasant. They gave passing thought to stopping until the next morning, but Nikki was too anxious to get home. By the time the clouds broke, they were still several hours from Boston, having inched through rush-hour traffic around New York City. At nine Nikki called the office to tell Joe Keller they were running late and might not be there until eleven, but there was no answer.

'He's either doing a late case or out to dinner,' she said. 'I shouldn't have told him when we were arriving, so he wouldn't wait, but now that I did, I'm sure he'll be there.'

Matt used the break to call his machine. There were two messages. The first was from Mae reporting that as far as she knew, there was no word about his patient, Dr. Solari, and that she was worried about not having heard from him all day, and hoped he was all right and that his absence was due to nothing more serious than the erratic behavior he had been exhibiting so much of lately. The second message was from Hal.

'Good news, Matt. Not great, but good. Fred Carabetta won't commit to any action regarding the mine, but he will meet with us in his office. Tomorrow at three. Two Hundred Constitution Avenue. Wherever you are, I hope you can make it. Call and confirm.'

Matt left a message on both his uncle's office and home machines that he would be there, and then dictated a message on his own office machine telling Mae he was all right and would be in touch. After he set the receiver down, he shared Hal's breakthrough with Nikki.

'I'm going to take the bike back to D.C. tomorrow,' he said. 'Wanna come?'

'Do you get frequent flyer miles on this thing?'

'Double miles to D.C. It's the shuttle.'

'Well, thanks. I really want to be with you, but for the moment I think I need to stay here. For one thing, I feel like my body can't take too much more, and for another, I have this job cutting up dead people that I get paid pretty well for doing, but only if I show up. It says so in my contract.'

'I understand. I'll be back up as soon as I deal with this mine thing.'

It was nearing eleven by the time they cruised up the Southeast Expressway toward the shimmering lights of Boston. The rain had stopped, leaving the air cool and fresh.

'Have you been back here since your residency?' Nikki asked.

'Nope,' he called back over his shoulder. 'In the beginning, after I returned to Belinda, I was working like hell in the ER, then to set up a private practice. Ginny got sick soon after that, and never really had much of a remission. Since she died, it's been hard enough much of the time just to get up and go to the office, much less embark on a nostalgic journey to Boston. I did like the place, though. Lots.'

The medical examiner's office was located just off the highway. Except for some low nighttime lighting, the three-story building was dark. Nikki rang the front buzzer half a dozen times. They could hear the sound of it echoing through the empty reception area, but there was no movement inside.

'Strange,' she said, 'there's usually a maintenance man here all night. Even if he's not, Joe often works past midnight. Knowing we're coming, I have trouble believing he went home.'

'Maybe he wasn't feeling well,' Matt offered.

'Maybe. The front door opens with a swipe card that is back in West Virginia with my things. But there's a security door in the back that has a keypad. Joe's office is toward the back anyhow. Maybe he can't hear the buzzer.'

Matt followed her through a dimly lit alley to the rear of the building.

'See,' she said. 'That's Joe's office, that light right there on the second floor. I knew he was here.'

'I think you're right about him not hearing us. This is a long building – sort of like an aircraft carrier.'

Nikki punched in the code and they stepped into the concrete rear stairway, eerily illuminated by a red EXIT sign. The air was imbued with the distinctive, though not overpowering, aroma of formaldehyde. With Matt following, Nikki quickly ascended to the second floor and opened the door onto a carpeted corridor with offices on either side.

'Joe, it's us,' she called out.

She knocked on the door marked JOSEF KELLER, M.D. CHIEF MEDICAL EXAMINER, then pushed it open. The office was brightly lit by an overhead fluorescent fixture and a desk lamp. Joe Keller was at his desk, his back to them.

'Joe,' Nikki said, 'why didn't you – ?'

Then she saw the blood on the carpet. She raced to the chair, with Matt right behind, and cried out loudly. There was dark, clotted blood all over the desk and splattered across the face and clothes of Joe Keller. His head drooped over his chest. Nikki lifted it gently, exposing a battered face with a bullet hole just above the nose. Keller's eyes were open wide and glazed with death. His wire-rimmed spectacles dangled from one ear.

'Look,' Matt said, gesturing to Keller's right hand, which rested in the dead man's lap.

The index finger had been cleanly severed off at the middle knuckle.

'Oh, Jesus!' Nikki cried, stumbling backward, her limbs suddenly in spasm. 'Oh, Christ, how could someone do this to him?'

Matt put his arms around her and held her closely.

'Honey, please don't touch anything anymore,' he begged.

'Who would do such a thing? Why? He was such a dear, sweet man. Why? Oh, Jesus. Oh, shit! No.'

She couldn't stop moving, shifting from one foot to the other, pounding her fists against the sides of her thighs. Matt led her away from the body of her mentor, trying at once to comfort her, evaluate the scene, and stay alert in case the killer was still in the building. He thought about the gun in his saddlebag, and cursed himself for not bringing it along when Keller failed to answer the door. He had an inkling of trouble at that moment, but simply hadn't paid enough attention to it. There wasn't the slightest doubt in his mind that the ME's torture and murder were somehow connected to Kathy Wilson. Was Grimes nearby – or his stooges?

There was a small, round conference table at one

end of the office. Matt helped Nikki into the chair that was facing away from Keller.

'Nikki, I'm really sorry about this – sick and sorry.'

'You think it had to do with Grimes?' she sobbed.

'I'm going to try to figure that out, but yes, yes I do.'

He chose not to question her again about what she might have said to Grimes either at the memorial service or in the cabin.

'I – I want to help you,' she said.

'In a little bit. Nik, can you sit here while I look around?'

'Yes.'

'Good. Just keep your hands in your lap. I know there's a logical explanation for your prints being in this building, but I'd rather not have them be the only employee's fresh prints in this office.'

'I understand. Matt, they *tortured* him.'

Matt paced around the desk and scanned the rest of the office. No gun, no knife, no finger. He squatted down and examined Keller's contused, distorted face. His nose had certainly been shattered, and there was probably a fracture of the orbit bone above his left eye.

Earlier in the evening they had again discussed calling in the police and had voted unanimously against it for the time being.

'Nikki,' Matt asked, 'can you estimate when he was murdered?'

'I would need to examine him to be really accurate, but from what I saw I would guess a couple of hours ago.'

'So we can wait to call the police.'

'And maybe do it from a pay phone.'

'In that case,' Matt said, 'come back to the bike with me.'

'Don't you want to look around and try to find out why they did this?'

'Oh, I do. But there's something in my saddlebag I want to get first, on the chance they're still around.'

Minutes later, with Matt cradling Larry's snub-nosed revolver, the two of them began a systematic search of the building.

'Assuming this has to do with Kathy,' he asked, 'what do you think they could have wanted?'

'I don't know. Let's start with our files. They're in a locked room right behind the autopsy suite.' Covering her fingertip with her shirt, Nikki punched in her code on a keypad and they entered the long, narrow file room. 'The charts on the shelves are arranged by case number,' she said as she crossed to a narrow six-drawer cabinet. 'This card file is alphabetical.'

'And?'

'I can't find her card. There are seven Katherine Wilsons, but none is the right one.'

'Look,' Matt said, pointing to a dark smear on the corner of the long table in the center of the room.

Nikki peered at the stain. 'They had Joe in here.'

She flipped through the cards again, then took out all the Wilsons and set them on the table. Matt went through them, and shook his head.

'Nada.'

'We have the cards backed up.'

Nikki sat down at a computer terminal and after a few maneuvers wrote down a number.

Kathy Wilson's chart was missing, too, and with it, all the autopsy data.

'Do you use a transcription service for your dictations?'

Nikki was already back at the terminal.

'We have our own in-house. The record's been deleted from the database. They thought of everything except the backup chart list. Joe somehow managed not to tell them about that. Let's go down to Histology. It's right below the autopsy suite.'

They carefully closed the file room and entered the large, open autopsy suite with three stainless-steel tables. The center table was occupied. A copper-skinned man, garbed in work boots and stained chino overalls, lay peacefully, thumbs hooked under his suspenders, staring unseeingly up at the drop ceiling. There was a thick smear of clotted blood and tissue where his left eye had been. Beneath the gore, they were certain, was a bullet hole.

'Oh, Christ,' Nikki said, turning away.

'The maintenance man?'

She nodded. 'Santiago.'

'Cute touch hooking his thumbs in like that.'

'The stairs to Histology are over there.'

To the surprise of neither, the slides for Kathy Wilson and all unsectioned tissue specimens were gone.

'Nothing,' Nikki said after she had checked the last possible place where any of Kathy's tissue might be.

'Two men died so someone could be certain of that.'

'Matt,' Nikki blurted out, 'let's get out of here. I want to go to my place right now.'

'I'm not sure that's wise.'

'I don't care. You've got a gun. If you're not

334

comfortable using it, I promise you I just became totally ready. I want to go home. I want to sit down and have a cup of tea in my own chair and figure out what to do next.'

'Okay, okay. Show me the way.'

'Thanks.'

'And Nikki?'

'Yes?'

'I'm really sick about Joe.'

'I know you are.'

In silence, through largely empty streets, they rode the few miles to South Boston and parked a block away from Nikki's apartment. Matt secured the revolver in his belt and pulled his shirt over it, keeping his hand in touch with the grip. Warily, they made their way along the colorful row of tightly packed duplexes and triplexes, keeping an eye out for movement in any of the cars parked along the street.

'How are we going to get in?' he asked.

'We keep a spare key wedged in a little magnet box behind the drainpipe. Kathy started losing hers all the time.'

The key was right where she expected it to be. Cautiously, they made their way up to the second floor. Matt slipped the gun out and held it ready as Nikki slid the key in the lock, turned it silently, and eased the door open.

'Oh, no.'

Her flat was in shambles. Books were strewn everywhere, shelves stripped bare. Lamps were knocked over. Every drawer was pulled out and emptied, every cushion and framed painting thrown in the middle of the floor. Figurines and candy dishes were smashed. Mindless of the possibility that men were still in the apartment, Nikki dropped to her knees, sobbing hysterically. Matt knelt beside her and did the only thing that felt right – he kicked the door closed, set his arm around her shoulders, and let her cry.

Fifteen minutes later they were still in the same spot. Finally, numbly, Nikki rose and shuffled into her bedroom. She emerged with a medium-sized backpack filled with clothes.

'Let's get out of here and out of Boston,' she said flatly. 'I feel as if I've been raped.'

Matt followed her out of the ransacked apartment, down the stairs, and around to the bike.

'They're not going to get away with this,' he said. 'I promise you they aren't.'

'We're going to the police,' she said firmly, turning suddenly to face him, her expression an unsettling mix of fury and bewilderment. 'I'm not going to let you talk me out of doing it this time. If we had gone when I said, maybe Joe would still be alive.'

'Nikki, that's –'

'Don't tell me that's nonsense!' she snapped. 'Maybe it is and maybe it isn't. I just want to go to the police.'

Matt checked around quickly to see if anyone had been roused by her outburst.

'Go now?' he said. 'But –'

'Dammit, Matt, my dear friend is dead, and Grimes killed him! I don't care about your fucking coal mine or . . . or your theories about toxic waste, or your goddamn insane town. Joe Keller was the gentlest man on earth. Why in the hell would they do this? Why?'

Sobbing wretchedly again, she threw her arms around him and buried her face in his chest.

Matt held her tightly. Going to the police was asking for trouble. He still felt certain of that. Joe Keller had already been dead for a couple of hours when they found him, and those who had killed him and destroyed her apartment were not going to be any easier to catch up with this minute than they would be after an anonymous call an hour from now. Reporting Nikki's kidnapping would be their word against Grimes's, and they would be exposing themselves at a time when freedom and mobility were just about the only elements on their side.

'Look,' he said, 'let's get on the road. We'll stop at a pay phone in a little while and call the Boston police. I hope I can talk you out of actually showing up in an FBI office or police station, but that'll ultimately be up to you.'

Nikki's racking sobs gradually diminished. Finally, without a word, she mounted the Harley and waited for him to step on.

Matt stuffed the revolver back into his jacket pocket, took his spot in front of her, and fired up the bike. If going to the police was what she needed, the police she would get. She had been through so much. He drove off, sensing her sitting rigidly behind him, staring off into the night. He was grateful she had gone into her bedroom to gather her things, grateful he had had time to pace around her living room before she returned, grateful he had happened to look over at the mantel. Somewhere in the next half hour or so, he would ease the Harley toward the soft shoulder, and when he was certain she wasn't paying attention, he would flip what he had found on her mantel into the woods.

And the whereabouts of Joe Keller's missing finger would forever remain a mystery.

Chapter 26

It was past two in the morning when Matt and Nikki found a motel vacancy just outside of Stamford, Connecticut. Confused, bewildered, and more than a little frightened, they checked in and carried their small cache of belongings up one flight to a fairly standard, well-maintained room with a view of I-95.

After leaving the shambles that was Nikki's apartment, they had ridden south in light traffic through Providence and on into Connecticut. It was a somber, silent ride, made well under the speed limit. Each of them was experiencing some tension born of Nikki's continued determination to involve themselves with the police and possibly the FBI in the face of Matt's desire to remain as much of a mystery to Bill Grimes as possible until his business with Belinda Coal and Coke was completed. Two exits past Providence, she asked him to leave the interstate. There, at a rest stop, she called the Boston police.

'There's been a double murder at the medical examiner's office on Albany Street,' she said, surprised by the composure in her voice. 'Chief William Grimes, G-r-i-m-e-s, of the Belinda, West Virginia, Police Department is responsible.'

A minute later they were back on the highway.

'Feel better?' Matt asked over his shoulder.

'Not much. Grimes will probably say that he doesn't know anything, and that some nutcase he once arrested is out to cause him trouble.'

'Once those bodies are discovered, I'm sure the police will begin to search out everyone who works in your building. It won't take long for them to figure out that it might be you who made the call.'

'I don't care. I know you do, but I don't. You and I are the only ones who can connect Grimes to Joe. It'll be our word against his, but two M.D. degrees have to count for something. After we wake up, I want to go to the FBI to report the murders and also being kidnapped. That's definitely a federal offense. If you want, I'll tell them I don't know where you are. That way you can get to Washington and meet with the guy your uncle spoke about.'

'Do whatever you have to do,' Matt replied.

'I'm really sorry if I end up interfering with your plans.'

'Let's hope it doesn't come to that.'

'You're angry.'

'I'm not angry. I would have liked to have, I don't know, solidified our position before involving the police – maybe speak to a lawyer.'

'Sorry.'

'Don't apologize. You've been living a nightmare ever since you set foot in Belinda. You have a right to do whatever you want.'

'And so do you,' she said.

'So do I,' Matt replied, just before accelerating up the entry ramp and back onto the interstate.

So do I.

Nikki showered and dressed for bed in the bathroom. Matt had changed into sweats by the time she emerged. He was reading a hostelry magazine in the armchair beside the small writing desk, as far away from the bed as possible.

'You coming in?' she asked unemotionally.

'Soon, maybe,' he responded in the same tone. 'I'm a little wired from the ride and all that's happened. Will the lamp bother you?'

'Not really.'

'Good.'

There were differences between Ginny and this woman, Matt was thinking, but not when it came to digging in. God, but he wanted to take her in his arms right now. Instead he stayed in the chair, flipping pages one moment, staring sightlessly at a bland photo of some snow-covered mountain inn the next.

Nikki rolled onto her side, facing away from him, but he could tell by her breathing and posture that she wasn't asleep.

'You sleeping?' he asked finally.

'No.'

'This has been a really hideous night.'

'Yeah. Joe was such a wonderful man.'

Several silent minutes passed.

'You know,' he said finally, 'in case you couldn't tell when I didn't even know how to pronounce the word, I don't know an awful lot about prion disease. If you're up to it, since we're both still too awake to drift off, I was wondering if you might be able to share some of what you know from your reading and that guy's presentation you went to.'

Nikki slowly rolled over to face him and propped her cheek on one hand.

'You mean Stanley Prusiner?'

'Yeah, him.'

'Is this a ploy because things are a little tense between us right now?'

'No ... Well, I mean, yes ... I mean I really don't know anything but the basics about prions, so I wouldn't exactly call it a ploy. More of a fact-finding mission.'

'You going to stay over there?'

'I don't want to.'

'And I don't want you to.'

'So, what am I doing over here?' He sat down beside her. 'Tell you what. How about I work some of that tension out of your shoulders while you enlighten me on spongiform encephalopathy?'

'I think Stanley would like that.' She turned onto her stomach as he began to knead at the considerable tightness radiating from the base of her neck. 'Mmmmm. Just a little softer. Oh, that's it, that's perfect. Okay, let's see, you already know that prions are little particles of protein that have the ability to reproduce themselves. No DNA, no RNA, yet they can reproduce. Amazing.'

'That's pretty much the sum total of my knowledge.'

'You're slowing down. You want to learn about this stuff or not? Much better. Okay. Prions are present normally in humans and possibly in every other organism with a nervous system. PrPC is the abbreviation for these normal prions. Some people and animals are unfortunate enough to have a mutation occur in one or more of their PrPC prions. The result is a gradual buildup of a toxic prion known as PrPSc. The brain and nervous system unknowingly adopt this imposter prion. Then the normal nervous tissue slowly comes apart, and the host organism dies.'

'Humans and cows.'

'And minks, and deer, and cats, and even monkeys. I suspect that the more we look, the more spongiform diseases we'll find. And prions may be at the center of some other neurodegenerative diseases, as well, such as Alzheimer's.'

'My mother's disease,' Matt said.

'Yes. That made me so sad this morning when you told me about her.'

'Most of the time I think she's handling it better than those around her.'

'Well, it's still too early to know, but possibly she has a prion-mediated disease. Are you getting tired doing that?'

'Nope.'

'In that case, a little farther out toward the shoulders, please. Nice. That's it. Oh, doggies, that feels good.'

'So, is mutation the only way to get prion disease?'

'No. Any means that gets the germs into the body will do the trick. The prions that cause Mad Cow disease or kuru are eaten. Patients receiving corneal transplants from someone infected with spongiform disease can get it that way. I would suspect that other routes of administration would do it as well.'

'And there is a long delay before symptoms develop?'

'Maybe decades. So far there have only been a hundred or so cases of Mad Cow disease in Great Britain, despite the tons of beef that those people ingested before the condition was recognized and warnings were sounded. That could mean there are thousands of cases still brewing. But I don't think so.'

'What do you think?'

'The arms. I think you should work on the upper arms. You're very good at this.'

'Thank you.'

'Are you like all those guys who say they love giving back rubs, then after a girl starts dating them, it turns out the *first* back rub is all they really enjoy giving? From then on it's do me, do me.'

'Maybe. That's for me to know and you to find out. So, don't leave me hanging. Why do you think there won't be thousands of cases of BSE in humans?'

'Partly because there haven't been thousands – tens of thousands – already. It seems to me that only a very small percentage of those who are exposed to PrPSc prions get infected. How could it be otherwise?'

'Why is that?'

'Why do *you* think that is?'

'Genetic factors?'

'Quite possibly. As with most diseases, we really don't have any idea why one person exposed to a germ gets sick and the person standing right next to them during the exposure doesn't. A little harder, Doc. Perfect. You tell me bad luck, and I'll tell you that right now for most infectious diseases, that's as good an explanation as any. I believe that those who develop spongiform disease are either lacking some sort of protective gene or else have a gene that in essence invites the altered prions in.'

Nikki rolled over, drew Matt's face down to hers, and kissed him lightly on the mouth.

'Tell her what she just won, Merv,' he said as she finished. 'Congratulations, you just won another two hundred hours of massage.'

Matt cupped his hands over his mouth and imitated the roar of a crowd.

'I'll tell you what, big guy,' she said. 'We'll stop in some city in New Jersey and I'll just file a report with the FBI office there. Then I'll go with you wherever it is you want to go. Deal?'

'I'm agin it.'

'I know you are.'

'Okay, deal . . . There's something else you want to add. I can see it in your eyes. What is it? What?'

'Matt, I hate to say this, and I don't want you to get upset or discouraged, but the mine theory isn't holding together well for me.'

'What do you mean?'

'I mean the connection between the toxic exposure and the syndrome we've encountered.'

'The waste dump is there. I saw it.'

'Given. Let's assume the two miners had the same spongiform disease that Joe found in Kathy. Spongiform encephalopathy, at least the four or five different types we know of, is caused by prions, but I just don't know how a toxic exposure can cause a prion infection.'

'Well,' he said after some thought, 'let me take a crack at that. There are good, life-sustaining prions that everybody has and loves, right?'

'Yes.'

'And there are bad, spawn-of-the-devil, PrPSc prions that cause spongiform disease, right?'

'Essentially, yes.'

'Then, how about the toxic exposure increases susceptibility to bad prions . . . or . . . or causes mutations from good to evil? Organic toxins cause mutations that go on to cause cancer.'

'That's a fact. But remember, these conditions seem to take years to develop – in some instances, decades. So if a toxic exposure did occur affecting our three cases, I would think it occurred before any of the subjects was old enough to be working in the mine. And what about Kathy? She never even came close to the mine as far as we know.'

'What about groundwater contamination?'

'The toxins from the mine get into the water and accelerate prion mutations. Is that what you wish to believe?'

'That *is* what I would like to believe, yes,' Matt said.

She kissed him once again, then pulled her pillow in tightly as she drew her knees and arms in.

'Works for me,' she said dreamily.

But Matt could tell that it didn't. He waited until her breathing said that she was asleep.

'G'night,' he whispered.

He rolled over and drifted off, his mind playing images of an underground river churning past countless barrels of poison, then coursing off into the darkness.

Newark, New Jersey. With four stops for directions, which were invariably given to them in dense Newarkese, it took longer to locate the FBI office than it had to make it to Newark from Stamford. They chose Newark because they expected it would have a good-sized office, and because neither of them wanted to drive into Manhattan. Matt rolled slowly down a tree-lined street, past the tall, nondescript Gateway Center on Market Street, and stopped half a block away.

'So,' he said as Nikki stripped off her helmet,

buckled it to the bike, and ran a brush through her hair, 'here we are.'

'Here we are,' she echoed, hands on hips. 'Matt, you're looking distressed. I thought we had decided on a plan.'

'I just don't feel comfortable about this.'

'I understand. How about making it a little easier on me.' She reached her arms out to him. 'Come on,' she cooed.

'Sorry,' Matt muttered, accepting the invitation to hold her. 'I still have trouble coming to grips with why people don't accept my point of view on any given subject as the only viable one, let alone the best one.'

'You can come in with me if you want.'

'The FBI agents might not look charitably on any guy with a ponytail who isn't Steven Seagal. Tell you what, I'm going to call my uncle from that pay phone we saw on the next block. After that I might come in.'

'It shouldn't take too long just to file a report.'

'We're talking government agency here. "Shouldn't take too long" is not a well-understood concept in that world.'

'Hold down the fort.'

Matt watched as she strode away, took a tentative step to follow, then turned, climbed back on the bike, and rode to the next block. There were two messages on his answering machine. One was from Mae, reminding him of a three o'clock appointment with his dental hygienist, and assuring him that his patients for the day had been moved to other slots.

'I certainly hope you are all right,' she added, the concern in her voice unmistakable.

The second message, recorded yesterday evening, was from Hal.

'Everything's set, Matthew. Fred Carabetta will see us at three o'clock tomorrow afternoon at his office in D.C. Call me for details.'

Hal answered on the first ring.

'Hey, Matt. Are you okay?'

'No.'

Quickly, Matt reviewed the events of the previous night.

'God, that's just awful,' Hal said. 'And where are you calling from?'

'Newark. Nikki's in with the FBI right now, filing a report.'

'Well, I think you've got to get her out of there,' Hal said. 'I was just going to leave another message on your machine. Grimes has an APB out for your arrest – both of you.'

'I was afraid he might do something like that. What's he charging us with?'

'Murder.'

'What?'

'Grimes called me early this morning, then came by and drove me out to view a body and bring it back to the morgue. Big man, what's left of him.'

'I think I know who he is,' Matt said, feeling the acid in his stomach beginning to percolate. 'Name's Larry. He worked for Grimes.'

'Extra crispy. From what I could tell he was shot in the head in a cabin off Tall Pines Road, then incinerated when it was burned to the ground. Quite well done, the man was. Then, while we're driving back to town, Grimes casually tells me that you and Dr. Solari are wanted for the guy's murder.

Wants to know if I might happen to know where you are.'

'How does he get off making me a suspect?'

'There are hospital medications and supplies in the woods near the cabin with fingerprints on them, and motorcycle tracks all around. Grimes is speculating that the big man was working for you when he kidnapped Dr. Solari and that you killed him to keep him quiet or from squeezing you for more money.'

'Slick. He's setting both Nikki and me up to die, Hal. Maybe a murder-suicide by this deranged doctor who became obsessed with his patient to the point where he had her kidnapped. All Grimes has to do now is get his hands on us. Hal, I've got to get to Nikki before she speaks with the FBI people. I'll call you later.'

'We're expected at Carabetta's office at three this afternoon. Constitution Avenue.'

'We'll be there,' Matt said.

He sped around the block and dismounted the Harley across the street from the office building.

'FBI, please.'

'Twenty-second floor,' the uniformed security man at the lobby reception desk responded, glancing up from his magazine only long enough to ensure that the questioner wasn't encased in dynamite and brandishing an assault rifle.

The six elevators were all between floors ten and fifteen of the twenty-four stories. Their descent was so painfully slow that Matt actually gave passing thought to sprinting up the twenty-two flights. He was the only one in sight as he stepped into the car, but predictably, three others – a man and two women – materialized just as the doors were about to close, and pressed buttons for floors five, nine, and seventeen. Matt tapped his toe and drummed his fingers over the upward journey, which seemed to take an hour. The elevator opened directly into the waiting room.

Thank God!

Nikki was there, seated opposite a receptionist, thumbing through a copy of *People*. A wizened Asian woman occupied one of the other chairs. Just as Matt stepped off the elevator, a darkly handsome young man with a Hollywood chin emerged from one of the offices, crossed to Nikki, and introduced himself as Duty Officer Sherman. Nikki, clearly startled by Matt's sudden appearance, didn't respond immediately to the agent. The hesitation was all Matt needed. He moved quickly to her side, slipping his hand around her arm, and applying as much force as he dared. Nikki looked momentarily shocked, but then came through and handled the assault coolly, her expression saying, *This had better be good.*

'I'm sorry to bust in like this, Officer,' Matt said, 'but we're going to have to come back a little later. There's been a death in the family.'

'Now, you jes listen here, Sara Jane Tinsley. You gotta stop actin' up an' let me get some damn work done. There ain't no one followin' you an' there ain't no one tryin' to hurt you. Now go on out an' find somethin' to do or someone to play with. If'n you can't occupy yerself, then jes get out back an' start pickin' corn.'

'Corn ain't ready, Ma, an' you know it,' Sara Jane snapped.

'It's plenty ready.'

'Besides, you jes want me out there so those men can have me. You hate me. You hate how ugly I done become. You think it's my fault. You think I'm staying up all night jes to git under yer skin. You don't understand that I cain't sleep. No matter how hard I try, I cain't sleep.'

She was twelve, tall and willowy, but yet to show any outward signs of becoming a woman. Right now, she thought, she really didn't care if she became a woman er not. She cared about the men who had tried to git her into their car as she 'uz walking down the road. First they called her by name an' offered her a big stuffed panda to come with them. Then one of them – the thin one with the cowboy hat – got out of the car with a fist fulla money an' held it out for her. At the sight of him, Sara Jane had whirled and taken off through the woods. The man came after her, but there was no way in hell he 'uz gonna catch her. Those were her woods. No one caught her out there less'n she wanted 'em to.

'You're making a big mistake,' the man had called after her as he gave up chasin'.

Sara Jane reported the incident to her ma, but it 'uz clear she didn't believe her. All she said was that Sara Jane wouldn't be gettin' in such trouble if she'd jes stop runnin' off ever' chance she got an' stayed closer to home. Seven kids an' Sara Jane was the only one actin' out the way she was. Stayin' up all night. Makin' up stories. Havin' tantrums. Screamin' at her ma. Gettin' into fights with her brothers and sisters. Racin' off into the woods.

It were the bumps on her face that were poisoning her an' makin' her do bad things, Sara Jane had tried to explain. The bumps. The doctor in Ridgefield disagreed. He said she 'uz jes becoming a woman an' doin' it harder 'n most. The lumps'd go away as soon as her monthlies started. Maybe so. But this mornin' she had found another one, this one jes above her eye – nearly as wide as a dime an' hard as a knuckle. It was the sixth one, plus two right on the top of her head. Them monthlies had better come soon or there wouldn't be nothin' left of her face.

It was clear that her ma had said all she was of a mind to say on the topic of Sara Jane Tinsley. *Well, to hell with her.* If she wanted the corn picked so damn bad, her fav'rite daughter would pick it.

Sara Jane stormed from the house, slamming the torn screen door behind her, and grabbed one of the plastic baskets. Takin' in laundry an' ironin' was her ma's main source of money, but the corn, half an acre of it, helped. Only this year had been dry, real dry, an' many of the ears was runted. Well, she wanted 'em, she was gonna get 'em, runted or not.

Furious, Sara Jane marched to the end of the farthest row and began tearing off all the ears she could find and throwing them into the bucket. The bending and shaking stalks made a sound like a thresher was going through them. The noise and her own wild movements kept her from hearing the man stealthily approaching her from behind, or sensing his presence until it was too late. Simultaneously, one of his strong, bony hands pinned her to him across her chest, while the second one clamped a cloth over her mouth and nose – a cloth soaked with something that smelled sickly sweet. Sara Jane tried to fight and bite, but he pulled her down to the ground and smothered her with his hand and his body. She knew it was the man with the cowboy hat, but there was nothing she could do. Quickly, her struggles lessened.

I told you, Ma. . . . I told you they 'uz after me . . .

Her head began to spin. Then, just as she thought she was going to throw up, peace and darkness settled over her.

Chapter 27

Ellen sat alone, nestled in the well-worn leather easy chair in Rudy's pine-paneled den, a barely touched avocado and Swiss sandwich on the TV tray in front of her, a nearly drained glass of Merlot – her second – cradled in her hand. She had never been much of a drinker and couldn't remember if she had ever drunk wine in the morning. But the Omnivax 'documentary' she was watching, put together by the Marquand campaign, coupled with the letter in her purse that she had yet to deal with, had generated a level of tension that simply could not go untreated.

It was just after twelve noon on the day following her remarkable interview with Nattie and Eli Serwanga, and a few hours after that, with Lassa victim John Gendron, a thirty-seven-year-old schoolteacher from Baltimore.

It was a frantic dash, with some luck from the traffic gods thrown in, but Ellen managed to catch a return flight from Chicago to BWI Airport. Her car was at Reagan International outside of D.C., so she rented one and drove to Gendron's place – a modest town house on Fayette, several blocks from the sparkling Baltimore waterfront.

Before his infection with the Lassa virus, Gendron had taught English in an inner-city junior high school. He was now eighteen months past his close brush with death, and believed he was too disabled ever to teach again. Ellen's conversation with him was limited by his hearing, which was 70 percent gone in one ear and 100 percent in the other as a result of his illness.

'I went to Sierra Leone to visit my sister, who is a nurse with an international aid organization,' he said. 'About a week after I returned, my throat began to burn when I swallowed anything – even water. Within three days, my temperature was spiking to a hundred and five. Blood was coming out of my nose and rectum.'

The man's eyes began to glisten, and Ellen could see that, however gracious he had been about inviting her to his home, this exchange was exquisitely painful for him.

'Mr. Gendron, please feel free to send me packing if this is too hard for you,' she said. 'I live close enough to come back another time.'

'No. No, I'm okay. You promised to tell me what it is you're working on.'

'And I will,' Ellen said.

'Well, I became delirious around the end of the second week, and was put in the hospital. They . . . they had to remove my intestine to keep me from bleeding to death. Even so, I nearly did. I'm divorced and live alone, so my sister flew back here from Sierra Leone and took care of me for nearly two months. My colostomy is a souvenir of my trip to Africa.'

It may actually be the souvenir of your flight home, Ellen was thinking.

'Go on,' she said.

'As far as I know,' he went on flatly, 'I infected six of my students, plus my son and one of his friends.

354

The friend made it okay. Two of my students and my son, Steven, weren't as fortunate.'

Oh, no.

'I am so sorry.'

'He was my only child. Every day I wish I had died and pray that I will soon.'

'I've had personal tragedies, too,' Ellen said. 'Making any sense of life afterward is terribly hard. Therapy and time. That's all I can tell you. Therapy and time and reaching out to help others.'

'Thank you.'

Once again, Gendron assured Ellen he was able to continue.

'Is there anything unusual you can recall about your flight back to the States?' she asked, taking pains to avoid any leading questions.

'The flight back here was uneventful. But I did meet one unusual character on the flight from Freetown to London, if that's what you mean.'

'That's exactly what I mean.'

'He was an American engineer – interesting and very outgoing. Specialized in inspecting bridges, I think he said.'

Ellen gripped the arm of her chair. 'Can you describe him for me?'

'I think I can, although my memory hasn't been so good since –'

'Just do your best,' Ellen said, deciding not to put the man through Rudy's writing exercise.

'Well, first of all, he was big. Not just tall, but big. Like a football player. His hair was sort of blondish and he wore thick glasses with a heavy frame.'

'Anything else?'

'I can't think of anything . . . except, wait, he had a scar – an unusual scar – right here above his lip.'

Bingo!

With some prompting now from Ellen, Gendron even recalled being bumped by the man while waiting in line at Gatwick Airport in London.

'He tripped, I think, and stumbled into me. It was like getting hit by a train. We both went down.'

After extracting the same pledge of silence from Gendron as she had from the Serwangas, Ellen explained her interest in the Lassa cases and the man with the scar. Then she drove to Reagan and exchanged the rental for her Taurus. She arrived back at Rudy's cabin just after two in the morning and was relieved to find that he hadn't waited up for her.

Now she sat in his den watching the Omnivax campaign special, breathing in the lingering, earthy essence of his pipe tobacco. His Merlot was gradually stoking the fires of her resolve to speak to him. Rudy was upstairs in his study, poring over the passenger manifests, making phone calls, and being a rock of support to a woman he considered a good friend – a woman who just happened to know that he had been in love with her to the exclusion of all others for almost forty years.

How was she going to tell him what she had done? And perhaps even more important, how did she truly feel about what he had written? There was no way to answer the first question without being ready to respond honestly to the second.

Ellen splashed in another glassful of wine. This was last call, she resolved, even as she felt warm fingers working through the muscles of her face. Three glasses were quite enough. Or had it been four? The glasses weren't that big anyway.

Omnivax had clearly become the flagship of the

Marquand campaign. With just over two months remaining before the election, the President's camp was laying out big bucks to get their message of beneficence, progress, and commitment to campaign promises through to the public. The documentary had initially focused on vaccinations in general and now had moved on to Omnivax. The narrator – unseen at the moment – was a movie star with a voice that inspired confidence and radiated authenticity. James Garner? Donald Sutherland? Ellen didn't watch enough movies or TV to be certain.

'And so,' the voice was saying, 'estimates are that between fifty and sixty thousand cases of potentially lethal infections will be prevented by this astonishingly potent vaccine over just the next year. I am honored to introduce to you the First Lady of the United States, Mrs. Lynette Lowry Marquand.'

Marquand strolled the pediatric ward of a hospital as she spoke.

'At three o'clock in the afternoon on September second, two days from today, a four-day-old child will receive the first official dose of Omnivax. I will be there for that most significant occasion, as will Secretary of Health and Human Services Dr. Lara Bolton, who will administer the supervaccine using this pneumatic device, especially developed for this purpose.' She held up a small gun that looked something like a derringer with a flattened muzzle. 'We are on the verge of the greatest advance in preventive medicine in our history – an advance that could signal the beginning of the end of infectious diseases as we know them. . . .'

'What about the thimerosal mercury a gazillion kids have gotten dosed with?' Ellen asked out loud, aware at the same instant that her speech was thick and her glass was empty. 'What about the autism? What about the seizures and brain damage and sudden death? What about the asthma and learning disabilities and ADHD? And what about the man who's flying around sowing disease and death to peddle his goddamn vaccine? What about all those?'

'What about all what?'

Rudy had entered the den carrying the manifests and other papers.

'. . . I am proud to say that all of our major networks will be carrying the ceremony from the Anacostia Neighborhood Health Center here in Washington, where a four-day-old child will take her place in medical history as the first official recipient of Omnivax.'

'I'm watching a program that could have been written by the pharmaceutical industry's public relations unit,' Ellen said, 'but instead was written by Jim Marquand's. There is something about that prissy wife of his that really bugs me.'

She tried to modulate her voice, which seemed like it might be too loud. Was there ever a time she had drunk like this? She followed Rudy's bemused gaze to the bottle on the table next to her. There was, at most, two inches remaining in it. Lying beside it, the corkscrew and Merlot-stained cork, proof that, not long ago, the bottle had been a virgin.

'It's the best Merlot I've found for the money,' he said, gently commenting because the situation demanded he say something.

'Rudy, I'm sorry. I'm overtired and . . . and was lost in this show and . . . and I didn't realize I had finished so much of it.'

'Nonsense. Good wine is to be enjoyed.'

'But I really don't drink very often,' she said thickly.

Rudy sank onto the tan leather couch. There was no judgment in his expression.

'So, what's the status of our friendly neighborhood vaccine?' he asked.

'Day after tomorrow a little four-day-old girl will be starting the ball rolling.'

Brought to You by the Four More Years for a Better America Committee, the final credit announced. Ellen realized that she had neglected to learn who the narrator was.

'If nothing else,' Rudy said, 'I certainly expect the number of Lassa fever cases to drop dramatically.'

'You have a point. No reason for Old Scarface to fly around infecting people anymore. Let the epidemic be cured.'

'It's a little chilly in here. Would you like a blanket?'

'No, I mean yes, I mean, you stay there. I can get it myself.'

Ignoring her request, Rudy withdrew a maroon throw from a refurbished old sea chest and floated it down over her lap.

Stop being so nice to me, she thought. *I'm a jerk.*

'Thank you,' she said thickly. 'I don't know how I would have done all this without you.'

'Nonsense. You're the pro. I'm just the caddy.'

'No, I mean it. Rudy, I –'

Rudy sighed. 'Let there now be eternal ambiguity surrounding the phrase "the shot heard round the world". You know, before you brought me into this world of vaccinations, I more or less took the whole thing for granted. The scientists and pharmaceutical companies produce their vaccines, and their PR people make sure we know why we need their products and what horrible things will happen to us if we don't embrace them. It seemed that simple. And after their vaccines are approved by the FDA, and the CDC tells everybody they should get them, we smile gratefully and say, "Thanks, here's a clear shot at my body. Take it."'

'When drug companies make a mistake, more often than not it's a lulu,' Ellen said, still trying to direct their conversation toward the letter. 'That's what I have in common with them. When I make a mistake, it's a lulu, too.'

'Tell me about it. I used to call myself the King of Screwupville.'

'Rudy,' Ellen said, 'I don't know what made me do what I did, but –'

'You did it because, unlike some First Ladies we know, you are a seeker of the truth. You have a granddaughter who looks as if she has been damaged by her vaccinations and you want to help determine if that is the case, and also to protect other children and parents from paying the same price.'

'I s'pose.'

Ellen looked about blearily and then emptied half of the remaining wine into her glass.

'You know, Rudy,' she tried once more, 'I've always been a very curious person – some would even say nosy. Howard used to say my nosiness was going to get me in big trouble someday.'

'If you hadn't been curious about all this, we would have already packed up and slipped back into our mundane existences.'

'Some things you do and the moment you've done them, you wish you hadn't.'

'That's how that creep who paid you a visit is going to feel when we get to him. Ellen, I've found some stuff for us to work with. We're closer to figuring out who the guy is than you might think.'

Ellen felt dizzy, queasy, and unable to focus fully on what she was seeing or hearing. She had badly overdone the wine, and she sensed that she was in the process of making a bad situation worse.

'I'm anxious to hear about it,' she managed. 'And I've got something I need to talk with you about, too.'

Had she actually said those last words or merely thought them?

'Well, then,' Rudy said, 'I'll tell you what I think is the significance of what you've found out.'

'It was a mistake,' Ellen said. 'I know I shouldn't have done it, and I really am sorry. But just the same – Rudy, are you listening to me?'

Rudy was leafing through the passenger manifests and a small sheaf of notes.

'But just the same . . . Go on, I'm listening.'

Ellen sighed. Next time, when she was clear-headed, she would try to do things right. Rudy didn't deserve to have a slobbering, slack-jawed inebriate blubbering about how she had invaded his privacy.

'What did you learn?' she asked, clicking off the TV.

'Okay,' Rudy said excitedly, moving the TV tray table aside, pulling a coffee table over, and taking a seat on the arm of Ellen's chair. 'I took as my criteria any male who was on multiple flights with a person who subsequently became infected with Lassa. That includes flights out of Freetown and from Ghana as well. By my thinking, our extortionist has to be one of these four men.'

Ellen was hearing Rudy's words, and at least some of them were registering, but the queasiness in her gut was intensifying.

'Go on,' she said, wondering if a bite of sandwich would help matters or hurt.

'Of course,' Rudy continued, 'I think it's a possibility – a good possibility – that all four of these men may be one and the same. Forged passports and IDs aren't all that hard to come by for someone with enough money.'

'And whoever is bankrolling this extortion has enough, or will.'

'I suspect you're right there. I have all of their names and addresses and . . . Ellen, do you want to take a break and maybe continue this in a few hours – or even in the morning?'

'You mean the wine?'

'I don't see you as much of a drinker, and you *have* had a bit.'

'I'm fine,' she replied with far more snap in her voice than she had intended. 'Really I am. Let's just try calling information and shee . . . *see* if any of these four men are listed where they say they live.'

'Great idea!' Rudy exclaimed, seeming genuinely surprised and pleased with her contribution.

Three of the names Rudy had culled from the passenger manifests weren't listed at all. The fourth, Vinyl Sutcher of Tullis, West Virginia, had a number that was nonpublished, at the customer's request.

'I suppose we start with him,' Ellen said, now battling exhaustion as well as the nausea and dizziness. *Be brave,* she told herself. 'Vinyl. It's hard to believe he'd make up a name like that for a fake passport.'

'Must be some sort of family name,' Rudy said. 'Or else a mother who liked to name her kids after her furniture coverings.'

'He's a cute little baby. I think we'll call him Naugahyde.'

'Maybe we should try and get an artist who will do a composite sketch,' Rudy suggested. 'Or else we might try to get a photo of these four guys from the passport files at the State Department.'

'At some point we may have to,' Ellen managed. 'But I am anxious not to lose that kind of time.'

'You know, I was quite impressed with that little air injector the Secretary is going to use on that baby.'

'You think that's how Vinyl, or whoever, infected those passengers?'

'Either with a pneumatic injection gun like that or some sort of flat, hollow plate that fits in his palm and uses compressed air from someplace up his sleeve. Technically it doesn't seem as if it would be too complicated to rig up. A little nudge, a jet of compressed air mixed with Lassa virus, and zap – instant disease.'

Ellen felt her eyes beginning to close.

'Rudy,' she said in the soft voice of a child, 'I need to close my eyes now, just for a little while. Need to sleep.'

'You do that, dear heart,' she heard him say as she floated off. 'You do whatever you need to do.'

Using the remote, Lynette Marquand flipped off the television that had been wheeled into her office.

'Well, Lara, what do you think?' she asked.

HHS Secretary Lara Bolton was beaming.

'Brilliant,' she said. 'Masterful. There's absolutely no way to tell that most of that program was shot a month ago. Those guys are good – no, better than good. They're grrrrrreat.'

'And my part?'

'Perfect. Just enough information, not too much. And you looked absolutely smashing.'

'Thanks. You liked the script, too?'

'It was right on – sincere and appropriately solemn, yet excited and humble. I loved it.'

'And the part about the kid?'

'You mean having you mention her but holding back on saying precisely who she is?'

'Yes.'

'I think it worked perfectly. Nobody can criticize you for putting her and her family on the spot or invading their privacy, but everyone everyplace will be wanting to know about her. We'll do the rest. It'll only take one or two anonymous-source phone calls, and in a few hours everyone will be buzzing about little, adorable Donelle Cleary.'

'And those calls?'

Lara Bolton made a pretense of checking her watch.

'I believe they've already been made, Mrs. Marquand,' she said.

Chapter 28

Hal Sawyer was waiting for Matt and Nikki in the lobby of OSHA headquarters on Constitution Avenue. He was dressed more like the commandant of a yacht club than a med school professor – white trousers, navy blazer, blue pin-striped shirt open at the collar, but his expression was grim. He embraced Matt, then shook hands with Nikki and introduced himself.

'I'm relieved you're both all right,' he said.

'Thanks to you,' Matt replied. 'We barely made it out of the FBI office without having to explain to them why a chief of police thinks I shot a guy in the head and then tried to burn the evidence.'

'They might not have even known yet. But Grimes is definitely turning up the heat, so to speak.'

Matt managed a weak smile.

'Is it safe to be here?'

'There's no reason to think Carabetta knows anything at this point. I wouldn't suspect OSHA is on the routing map of all points bulletins for murder.'

'Lord. Mom okay? Does she know I'm not around?'

'For a few minutes at a time she seems to. But then just as quickly she forgets. I'm really sorry for all you've been through. You, too, Dr. Solari.'

'It's Nikki, please,' she said. 'I appreciate your concern. This whole business doesn't seem to be getting any better.'

'It will. Grimes has a lot of power around where we live, but he doesn't have a lot of power everywhere.' He lowered his voice a notch. 'I know some excellent lawyers we can go see after we get this mine business straightened out. You still think Grimes is doing all this to protect BC and C?'

'I'm pretty certain of it, yes,' Matt said, pointedly ignoring Nikki's expression of doubt.

'In that case, maybe I'd better start watching *my* back. I've come in contact with these cases, too, you know.'

'I hadn't thought of that,' Matt said. 'All the more reason why we have to get our evidence and put the clamps on Grimes as soon as possible.'

'Oh, speaking of evidence, I've found Darryl Teague's brain, but so far Ted Rideout's is a no-show.'

'Could someone have taken it?' Nikki asked.

'Well, we like to think we take decent precautions against such things. For the moment I'd prefer to believe it's been misplaced. We have a storage facility for specimens over a year old. Even though Rideout's death was less than a year ago, maybe it's over there.'

'I hope so.'

'By the way, Nikki, I was very upset to hear about Joe Keller. I met him once at a meeting. He seemed like quite a guy.'

'Thanks, he was. The people who murdered him took all of Kathy Wilson's specimens. It seems possible they might be after the ones you have, too.'

'Maybe. I intend to be careful and to try and gather up all the specimens I have and get them someplace safe.'

'The man Matt and I are supposed to have killed was one of the thugs who kidnapped me. Grimes was at the cabin with him, questioning me about Kathy's death. It was clear Grimes was the boss.'

Hal whistled softly through his teeth.

'Well, he says you two killed the guy, then tried to burn the evidence, so to speak. I told him Matt wouldn't have bothered with the fire because he knew I was a sharp enough medical examiner not to miss the bullet hole in the guy's skull even if he was incinerated, but he wasn't interested.'

'Well, he either shot the guy or more likely had it done,' Matt said. 'At least now you see what kind of person he is.'

'Now I see,' Hal said somewhat ruefully.

'He's banking on support from those country club cronies of his who think I'm way off center to begin with, and probably capable of anything.'

'I've known Bill, pretty well I thought, since he came to town. Just goes to show how wrong you can be sometimes. Well, it's time for counterattacking. Let's visit with Fred. Matthew, I'm going to let you speak with him alone. Nikki and I will wait in the reception area. If he doesn't agree to the inspection you want, it will be my turn.'

'Whatever you say.'

Fred Carabetta was waiting for them in a neatly maintained single-windowed space with a worn leather couch and built-in bookcase. The office would have been relegated to a low- or mid-level manager in the private sector, but in government service, indicated some clout. There were pictures around suggesting a wife and two teenage girls, and interests in deep-sea fishing and golf.

Carabetta was a rotund, balding man around fifty, short enough to seem nearly as round as he was high. He had the tendency of constantly rubbing his fleshy thumbs across his sausagelike index and middle fingers. Probably aware of the nervous habit, he kept his hands in his lap much of the time. To the man's credit, Matt thought, Carabetta listened patiently to his account of locating the toxic dump, only occasionally interrupting to clarify a point. Matt purposely left out any mention of Joe Keller's death or the assault on Nikki. He didn't know Carabetta at all, and to this point at least, there was nothing about him that suggested fearlessness or a commitment to justice.

'Well, now,' he said when Matt had finished, 'that's certainly not a tale one hears every day around here. Knowing you were coming, I did a little research on Belinda Coal and Coke. There *have* been some complaints filed against the company over the past few years, but for whatever reason, all of them were submitted by you.'

'And there was never any action taken on any of them,' Matt replied, way too intensely. 'Most of the allegations were never even responded to.'

'I assume you've tried the EPA and Bureau of Mines?'

'Only a few dozen times in the past. The issues I wrote about were never this big or easily documented. But I don't have any credibility. I need someone with respect and clout to corroborate what I have to say. That's why Hal suggested you.'

'I appreciate that,' Carabetta said. 'I hope you won't take offense, Dr. Rutledge, but there is a great deal of speculation and hearsay supporting those allegations, and very little fact.'

'I'm aware of that, but –'

'And there is another consideration at work here as well.'

Matt knew what was coming.

'Namely,' he said.

'Namely Senator Nick Alexander.'

Matt rolled his eyes. Alexander, the influential, conservative – some might say moral rightist – senior senator from West Virginia, was in bed with the mining companies. He was a consummate politician who, over the years, had skillfully quashed any number of bills that would have caused hardship for the owners.

'The best I've ever been able to get from his office are a few "We'll be sure to look into it" letters.'

'Well, you may or may not know it, but Alexander is the chairman of the subcommittee that oversees this bureau and its budget.'

'I'm not surprised.'

'He may be in line for Secretary of the Interior in Marquand's second administration. There is no way I can just barge into a company like BC and C and demand a spot inspection without hard evidence.'

'This is crazy,' Matt said, struggling to keep his voice even. 'I was there. I saw that dump. You have a chance to be a hero.'

This time it was Carabetta who rolled his eyes.

'Dr. Rutledge, I have never been a mover or a shaker or a hero of any kind. I expect to work in this agency until I retire. By then I will have moved up the GS ladder a couple of more notches. My pension at that level will serve me and my family well enough. The last thing I want to do is jeopardize that master plan.'

'I understand,' Matt said, resigned.

'There's one more thing,' Carabetta said. 'I have a graduate degree in chemistry, but I studied a good deal of biology as well. Over the ten years I have been in this division of OSHA, I have been involved in the evaluation of more chemical accidents and exposures than I can count. To my knowledge and experience, there is no toxin that causes the sort of neurologic condition you have described – especially in a woman who lived five hundred miles away and had probably never been in a mine in her life.'

'But don't you agree that toxic chemicals can cause mutations?' Matt asked. 'And don't you wonder why the mine would send four thugs out to my friends' farm to stop them from telling anyone what we saw inside that cave?'

'Perhaps,' Carabetta said. 'Dr. Rutledge, I'm sorry. I just don't see how I can go any further with this matter at this time, given your lack of concrete evidence. Maybe a report to the police is the way you should go.'

With a sigh, Matt stood and shook the bureaucrat's hand.

'Thanks for listening,' he said, taking no pains to mask his frustration. 'Hal asked if you might have a few minutes to speak with him.'

'Of course. Send him in.'

Matt crossed the small reception area to where Nikki and his uncle were waiting.

'No go,' he said. 'Not enough hard evidence for him to risk taking any chances – especially crossing Big Nick Alexander.'

'Freddy, Freddy, Freddy,' Hal sighed. 'You two wait here.'

He adjusted his sport coat, flexed his neck, and marched into Carabetta's office. Fifteen minutes later he emerged and motioned Matt and Nikki out of the reception area and into the hallway.

'Are you sure you can get us back to the cave at night?' he asked.

'Positive. Once we're through the cleft, there are no real forks in the tunnel, just twists and turns. Finding the cleft may be the hard part.'

'Don't worry about that. I know where it is,' Hal said. 'I grew up running through those hills. Well, the news is, it's going to be tomorrow night. You'll both stay at my place until then. We'll put your motorcycle in the garage, Matt. You both can just relax, empty the fridge, and watch videos until Fred arrives.'

'You did it!' Matt exclaimed, pumping his fists. 'Way to go!' Then, just as quickly, he dropped his hands. 'Hal, you had to pay him, didn't you?'

'I was hoping your enthusiasm and persuasiveness would win him over, but the truth is, all along I suspected it would come down to money. Fred and I have had such dealings once before, and believe me, I'm not the only one.'

'Can you tell me how much he cost? I want to help if I can.'

'Being right about this cave is all you are required to contribute. And as for how, um, difficult Fred was to convince, let's just say that at the moment my uncle points should be at an all-time high.'

'Well, you sure have a hell of a grateful nephew. And don't worry – unless they buried it, the dump's still there. Speaking of which, the guards may be there as well.'

'I thought about that,' Hal said. 'I actually have made a few inquiries searching for someone who deals with such things professionally and might accompany us. Now that I know when we'll be going, I'll make a call.'

Matt gave his uncle a hug.

'You know, there's no reason you have to go in there,' he said.

'On the contrary,' Hal replied. 'With the sudden investment I have in Freddy Carabetta, I wouldn't miss this for the world.'

Ellen awoke to an unpleasant buzzing in her head. An unnatural film covered her tongue and palate. Well, she thought disdainfully, it had certainly been a blue-ribbon day. All she had done was gotten drunk in front of Rudy, passed out, and now was in the slow process of waking up with a nasty Merlot hangover, having managed still to say absolutely nothing of what she had done. And to make matters worse, a two-day-old girl was just forty-eight hours from the first formal dose of a supervaccine containing a component specifically included to halt a lethal epidemic that Ellen now knew was totally man-made.

She held her eyes closed tightly, wary of the dreadful spinning likely to ensue from opening them. Finally, more to check the time than anything else, she forced her lids apart a bit. The walls and ceiling stayed reasonably still. She was in Rudy's guest room, not, she suddenly realized, in the chair where she had nodded off. She was dressed as she had been, and still covered with the maroon throw. The curtains were drawn, but there was enough light to check her watch. *Five*. Assuming it was the same day, she had been out for four and a half hours. Not bad for a rank amateur.

She rolled over and switched on the bedside lamp. There was a single, beautiful, long-stemmed rosebud in a vase beside the lamp. And propped against the vase was an envelope identical to the one she had torn open. Her name and address were written on the outside in Rudy's hand, and in the upper right-hand corner was a stamp with today's postage. Her hands shaking, she gently opened the envelope.

Dear Ellen,

So, now you know. What a relief! I have debated more times than I can count whether to send the letter or hand it to you or wait. Now whichever fate decides such things has taken the choice from me. Well, so be it. I love you, and the next time I see you I'll probably tell you to your face. There is no need for you to respond one way or the other when I do.

Please don't let what I wrote change our friendship. That would hurt me as no rejection from you ever could. I have dealt with my feelings for you for many years. If necessary, I'll deal with them for many more. Please don't feel bad over having opened the letter. It was meant to be.

And for God's sake, no more Merlot.

With love,
Rudy

Ellen washed her face with cold water and brushed her hair and teeth.

A fine-looking woman for your age. That's what

Howard had said. Rudy Peterson hadn't even mentioned her age – or his, for that matter. He loved her thirty-nine years ago; he loved her today. She had, in many ways, been frozen since the day Howard left – her feelings tightly bound. Maybe it was time to open up. How much better could a woman ever do than her oldest, dearest friend?

A final check in the mirror and she went out to meet him. Rudy was seated at his dining room table, his unlit pipe resting loosely between his teeth, pages of data spread out before him, along with a large atlas of the world. Ellen slipped into the seat across from him, then slowly reached her hands over the table and took his.

'Thanks for the rose and the note,' she said.

'Thanks for taking the pressure off.'

'I can't really say anything in response right now.'

'I didn't expect you to.'

'But I'm going to be looking hard at my feelings and I'll certainly keep you posted.'

'What more could a guy ask?'

'You're really a very wonderful man, Rudy.'

'I know,' he said. 'Just cursed by being really, really choosy.'

Ellen felt herself blush.

'So,' she said, clearing her throat, 'what do you have there?'

'Well, I have an old friend, a lawyer, who works at the IRS. He wouldn't give me any more information except to say that Vinyl Sutcher exists, filed a tax return last year, and lives right where his passport says.'

'West Virginia.'

'Tullis, to be exact. It's right here, not too far from the Virginia border.'

'I know the police chief in my town pretty well. I'm sure he'll run this man Vinyl through his computer for me. Maybe he could even check with the police in Tullis to see if they know anything about him. If I have to, I'll just take a drive over there and meet with the police myself. Let me just call Beth and make sure she's still okay with getting Lucy to school.'

Ellen caught her daughter just as she was leaving the house.

'Hi, Mom. I only have a minute. Lucy's got a dentist appointment. We can't be late because they clear the office out when they have to work on her.'

'I know,' Ellen said understandingly.

'It takes the whole damn staff to keep her still and she screams like a banshee. It makes sense they should clear the place out. I mean, who would ever want their kid to hear that in a dentist's office? Everything else she doesn't react enough to, but this –'

'I know,' Ellen cut in quickly. 'Honey, just hang in there. That's all you can do. You're doing a great job.'

'Last night Dick started talking again about adopting. Mom, I just can't, I . . .'

Ellen could tell Beth was coming unglued. There was a time when she was strong, competent, and centered. Not anymore.

'Beth, I was calling to see how things were going, and also to see if you're still able to handle the school run for a couple of days.'

'Sure. Is everything okay?'

'Everything's fine. Just some commission stuff I need to take care of. I'll call you.'

'Okay.'

'And Beth?'

'Yes?'

'I meant what I said. You're a terrific mom.' She set the receiver down. 'Dentist day is even tougher on Beth than on Lucy.'

'You're right, she is doing a great job.'

Ellen shrugged off a sudden wave of melancholy.

'So, if need be,' she said, 'I'm all set for a trip to West Virginia. If I can get this Sutcher arrested, then I'll feel much safer about Lucy if we decide to take any action.'

'I like that approach so long as you're very careful. Meanwhile, I'll do a little more research on these men – starting with a trip into the passport office in D.C. to see if I can get a look at their pictures.'

'Terrific.'

'Tullis doesn't look like much on this map,' Rudy added. 'Just a speck, really. The nearest town of any size is right here. Belinda. Belinda, West Virginia.'

'Pretty name,' Ellen said.

Chapter 29

Ellen was humming along with a Sinatra CD as she crossed the Shenandoah River. She was in northern Virginia, heading southwest toward the West Virginia state line. The late morning sun was therapeutically warm, the highway was newly paved and virtually empty, and soon, very soon, she might be helping to cage the beast who had threatened her family and single-handedly infected a large number of people with a hideous, deadly disease. It wasn't at all a sure thing yet that Vinyl Sutcher was the man she wanted, but getting a look at him was the only way she would ever know for sure.

Her first stop of the day had been at the police station in her hometown of Glenside. Chief Ed Curran was a member of the club where Howard had played golf and she had played tennis, quite often with Curran's wife, Lorraine. She arrived at the station only to discover that the Currans were away in Italy for another week, celebrating their thirtieth anniversary. Ed's stand-in, a much younger man named Wes Streeter, was a home-grown product – a former high school football hero – totally lacking Curran's warmth and, Ellen quickly discerned, much of his intelligence as well.

'So this man with the scar, he broke into your house, waited for you to come home, and then threatened to kill your granddaughter. Why?'

'I don't want any publicity about the reasons why. Can you promise me that?'

'Mrs. Kroft, I can't promise you anything until you tell me what's going on.'

'Never mind. I'll take care of matters myself.'

'You should file formal charges against this man right here,' Streeter said. 'This is where the crime occurred.'

'I don't even know for certain if the name I have is the man who broke into my house. I just want to get a look at him. One look. A photo or in person, I don't care which. The moment I see him I'll know if he's the one or not. Isn't there some sort of police computer site where you can punch in his name and address and see if he's been in trouble before?'

Streeter, clearly feeling that there might be more to the matter with the woman seated across from him than with the alleged criminal, ran the name Vinyl Sutcher of Tullis, West Virginia, through his computer, but came up empty. Eventually, with some hardly subtle prompting from Ellen, he determined that Tullis, West Virginia, had no police department of its own, but was serviced by the adjacent town of Belinda. By this time, the policeman was bewildered by Ellen and her story, and most anxious to move on to other business. He presented her with the number of the Belinda police, the name of the chief, William Grimes, and a quiet room where she could make a call. She had an image of Andy Griffith, Don Knotts, and Mayberry in mind as she dialed, so after she told the officer who answered why she was calling, she wasn't that surprised to be told that Chief Grimes would be right with her.

'Chief Grimes.'

Ellen's mental image was of a man older than Wes Streeter and younger than Ed Curran. Andy Griffith.

'Chief Grimes, my name is Ellen Kroft. I'm calling from the police station in Glenside, Maryland, where I live, at the urging of the acting police chief here. A few days ago a man broke into my house and threatened me and my family if I didn't do something he wanted. I have reason to believe the man might be from Tullis, next to your town. His name is Sutcher, Vinyl Sutcher. Do you have a few minutes?'

'We always try to make time for our neighbors in Maryland,' Chief Grimes replied.

The truncated story she told to Chief Bill Grimes included her suspicions regarding the Lassa fever outbreaks and the way she had ultimately derived Sutcher's name from the passenger manifest.

The Vinny Sutcher the chief recalled didn't fit the description Ellen gave him all that well. From what Grimes remembered – and he admitted he wasn't at all sure he was thinking of the right man – Sutcher was stocky, but not that tall, and had no scar like the one Ellen described above his lip. He was a woods-man and occasional bodyguard of some sort who did live in the next town. Grimes recalled seeing him briefly a year or so ago after he allegedly shoved a man who rear-ended him at a traffic light. The police chief couldn't remember how that incident had been resolved, but he didn't think formal charges were ever filed.

If she wanted to drive down to Belinda, he would be pleased to meet with her, take a statement, and share what information he could obtain on the man, including a photo if, in fact, Sutcher had actually been arrested. And if the evidence she presented was compelling enough, he would certainly contact the FBI and assist them in putting together an arrest warrant, he said.

'I'll give you my cell phone number in case there are any problems,' he said.

'And I'll give you mine.'

It was just after two when Ellen rounded a sweeping curve on a mountain road and got her first glimpse of Belinda, West Virginia, a postcard-perfect town, nestled in a broad valley just to the east of a range of rolling foothills. Beyond the hills, the craggy Allegheny Mountains probed upward into the azure afternoon sky. It had been more than three hours since she left home, but the uninter-rupted drive, with CDs by Carly Simon and Natalie Cole alternating with Lyle Lovett and Sinatra, seemed much shorter.

Throughout the trip, Rudy was very much on her mind. Not surprisingly, he had said and done all the right things to make her feel less humiliated at having opened the letter from his drawer. Now it was just a matter of sorting through her feelings for him, searching beneath the enduring warmth of their friendship for the spark of passion that, even at sixty-three, she wanted to have. Rudy loved her truly, of that she had no doubt. And he was certainly a man she could grow old with. The question she was mulling over as she swung onto Main Street was whether or not he was a man she could grow young with.

Her meeting with Police Chief Grimes wasn't scheduled for almost three hours, and except for a doughnut and the coffee she had brought in a thermos, she hadn't had a thing to eat since leaving Glenside. Her hangover was essentially gone, but the pledge she made about drinking wine in the morning would, she hoped, live on forever. She thought about driving through Belinda and into Tullis, just to check out what the place might look like, but the Belinda Diner, a classic, railroad-car eatery on the edge of town, was just too inviting to pass up. The place was nearly empty. A competent-looking, middle-aged waitress in jeans and a T was serving two elderly women in one booth and two grizzled men in another.

'Anyplace you like,' she called out cheerily.

Ellen took a copy of the *Montgomery County Weekly Bugle* from a rack and brought it to a booth in the corner, well away from the other patrons. She ordered the meat loaf special and turned to the police report, as she inevitably did when reading any small-town newspaper, including her own. Barking dog . . . Stranger lurking . . . Fight . . . Deer hit by truck . . . Disturbance . . . Drink dispenser vandalized . . . Patient kidnapped. Tucked in among two dozen or so police calls was a two-sentence report of the kidnapping of a hospital patient from an ambulance. Ellen found the article dealing with the crime on page 1 and read the skimpy account until the waitress came with her meal.

'What's this kidnapping thing all about?' Ellen asked.

The waitress shrugged. 'No one knows,' she said with a pleasant twang. 'Rumor I heard is that her doctor did it. Doc Rutledge. The patient was a doctor herself. Now she's gone an' he's vanished, too. Maybe he jes got obsessed with her – you know, couldn't live without her. So he hired a couple of thugs to snatch her, then acts like he's as surprised as the next fella.'

'And I thought I was coming into a sleepy little town. Doctor kidnaps patient. Sounds like a TV miniseries.'

'Poor Doc Rutledge. Ain't been the same since his wife died a few years back. He's a darn good doctor, though, from what I've heard. If I ever went to a doctor I jes might 'uv gone to him. So, what brings you here?'

'I . . . have a business appointment. This sure is a beautiful town.'

'Thank you. We think so. Your appointment here in Belinda?'

'Actually, no,' Ellen replied after pausing while deciding if any harm could come from trying to determine where Vinny Sutcher lived. 'It's in a town called Tullis.'

'Well, heck, that's jes the next town over. Parta Belinda more or less.'

Ellen consulted a pad she took from her handbag.

'Deep Woods Road,' she said, reading back the address they had gotten from the passenger manifests.

'Never heard of it,' the waitress said.

'I have,' called out one of the old men, who was sitting four or five booths away. 'Take Main Street all the way inta Tullis. Then go rot through Tullis, left onta Oak, then 'bout two mile up inta the hills. You'll be lookin' fer a gravel road on the rot. I don't b'leive it's got no sign, but some a the mailboxes at the corner say Deep Woods on 'em.'

'Thank you,' Ellen called over.

'Belinda Road is jes the continuation of Main Street into Tullis,' the waitress said. 'Go right out the parkin' lot an' jes keep on goin'. You'll see a little sign for Tullis.'

382

'Place don't deserve nothin' no bigger,' the eavesdropper hollered.

His tablemate and the two ladies in the booth near them hooted and whooped at his humor.

Not surprisingly, given Ellen's experience with such diners, the meat loaf was commendable and the mashed potatoes and gravy appropriately decadent. She left a decent tip and walked out into the late afternoon sun. There were still almost two hours to go before she was to meet with Grimes. From the moment the old eavesdropper gave her directions to Deep Woods Road, she was obsessed – driven by her own anger and curiosity to want even a glimpse of Vinyl Sutcher. If he was as Grimes described, it was back to the drawing board and the other passenger names for her and Rudy. If Grimes's memory was off, if she could determine that Sutcher's cinder-block head featured a flat face and distinctive scar, she was on the verge of sweet, succulent revenge. She just needed to be careful and stay in the car. All she wanted now was one look at the man or at least the place where he lived.

With the same tiny voice that had lost the battle over Rudy's letter begging her to wait until her meeting with the police chief, Ellen eased the Taurus out of the parking lot and headed for Tullis and Deep Woods Road. The directions were fairly accurate, but the mileage was off on the low side. The far end of Tullis was nearly six miles away, and Oak Street snaked upward for three miles more before she spotted the cluster of ten or eleven mailboxes, several of which had 'Deep Woods Road' painted on one side. One of the boxes had the number 100 in neat stick-ons, and beneath it the name SUTCHER. Maybe Grimes was right after all, she thought. This was hardly the place one would expect to find a world traveler, who had made at least four trips to an obscure country in West Africa over the past three years. But then, if she and Rudy were right, the trips, along with a dozen others, were strictly business.

Deep Woods Road, graded dirt and pebbles, coursed gently upward through a continuous arch of dense foliage. It was one car wide, with shallow drainage ditches on either side, and periodic spots to pull over so that an oncoming vehicle could pass. Ellen inched ahead, feeling a strange, almost perverse pleasure at operating on the edge of a situation she knew might be dangerous. Despite the mailboxes, there were no houses visible. Instead, there were dirt drives wending off into the forest on either side, most with a board nailed to a tree announcing the house number.

62 . . . 70 . . . 83 . . .

Ellen slowed even more. Several dirt drives had no number. Was one of them to Sutcher's place?

90 . . .

Her heart pounding, Ellen stopped and, using one of the unmarked drives, turned her car around. Then she carefully opened her door.

This is stupid, the tiny voice was saying. *This is absolutely dumb.*

She dropped the keys into the pocket of her slacks, shut the door softly, and cautiously made her way up the narrow road. Ahead the natural light was considerably brighter.

100.

The number, painted in black on a plain piece of pine board, was nailed head high on the trunk of a small birch. Just past the birch, the forest fell away, yielding to a clearing, beyond which was a spectacular vista – a broad valley streaked with rivers, stretching out to lush foothills and gray-blue mountains. In the center of the clearing was a new house, or an old one that had recently been extensively renovated – one story, modern, with large picture windows and mahogany-stained cedar siding. There were remnants of the construction still lying about. The lawn had not yet been laid, although the piping for an underground sprinkler system was piled up and ready to be installed. There was no garage, but to one side of the lawn-to-be was a gravel parking space large enough for two cars.

Despite her certainty that the property was empty, if not unoccupied, Ellen stayed in the relative safety of the forest for more than five minutes, watching. There was no movement.

Desperate now to glimpse the inside, she stepped from the shadows and moved toward the house, her pulse still hammering. The construction-in-progress notwithstanding, the place was clearly someone's home. Through the windows she could see that it was fully furnished in a manner that was quite masculine – thick leather couches and easy chairs, heavy unadorned end tables. Encouraged, Ellen pressed her face to the glass and peered more intently inside. There was a huge bull-elk head mounted above the mantel, and several shotguns hooked on the wall. She scanned the interior, looking for photographs. There were none. A window at a time, she worked her way around to the side of the house.

The panorama was truly magnificent, made even more so by the sun, now in descent toward the mountains. The house, while not built on a sheer drop, was set on the top of a steep slope. Ellen

385

stepped to the edge. The slope was mostly dirt, weeds, and rocks, littered with boards, strapping, and chunks of concrete from the construction, left to be cleaned up when the place was finally landscaped. It was then she realized that the house wasn't one story as it appeared from the road, but two and possibly even three, the others having been hewn into the hillside. She took a few tentative steps down the hill and gasped. There were two stories of living space – the floor she had examined and another beneath it. Each featured a solid wall of tinted glass, running the entire length of the house. And underneath the lower story was a garage – also built into the hillside, and accessed by a narrow driveway that arced far out to her right, then undoubtedly upward to a spot not far from where she had parked.

In the garage was a large, black Jeep 4×4.

Ellen felt a sickening tightness in her chest at the sight of it.

'Well, now, what have we here?'

Vinyl Sutcher's booming voice was a spear through Ellen's heart. Startled beyond measure, she whirled, stumbled, and fell to one knee, landing on a jagged piece of concrete. She leapt to her feet, mindless of the pain, the tear in her slacks, and the circle of blood rapidly expanding around it. Sutcher was standing above her, twenty feet or so away, hands on hips, his huge, flat face grinning down at her.

'I knew it was you,' Ellen said contemptuously.

'Get up here. . . . I said, GET THE FUCK UP HERE!'

Ellen hesitated, then slowly did as he demanded. She had made a terrible, terrible mistake and now she was going to pay for it in pain, and then, sooner or later, with her life. If the slope behind her was just a little steeper, she might have ended it quickly right there, or at least have tried to pull him over with her. As things were, the driveway below would stop any fall. All she could do was stand there and face up to him.

'How did you find this place?' he demanded.

'Isn't it a horrible moment when you realize you're not as smart as you think you are?' she said, as much to herself as to him.

Sutcher was dressed in black jeans, a black short-sleeved dress shirt, and black boots, and looked to Ellen as malevolent as any person could. His narrow rodent's eyes glared down at her.

'I asked you a question,' he snarled.

He closed the last ten feet between them, grabbed Ellen's wrist, and, with his other hand, forcefully flexed her knuckles inward until she dropped to her knees, crying in pain.

'I know who you are and I know what you did,' she managed.

Sutcher pulled her to her feet, but maintained his grip on her hand.

'What are you talking about?'

'Do you get much pleasure out of hurting ladies that are old enough to be your mother?'

'I get pleasure out of hurting anyone. Now, I'm going to ask you one more time before the real hurting begins, how did you find me?'

Ellen pictured her granddaughter, sleeping in her room while this monster took photos of her.

'I just stood downwind and sniffed,' she said. 'Then I followed the smell and here you are.'

Without hesitation, Sutcher hit her – a vicious openhanded slap that spun her around and sent her tumbling down the slope like a rag doll. Battered and bleeding, she came to rest halfway down to the driveway, on her belly, her arms and legs splayed, her gashed cheek grinding into a chunk of concrete. She was awake and alert, but hurting in so many places that in some strange way she wasn't hurting at all. She remained motionless, her eyes closed. *What was next?* From up above, she could hear Sutcher's grunts and the clattering of stones as he worked his way down the slope toward where she lay.

She opened her eyes a slit. Resting beneath her right hand was a three-foot-long thin slat of wood, and protruding from the far end of the slat was a nail – two inches long, maybe two and a half. She was going to lose to the monster, that was a given, but not without at least trying to hurt him first. Moving nothing but her fingers, she closed them about wood. Her only chance, if there was a chance at all, was to swing at his face and hope to catch an eye. Her hatred for the man was such that the idea of blinding him brought no distaste.

His labored breathing was getting closer. At least once she thought she heard him stumble. *Good!* . . . He was there now, next to her, nudging her over with the toe of his boot. If he noticed her hand clutching the slat and stepped on her wrist, her one chance to inflict any damage would be gone. But he seemed more intent on determining whether or not she was alive. To make it more difficult for him, she held her breath.

'Come on, over you go,' he said, working the toe of his boot underneath her.

Ellen allowed him to turn her nearly over before she finished the job. With a loud screech, she rolled to her back and swung her weapon in the same motion. The nail sank to the hilt through Sutcher's cheek, less than an inch below his eye. He howled an obscenity and lurched backward, clawing at the wood. Just as he pulled it free, he fell heavily, tumbling over and over down the steep, rubble-strewn hill. Ellen was on her feet before he reached the driveway. Ignoring the pain of many wounds, she scrambled up the slope.

'You bitch! I'm going to kill you!' Sutcher bellowed. 'You're dead meat!'

Even if he had the key to his Jeep in his pocket, there was no way he could get to her before she reached her car. Half stumbling, half running, gasping for air, she charged across the dirt lawn to the Taurus. Moments before she reached it she was seized with the fear that he had flattened a tire or in some other way disabled the car. Neither was the case. Turning her car around before leaving it stood out as the lone bright spot in an afternoon of stupidity. She scrambled awkwardly behind the wheel and in seconds was skidding off down the road.

With her eyes darting from the narrow roadway to the rearview mirror and back, she negotiated the dirt track as rapidly as she dared. Nearing the end, she chanced fishing out her cell phone from her purse. Praying she was in range of a transmitter, she dialed the number Chief Grimes had given her. She was surprised when he answered himself.

'Mrs. Kroft, that certainly wasn't a very wise thing to have done,' Grimes said after she gave him a quick summary of her situation.

Tell me something I don't know, she thought. 'I think he's coming after me,' she said. 'What should I do?'

'I'm in the cruiser right now,' he replied. 'Just keep driving as fast as you can until you see me coming the other way, then pull over. I'll have the flashers on so you can pick me up.'

'Oh, thank you,' Ellen said, feeling her pulse rate begin to recede into the thousands.

'It's okay, Mrs. Kroft. You've done a really dumb thing, but luckily you're okay. I'll take over from here. Just take a deep breath and let it out real slow. You're safe now.'

'No! Absolutely not! We've got a baby sleeping in here. Now go away, please. No more interviews.'

Don Cleary slammed the door shut and stalked back into his apartment, cursing the locked downstairs door and buzz-in security system, neither of which had been functional for a year or more. Damn, but it was going to be good to get out of the projects once and for all, he thought.

'More reporters?' Sherrie asked sleepily, from her spot on the sofa.

'They're crammed on the stairway like rabbits, and there're camera crews on the walk outside.'

He, Sherrie, her mother, and some friends had watched the Omnivax television program after being told about it by a woman named Tricia from Lynette Marquand's office. As the woman promised, in order to protect their privacy for the moment, their names weren't broadcast on the air. Of course, after the actual injection was given, things were going to change. That, they could count on. Mrs. Marquand, Tricia said, would be happy to provide them with a publicity person who would help them after the injection to deal with the press and also to benefit financially in any way possible – and there were bound to be a number of offers.

Then, just an hour or so after the program ended, the phone had started ringing. No one who called seemed to know exactly how they had gotten the Clearys' phone number or Donelle's name. At first, he and Sherrie had been excited. They gave a taped interview to a reporter from one of the Washington television stations and allowed a photographer from the *Post* to come in and take a photo of them with the baby. After that, as the media crush intensified, they began saying no. Now they were getting angry.

In her cradle by the sofa, Donelle began crying.

'Damn, I woke her up,' Don said. 'I'm sorry, honey.'

He hurried to the cradle, lifted the precious bundle in his arms, and sat down next to his wife. The baby's bleating stopped immediately. Her dark eyes opened widely and seemed to fix on his face.

'Is she lookin' at you?' Sherrie asked. 'What a flirt.'

'Yeah, just like her mother.'

'You get out! Donny, look, isn't she perfect?'

'Yeah.'

'What do you think she'll be? A dancer? Or . . . or a doctor? Or maybe a famous athlete?'

'I don't know and I don't care,' Don said. 'The truth is, there's only one thing I want her to be.'

'What's that?'

'Healthy.'

Over in the corner, the phone started ringing again.

Chapter 30

It was just ten-thirty when Fred Carabetta arrived at Hal's place – a rustic but expansive lodge with half a dozen bedrooms, three fieldstone fireplaces, and a boathouse, built atop a high ledge over a pristine, five-mile-long lake. Matt and Nikki watched through the kitchen window as he maneuvered his considerable bulk out of what appeared to be a Cadillac of some sort.

'Carabetta's here,' Matt called out. 'It's going to be a tight squeeze in some of those tunnels, but I think he'll make it.'

Hal came in from the kitchen, a camera case looped over one arm and a shotgun nestled in the crook of the other. He was dressed for their expedition in black, as Matt had suggested, and was clearly keyed up. But if he was the least bit frightened or tense, he hid it well. Knowing his uncle's sense of adventure, Matt wasn't at all surprised.

'And Freddy makes four,' Hal said cheerily. 'Our security man should be along soon. With whatever weapon he's bringing, plus old Hawk-Eye here, plus the handgun you have, we should at least be better prepared than you were when you and Lewis Slocumb waltzed in unarmed.'

'Believe me, I am much more competent at running than shooting anyway. Hopefully, though, nothing's going to happen. It was just a fluke that the guards happened to be making their rounds when they did. They waltzed into the cave with no idea we were there. We'll just stay alert tonight. There isn't going to be any trouble.'

'I expect not,' Hal said. 'You feel pretty sure you can get us in there?'

'I was paying really close attention on the way in. You'll have to trust me on that. After what happened to Lewis, I just don't feel right involving the Slocumbs again, even though I think one of the other brothers would come if I asked. They've done enough. It's really a miracle Lewis is still alive.' *If he is still alive.*

Carabetta knocked on the front door and was let in. He looked slightly ridiculous in a black pullover and watch cap, but he did have a rather sophisticated Pentax slung over his shoulder, as well as a narrow leather case that Matt suspected contained sampling gear. From the moment the OSHA official stepped through the door, he looked uncomfortable.

'Greetings, Freddy,' Hal said. 'Are you ready to become Numero Uno at that agency of yours?'

'I'm not certain this is such a good idea,' Carabetta said. 'What's the gun for?'

'We want to be prepared for any situation,' Hal explained. 'I don't expect any problems. But if there are, at least we'll be able to negotiate from strength.'

'That shotgun is strength?'

'Actually, we have another man coming with us – a professional protector, if you will. Believe me, Fred, there's nothing to worry about.'

'Go in, observe, maybe bottle some samples of the material, and get out. That's all we want from you,' Matt said.

'I . . . I need to talk to you, Hal – in private,' Carabetta said.

'Talk to *me*,' Matt said firmly, sensing he knew now what the man was about. 'This is my project. Come on, let's go someplace quiet.'

'The master suite is fine,' Hal said.

Heidi, Hal's significant other, was off visiting her mother for a week. Matt led Carabetta to the expansive suite, which featured a lush sitting area, a beamed cathedral ceiling, and a panoramic window overlooking the lake. He could see Carabetta staring into the master bath, which included a rock wall waterfall that cascaded into a large hot tub. *The kids' college tuitions I never had to spend* was the way Hal explained the spectacular bedroom. Matt could read Carabetta's thoughts.

More.

'Okay,' he said, 'what's the deal?'

Carabetta pulled himself up straight and met Matt's gaze defiantly.

'The deal is, this whole affair is way more complicated than I was originally led to believe. And now there are guns and . . . and bodyguards, and security people who may or may not show up while we're there.'

'And?'

'And I don't think what I'm being paid is worth the risk.'

Matt suppressed an explosion. Without Carabetta, they really had nothing.

'How much?' he asked.

Carabetta again peered through the bathroom door.

'Another five thousand,' he said quickly.

Matt had not been told specifically what the

original deal with Hal was, but something his uncle said had him thinking it was around fifteen. Now Carabetta wanted five more. Twenty thousand – not a bad night's work. Matt flashed on his own anemic bank account, which could handle a five-thousand-dollar ding, but only just. Then he flashed on Armand Stevenson, and Blaine LeBlanc, and Don't-Call-Me-Bob Crook, and the security men who had rousted him from the mine offices and then attempted to eliminate the Slocumbs, and finally, on Bill Grimes.

'Five thousand and not another penny after that,' he said.

'I expect to be paid first thing tomorrow. No money, no action from me regardless of what we find tonight,' Carabetta countered.

You are really a credit to your profession, Matt wanted to say. 'You'll get your money,' he said instead.

They returned to the living room where, with a minute nod, Matt indicated to Hal that the deal was done. He then motioned Nikki into the privacy of the hallway, where he held her for a time, then kissed her lightly on the mouth.

'Thanks,' she said. 'I was just thinking that it's been too long. So, how much did Carabetta try and gouge you for?'

'He didn't just try,' Matt replied. 'The man is really a sleazebag.'

'But a well-placed sleazebag, at least for our purposes.'

'Keep reminding me. How're you feeling about all this?'

'Nervous, maybe a little scared. What about you?'

'More angry than anything else, I think – for my dad, for all those other miners, for all the humiliation I've had to endure for just trying to do the right thing. Listen,' he went on, clearly searching for the right words, 'there's really no reason you can't wait here until we get back.'

'You mean just hang out on the couch and watch Home Shopping Network while you men tromp off to even the score with the people at the mine and maybe the man who kidnapped me and killed Joe? Now, doesn't that just sound like an opportunity I'd jump at?'

'I just –'

'You just kissed me,' Nikki cut in. 'That means I'm going. Plus I want to make certain you come through this in one piece. You and I have some unfinished business when all this is over.'

Despite the beauty and sensual comforts of Hal's home, Joe Keller's terrible death was still too raw. They had spent the night in each other's arms, talking and touching and knowing that soon, very soon, they would be lovers. Matt's kiss this time was much less inhibited. Nikki dug her nails into the nape of his neck as she responded.

'We'll do fine,' she whispered as they drew away from each other. 'We'll do just fine.'

Minutes later, a pair of headlight beams lanced through the darkness of Hal's driveway.

'This must be our protector,' Matt said, gesturing out the window. 'How did you find him, anyway, Unk?'

'I know you think of me as lily-pure and without fault,' Hal replied, 'but the truth is that after spending much of my life around here, I know a few people. Just as you have your strange little connections around the valley, I have mine. I spoke to a friend with knowledge of such matters. He agreed to arrange for what we needed, and a few hours later, this is the man who called me.'

'What better recommendation could anyone get than that?' Matt said. 'Do you even know his name?'

'I will soon enough. Remember, nephew, we are not hiring this gentleman to prune our rhododendrons.'

'I gotcha.'

The twin raps on the front door were like pistol shots – magnitudes louder than Carabetta's had been. Hal swung the door back, revealing a man whose shoulders nearly filled the span and whose massive head barely cleared the overhead frame. The man nodded a greeting and stepped into the room. His impressive head and flat, pinched face reminded Matt of a villain in a Dick Tracy cartoon. There was a rather large bruise and healing abrasion over his right eye, and a square Band-Aid patch covering some sort of wound on his left cheek.

The man we want is the one who did that to him, Matt was thinking.

'Sutcher,' the man said gruffly, 'Vin Sutcher.'

His name rhymed with 'butcher.'

Hal and Matt had decided they would park in a small public lot at the base of a series of hiking trails. From there, the walk to the cleft would be half a mile or so over terrain that Hal felt Fred Carabetta, clearly the physical weak link of the expedition, would be able to negotiate without too much difficulty. The tunnel to the cave might be another story, but Matt felt confident there was enough room for the man, even in the tightest passageways. They took two cars to the spot – Hal, Nikki, and Carabetta in Hal's Mercedes, and Matt in Vin Sutcher's Grand Cherokee.

Matt was surprised to find the man erudite, well-read, and quite willing to discuss his life and profession. Sutcher had gone to Penn State on a football scholarship, but tore up a knee and ended up leaving school after his second year. He sold automobiles for a time, then insurance. Finally, because of his size and willingness to 'mix it up,' he found employment with an agency that provided bodyguards for rock stars and occasionally movie stars as well. He traveled a good deal, but had chosen a house in the hills just west of Belinda as his home base because the hunting and fishing were excellent in the area, and he had always liked the privacy. It was sheer luck that he happened to be around when Hal's friend called.

Sutcher's choice of weapons included a handgun stuffed in a shoulder holster over his black, long-sleeved T and some sort of semiautomatic submachine gun, which he cradled with a loose familiarity in his right hand. Matt wondered if he had ever killed or even shot anyone, but there was no way he was going to ask. Regardless, he felt much more confident and secure knowing the man was coming along.

It took half an hour to make the walk to the cleft along an ill-defined path. Hal knew the way, though, and led the silent, single-file procession. Carabetta followed Hal, then Nikki, Matt, and finally Sutcher.

'I'm really glad you're here,' Matt said to Nikki as they trudged along.

'You're very cute when you're intense,' she whispered back.

Although they all had flashlights, only Hal had his turned on and then only as necessary. The cloudless night was lit by a silver gibbous moon that was bright enough to illuminate the trail. The group crossed the broad steam now familiar to Matt, and reached the cleft without difficulty.

'Okay, Doctor,' Hal said, 'you're up. Get us in, get us out.'

'Roger that,' Matt said, taking over at the head of the line. 'Fred, why don't you stay right behind me. There's going to be some pretty narrow squeezes, and one place where we're probably going to have to crawl on our bellies for a few feet, but I believe you'll make it okay.'

'Jesus,' Carabetta whined, 'no one said anything about wriggling along on our bellies.'

'Just keep on thinking about all that money and the citations you're gonna be awarded, suitable for lamination. It'll make you thinner. Also, we'll be edging our way along some drop-offs. Just don't pay any attention to them.'

'Aw, Christ,' Carabetta said.

The second time along the damp, narrow tunnel was considerably easier for Matt than the first. He moved silently ahead with some confidence despite, at times, actually having to hold the hand of a softly cursing Carabetta to get him around a drop or across a ledge. Whether it was his familiarity with the passageway, or the distraction caused by being the leader, Matt's claustrophobia was less of a strain than he had expected it would be.

With surprising ease, Carabetta made it through the tight passage that required them to drop onto all fours and crawl. But at the still narrower one, where Matt motioned them onto their bellies, he balked.

'No fucking way,' he said loud enough for all of them to hear. 'This is as far as I'm going. You can keep your damn money.'

'Fred, come on,' Matt urged. 'You can make this. And after about ten feet, you can stand. On the way back, there are other trails we can take that won't be so narrow.' *Provided I can find them.*

'No way. I'm staying here.'

'Mr. Carabetta, come speak with me,' Vin Sutcher rasped.

Without questioning the order, Carabetta worked his way past Hal and Nikki to confront the giant. Sutcher bent over and whispered something brief into his ear. Even in the nearly black tunnel, Matt thought he could see Carabetta blanch.

'All right,' he said, pausing midsentence to clear a bullfrog from his throat, 'but if it looks the least bit like I'm going to get stuck, I'm going back.'

'What did you say to him?' Matt whispered to Sutcher after all five of them had negotiated the low schism without major difficulty.

'I told him that if he didn't get moving, I was going to rip his arm off,' the bodyguard replied, without a fleck of humor.

'Very effective.'

Now, for the first time, Matt caught the pungent aroma of the chemical dump. Four days had passed since he and Lewis had penetrated the cavern – probably not enough time to empty it even if Armand Stevenson had decided to do so. Hiring killers and bribing officials was so much cheaper and more efficient – especially with the chief of police already on his payroll. Matt found himself momentarily wondering about the person – man, he suspected – who had slipped the note about the toxic dump under his door. Whatever ax the writer had to grind with BC&C was about to be made razor sharp.

'Smell it?' he whispered.

'Oh, yes,' Nikki said.

'Toluene,' Carabetta opined. 'Toluene and maybe creosote.'

'Cameras ready,' Hal ordered. 'Mr. Sutcher, would you please take the point.'

'Be happy to,' Sutcher said, tightening his grip on the submachine gun.

'Straight ahead,' Matt said. 'Keep your flashlights turned off as much as possible and your voices low. If there is any interference, it'll come from the entrance on the far side.'

Cautiously, with Sutcher now in the lead and Hal bringing up the rear, the column moved through the narrow, stygian tunnel, following the increasingly potent chemical smell.

'There,' Matt said.

Not far ahead, a faint, gray light pierced the darkness.

'Go ahead,' Sutcher urged. 'I'll be watching for trouble.'

Matt led the way into the cavern. The rushing underground river, the huge, three-dimensional pyramid of barrels, stretching upward twenty feet or more, the unpleasant, sickly sweet odor, the protective gear hanging along one rock wall – all seemed unchanged from the way he and Lewis had seen it a few days ago. Using his flashlight, he motioned Carabetta to move closer and led him, then Nikki, around the perimeter.

'Okay,' Matt said, 'let's take some pictures and get some samples.'

'Rutledge,' Carabetta exclaimed, pointing past the barrels, 'what's that lying over there?'

Matt never got the chance to answer. With a deafening roar, brilliant light, and a force unlike anything he had ever experienced, the two entrances to the cavern simultaneously exploded. Instantly, the entire space filled with acrid smoke and choking dust. Boulders the size of automobiles and all manner of rock hurled through the air. Flung sideways, Matt was slammed viciously against the wall. He collapsed onto the floor as dust filled his lungs. Rocks rained down upon him. A basketball-sized boulder thudded against his back. Other chunks buried his legs and pelted his arms with enough force to shatter bone.

In just moments, the explosions were over. The pitch-black cave was filled with suffocating silt and the smell of chemicals freshly released from their drums. Matt lay there, his face half-buried in rubble. The only way he could get enough breathable air in was to force his mouth and nose against the shoulder of his shirt. His ears were ringing mercilessly, and he sensed that his nose was bleeding. Then, through the darkness, he thought he heard whimpering.

'Nikki?' he tried calling out, but his dirt-covered vocal cords barely made a croak.

He coughed, then spat, then coughed again until it seemed like some of the grit cleared from his throat. He also noted that the pain in his back was bad, but not incapacitating. Probably nothing but bruises there. He rubbed his hand across his nose. It wasn't broken, but it was definitely bleeding – how much was hard to tell. Quickly, he tested his arms, which seemed intact, and his legs, which were totally buried beneath many pounds of stone.

'Nikki?' he called out again.

'Matt?'

He thought he heard her voice, faint and strained, from somewhere to his left, but he wasn't certain. His damaged eardrums muffled the sound, but the lack of intense pain made him believe that, while the membranes and ear bones were swollen and bruised, neither drum had been torn. It had to have been Nikki's voice.

He pulled his shirt up over his mouth and nose, making breathing much easier. With great effort, he managed to roll over enough to begin moving debris off his legs.

'Nikki?' he tried once more.

This time there was no answer.

The backs of his hands were raw, and he felt battered all over, but stone by stone he was able to free up his legs. It seemed logical that the people who had blown up the cave had counted on the roof collapsing and sealing the whole deal instantaneously. Clearly, since he wasn't permanently pancaked under a few dozen tons of rock, that hadn't happened. He pulled his legs free and flexed them. Aches, but none of the pain that would have indicated a broken bone. Given what he had just been through, he was as intact as he had any right to be.

'Nikki? . . . Hal? . . . Anybody?'

The sound barely echoed. There was no way to tell how much of the cave – how much air – was left. He rolled onto his hands and knees and crawled over the sharp stones toward where he sensed

Nikki's voice had come from. He hadn't moved more than a few feet when he hit against a body. It was a woman, lying facedown, covered with dust and debris. Her hair was much longer than Nikki's, and her body, clothed in jeans and a T-shirt, was very slight – not much more than a hundred pounds. A girl, he thought, not a woman. He checked for a pulse at the carotid artery in her neck and found one easily. At that moment, the girl took a breath.

'What in the hell?' he muttered. 'Can you hear me?' he said into her ear. No response.

Gently, careful to stabilize her neck as best he could, he turned her over. Reaching through the absolute darkness he brushed her hair and some of the dust off her face.

'Oh, God,' he moaned the moment he touched the hard, neurofibroma nodules scattered over her face and scalp. 'Oh, God, no.'

Chapter 31

The darkness in the cave was total, oppressive, and, for Matt, claustrophobic as well. The fumes were pungent, though not caustic in the way that chlorine fumes were – at least not yet. He sat for a time, composing himself, breathing through his shirt, with the unconscious girl resting beside him. Clearly, Armand Stevenson and his confederates had chosen to bury the human evidence of their transgressions along with their accusers. How many others like this girl were in the cave? Matt wondered.

His ears were continuing to buzz unpleasantly, but from what he could tell, the bleeding from his nose had subsided. Every few seconds another chunk of rock dropped from someplace in the cavern. The roof hadn't caved in but clearly it was unstable. For a time, Matt knelt there, listening to the rattle of falling rock, unable to shake the image of the delayed collapse of the World Trade Center towers. He was finally able to orient himself by focusing on the churning and splashing of the river, which ran behind where the chemicals had been stacked. The continuous white noise of the moving water echoed through the midnight blackness, and had a strangely calming effect.

'Nikki?' he called out. 'Hal?' From somewhere to his right, he was sure he heard a man groaning. 'Fred?'

He brushed some more dust and shards of stone from the girl's face and hair. Her narrow face seemed intact, although there was no doubt she was badly disfigured. *Poor baby.* Clavicles, chest wall, arms, hands, abdomen, pelvis, legs. From what little he could tell, she had sustained no major injuries.

'Nikki?' he called again. 'Anyone?'

For a few seconds there was only the sound of the river, then, 'Matt? . . . Matt, it's me.'

This response was definitely not his imagination. Nikki's voice, weak but composed, came from his left, some distance away.

'Nikki, it's Matt, are you hurt?'

'I . . . I hear you, but I can't make out your words. My ears . . .'

'I know,' Matt said, speaking slower, louder, and more distinctly, 'mine, too. I asked if you were hurt.'

'I . . . I don't think badly. My ears are messed up. They won't stop ringing. I got hit on the head pretty hard, too. I don't think I was knocked out, but I'm a little dizzy.'

A second concussion, Matt thought. The word was often thrown around casually, especially in the ER, where head injuries weren't considered serious by most unless there was a period of unconsciousness, X-rays showing a fractured skull, or a CT scan demonstrating a hemorrhage or brain contusion. But he had seen many lives ruined and families torn apart by post-concussion syndromes, sometimes with as little trauma as a minor fall or fender-bender. He pushed himself up from the stone floor. His back and legs throbbed, and the backs of his hands were stinging, but the discomfort was tolerable – especially now that he knew Nikki had survived.

'Nikki, can you stand?'

'I think so.'

'Walk?'

'Let me see. . . . Yes, yes, I can walk.'

'Wait!' he cried out suddenly. 'Don't move! Do you have any idea where your flashlight is?'

'Pardon?'

'Your flashlight.'

'I . . . I was holding it when the blast went off. There's so much rubble. I have no idea where it might be. I'll look around and –'

Her words dissolved into a fit of coughing.

'Pull your shirt over your mouth to breathe. It helps. Nikki, just stay where you are and keep talking. I'm going to walk toward your voice. We'll look for the light together.'

Matt guessed she was twenty-five or thirty feet away. Shuffling through boulders, arms extended like Frankenstein's monster, he inched his way through the blackness, guided by Nikki's recitation of a country song he knew well.

Silver threads and golden needles cannot mend this heart of mine . . .

Matt twice dropped to all fours to negotiate piles of rock.

. . . and I dare not drown my sorrow in the warm glow of your – Hey, I found it! I think it's okay.'

An instant later a beam of light filtered through the suspended silt, panning about until it locked on him. Seconds after that, they were together.

'Oh, baby,' Matt said as they held each other. 'I was so frightened you were hurt or – or worse. I can't believe they would do this to us.'

He took the light to check her. Blood was flowing

from a gash not far from her healing gunshot wound. He pulled off one of his socks and used it to apply pressure to the cut.

'Are you okay?' she asked. 'There's a lot of blood on your face.'

'My nose has been bleeding but I don't think anything hit it. Probably the shock from the blast. No bones broken anyplace as far as I can tell. Weird as it sounds, we're lucky. I think they expected the ceiling of this vault to collapse. From the way the rocks keep dropping, it still may.'

Nikki swung the beam around the void. Because of the dust, visibility was limited.

'What about the others?' she asked.

'I don't know. But there's a girl over there – at least I think it's a girl and not a woman.'

'What?'

'She's unconscious. I bumped against her while I was crawling around. And guess what her face and scalp are covered with.'

'Neurofibromas. Matt, this is awful. Could you tell if she was badly hurt?'

'I don't think so, but she's unconscious. And I think I heard a man out there moaning as well.'

'Hal?'

'No idea. I'm worried sick about him. Wasn't he right behind you?'

'From what I remember, yes.'

'Well, that would put him someplace over there, not where the sounds came from. Hal? Hal, can you hear me?'

Nikki panned the flash along the wall. If Hal Sawyer had been standing behind her, he would have been virtually under the entrance from the tunnel, which was now an impenetrable pile of huge boulders and debris that extended up to the roof of the cavern.

'I don't see how he could have avoided being buried under that,' Matt said. 'Hal? Hal, it's Matt.'

Silence.

'Let's try to find him, Matt.'

They shuffled to the pile and moved a couple of rocks. Then they looked at each other and shrugged helplessly. If he was buried beneath this mass, there was nothing they would accomplish by digging except to exhaust themselves.

'He was such a good egg,' Matt said finally. 'Eccentric and quirky, but a real good guy just the same. He was so kind to Mom, and . . . and he loved me to pieces.'

'I know he did.'

'I just can't believe this. Hal? Dammit, Hal, answer me. It's Matt.'

She put her arms around him and pulled him tightly against her.

'Stevenson and those other bastards are going to pay for this,' he said.

Nikki was reluctant to point out the obvious – that at this moment, their chances of surviving to make anyone pay for anything seemed remote.

'Listen,' she said, 'let's get back to that girl.'

The dust seemed to be settling a bit, making the beam of light more effective. The girl was there, twenty or so feet away, lying on her back, still unconscious. She was eleven or twelve, with long, corn-silk hair. Her narrow, distorted face, possibly pretty at one time, was filthy and battered. Matt was checking her more thoroughly than he had initially been able to, when they heard a groan from off to their right. A man lay there, supine, semiconscious, buried from the waist down. His head was lolling from side to side, and every few seconds his arms flailed impotently at the jagged rocks that pinned him down.

'Oh, my God, look!' Nikki exclaimed.

Not ten feet away from the man lay the lower half of a body – men's work boots and overalls, protruding from under a huge pile of collapsed rock. And not far from him, lying faceup, only partially buried in rubble, was yet another man, minimally covered with debris, unconscious but clearly breathing. Nikki rushed to him, leaving Matt temporarily in darkness.

'Oh, no, Matt! Quick!' she cried, setting the light down to remove dirt and stones from the two. 'He's another one.'

Matt hurried over, took the flash, and knelt down. The man's silt-covered face was badly disfigured by neurofibromas. Probably in his twenties, he had a gash and a deep bruise on his throat where a rock had apparently hit. His respiration was labored and accompanied by stridor – the whooping noise produced when air is drawn in past a significant obstruction.

'Well?' Nikki asked.

'Hell, I don't know, except that it's a miracle any of us are alive. This cave was supposed to be a mass grave for all of us. We have at least one person dead and three – my uncle, Vinny, and Carabetta – missing. We have three people that we know of who are unconscious. That man thrashing around over there looks like he might be badly hurt, and this guy's breathing doesn't sound good.' Matt reached into the man's hip pocket, produced a thin billfold, and withdrew his driver's license. 'Colin

Morrissey,' he read. 'Age twenty-two. From Wells.'

'Where's that?'

'Thirty miles south of here.'

'So now we have two with neurofibromas. Do you think there are more?'

'I wouldn't be surprised. I can't make much sense of this yet. But I do know one thing. We have a limited amount of air that's loaded with fumes that are probably toxic, and one meager source of light with batteries that could last an hour or a minute.'

'Not so good,' Nikki said.

'We need to find some more light. If your flashlight goes out before we come up with something, we're finished. We've got to find the one I had.'

'Think we should try and help that poor guy over there first?'

'Your call.'

'Let's see if we can free him up. He's more awake than the rest. After that we can decide whether to help the others or look for your light.'

'Okay. Once we're oriented, let's shut the flashlight off and move the rocks in the dark.'

The man, heavyset and balding, kept crying out as Nikki and Matt cleared the fallen rocks off of him. They both knew the potential for disaster from his situation. Pelvis, abdomen, groin, legs, spine, muscles – in addition to fractures and internal injuries, there was the possibility of sudden death, usually from the release of clots formed in injured legs.

By the time they had removed enough rubble to pull the man free, he was beginning to speak. His invective-laden babble was disjointed and garbled, but there was no mistaking his anger.

'Fuckin' double-crossers . . . you die, you die . . . Tracy . . . I love you, Tracy . . . can't move . . . bastards . . . fuckin' double-crossers . . .'

'Hey, calm down, fella,' Matt said. 'Easy does it. We're doctors. We're here to help you. Nikki, put the light on my face, maybe that'll help.'

Another minute passed as first Matt and then Nikki attempted to get through to the incoherent man. It was Nikki who succeeded. She held her hand under his head, and had Matt hold the light away so that it illuminated both her face and the victim's.

'My name is Dr. Solari,' she said kindly. 'Do you understand?'

'Doctor,' he murmured.

'Yes. What's your name?'

'Name . . . Sid,' he replied sluggishly, shaking his head as if to clear it.

'Sid, what happened? How did you end up here?'

'Double-crossed . . . bastards . . .'

Nikki lifted his head slightly and brushed some of the remaining dust from his face. He responded to her touch. His head stopped moving and his gaze fixed on her.

'Sid, what do you do? Who double-crossed you?'

'Are you . . . really a doctor?'

'I am.'

'My legs . . . don't think I can feel my legs.'

Matt checked both of the man's legs, then looked up at Nikki and shook his head grimly.

'We'll go over you and do what we can,' she said.

'Wh . . . what happened?'

'There was an explosion. We're in a cave where they store chemicals. The entrances are sealed off. Whoever did this meant to kill us, but the ceiling hasn't collapsed. So here we are. We have only this one flashlight, so we're going to have to keep turning it on and off. Do you understand?'

'There are . . . plenty of flashlights. . . . Big ones.'

'What?' Nikki and Matt exclaimed in unison.

'Cabinet on other side of . . . river. Gloves, lights, gas masks, first-aid kit, tools.'

Sid began coughing spasmodically. Nikki lifted him and propped him against her knee, taking pains not to move the area around his lower thoracic vertebrae where it seemed his spinal cord was compressed or severed.

'Who are you?' Nikki asked.

'I'm . . . a guard here. Tommy . . . Where's Tommy?'

Nikki glanced over at the motionless lower body protruding from beneath a ton of rock. Sid followed her gaze.

'Oh, shit! Oh, no! Double-crossing bastards. Sonofabitch. He had a little kid.'

'People from the mine double-crossed you?' Matt asked eagerly.

'No,' Sid said vehemently. 'It was Grimes. . . . Fucking Grimes, and some guys.'

'What did they pay you to do?'

'Just look the other . . . way while they worked inside this place. I thought they were just going . . . to bury it all because of those guys who showed up here last week. . . . No one said nothin' about people being in here when it blew . . . especially not us. . . . They shot us up with something to knock us out and left us to . . . Doc, my legs. You got to help me.'

Nearby, the girl and Colin Morrissey had begun moaning loudly.

'Whatever they used on you all must be wearing off,' Nikki said. 'Matt, we ought to check that cabinet.'

'Don't leave me,' Sid cried. 'I can't move my legs.'

'We'll be back.'

Nikki set him back down and took Matt's arm as they made their way around the mass of barrels, many of which had spilled their oily contents onto the stone floor. Surprisingly, a number of them, mostly those at the bottom of the pyramid, remained secure.

'Why do you suppose Grimes knocked them out with an injection and not a bullet in the head?' Nikki asked.

'I suspect he was hedging his bets against the remote possibility that anyone ever dug in here and found us. There would be no evidence we were all murdered. A tour group, maybe, or else some environmentalists unfortunate enough to be in the wrong place at the wrong time. Hell, mines and explosions are like Thanksgiving and turkey – especially *this* mine.'

The river, about ten feet wide, flowed from their left to right with a modest current, its surface a foot or so below the floor of the cave. Two flat bridges with rustic wooden railings had been built across it, but one of those had been destroyed by several enormous chunks of rock. The river was already having difficulty negotiating the obstruction, and some water behind the new dam had begun splashing over the stone bank onto the cavern floor. The second bridge looked passable.

'If this place begins to fill with water,' Matt said, 'which do you think will happen first? We suffocate, or we drown?'

'We're going to find a way out of here, Dr. Rutledge,' she replied firmly. 'Any more negative thinking on your part will be dealt with most severely.'

'Well, let me ask you this way: Do you think we should be focusing our energies and oxygen on getting out of here or on stabilizing everyone who's injured?'

'Could you just ignore them?'

'Probably not.'

'Then why did you ask?'

'I was hoping you'd talk me into it.'

The cabinet, made of hard, gray, molded plastic was where Sid had described. Fixed to the rock wall, it was seven feet high, at least that wide, and a foot and a half deep. It contained four powerful battery-run lanterns, three gas masks, surgical masks, tools of all kinds, rope, duct tape, what appeared to be an exposure suit, and a large, fairly well-stocked first-aid kit.

'We're in business,' Matt said, pulling a surgical mask over his face and handing one to Nikki. 'You ready to play doctor?'

'Let's.'

They tested the lanterns, all of which worked, and carried them to the others along with the first-aid kit. On the way they got a better sense of the condition of the cavern. The two entrances, perhaps a hundred feet apart, were completely sealed by massive amounts of rubble. Most of the drums of toxic waste, though no longer piled in a neat pyramid, were still in the center of the cave. The ceiling, twenty-five feet up, was holding, leaving them with a good amount of air, albeit air heavily tainted with fumes.

'No telling what this stuff is doing to our lungs,' Matt said.

'Probably not the greatest of our worries right now. Where do you want to start?'

'Colin Morrissey's throat trauma looks like potential trouble to me, but I suggest we make sure there aren't any people we don't know about lying around, and take another look for Hal, Vinny, and Fred at the same time. Then we can move everyone to one area, triage, and do what we can.'

The dust and silt were settling, but each of their steps sent plumes of it floating back into the air. The cries of pain had increased, and with them the sense of urgency. Matt and Nikki set the equipment down next to the young girl, who was beginning some purposeless movements. Then, each carrying a lantern, they began picking their way around the cave, scanning the rocks for bodies.

'Over there!' Matt exclaimed after they had covered just a few yards.

Fred Carabetta lay semiconscious on his belly, face turned to one side, pinned under a mound of rock that extended from his mid-back to beyond his feet. There was blood trickling out of his left ear, and what they could see of his face looked like a battered prizefighter's.

'Help . . . me. . . . Help . . . me,' he was moaning over and over.

'Fred, it's Matt. Can you hear me?'

'Hear . . . you. . . . Help . . . me.'

'Should we try and get him out now or check around for others?' Nikki asked.

'We need more hands.'

'Matt, we can only do what we can do.'

'Then let's try to free him up. Fred, we're going to get these rocks off of you.'

The pile holding Carabetta down was considerably smaller and easier to move than the one that had covered the paralyzed guard. Still, by the time they had removed enough to free him, both were perspiring heavily and working at sucking in air.

Carabetta cried out in pain as they rolled him over. The two of them winced at what they saw. His black sweat pants and shirt were sodden with blood, most of it oozing steadily from a wound to the right of his groin.

'With all these rocks, there isn't even enough space to kneel down here,' Matt said. 'Let's try to haul him over near the others and work on him there.'

'I'll do my best.'

'Fred, we're going to pull you over to where we have enough room to help you out.'

Moving the man was no small feat. Ultimately, success involved Nikki and Matt each seizing a wrist and dragging him a foot or so at a time, past the girl, who was now randomly moving all her extremities, to the area where the security guard and the man with the Belinda syndrome lay. Exhausted from the effort and from breathing through the surgical masks, they stood for nearly a minute, hands on knees, gasping for breath.

'No more sundaes for Fred,' Matt panted.

At that moment, with a bansheelike screech, a figure flew from the darkness, off a tall pile of rubble, onto Nikki, sending her hurtling backward, shattering one of the lanterns.

Nikki cried out in pain as the attacker – a stocky woman – quickly set upon her, hands around her throat. From the remaining illuminated light, Matt could easily discern the dense growth of neuro-fibromas virtually covering the woman's face. He dove at her, hitting her shoulder-to-shoulder, and tackling her onto the cave floor. Growling and spitting, she flailed at his face and arms, landing several effective blows. Matt hit her in the face, first with an open hand, then full force with his fist. It was the first time he had ever punched someone that way in his life. Stunned, the woman sagged back-ward. Matt set his knee across her throat, tore off her cotton work shirt, and used one sleeve to tie her hands tightly together and the other to bind them to her ankles. Then he used adhesive tape from the first-aid kit to immobilize her more effectively.

'You okay?' he asked, turning to Nikki.

'My left ankle,' she groaned, in obvious pain. 'It went over when she hit me.'

'Are you hurt anyplace else?'

'Not badly.'

He knelt by her and examined the injury. Swelling had already begun across the outside of the ankle. In addition, there was impressive tenderness over the lateral malleolus – the bony prominence. If the end of her fibula hadn't broken, ligaments had surely torn. Either way, her mobility was, to all intents, gone. Nikki moaned softly as Matt wrapped the ankle with gauze. Then he activated a bag of chemical ice and secured it against the joint with an Ace bandage. A second Ace completed the bulky splint.

With great effort, Nikki rolled onto her hands and knees.

'Let's get to work on Fred,' she said. 'I don't know how much longer he can stay alive.'

'You can do this?'

'I can try,' she replied, wincing.

'I'm going to get that duct tape and do the other two while you check Fred out. I don't want a repeat of Tarzana, here, when they wake up. Jesus, what a mess we're in.'

Moving slowly and painfully on her hands and knees, Nikki propped two lanterns on piles of rock, took two pairs of rubber gloves from an as yet unopened box, and set to work. Using a bandage scissors and her hands, she cut and tore away Carabetta's clothing. If he wasn't in shock yet, he was close – filthy, pale, bloodied, and sweating, with a pulse that was ominously rapid and faint. There were four or five lacerations over his fleshy body and tree-trunk legs, which were still oozing crimson, but the real trouble was a deep, three-inch rent in his groin, where dark blood was flowing freely.

Breathless, Matt returned from his task.

'Arterial?' he asked.

'I think venous. You're bigger. How about some pressure.'

Matt set a wad of gauze pads over the wound and leaned down on it with all the strength he could muster. Carabetta's thick layer of saffron-colored fat made it difficult to apply enough force. Blood continued seeping from beneath the gauze.

Meanwhile, Colin Morrissey's stridor was worsening.

'We need more hands,' Matt said again as Nikki crawled over to check on the man.

'We have what we have,' she said over her shoulder. 'Matt, this guy's in trouble, too. I don't think he's going to make it too much longer without a tracheotomy.'

'Well, I can't maintain enough pressure to stop

419

Freddy's bleeding. My guess, he's torn his saphenous vein.'

'So what can we do?'

'Get some narrow gauze bandage underneath the saphenous and tie it off.'

'Have you done anything like that before?'

'If you count my cat cadaver in comparative anatomy, I have. You?'

'Well, between my year of surgery and my job cutting up the unfeeling, I know the anatomy pretty well.'

'That settles it. I first-assist and you take a crack at it.'

'What about Colin?'

'Right now, he's breathing. If we don't stop this bleeding, Freddy's toast.'

'Okay, okay.'

While Matt kept pressure on the wound, Nikki opened the first-aid kit and extracted a roll of one-inch gauze and a pair of forceps – the pointy-tipped kind used for removing splinters.

'Any snaps?' Matt asked, referring to self-locking hemostats.

'I don't see any.'

'A scalpel?'

'Nope.'

'Novocain? Xylocaine?'

'You wish. Wait, there is a disposable scalpel.'

'Ah, something to be grateful for. Fred, can you hear me?'

'Help . . . me.'

Matt abandoned the notion of a medical explanation. He leaned close to the man's ear.

'Fred, this is going to hurt,' he said emphatically. 'Nik, how's the ankle?'

'Numb. As long as I don't make any quick movements, it's bearable. I don't think I'm going to be able to stand on it, though.'

'Well, I can keep pressure on this and hold the lantern, but you'll have to serve as your own scrub nurse.'

'I'm afraid,' she said suddenly.

'I know,' Matt replied. 'I wouldn't trust you if you weren't. Just do your best and do it fast.'

'I think I need to open up the area better.'

'Just do it.'

Nikki shrugged and made a deep, four-inch incision at right angles to the middle of the gash. Blood oozed from the skin margins of the cut and from the bright yellow fat beneath it.

'Oh, Jesus!' Carabetta howled as the slice was made. 'Oh, fuck!'

At the man's scream, Nikki pulled back, but Matt shook his head.

'You can do it,' he said firmly.

'Okay,' she replied, 'put pressure below the cut – a lot of pressure. Look, it is the saphenous vein – almost chopped through. It's a miracle he's still alive.'

'You're the miracle. Tie it off – top and bottom – then we can move on to he who cannot inhale.'

Behind them, they could hear Colin's labored breathing getting worse.

'If that guy and the girl are anywhere near as crazy as Tarzana was, we'll have our hands full when they wake up,' Nikki said.

'This guy, *then* that guy, then the girl,' Matt said.

'Right.'

Nikki used her fingers and the blunt end of the forceps first to spread the tissue around and under the torn vessel. Then she forced the ends of two twelve-inch lengths of gauze through the tunnel she had created. With each movement, Fred cried out, but his response to the pain was getting feebler. A large percentage of his blood volume was in his clothes and on the dusty floor. Unless his bleeding was stopped, he might have a minute or two before drifting into unconsciousness for good – maybe a little more, maybe less.

'You're doing great,' Matt encouraged. 'Get a knot in that lower tie, and I'll switch the pressure to stop the backflow. For someone who hasn't touched a live patient in years, you're pretty darn good.'

'Come on, baby,' Nikki murmured to the vein as she gently worked the second gauze tie into place, 'don't tear apart on me now.'

'You've got it! You've got it!'

'I hope so, because here goes.'

Nikki pulled the gauze tight, and a moment later Matt released the pressure he had maintained through most of the procedure. There was some oozing from the incision and the gash, but the area around the lacerated vein was dry. The saphenous was the vein usually harvested for cardiac bypass grafts. Collateral veins would take over the job of returning blood to the heart. If Carabetta made it through this episode and out of the cave – both enormous ifs – he might be left with little more than some periodic ankle swelling.

'Nicely done,' Matt said. 'Getting around that vein without ripping it in two was really something.'

At that moment, Colin Morrissey's breathing seemed to become even more labored.

'We might need to trach him,' Nikki said. 'Can you go check him again?'

'I would, but Fred here still needs pressure on this wound.'

'I'll do that,' a voice beside them said. An older woman, battered as the rest of them, had crawled over from some part of the cave they had yet to inspect. 'You go check the boy,' she said. 'I'll do my best here. My name is Ellen. Ellen Kroft.'

Chapter 32

Nikki knew her ankle was broken. She had felt the crack of bone and the explosion of pain when the woman Matt was calling Tarzana – 160 or 170 pounds – blindsided her. Now she simply bit at the inside of her lip and did her best to cope with the pain. They were in a fearsome predicament with a finite air supply and no obvious way out of the cave. The last thing the others needed was to worry about her.

The newcomer, Ellen Kroft, essentially uninjured, kept pressure on Fred Carabetta's wound while Matt used his ear as a stethoscope to examine the lungs of Colin Morrissey.

'I think he's moving enough air,' he said, 'at least for the moment. His coma seems to be getting a little lighter, too.'

'Let's hope he's sane when he wakes up.'

'With his larynx swollen nearly shut, I don't think he's going to pose much of a problem. How's your leg?'

'Fine,' Nikki said perhaps a bit too quickly, adding, 'It aches some.'

'Think you can put weight on it?'

'I . . . I doubt it.'

'I watched you working on this man from over there,' Ellen said, gesturing toward the darkness to her right. 'You're both doctors?'

'I'm Matt Rutledge, an internist from Belinda, and this is Nikki Solari from Boston. She's a pathologist.'

'How many others are there in here besides us?'

'Do you know of any?'

'No. I was tied up here for a time, then injected with something that knocked me out. When I came to, I was covered with dust and pieces of rock. I assume Grimes untied me while I was unconscious, then blew up the cave. He's the police chief here.'

'Oh, we know who he is. You assume right about him. In addition to that guy and the four of us, there are two people – a woman and a girl – with lumps on their faces like his. They don't seem to be badly hurt, but the woman is pretty wild. We've tied her up for now. The girl's still unconscious.' Matt lowered his voice. 'Then there are two security guards from the mine over there. One of them's dead, the other probably paralyzed.'

'And two more men who came in with us are missing,' Nikki added.

'Do you know why Grimes did this to us?' Ellen asked.

'I don't know why he included you,' Matt replied, 'but as you can see, the local mine has been illegally storing toxic chemicals in here. We were about to expose the whole business. Grimes is in bed with the mine owners.'

With Kathy's fatal prion disease not adequately accounted for, Nikki had never felt completely comfortable with Matt's contention about the mine.

'Not to muddy the water,' she said, 'but what Matt didn't say was that a number of people from this area have developed a syndrome of horrible facial lumps and progressive paranoia. Matt thinks it has something to do with these chemicals. I'm not as certain about that as he is. Do you have something to do with the mine?'

'No. I've never been in this area before.'

'Then, why?'

'Well, believe it or not, I came because a man broke into my home in Glenside, Maryland, and swore he would kill my granddaughter unless I did what he wanted me to. I was able to learn who he might be, and traced him back here to Tullis, but I needed to get a look at him before I could be certain he was the one. Your police chief was supposed to help me do that and also take a statement from me, but we never got that far.'

'I don't understand,' Matt said, turning back to check on Morrissey. 'Who was the man you came about?'

'His name was Sutcher. Vinyl Sutcher.'

Stunned, Nikki and Matt stared at one another.

'Perhaps you'd better tell us more,' Nikki said.

Fred Carabetta had lapsed into unconsciousness. His steady, sonorous breathing formed the background for Ellen's account of her place on the blue-ribbon Omnivax commission; of Lynette Marquand's politically motivated pledge to the American people; of her terrifying encounter with Vinyl Sutcher; and finally, of the fruits of Rudy Peterson's dogged pursuit of the truth behind the outbreaks of Lassa fever. For a time after she had finished, nothing was said. Matt's eyes closed as he spun through the kaleidoscope of his memories, searching to connect with something . . . something he knew was there.

Suddenly he looked up at the two women, his expression grim.

'The Lassa fever vaccine was tested here,' he said.

'What?'

'I don't know exactly when, sometime between when I left for college and when I came back to practice. A drug company paid all the doctors in the valley for each patient they could convince to get the shot. After I came back to go into practice here, a bunch of the older docs were joking about it one day in the lunchroom at the hospital. Here none of them had ever even seen a case of Lassa fever in their lives, and now, with a bunch of the town immunized, none of them ever would. That was the gist of what they were laughing about. A couple of them didn't even know what the disease was, even though they signed up a number of their patients and gave them the shot. I actually think I remember them saying that they got a hundred dollars a head, and that some of them shared that money with the patients. It was all perfectly legal as far as I know – docs and patients are both paid all the time for participating in research protocols or drug testing. I don't know how many in the valley were given the test shots.'

'Four hundred,' Ellen said. 'Four hundred of all ages. I saw the summaries of the field trial, but I never noted down where it was conducted.'

'How many years ago?' Nikki asked.

'I don't know,' Matt replied. 'Maybe ten.'

'Oh, God,' she exclaimed.

'What?'

'Matt, don't you see? Prions. The latent period between exposure to the germ and development of symptoms can be as much as ten years or even longer. That's where the Belinda syndrome is coming from – from the vaccine, not from these barrels of poison. The tissue culture cells that the virus was grown on must have been contaminated with prions right from the start. It seems likely they would have used monkey tissue. If so, maybe the monkeys that the cells came from originally were infected.'

'But –'

'You were right all along about the mine storing toxic waste. You were right and you were passionate about what you believed. Grimes knew about this dump and probably sent you that note to keep pushing you in this direction so you wouldn't ever search for the truth about the cases you discovered.'

'But why would he do that?'

'He must have a stake in the vaccine.'

'If he does,' Ellen said, 'he's on the verge of becoming an extremely wealthy man. Lasaject is one of the most expensive components of Omnivax. In the next year, especially when older children and adults are immunized in addition to newborns, tens of millions of doses are going to be administered. What's this about prions? What are they?'

'The germs that cause Mad Cow disease and other neurologic illnesses as well,' Nikki said. 'We think they're responsible for the condition that man has, and also the woman who attacked me, and the girl over there. The symptoms don't appear for years after exposure, and there's essentially no test to see if someone without symptoms has contracted the disease.'

'You think everyone who gets the vaccine will get infected with prions?'

'I doubt it. Those who get the disease probably have some sort of genetic predisposition to the effects of the prions. In Britain, despite the hundreds of thousands of people who ate contaminated beef, relatively few cases of Mad Cow disease have been reported.'

'How many of the original four hundred do you think have developed prion disease?'

Nikki shrugged. 'Let's see,' she said. 'Matt and I have encountered six cases, including these three. If, say, an additional six cases have disappeared thanks to the handiwork of Grimes and his men, that would make twelve.'

'Three percent,' Ellen said.

'That may be higher than with Mad Cow disease,' Matt said, 'but the jury is still out on the rest of those exposed, because we don't know how variable the latency period of the disease is. And the British *ate* the germ. These people had it injected.'

'Three percent at a minimum,' Ellen said. 'That's terrible. Do either of you know the date and time right now?'

'The second,' Matt said, checking his watch. 'One-thirty A.M. Why?'

'Because later today, at three o'clock this afternoon, I think, the First Lady is going to preside over a live televised ceremony featuring the Secretary of Health and Human Services giving a four-day-old girl the first official shot of Omnivax. She's going to be inoculated at a neighborhood health center in the Anacostia section of D.C. Immediately after that first shot, pediatricians all over the country will begin giving Omnivax to their patients. The vaccine is already in their refrigerators.'

'And probably none of those kids will get sick immediately,' Nikki said glumly. 'There'll be no warning that anything is wrong.'

'Oh, some will get sick,' Ellen said. 'A percentage

of children getting vaccinated inevitably get sick, some of their reactions are serious, some of them even fatal. The pediatricians and scientists and drug manufacturers tell us their lives are a trade-off for the greater good. I wonder how they would feel if it was *their* child's life. The real question now is one that has troubled me and others about inoculations right along: Who will be able to say what will happen five years after a child receives her immunizations, or ten – especially now that they're all rolled up into Omnivax?'

'These three can,' Matt said. 'Grimes must have realized the vaccine was flawed. With all that money on the line, rather than come clean about it or chance someone like us seeing enough cases to piece things together, he decided to eliminate everyone who has developed the prion disease. That gives him ten years before the next wave of spongiform encephalopathy and neurofibromas hits.'

'A wave maybe,' Nikki said, 'but possibly a tsunami.'

'Nikki, you told me Kathy was convinced men were following her, trying to kill her. Well, I think they might have been. I believe Grimes tracked down every single patient from the original vaccine test group. The three in here may be the last of them with the syndrome.'

'We have to stop the supervaccine,' Ellen said.

'Ellen,' Nikki replied gently, 'Grimes somehow arranged for your friend Sutcher to sign on as our bodyguard. I'm almost certain he was the one who threw the switch that blew up the entrances to this place. It's a miracle the ceiling hasn't collapsed. Clearly it was supposed to. But we're sealed in here, way inside the mountain. There's no way out.'

'There is, because there has to be,' Ellen countered with grim conviction.

'I hope you're right,' Nikki said. 'We've been around this cavern some and nothing's apparent to us. I think you can try letting up on the pressure now.'

Ellen did as she was asked. Save for a small amount of oozing, the gaping wound below Carabetta's groin remained dry. In silence, Nikki packed it with sterile gauze and partially closed it with adhesive tape. The OSHA investigator reacted to the painful procedure with nothing more than a muted groan.

'Ellen's right,' Matt exclaimed, his fist clenched. 'There's a way out because there has to be. There's too much at stake for us just to sit here waiting for a rescue we know isn't going to happen.'

'You want us to dig out? Matt, some of those chunks of rock weigh hundreds or even thousands of pounds. I can't even walk without help.'

'Well, then, Ellen and I will do it. Maybe the girl when she comes to, and even Tarzana if we can get her to calm down. What choice do we have?'

'Maybe there *is* one,' Nikki said. 'The stream back there. It's coming from someplace and going someplace.'

Matt latched on to the notion immediately.

'I think it enters right by the cleft where we came in,' he said, a hint of excitement in his voice, 'but that's a hell of a long way underground, and most of it steeply uphill from here. I doubt anyone could make it.'

'Maybe the way out is in the other direction, then.'

Matt looked from one of the women to the other

as he tried to imagine what such a journey might be like – and how it might end. He recalled the gut-tightening panic he experienced crawling through the low tunnels. What would it be like being carried along through a narrow, pitch-black, water-filled tube? What if he got stuck? What if the passage became too small and he couldn't back up? Could there possibly be a worse way to die than to drown, pinned between rock walls in an underground river? How long would it take before he finally lost consciousness?

'Let's go take a look,' he heard himself say.

Without asking permission, he bent down and lifted Nikki in his arms. Then, with Ellen carrying a lantern, and another one left illuminated to comfort and orient the others, they made their way through the rubble, around the barrels, to the river. Nikki wrapped her arms around Matt's neck and pressed her cheek tightly against his.

'Thanks for the lift, stranger,' she said as he set her down on her good leg and she braced herself against the railing of the bridge.

' 'Tweren't nothin', ma'am.'

He tipped an imaginary Stetson, then knelt and peered down at the inky, churning water. To their left, the river entered the cavern through a narrow opening – a foot and a half at the most between the surface and the rock. Ten feet toward them were the remains of the other bridge. On the downstream side, to their right, the opening was even smaller, maybe a foot. He reached his hand down and confirmed what he already knew – the water was damn cold.

He cast about for some way to measure the depth and settled on one of the railings from the shattered bridge. The piece, between three and four feet long, struck bottom just before the end would have vanished – a good sign.

'I can do this,' he said, aware of the ball of fear that was materializing in his chest.

'I should go,' Ellen said. 'I'm smaller than you are and I swim at the Y four times a week.'

Even after just a short time together, Matt had little doubt that Ellen Kroft had the tenacity to give the escape attempt a hell of a go. But he was younger and stronger and no less motivated.

'These woods and mountain people can be pretty inhospitable,' he said, 'especially in the middle of the night. You may still get your chance. If there's no sign of me in three or four hours, you might want to try going the other way. That'll be up to you. But I'll have you know there is little to worry about. I was a junior lifeguard at the Y.'

'In that case, I'll wait,' Ellen said. 'You're going to make it.'

'I am.'

Matt put his arms around Nikki and held her close.

'You want me to carry you back to your patients?' he asked.

'Ellen and I will get back to them okay,' she said, sniffing back some tears. 'Matt, I'm frightened. I . . . I don't want you to go.'

Matt kissed her – at first gently, then with intensity.

'I can think of a few things I'd rather be doing myself,' he whispered. 'But like Ellen said, I'm going to make it because I have to.'

He sensed there wasn't as much conviction in his voice as he had intended. The knot of fear beneath his breastbone was nearing the size of a bowling ball. He stared down again at the river, then over at the slim opening above the surface where it reentered the mountain. In college, a mind game he and his roommates had played from time to time centered around what they would do, what they would feel, if somehow they learned precisely when they were going to die. Now it felt as if he might actually be in a position to know.

Again the questions rattled through his mind.

Was there any other way – any other reasonable possibility of escape for them? If he became wedged, how much time would it take before he lost consciousness? How long could he hold his breath? What did it feel like to drown?

The revolver he had taken from Grimes's massive associate was nestled in the pocket of his sweat pants. The weapon might prove helpful if he ever made it out and then got into trouble. He knew enough about handguns to feel confident it would fire after being submerged for a short time, provided he remembered to empty the water out of the stubby, two-inch barrel before pulling the trigger. If he got trapped, it was doubtful he'd get the chance to use it on himself.

More questions . . .

Was there anything else that might be useful to take? Better to remove his shoes or leave them on? Hyperventilate or just go for it?

Matt knew that he was stalling. He galvanized himself by imagining the terrible loss of life down the road should their suspicions about Lasaject and spongiform disease be true. Holding that thought, he slipped over the rocky edge and into the chilly water. Nikki leaned down and touched her fingertips to his.

'I'll see you soon,' she said.

He walked chest-deep toward the opening in the rock. Once there, he took several deep breaths and looked back over his shoulder.

'You bet you will,' he said.

With that he took a final, lung-filling draught, ducked below the surface of the ebony river, and pushed off downstream.

Chapter 33

The burning in Matt's chest – the first sensation of air hunger – began after just fifteen or twenty seconds of swimming beneath the surface of the chilly, pitch-black water. His awkward swimming became even more uncoordinated. Fearing that if he tried to break the surface he would encounter only the ceiling of his tomb, he pulled himself ahead for another twenty seconds. The fire in his lungs was becoming unbearable. Terrified, he reached overhead. His hands broke water, but then, almost immediately, with his elbows still bent and his feet scraping along the bottom, his fingers touched rock. There was some air space above him, though it was difficult to be certain how much.

Battling a horrible, smothering sensation, he pinched his nose closed, tilted his head back as far as he could, planted his feet on the bottom, and pushed himself up. His face was level with his forearm when it broke water. There was not enough room for him to stand straight up, but there was a four- or five-inch space. With his forehead pressed upward against the rock, he took half a dozen grateful breaths of stale, heavy air. Next he lowered himself until his eyes were just above the water's surface and slowly turned 180 degrees. The darkness behind him was intense and absolute. It was doubtful Nikki and Ellen had already left the bridge, so he concluded that he had either swum farther than he reckoned or that the river had turned sharply. The cold water flowed steadily past his face. He worked his way around again so that the current was behind him, then tilted back so he could breathe once more.

Even pinching his nose shut, with his forehead pressed tightly against the ceiling, water still sloshed into his mouth, making it hard to get air in consistently. Fingers of panic, infinitely colder than the water, squeezed at his throat. He was alive, but nearly immobilized by fear. The oppressive, claustrophobic sensation was worse than he'd expected – much worse. There was absolutely no way he could go on. He had to get back – back to where he could straighten up, back to where there was more space to breathe, back to Nikki. He struggled unsuccessfully to swing around again, but his strength seemed gone.

The current, though not that forceful, kept pushing him downstream, lifting his feet off the stony bottom, and dragging him underwater. With effort, he could wedge himself between the floor and roof of the tunnel, but only for ten seconds at a time before the current won out. Aware of little beyond the hideous impotence of being confined, he floated on. An outcropping of rock struck his hand and forehead with surprising force, dazing him momentarily. The walls of the tube scraped at his arms. The energy it took just to hold himself in place quickly had him gasping.

He simply couldn't take it anymore.

He had to stand up straight.

Damn you, Grimes.

Matt braced himself once more and shut his eyes tightly. Vision was useless here anyhow. He calmed himself down some by imagining that there was a cave just ahead ... a vast cavern ... unlimited air ... space to move ... space to turn around and stand ... space to think.

Slowly, with his head dragging against the ceiling, he lowered his mouth and nose below the surface and took a controlled step downriver . . . then another, and still another. He sensed his pulse begin to slow and his thoughts to focus. The icy fingers loosened their grip. Every six or seven steps, he paused long enough to tilt his head back and suck in a few more gulps of air. Emboldened, he actually dropped down beneath the surface and propelled himself forward with several breaststrokes. However, this time when he broke water, he could straighten up even less than before, and the air space had become reduced by half – two inches, maybe three. There was the chance for only a couple of incomplete breaths before the current pushed him ahead. Another few feet and the space disappeared completely. With less than full lungs, he dropped down, leveled off, and began to swim forward again, this time desperately and with all his strength. Twice he tried to break through the surface. Twice he was met by rock.

This was it. This was the end.

The current was increasing now as well, and turbulence was becoming an additional problem. Frantically, he clawed through the churning water, trying to stabilize his body. His lungs were afire once more, and each heartbeat was a shell-burst inside his skull. The walls of the tunnel seemed to be closing together, tearing at him as he tumbled past.

Don't breathe! ... Hang on! ...

At the instant he had to inhale, his face broke the

surface of the water. Coughing and gagging, he struggled to adjust to the now powerful current, trying to keep himself upright as he sucked in some of the dense air from what he sensed might be a small cave or even a cavern. But his weakness and merciless coughing made regaining control impossible.

The river had widened and become shallower. No more than three feet deep, it churned ahead at intense speed through the pitch-black space. Matt tried to scramble to the right-hand bank, but water roiled about him, forcing him under, then flipping him over like a rag doll. Twice he was slammed into rocks protruding from the bottom. Over the years, he had rafted a number of West Virginia's rivers, traversing dozens of rapids either by oar or swimming. The goal either way was to avoid boulders, and the technique when in the water was to navigate feet first, in a near-sitting position, using one's arms as rudders. Constantly being hammered by rocks, he attempted to establish that position. But in the dark, with no visual cues and no warning of an approaching boulder, he had little chance.

Sputtering on aspirated water, he careened helplessly down a steep slope. The swirling, foaming river seemed to be moving closer and closer to vertical, and now he could hear a roar echoing off the rock – the roar of falling water. He tumbled on, slamming against the stony bottom and one boulder after another. His arms, which he was using to protect his head and face, were absorbing a fearsome pounding. His wind was gone, his consciousness was waning, and his lungs were filling with water. Suddenly, what had been a slope became a drop. Weightless and airborne, he hurdled over the precipice. He hit the shallow pool below awkwardly and with great force. Pitching forward, his forehead smacked against a jagged rock. Pain exploded through his brain from the impact.

An instant later, there was nothing.

For fifteen minutes, Nikki and Ellen stood silently by the bridge, a lantern fixed on the opening where the river left the cavern.

'I'm frightened for him,' Nikki said finally.

'I understand why. That was a very brave thing he did.'

'He has claustrophobia. He told me so himself.'

'The river has to come out someplace. He can do it.'

'You don't know!'

Ellen put her arm around Nikki's shoulders.

'Sorry. I was just trying to sound positive. I know how awful this must be for you. It's terrible for me, too.'

'Sorry to have popped off,' Nikki said.

'Nikki, what Matt chose to do was right. You and I both know that as things stand, we don't have much of a chance here. I'm going to wait a couple of hours, and if nothing's happened and we can't think of anything else, I'm going to try and make it out of here, maybe going upstream. Are you ready to go back and check on the others?'

Nikki peered toward the narrow slit between the river's surface and the ceiling of the tunnel. The lantern beam sparked off the water, then vanished into the darkness. Reluctantly, she picked up the light and lay her arm around Ellen's shoulders. Her ankle was throbbing with even slight movements, but it really didn't matter. She had always done pretty well with pain.

'You're a very good person,' she said as she hobbled and hopped back toward where Colin Morrissey lay.

'As are you,' Ellen replied, her arm around Nikki's waist. 'As are you.'

The girl, her flaxen hair matted and filthy, was sitting beside Morrissey stroking his hand. Nikki cringed at the fibromas that distorted what might have once been a pretty face. Morrissey, whose face was even more disfigured than the girl's, was still unconscious and not moving air at all well. The stridor, a sign that at least there was some airflow, was reduced to barely audible wheezing.

'He's dead,' the girl said in a distant, singsong voice that was devoid of emotion.

'No. No, he's not,' Nikki replied, kneeling next to her. 'My name's Nikki. I'm a doctor. This is Ellen. She teaches school. What's your name?'

'Sara Jane Tinsley. Are ya gonna help him?'

No fear, no anxiety, no questions about what had happened to her or where they were now. Nikki decided not to press the issue unless the girl asked pointedly. Clearly, shock and denial were at work, along with the residual effect of whatever drug she had been given, and maybe even the spongiform disease that was probably eating away at her brain.

Just as well, Nikki thought. The less aware the girl was of their circumstances, the better.

'I'm going to try, Sara Jane,' she said.

'Ah think he's dead, dead, dead.'

'No, see, he's br –'

Nikki stopped in midsentence. Morrissey's wheezing was gone. His contused, swollen throat had finally closed entirely. She checked his pulse, which was weaker than it had been but still present.

From this instant until irreparable brain damage, she had three to four minutes to bypass the obstruction and deliver some oxygen to his bloodstream. Almost in spite of herself, she hesitated, her mind unable to get past the likelihood that Morrissey already had an irreparable, progressive brain disease.

Rapidly, though, that notion gave way to thoughts of Kathy Wilson and Hal Sawyer, of Joe Keller and the dead miners, and of the other cases of the Belinda syndrome that Grimes and his crew had probably already dealt with. And suddenly all of her anger, all of her frustration and fear became focused on this young man, innocent of anything more malevolent than doing what his doctor and his mother recommended a decade ago.

Colin Morrissey was not going to die – not if she could help it!

Silently, Nikki cursed herself for not making preparations in advance for an emergency tracheotomy. She had been too wrapped up in their predicament and her pain to think clearly, and possibly she had also been influenced by the hopelessness of the untreatable disease that she believed was ravaging the man's brain. She reminded herself that hindsight was always 20/20. What had happened had happened. What she needed to deal with now was this moment.

'Ellen, I'm going to have to get some sort of airway into him. I'll need your help.'

'Just tell me what to do.'

Nikki tipped the young man's head back, straightening his windpipe. Morrissey responded with a single, surprisingly effective breath, regaining the precious seconds that had been lost since his last one. In Nikki's mind, the four-minute clock was reset.

'Please keep his head in this position,' she said. 'Do you by any chance have a pen or anything else that's hollow?'

'I'm afraid not.'

'Sara Jane, I'm going to do some things to help this man if I can. There may be some bleeding from his neck.'

'Ah seen blood,' the girl said, looking about at the cave as if for the first time.

There was no more time to explain. The skin above Colin Morrissey's collarbones was retracting inward as his lungs struggled unsuccessfully to suck in air. Nikki grabbed the first-aid kit and searched through it frantically. The disposable scalpel she had used on Carabetta was there, along with a pair of bandage scissors that she could use as spreaders. Now she needed something round, hollow, and sturdy – something wide enough to allow enough air through, but not so big that it tore the trachea apart. A large-bore needle would buy her a little more time, and a long pen cap would be perfect. Acutely aware of the passing seconds, she dumped the entire kit onto the stone floor. A 2cc syringe, still in its sterile wrapper, had been buried beneath some bandages.

Perfect!

'We're in business,' she said.

Nikki discarded the plunger and used the bandage scissors to cut off the end of the barrel where the needle would have attached. The inch-and-a-half-long hollow tube was as good as she could have hoped for.

Pain shot from her ankle as she shifted so that she

was hunched over Morrissey's swollen, discolored throat. Ellen clumsily tried to adjust the light while maintaining the neck extension Nikki required.

'Sara Jane,' she said finally, 'can you shine this lantern right here on this spot?'

'Ah kin do thet.'

'Good girl. We need you, Sara Jane. Be steady.'

Nikki had no idea how much of the four minutes had elapsed, but there would be no stopping for any reason.

'Not on my watch,' she whispered as she focused in. *Not on my watch.*

She located the spot just above Morrissey's larynx that she felt represented his cricothyroid membrane – the best place to make her incision. If she was wrong, she would make do. But she wasn't going to hesitate, and she was damn well not going to screw up. A dozen or more had already died to make Grimes and his people rich. Hundreds, maybe thousands more were in danger if they succeeded in getting their vaccine onto the market.

But not this man – at least, not now.

Using the precious scalpel, keeping it parallel with the cartilaginous rings of the trachea, she made a stab wound through the skin and straight down through the windpipe. Instantly, a bloody froth bubbled out. Reflexively, Morrissey coughed, spattering Nikki's shirt and chin. The drug he had been given was wearing off. His consciousness was returning. Deftly, mindless of the blood, Nikki inserted the scissors into the incision and spread them to open up the hole. Then she slid the plastic tube down into the trachea. There was a whistling, gurgling sound as the first rush of air entered the man's lungs. Quickly, his breathing calmed.

Minutes later, Colin Morrissey lifted one arm, and soon after that, his eyes fluttered open.

Two more hours passed as Ellen and Sara Jane tended to their four patients. Fred Carabetta remained comatose, although he seemed to respond a bit when cold river water was sponged over his face and lips. Sid, the guard, lay nearby, alternately sobbing and cursing. He was clearly paraplegic, and now was woefully aware of that fact. The woman who had attacked Nikki remained trussed up with tape. She slept much of the time and rattled on incoherently when she was awake. Seemingly mindless of their predicament, Sara Jane crawled from the woman to Morrissey and back, comforting them, sponging their foreheads, holding their hands, and even singing to them.

'They're lak me,' she said in one of the rare instances when she spoke to Ellen and Nikki. 'They're jes lak me.'

Nikki had insisted that Morrissey's hands be taped securely to his belt to prevent him from pulling the tube from his makeshift tracheotomy. Now, exhausted and more apprehensive each minute, she lay on the dusty floor, propped against a large boulder, her injured, throbbing leg elevated on a pile of stones. There was nothing more she could do now than wait. Horrible visions kept impinging on her mind – visions of Matt, his body wedged forever between two rocks, his limbs wafting lifelessly in the black water. In addition, the sickly sweet air seemed to be getting thicker and harder to breathe. Was it vanishing already?

Not with a bang, but a whimper . . . Not with a bang . . .

As she lay there, Nikki marveled at Ellen, who remained in almost constant motion, tending to the others, speaking cheerfully and hopefully with them and with Sara Jane. Periodically she would return to where Nikki lay to assure her that her patients were okay, and that Matt was going to make it, and so were they. On this trip, however, she had no such message. For the first time, tension etched her face.

'I'm going to try the river,' she said.

'What?'

'I won't go downstream, but I have to try something. It's been almost three hours and I think we might be running low on air. Do you think you can manage without me?'

What difference does it make? Nikki stopped herself from saying.

'I'll do what I can do,' she said instead. 'You don't think he made it out, do you?'

Ellen sat beside her and took her hands.

'I don't know what I think right now, except that we can't just sit back and let them win. For one thing, we both have new men in our lives. I want to see how that turns out for me. And for another, in just a few hours that vaccine is going to be the standard of care. Pediatricians all over the country have been primed by the public-relations people from the pharmaceutical houses and the dear President and his wife. I wouldn't be surprised if a couple of thousand doses of the stuff get administered by sunset today.'

'You're right,' Nikki said, pushing herself up. 'We've got to keep trying. You said you're a good swimmer?'

'A fish.'

'Let me hop you over. Sara Jane and I'll do fine here.'

'I know you will.'

Both women were breathing harder from the trip across the cavern than they might have expected. No comment was necessary. The supply of oxygen was definitely dwindling.

Nikki watched as Ellen made her way around the pile of wood and rubble that had once been the second bridge and lowered herself into the water. This was one hell of a woman, she was thinking – courageous, intelligent, resilient, and kind, precisely the sort of person she would like to be in her sixties. The notion of even reaching sixty brought a rueful smile. Several hours had passed since Matt headed off. It was doubtful that he had made it out of the mountain, and now what little remained of their hope for survival rested with a wisp of a woman who was nearly twice his age. Ellen would not only have to find a way out of the mountain swimming upstream, but she would have to avoid Grimes and his gunmen, find people who could and would help, and make it back to the cavern before it became an airless tomb. The chances of her pulling all that off were slim indeed.

But slim wasn't none.

Lantern in hand, Nikki settled down on the bank and waited. Her wait was not a lengthy one. Not five minutes after Ellen had paddled into the pitch-black tunnel, she came floating slowly back, feet first, facedown in the water. Nikki scrambled onto her hands and knees and reached for Ellen's blouse. The fabric slipped from her hand. Ignoring the stunning pain from her ankle, she pushed off the rocky bank in a clumsy dive and wrapped her arms

447

around the older woman's waist just before they reached the second bridge. Holding tightly, Nikki grabbed a fistful of Ellen's hair and pulled her face clear of the water. Then she braced herself against the bridge and managed to set her one good foot on the bottom. The river lapped by just beneath her chin.

Inch by painful inch, drawing on a reserve of strength that surprised her, Nikki pushed Ellen upward until she was sprawled out prone on the bridge, her legs dangling down into the water. Then, crying out in pain, she hauled herself onto the bank and crawled over to where Ellen lay. A single downward thrust on both sides of her back cleared much of the water from Ellen's lungs. A second thrust, and she began breathing on her own, sputtering and coughing reflexively. In less than a minute, she began to come around. For some time she lay that way, her chest heaving.

'Rocks,' she said finally. 'Tunnel was blocked by rocks.' Another minute passed before she spoke again. 'I . . . tried to move them. . . . Foot got caught. . . . Couldn't get free. . . . Water got down my –'

'Easy,' Nikki said, cradling her head in her lap. 'Easy. You gave it a great try. Just relax and catch your breath. I'm just grateful you made it back here.'

It was many minutes before Ellen could push herself up, still violently coughing out river water.

'God, but that was awful,' she said. 'The rocks collapsed on me. I couldn't get my leg out.'

Nikki hauled herself up using the bridge railing. The two women, soaked and shivering, held each other tightly. Then Ellen pulled away.

'Where are you going?' Nikki asked.

'Up on that pile of rock,' Ellen replied, gesturing toward what remained of the entrance Nikki and the others had used. 'Send Sara Jane up to help me move some of that stuff.'

Nikki started to protest, then merely shrugged and nodded.

Dead waiting around helplessly was no different than dead trying.

Chapter 34

Matt's first awareness was the smell of motor oil. His second was that he was alive and cold. He was in a large shed of some sort, lying in his sodden clothes on a bed of filthy rags. The walls were creosoted wood. The bare bulb dangling overhead was unlit, but thin, gray light filtered in through a foot-square, screen-covered window near the peak of the ceiling. Piled not far from him were covered plastic buckets of what looked like chemicals, and large, unmarked paper sacks of what might have been seeds or fertilizer. There were gardening tools in one corner of the coarse wood floor, several gas-powered weed whackers hanging on the wall, and a good-sized, partially dissected motor underneath them.

It wasn't until he tried to move that he realized his left wrist was handcuffed to a U-shaped pipe that seemed to have been built through the wall of the shed for precisely that purpose. He peered about again, trying to get a sense of who his captors might be. A pulsating pain encircled his head like a bandanna that had been knotted too tightly. His stomach, reacting to the odors and his dizziness, was sending acrid jets of bile into his throat. His watch was gone, as was the pistol he had shoved into his pocket. The backs of his hands were scraped raw and coated with clotted blood. There was no traffic noise from outside, but twice over fifteen minutes or so, he heard a motorcycle rumble away – two different ones, he guessed, both Harleys. Bit by painful bit, memories of his devastating trip down the underground river crystallized.

'Help!' he cried out. 'Hey, someone help me!'

He waited for a reply, then yelled again. Tentatively, the door across from him opened, and a slightly built woman in her twenties peeked in and put her finger to her lips. She had badly spiked purple hair, dense black eye shadow, and piercings through her nose, brows, and lower lip. Her black leather pants were frayed and dusty, as were her black T and leather vest.

'Quiet!' she whispered urgently. 'They'll tend to you when they're ready.'

'But I need to get –'

The woman had already pulled away and closed the door behind her. Matt waited a few minutes and then began hollering again. This time, when the woman reappeared, she had a child on her hip – a boy, two years old, filthy and frail, with a sallow complexion, thick greenish mucus draining from both nostrils, and a deep, nasty cough. She tossed Matt a tattered brown army blanket.

'Look, I told you to shut up,' she said, still in a pressured whisper. 'They ain't much likelihood they ain't gonna kill you. But yellin' like that an' disturbin' the children will take care a what little chance you got.'

The woman moved to go, but this time hesitated when he spoke.

'Wait, please, I'm a doctor,' he said quickly. 'My name's Matt Rutledge. Dr. Matt Rutledge from Belinda. I don't know how I got here or even where

451

I am, but I've got to get away and get some help. My friends are trapped in a mine cave-in and they're going to die.'

'You ain't no doctor,' she said. 'They said you had a gun. Doctors don't carry guns.'

'I can explain that. Look, your boy there has a bad sinus infection and probably a throat infection, too. I'll bet he isn't eating or sleeping well. He should be checked over by a doctor, and soon. He needs antibiotics.'

'We don't go to no doctors.'

'I can take care of him. I can get you the medicine he needs. What's your name?'

The woman's eyes narrowed.

'Becky,' she said finally. 'This here's Samuel. An' don't go callin' him Sam neither. His daddy gets mighty angry at that.'

'Well, I'm a really good doctor, Becky, and I can get Samuel better. Just let me go and get some help for my friends. Then I'll be back to take care of him.'

Indecision flickered across Becky's face but then just as swiftly vanished.

'I did that an' they'd never find all the pieces of me,' she said. 'You jes lay still an' keep quiet. If yer not a doctor, Bass'll kill you quicker'n you kin snap yer fingers. An' if you are, he'll most likely do you anyway. Now shut up!'

'But –'

This time the door slammed shut.

'Becky, please,' Matt called out.

There was no response. He looked up at the small window, trying to get a sense of the time of day. How long had he been gone? His damp clothes and the freshly clotted blood suggested it hadn't been all that long, but he couldn't be certain. The handcuffs were police-department grade and put on way too tight to slip out of. He set his feet against the wall, grasped the copper pipe with both hands, and tried to pull it loose. The futile effort sent a fusillade exploding through his head. Frustrated, he sank back onto the oily rags and kicked the walls until his strength was gone. There had to be a way out. Waiting for Bass or whoever was supposed to kill him did not seem like his best chance.

'Becky,' he shouted. 'Samuel is sick. Really sick. You know he is. He's not going to get better without medicine. That stuff draining out of his nose is serious. I can help him. He could get very ill. Please listen to me. People are going to die if I don't get some help. Don't leave me here like this.'

'Bass, no!' he heard Becky cry.

An instant later the shed door burst open. The man stood there, filling the space. He was six-five, with shoulders that nearly spanned the doorjamb; heavily tattooed, tree-trunk arms; and a massive gut. His thick, shoulder-length auburn hair and full beard hadn't seen a scissors in months, if not years, and his vest, perhaps once the covering for an entire cow, was studded with chrome spikes. His narrow, feral eyes held not a bit of warmth.

'Who the fuck are you?' he said, taking a step into the shed. 'And who do you work for?'

Behind him, Matt could see at least one other biker, as well as Becky, Samuel still riding on her hip. He pushed himself to his feet.

'I'm a doctor,' Matt said, certain that he had better state his case quickly. 'My friends and I were trapped in a mine explosion. I swam out in the river to get help.'

'Bullshit.'

'No, please, it's true. I'm from Belinda. I need to get to the Slocumb brothers' farm off 82. Do you know them? They can vouch for me.'

'I don't know them. I don't know nothin' except that you were where you shouldn't have been with a gun in your pocket. Now, we can do this the easy way or the hard way. You DEA?'

'No, I'm a doctor from Belinda.'

'I'm gonna find out, and I promise it ain't gonna be pleasant for you. Tell me who you work for and I'll see to it you don't suffer too much. Fuck with me, and I promise you'll be beggin' to die.'

'What I told you is the truth,' Matt pleaded stridently. 'I swear it is.'

Bass stepped forward, grabbed Matt's shirt in his massive fist, and lifted him onto his toes. Matt could smell the odor of marijuana wafting from his clothes.

'You have half an hour,' Bass growled.

He whirled and left, slamming the door with a force that threatened to collapse the shed.

'I'm tellin' you, he really is a doctor,' Matt heard Becky say. 'Ask him to look at Rake.'

'No!'

'Christ, Bass, he's your brother.'

'Shut up! This guy's a fed and in a little while he's gonna be a dead fed. This ain't no fuckin' game we're playin' here. I want to know how in the hell he found us.'

Drugs! Matt felt certain the bikers were either growing them, processing them, or more likely both. He again checked the single window. The overcast sky seemed brighter now. Time was running out – for him, for Nikki, and for the rest of those in the cavern. It was also running out for some children who were about to receive the so-called vaccination of a lifetime.

For a while, he lay in silence, assuring himself again that the handcuffs were unyielding, and trying to conjure up a way to expand on his primitive effort to exploit Becky, clearly a weak link in the chain. Twice a bike rumbled off. He couldn't tell for certain if either was one he had heard before. He imagined his own Harley and the indescribable sense of freedom and completeness he felt when riding the hills. Then, soundlessly, Becky eased open the door, slipped inside, and closed it behind her. Samuel wasn't with her. Instead, she was carrying a dirty pillowcase, partially filled with something.

'You are a doctor, ain't you?'

'Just like I said. Becky, I –'

'Tell me which of these will help Samuel.'

She dumped the contents of the sack onto the floor in front of him – dozens of bottles and vials of various pills and liquid meds, almost all of them legitimately labeled from one pharmacy or another.

'The guys 'mos always clean out the medicine cabinets a the houses they . . . um . . . visit,' she whispered. 'They all love Perks and Oxys, but a couple of 'em prefer codeine. The rest a the pills they jes keep around. Will any a these help Samuel?'

Matt fingered through the vials and picked out two different brands of amoxicillin, 250 milligrams – thirty capsules in all.

'This'll work,' he said, pulling one of them apart. 'Just take about half the powder from one of these capsules and mix it in his food three times a day. For the first dose, use a whole capsule's worth. Does Samuel have any allergies?'

'Any what?'

'Don't worry about it. Here, half a teaspoon of this liquid medicine will help his cough.'

'Thank ya, Doctor,' she said, gathering up the pills. 'I'm sorry Bass don't believe you.'

'Becky, you've got to help me get out of here.'

'Oh, I cain't do thet.'

'They're growing drugs here, aren't they. Is that what Bass is afraid I'll find out?'

'I gotta go now.'

'Becky, I swear I won't tell anyone. I just want to help get my friends out of that mine. Please, he's going to kill me.'

'I know. I sure wish he wasn't.'

'Who's Rake?' Matt asked suddenly.

'How did you – ? Ah, you heered me talkin' ta Bass.'

'What's wrong with Rake?'

'He's . . . sick. Some kinda cancer or somethin' in his back, they said. He kin barely walk, an' he cain't ride his bike atall.'

'Show me on you, Becky. Show me where Rake's cancer is.'

Becky hesitated, then turned and pointed to her lower back.

'I gotta go now. Thanks for helpin' Samuel.'

'Becky, get Bass,' Matt said desperately. 'Tell him I'm ready to talk. I'm ready to tell him everything.'

'You ain't a doctor?'

'I am. Now, please, get him.'

'I'm sorry,' he heard her say as the door closed.

Matt sensed the woman hurrying away. He should have been harder on her. If she didn't agree to help him, he should have threatened to tell Bass that she had. *Stupid*. Frustrated, he whipped his manacled hand up with such force that a slice of skin peeled back from his wrist. He barely noticed the pain.

'Bass, I'll talk,' he called out, certain his voice hadn't carried past the walls. 'Let's make a deal. Come on.'

Nothing.

Ten minutes passed, maybe more, before the door opened again. Two bikers, both in black, but neither needing to dress tough in order to look tough, strode in and pulled him roughly to his feet. One of the men – shaved head; broad, flat nose; tattooed neck – unlocked the handcuff on the pipe and secured it to his own wrist.

Thank God, Matt thought. But then, as they led him outside, another, far more ominous thought came to mind. The bikers were making no attempt to conceal their compound from him. In all likelihood, no matter what he did or said, he was a dead man. Scattered in the dense woods, well hidden from above, were ten wooden structures of various sizes. The largest, looking something like an Indian longhouse, had smoke curling from two chimneys. Above the chimneys a broad metal roof, suspended from the trees, diffused the smoke, which carried a distinctive, chemical odor. Opium, Matt guessed. No way they were going to let him go having seen this.

The two men led him across a dirt and pine needle courtyard to a modestly sized rough-hewn house with a small, low front porch. Bass was inside, standing by a bed in what might have once been a living room. Lying on his side on the bed, knees drawn up, was a man so like Bass in appearance that Matt guessed they were twins. A husky woman, her face deeply pocked from burnt-out acne, sat in a wooden rocker in one corner of the room, breast-feeding an unkempt infant who looked as if it might be battling the same germ as Samuel. Rake, pale and sweating, was obviously ill and in pain.

'This here's my brother, Rake,' Bass said as the bald one unlocked Matt's manacle. 'He's been sick for a couple a weeks with like a cancer on his back. If you're really a doctor, fix him up. If you ain't, I'm gonna put yer eyes out, for starters.'

'You're going to kill me anyway,' Matt said.

The moment he spoke the words, he knew they were a mistake. Moving like a cobra strike, Bass snatched him by the shirt again, this time lifting his toes clear of the floor.

'Don't fuck with me,' he rasped. 'And don't fuck with my brother neither.'

'Okay, okay. Put me down.'

Praying his instincts about Rake's problem were correct, Matt walked around the bed and drew down the sheet. It was as he'd suspected, a gigantic abscess of a congenital remnant, known as a pilonidal cyst, located directly over the tailbone just above the crack between Rake's enormous buttocks. Partially obscuring the abscess, which was six inches from top to bottom and almost certainly down to bone, was a large, geometric tattoo that looked like something drawn with a Spirograph.

'I can fix this,' Matt said.

'Ain't no one can fix cancer,' one of the bikers said.

'Shut up,' Bass snapped.

'This isn't cancer,' Matt replied. 'It's infection. I need to open it up and wash the pus out. You have anything like a bathtub here? I mean one with hot water. It's got to be big enough for him to fit into.'

'Tub's back there,' Bass said. 'We kin get plenty a hot water from . . . we got it.'

'And soap, like the kind you wash dishes with.'

Bass looked over at the nursing mother, who nodded.

'We got that,' he said.

'And some rags, a lot of them – the cleaner the better.'

Another look, another nod, this time in the direction of the kitchen. One of the bikers went in there and returned quickly with a small armload of rags. He set them where Matt indicated at the foot of the bed.

'Okay, I need a knife – a sharp one.'

In an instant, all three bikers had produced blades from nearly invisible sheaths, the smallest of which was half a foot or better.

'Pick one an' don't do nothin' stupid,' Bass warned.

Matt chose the smallest knife and hefted it in his hand, examining the point at the same time.

'Finally, I need some hot, soapy water,' he said. 'Half a pail.'

Bass grunted something, and in a minute, the bald biker had left, returned, and set a bucket half filled with sudsy water at Matt's feet.

'Tell him this is going to hurt like hell,' Matt said. 'A little while after I'm done, much of the pain he's been having should go away.'

'You hear that?'

'Tell him to do whatever the fuck he has to,' Rake groaned.

Given what awaited within Rake's infected

pilonidal cyst, there was no sense in bothering to sterilize the knife or his skin. Matt wrapped a cloth around the blade and held it in place about an inch from the tip.

'Okay, Rake. Ready . . . and . . . now!'

He thrust the knife straight in and pulled it straight down through the tattoo, almost two inches. Rake hissed through clenched teeth, but made no other sound. Bloody, foul-smelling pus, under tremendous pressure, spewed from the wound. Much of it hit the cloth surrounding the blade. Some of it actually spattered Matt.

'Soon as he can move, get him into the tub of hot, soapy water,' Matt ordered, cleaning the wound out as best he could and rinsing his hands in the bucket of water. 'It might sting, but it'll help a lot. Does anybody here have any antibiotics? Now that the infection is open, they might help.'

'You're a shitty liar,' Bass said. 'Becky already told me what you did with Samuel.'

Obviously anticipating the need, he tossed over the pillowcase of purloined medications, and Matt selected out the most powerful of them.

'Two of these four times today,' he said, wondering if being caught in this particular lie was a minus or a plus, 'then one four times a day. He really should be seen at a hospital, but even if you don't take him, this cavity should heal from the inside over two weeks, three tops. Send someone to a store for ten or twelve bottles of peroxide and some gauze bandages. You can wash out the hole with the peroxide and then pack it with the gauze.' He glanced down at his unprotected hands and added, 'Get a few boxes of rubber gloves, too.'

He hesitated, carefully choosing the words to

make a sort of deal with Bass. Before he could speak, though, without a word of thanks or warning, Bass motioned with a jerk of his head, and Matt was unceremoniously pulled, almost dragged, from the house and returned to the shed.

'Wait a minute,' he complained as Shaved Head locked his cuff back onto the copper pipe. 'Wait one fucking minute. I just saved that man's life. No questions asked. Listen, I need to get out of here. My friends are going to die if I don't. Tell Bass I won't ever say anything to anyone about having been here. I promise.' The bikers were already headed out. 'Stop! This isn't fair! I saved your friend's life!' He was railing at the inside of the closed door. 'Goddamn it.'

Matt kicked the wall and made yet another fruitless attempt to pull the pipe free. No chance. He was as good as dead. If they let him live, it would only be to care for the cavity he had created in Rake's back.

'You bastards!' he yelled. 'Ungrateful bastards!'

He slumped down onto his bed of oily rags, pulled the blanket over him, and closed his eyes. Nikki and the others had virtually no chance now, either. For a time he thought about slow suffocation. Breathing gets more difficult, you feel sleepy, you lay down and close your eyes, you don't wake up. There were certainly worse ways to die, probably including whatever the bikers had in store for him.

Time passed. He might have actually dozed off when the door flew open again. Bass stood there as he had initially, all but blocking out the scene behind him. But this time there was a difference. This time his left hand was behind his back and his

461

massive right paw, dangling loosely at his side, had a gun nestled in it.

'Shit. Bass, don't do this,' Matt begged in a half whisper. 'I won't tell anyone about you. I promise.'

'You better mean that,' Bass growled. 'It's a good thing fer you yer such a crummy liar.'

He bent down and skimmed Matt's pistol across the floor to where he lay. Matt hadn't fully absorbed the significance of the gesture when the key to the handcuffs followed along with a pair of dry jeans and a work shirt. Without another word, Bass turned and left the shack.

Standing in his stead, taking up considerably less space, was Frank Slocumb.

462

Chapter 35

'Ain't it jes the balls, Lewis? Har this boy survives a friggin' mine cave-in, goes o'er a thirty-foot unner-ground waterfall, an' then ends up gittin' hisself captured by Bass Vernon an' his lunatic gang.'

'Y'are somethin',' Lewis Slocumb said to Matt.

Lewis, his jury-rigged chest tube pinned to his shirt, sat crammed between his brother Frank and Matt in the cab of their battered 1940-something red Ford pickup. In the back, amidst boxes and tarps, was younger brother Lyle. Kyle had been left to guard their farm.

'Frank,' Matt said, still giddy from his close call with the bikers, 'except maybe for when you popped out of your mother's womb, I swear no one has ever been happier to see you than I was back there.'

'Who sez Mammy 'uz happy?' Lewis chimed in. 'She 'bout slit her throat when she first saw him.'

'An' she 'bout slit yourn when she saw yew.'

Matt joined in their laughter. It was just past ten on a heavily overcast morning. The truck had been jouncing up a steep, rutted dirt road for nearly half an hour, circling the mountain that contained both the Belinda mine and the toxic storage dump.

'Ya done took yerself quat a trip, Matthew,' Frank said. 'Five mile allagether, mebbe six from whar ya started ta whar Vernon's people foun' ya. You are some lucky man.'

'I thought I was dead going over the falls, then I really thought I was dead when Bass came in with that friggin' gun in his hand.'

'Thet's his way. Bass is crazy as a bedbug. Mean, too, dependin' on whut drugs he bin takin'. Ah don' know if'n Ah ever seed him let someone go after they done been ta his camp. You, Lewis?'

' 'Ceptin' us,' Lewis said.

'He knowed we mak the best damn hooch inna valley. We got no intrest in the stuff they grow in thet hellhole. But they got more guns an' ammo than the U.S. Army, an' we're always intrested in thangs thet go bang.' Again he and Lewis laughed heartily. 'O'er the years they come ta trust us – leastways, much as Bass is capble a trustin' anyone. Ya musta done somethin' purdy special fer him ta b'lieve us thet ya kin be trusted, an' let yer ass go.'

'I saved Rake's life,' Matt said simply.

'Ain't no one's gonna give ya no medal fer thet,' Lewis said.

Matt checked his watch. There had to be enough air in the cave to get Nikki and the others this far. He prayed that Nikki or Ellen hadn't given up on him and tried to get out via the river. It was doubtful the gods would let two survive that trip in a single morning.

'How much longer?' he asked.

'Almos' there,' Frank said. 'They's no way ta git direct from Vernon's place ta the tunnel we plan on usin'.'

'And Vernon explained what I needed? I mean, you brought some explosives?'

Frank smiled.

'Ah think ya kin say thet,' Lewis replied.

'Wha d'ya think Ah been drivin' so slow,' Frank added.

Matt gulped and looked back through the window at Lyle, who was stretched out calmly among the bundles, smoking a cigarette.

'I owe you guys big-time,' Matt said.

They drove the last quarter mile off-road, weaving through the trees and rolling over roots. At the spot Frank pulled over, there was no hint of a tunnel along the rocky base of the broad, wooded hill.

'Where are we going from here?' Matt asked as they unloaded two large rucksacks from the truck, as well as two smaller nylon bags and a long, khaki canvas bag with a U.S. Army insignia stenciled on it.

'Jes 'cause ya cain't see somethin' don't mean it ain't there,' Frank said, passing Matt one of the large backpacks and two thick coils of rope. 'They's a bunch a entrances inta this here moun'in. Trick is ta know which one of 'em end suddenly in big, deep holes.'

Only Lewis wasn't loaded down as the four of them made their way across twenty yards of shrub- and leaf-covered ground to the hill. Matt felt his excitement beginning to surge at the prospect of seeing Nikki alive.

Hang on, baby. Just a little longer.

This entrance to the tunnel, completely obscured behind an outcropping of rock, was no more than four feet from top to bottom – a jagged crack large enough to admit a person on hands and knees, but certainly not one with a pack. They piled their gear by the entry, and Matt and Frank made their way inside, each pulling one end of rope. Matt was not the least surprised to realize that his pulse remained relatively slow and stable, despite the tight passageway.

Step right up and get it, ladies and gentlemen, Dr. Rutledge's Famous Cure for Claustrophobia.

Guided by powerful flashlights, they made their way thirty feet along the narrow tunnel before arriving at a vestibule high enough to stand and wide enough for all of them and their gear. Frank tied the ropes together, forming one end of a long loop, with enough cord extending from the knot to lash onto a strap. Lewis was doing the same outside. One piece at a time, they hauled their gear in, while the empty cord was returned to Lewis and Lyle for reloading.

Hurry! Matt wanted desperately to yell out. Hurry!

The trip into the mountain by this route seemed longer and narrower than the one from the cleft, but there were no drop-offs and no water until they passed over the river on some planks near the very end of their journey.

Ten-forty.

The landscape of what used to be the entrance to the toxic dump had been completely transformed. Much of the overhead wall had collapsed, making a new cave outside the old one. The ceiling of the new cave, perhaps twenty feet above them, could be reached by climbing up a wall of rock that was just ten degrees or so short of vertical. The floor was littered with rubble but passable, and some of the right-hand wall had collapsed, leaving a strangely smooth gouge that looked as if it had been produced with a giant ice-cream scoop.

'Oooeee,' Frank said, inspecting the massive front wall. 'Them boys 'uz playin' fer keeps.'

Matt felt sick. He had images of putting a stick of dynamite among some boulders, lighting a match, and blowing a new entrance to the cavern. *Piece of cake*.

As if reading his thoughts, Lewis put a hand on his shoulder.

'We'll git in thar fer ya, Matthew,' he said.

Largely in silence, the three Slocumbs functioned like a highly skilled military unit. Lyle set out several kerosene lanterns, making the space nearly daylight bright, and then began unpacking their gear. Lewis, hands on hips, slightly short of breath, watched as Frank scuttled to the top of the pile of rock, then across from one side to the other.

'You'd best be darn good, Lewis,' he called as he scrambled back down the wall.

'Ah am,' Lewis replied simply. 'Okay, Matthew, here's the deal. This here's the head-wall. It's lak a plug whar there useta be a hole. Ain't no big trouble blowin' it up. The trick is ta do it without killin' us an' anyone whut mot be behin' it.'

'But you think you can?'

'Ah think Ah kin try. Ain't no one kin do more'n thet. Lyle, lis'n up. I wanna soften up this here baby with a shell from Little Bertha, jes 'bout two-thirds a the way up. Kin ya hit thet big, pointy rock rot thar?'

'From whar?'

'Far 'nuff back so's ya don' git kilt, Lyle.'

Lyle scanned the cave.

'No sweat,' he proclaimed. 'They's a spot ta shoot from rot back thar.'

He opened up the long army-issue bag, removed a compact rocket launcher, and began preparing it to be fired.

'Ain't she a beauty,' Lewis said to Matt. 'A Javelin Anti-tank Missile with HEAT – hah-explosive antitank warhead. It'll penetrate more'n twenny inch a armor. Jes far an' ferget – thet means ferget whut yer shootin' at an' ferget about standin' round ta watch. Range a twenny-fahve hunnerd meter. Thet's goin' on two mile.'

'Jesus, Lewis. How'd you guys get this?'

Lewis replied with a wry look that said, 'Ya know better'n ta ask a queschin ya really don' want ta know the answer to.'

'Frank,' he said, 'les you an' me git the Gel-Paks ready. Three rows up an' down, beginnin' with a pound at the very top an' finishin' with, say, ten pound at the bottom. We'll use det cord ta link 'em up.'

Frank quickly produced several dozen sausage-like packages from one of the rucksacks and laid them on a tarp by Lewis, along with the detonating cord. Skillfully, the brothers began linking them together.

'Ready,' Lyle called out.

Frank dragged the Gel-Paks away from the target and threw another tarp over them.

'This way, Doc,' Lewis said, leading him and Frank back into the tunnel until they couldn't even see the head-wall. 'It'd be fun ta watch this, but it'd also be a mot dangerous. Ah s'pect Lyle'll be back here purdy darn quick, too.'

Matt heard a loud *woosh* from around the bend, followed by Lyle diving headfirst at their feet. At the same instant a sharp, near-deafening explosion resonated through the tunnel, followed by the clattering of rock. When Lewis nodded that it was okay to revisit the head-wall, they found the center of it largely pulverized, and the topmost rocks displaced and loosened.

'I'd hate to see *Big* Bertha,' Matt muttered.

'Fahn shot, Lyle,' Lewis said. 'Ah guess they's hope fer ya yet. Frank, les git these here sausages in place an' mak us a hole.' He turned to Matt. 'We're gonna use de-lay detinaters ta blow this here thang so's it clapses from the bottom up. If'n we do it rot, a space oughta 'pear et the top. If'n we miss, it had best be on the sod a too little rather'n too much. If'n we don' git no hole the first tom, we got enuff Vibrogel ta try it again. Mebbe twice more.'

'Hurry,' Matt said, in spite of himself.

'Wha on earth 'uld we e'er want ta tak our tom?' Lewis replied. 'Ah mean, t'ain't lak we're workin' with hah explosives er nothin'.'

'Sorry.'

'Ah thank Ah'm ready,' Frank said, looping the det cord around his elbow before he ascended the wall.

'Ready for what, pervert?'

Bill Grimes, his service revolver leveled at the four of them, stepped into the cave from the tunnel, followed immediately by Vinny Sutcher, still in black, who casually panned the group with a submachine gun. Last to step into view, his gun also at the ready, was the thin man Matt had outwitted at Shady Lake Manor Estates.

'See, Vinny,' Grimes said. 'I told you it was worthwhile having you and Verne hang around for a day checking the entrances to this place. This here doctor is as slippery as an eel.'

'What an imaginative metaphor,' Matt said, noticing how incredibly calm Lewis Slocumb and

469

his brothers appeared at that moment. He had no way of knowing for certain, but he felt some sort of information was being silently exchanged among them.

Grimes may have sensed the same thing. His expression darkened, and his heavy pistol steadied on Lewis.

'Step away from that stuff, Slocumb. Your brother, too,' he said. 'Vinny, get around there and move that shit away.'

Sutcher shouldered his weapon, circled around to the base of the head-wall, and eyed the pile of Gel-Paks suspiciously.

'Ya'd best not e'en fart near thet stuff,' Lewis said, mimicking an explosion with his hands. 'Ka-boom.'

Frank, who was about ten feet to Lewis's right, and Lyle, who was on one knee about fifteen feet behind him, both snickered.

'So,' Grimes said, turning his attention to Matt, 'I must conclude from your presence here that you are not the only one who managed to survive that devastating accident.'

'They've all escaped except the guards you double-crossed,' Matt replied, sensing he needed to stall. 'We're digging those two out because they both swore to kill you if they ever saw you again. What are you, Grimes, some sort of major stock-holder in the company that makes Lasaject? Is that what's going on?'

Surprise flashed across the policeman's face, then just as quickly vanished.

'Oh, yes,' he said. 'Mrs. Kroft. Well, if you must know, I have a proprietary interest in the company, yes.'

'Do you know how many people – how many

children – will die if that vaccine of yours gets into general use?'

'There's no proof that's so.'

'Spare me. Those people you tried to kill in there are proof, and you know it. That's why you did this to them. Well, Grimes, they've escaped just like me. They're headed to Washington right now, along with Ellen Kroft and Nikki. You're finished.'

Matt saw uncertainty in the man's eyes.

'I don't believe you,' Grimes said. 'We'll deal with the problems in there as soon as we've dealt with the problems right here. Verne, pat each one of them down, beginning with that one back there. Then get them together over in that corner. Then the good doctor and I need to have a little chat. If any of them give you any crap, shoot 'em in the knee. We'll save the other knee and the balls for later.'

'Don't ferget ta check me fer rocket launchers,' Lyle said, choking himself on a laugh.

Despite the obvious advantage his side held in terms of weapons and age, Verne approached Lyle cautiously.

'Stand up,' he ordered.

'Cain't,' Lyle said. 'Ma laig's broke.'

'If he doesn't do as you tell him to, just kill him,' Grimes said. 'He's not going to hurt you, Verne. He's a fucking old man and you have the gun.'

'Yeah,' Lyle said, 'Ah'm a fuckin' old man.'

He smiled toothlessly and shifted his weight as if he was going to stand.

At that instant, there was a scraping sound from high on the head-wall. All seven of those below turned to the noise. Ellen, a gaunt, dusty apparition, was standing straight up, twenty feet directly above

471

Vinny Sutcher. The broad, flat rock she was holding over her head looked as big as her chest. At the moment Grimes spun and fired at her, she hurled the rock with all her strength, straight down at Sutcher. With his head tilted back, the heavy missile caught him flush in the face, producing the sickening sound of a pumpkin dropped onto pavement from a second story. Instantly limp, blood spattered across his face, Sutcher crumpled backward onto the stony floor.

The seconds that followed were a blur to Matt. He was still fumbling for the gun in his pocket when all three Slocumb brothers produced pistols, seemingly out of thin air. Instantly, the cavern sounded like a Chinese New Year. Gunshots seemed to be coming from everywhere. But the only muzzle flashes Matt saw came from the Slocumbs. Grimes was instantly hit in the chest, neck, and face. His eyes wide with disbelief, he danced sideways like a giant marionette, arms flapping, legs disjointed. Then he crumpled as if his strings had been sliced, held a sitting position for a single beat, and toppled lifelessly onto the dust. Verne caught bullets in his throat, mouth, and the center of his forehead, and was dead before he hit the floor.

Matt raced over to the head-wall. Above him, Ellen was down, but he could see that she was moving.

'Ellen?'

'I'm okay,' she called back. 'I slipped when I threw the rock. My pride's going to hurt when I sit, but otherwise I'm not hurt badly.'

'Is Nikki all right?'

'She's back there with the others. It's slow going with her ankle. I think it's broken.'

'Is there enough air in there?'

'There is now, thanks to whoever created that hole.'

Ellen began making her way down to where Matt waited. Vinny Sutcher lay at his feet, deeply unconscious, breathing shallowly and intermittently. His broad pancake face was a pulpy mass, his eyes obscured beneath twin pools of blood. His head was cocked at a sharp angle, leading Matt to suspect that his neck had been fractured. Ellen moved in beside him, her jaw tightly set, her eyes fixed on the horrific damage she had wrought. Then, without a word, she bent down and, with great effort, picked up the rock again and leveled it over Sutcher's face.

'Ellen, don't,' Matt urged. 'It's over. Trust me, it's over.'

Tears glistened through the dust on Ellen's cheeks. Her arms were shaking from the effort of holding the rock. Sobbing, she turned and dropped it to the floor, where it split in two. Matt put his arms around her and held her. A few seconds later, Sutcher took a single, shuddering gasp, and stopped breathing forever.

Matt led Ellen over to where Frank was once again arranging the Gel-Paks, and introduced the two.

'I'm going in to see Nikki,' he said.

Ellen pointed to his watch. 'Matt, listen. That first shot of Omnivax is going to be given to that baby in a little over three hours. As soon as it is, other kids all over the country are going to start getting it. We've got to stop them.'

'Is there someone we can call?'

'This is the biggest campaign stunt of this election. I don't know anyone in a position to rein in the First Lady at this point. Do you?'

'No. We could try calling in a bomb threat.'

'I hate that idea, but I suppose we could try it if we absolutely had to. I can see us accomplishing nothing except to give them more publicity and land us in serious hot water.'

'If they go ahead with the shot, how many kids do you think will be vaccinated by the end of the day?'

'I really can't do more than guess,' Ellen replied, 'but I think it could be lots, especially on the West Coast, where pediatricians' offices will be open three hours later than the ones on the East Coast. Thanks to the President's publicity people, the papers are calling today's injection The Shot Heard Round the World. The public and the pediatricians just love vaccines. Omnivax is the most eagerly awaited advance in immunizations in decades, but it's been made clear that even though tens of thousands of doses have been shipped to offices and clinics around the country, administering it to patients won't be legal until after Lynette Marquand and Secretary Bolton have had their worldwide TV photo op. So . . . What? Maybe a few thousand doses by the end of the day? Maybe more. Who knows?'

'With a three percent prion infection rate.'

'Or more.'

'Or more,' Matt echoed.

He peered up at the hole high on the rock wall and made his decision.

'My Harley's at my Uncle Hal's place. I can probably get you to D.C. on time, but I don't want to leave before I see Nikki. We've been through too much together.'

'I understand, but please, let's get going as soon as you can.'

'We will.'

'And Matt, I apologize for getting so wrapped up in my issues just now. I'm sorry about your uncle. I really am.'

'Thanks. Me, too. Lewis, can you wait a little before setting off those charges?'

'Ain't no place we got ta be. We don' 'specially need Lyle, neither. He kin drahve ya ta yer bike.'

'Great. Lewis, tell me something. How on earth did you guys get your guns out so fast?'

Grinning broadly, Lewis pulled up the sleeve of his jacket, revealing an arrangement of leather straps and springs.

'Ma brother Frank, thar, invented this here gizmo a couple a year ago an' built one fer each a us. We ain't really got ta use 'em, but we put 'em on taday 'cause we jes don' truss Bass Vernon much. An' the older we git, the more careful we git. That rot, Frank?'

'Thassit.'

'So that's why you guys were looking at each other like you had a secret.'

'We knowed somethin' they dint, thet's fer sure,' Lewis said. 'The moment Grimes tol' his boy thar ta git our guns an' dint jes pull the trigger, we knowed he 'uz a dead man, providin' Frank's gizmo worked the way it's s'pose ta.'

'And did it ever. Ellen, I'll be right back. We'll make it. My uncle's place isn't too far from here. His girlfriend is away, but I know where he keeps a spare key.'

'Good, because there's someone I need to call.'

'I'll be back.'

Matt was halfway up the head-wall when he heard Nikki's voice.

'Hey, sailor, come up here and get your Red Cross advanced swimmer's badge.'

Looking about as grungy and disheveled as a person could, she sat perched on a slab to one side of the rent Lewis had made in the massive wall. Matt hustled to her side and kissed her unabashedly.

'I knew you'd make it,' she said. 'I just knew it.'

'You did not.'

'Okay, I didn't. But you made it just the same, and that's what counts.'

'How's your ankle?'

'Better now than it was a few minutes ago. You know any decent orthopedists?'

'As a matter of fact, I do. How many people are still alive down there?'

'Believe it or not, all the ones that were alive when you left.'

'Even Fred?'

'He's actually a little better. I did a trach on Colin.'

'Incredible. You dun need no steenking OR.'

Nikki looked down at the three bodies sprawled in blood amid the stones and dust.

'Did you do that?' she asked.

'In my mind I did, especially Grimes. But I didn't even get a shot off.'

'I never trusted that Vinny.'

'I know. Listen, it's almost noon. Let me help you down. I've got to get Ellen to D.C.'

'Oh, yes, that first shot is due this afternoon. Hurry. I can get down myself.'

'You can let me help you.'

It was a slow, awkward descent. When they finally reached the bottom, Matt carried her to a safe spot in the tunnel and set her down. Even beneath the bandage he had applied, he could feel the enormous swelling in her ankle. He kissed her hand, then her neck, and finally her lips.

'You think you might like to, I don't know, hang with me after I get back?'

'Only if you promise me we get to do something really, really dull.'

'I promise.'

They kissed once more before he headed back to Ellen. As he passed Grimes's bullet-riddled body, he paused.

'See, I told you there was proof,' he said.

Chapter 36

Clearly pleased with the responsibility Lewis had bestowed on him, Lyle Slocumb hopped up behind the wheel of the old Ford pickup. Matt saw Ellen mulling over how best to negotiate the gearshift protruding up from the floorboards and saved her the maneuvering by taking the center seat.

'I could have handled it,' she said, sliding in beside him.

'Hey, after watching what you did with that rock, I would say you can handle just about anything. I just figured since me and Lyle have known each other from when I was a boy, he might enjoy rubbing elbows with me.'

'Yer nuts,' Lyle said.

'Yes, and don't you ever forget it.'

As they pulled away, Matt looked back toward the mountain, feeling an odd mix of horror, relief, and foolishness. True, there was a toxic waste dump just as he'd suspected. Soon the mine owners were going to be exposed for the callous, unscrupulous profit-mongers they were, and the cave would be cleaned out. But his narrow-mindedness regarding the mine owners and the cause of the Belinda syndrome had kept him from the truth and had, to some degree, cost lives – most notably for him, his godfather's. He also knew that there was going to be trouble for Lewis and his brothers. The Slocumbs had become legendary for their mysterious, hermit-like existence. Now, unless a way could be found to dissociate them from the carnage in the tunnel, there was going to be publicity, inquisitions, and scrutiny, and probably weapons charges as well.

Inwardly, he shrugged. He had done what he thought was right and had tried his best. That was the way he had been taught to live his life. There was nothing more he could ask of himself. But there was also no hiding the fact that his exuberance about the mine had almost enabled Grimes and his Lasaject cronies to pull off their lethal deception. Over time, he would have to deal with the way he had handled matters, perhaps with Nikki's help. For the moment, though, it was essential to focus on other things. All that mattered right now was beating the clock to Washington, and placing Ellen in a position to stop the initial injection of Omnivax and all subsequent injections as well.

Three percent.

The figure reverberated in his mind. Three percent of tens of thousands – biological time bombs with an untreatable, communicable disease that had no diagnostic test and didn't manifest itself for a decade or more.

Three percent.

'It'll be close, but we'll make it before that first shot is given,' he pledged.

'Not if we try too hard and end up as roadkill.'

'Okay, okay. I'll introduce myself to the speed limit. Have you ever been on a motorcycle?'

'Once.'

'And?'

'I've been around for a long time, Doctor. Over those years, there have been plenty of motorcycling

479

opportunities. Doesn't my saying "once" tell you anything?'

Matt grinned.

'You'll love my bike, Ellen. I promise. Lyle, make the next left. My uncle's road is about three miles from here.'

'Ya got it,' Lyle said.

Studying the man – thinning gray hair, aquiline nose, weathered skin, engaging, toothless smile – Matt wondered if Lyle, or any of the brothers, for that matter, had ever had a driver's license. They were certainly a strange lot, but they also seemed to be living lives that were quite fulfilled on many levels. And now, once again, Matt owed them his life. Becoming their friend was certainly an unmerited gift of that bicycle ride to their house so many years ago.

'Know whar the key ta yer bike is, Doc?' Lyle asked.

'In the kitchen on the counter.'

'Jes in case, Ah'll wait round 'til Ah'm sure ya foun it.'

'Thanks, pal. So, Ellen, what's our plan once we get to D.C.?'

'I don't really know. The community health center is in the Anacostia section of the city. I suspect security will be exceedingly tight, what with the First Lady there and everything else that's been going on since nine-eleven. I don't know anyone I could call, and I don't think phoning someone would accomplish anything in time. But once the people at the clinic see that I'm no menace and hear who I am, and assure themselves that the wild man who's with me is no threat, I imagine they'll let me speak with someone in authority. Whether whoever *that* is believes us in time or not is another story. There's a heck of a lot of votes at stake here, and I'm sure the last thing the Marquand camp needs is something that looks like a screwup on their part.'

'Maybe you can get in front of the cameras to explain what's happening.'

'I doubt it, but I suppose anything's possible. The bottom line is, we've got to get there in time to find someone who'll listen to me.'

'If we don't, doctors all over get the green light to start shooting Omnivax.'

'Four days to two weeks old,' Ellen said. 'That's the age range where Secretary Bolton says they're going to start administering the inoculations. But soon, Omnivax will be available to all.'

'Oh, that's just great.'

'They're justifying that decision by stating that except for those who are allergic, there's no evidence that being overimmunized is dangerous.'

'And every single man, woman, and child in this country should be grateful for the protection against Lassa fever.'

Ellen laughed sardonically. 'Exactly,' she said.

'But nobody's ever studied the adverse effects of vaccinations over the long term.'

'Not in any organized study that I'm aware of.'

'I feel like I've been such a medical ostrich about this stuff.'

'Believe me, you have company. It's not that on balance vaccinations do more harm than good. It's just that no one really knows.'

'Well, then, let's get us to Washington. Lyle, that's Grandview Road, right there. Hang a left. The house is at the very end. Wait until you guys see my uncle's place. You won't have any trouble understanding why they named the street Grandview.'

The road remained paved throughout. Hal's house was at the end of a long, gravel driveway that cut through a peninsula covered with low-lying shrubs and scattered pines.

'I'm sure coming here like this will be hard for you,' Ellen said.

'I still can't believe this has happened. Hal's always been very good to me and my mother. I'll miss him, and I know she will, too.'

Matt decided against going into any details about his mother's deteriorating mental state.

The thin woods gave way to a broad, beautifully landscaped lot, at the end of which was Hal's expansive lodge, perched on a promontory two hundred feet above a large, pristine lake.

'Magnificent,' Ellen whispered reverently. 'Just beautiful.'

'Wait! Stop!' Matt cried.

Lyle skidded to a halt.

'What is it?' Ellen asked.

'There, parked in the driveway on the side. That's my uncle's car.'

'So?'

'Something's wrong. He drove us to the mine last night. If he's buried there, how did the car get back here? Lyle, do you have your gun? I left mine with Lewis so that we wouldn't have any trouble with the security people in D.C.'

'Frank's got m' pistol, but they's a shotgun in the back.'

'Bring it, please.'

Cautiously, the three of them approached the lodge.

'Look!' Ellen exclaimed in a loud whisper.

Through the broad living room window, they could see a man polishing a vase.

'That's Hal! That's my uncle,' Matt said. 'Lyle, stand over there and keep the door covered. I . . . don't know what's going on.'

His confusion did not last long.

He was moving toward the front door when it opened. Hal, nattily dressed in white trousers and a light blue button-down shirt, stepped out onto the low front porch. At the sight of the man, showered, relaxed, and clear-eyed, Matt knew.

'Matthew! God, I'm so relieved to see you. I've been worried sick about you since the explosion. I've called the police and –'

'Pardon me for saying it, Hal, but you don't seem very frantic. In fact, you look downright rested – not at all like someone who's spent the last twelve hours trying to get his nephew rescued from a mine explosion.'

'I've made many desperate phone calls for help, Matthew. I –'

There was no sincerity in his words. Matt's lingering disbelief vanished.

'Can it, Hal,' he snapped. 'You're demeaning yourself. You know what's been bothering me ever since we figured out that the Lassa vaccine was really behind those deaths? Grimes. That's what's been bothering me, Hal. He's not exactly a dope, but he's no Einstein, either. I couldn't understand how a man like that could have gotten involved with the manufacture of Lasaject in the first place. Then he goes and masterminds an epidemic to get his vaccine included in Omnivax; then he discovers that the vaccine has a fatal flaw; and finally, he sets about systematically destroying all the evidence of that flaw. That make any sense to you, Hal, that he was capable of doing that?'

Hal looked as if he was about to issue another denial, then he shrugged nonchalantly.

'Grimes is a jerk,' he said. 'A violent and avaricious jerk, and therefore quite useful to me, but a jerk nonetheless.'

Hearing his uncle openly admit what he had done brought Matt a wave of sadness. 'When did you first learn about the prion disease?' he asked.

'Not that long ago, really. Would you please tell your friend to stop pointing that thing at me?'

'No. Go on.'

'Well, two cases were brought to me for autopsy a couple of weeks apart. One had killed herself, the other had been shot in a bar fight. I recognized the names from our initial field trials and began to suspect that was the connection. Then you got involved with that miner, Rideout, and I was certain. Lasaject was too close to being included in the supervaccine to allow anyone to stumble on the connection, so I simply had to identify those unfortunates who had the side effect and send the late Mr. Grimes and his people to deal with them. I assume he is late.'

'Actually, he's very much alive and talking to the state police right now.'

'Nephew, nephew, you never were a very good liar. And Mr. Sutcher?'

'Well, let's just say things got a little rocky for him.'

Matt glanced over at Ellen.

'Ah,' said Hal, 'the redoubtable Mrs. Kroft, yes?'

'A lot of people are dead because of you,' Ellen said icily.

'Life can be very hard sometimes.'

'Jesus, Hal, who in the hell are you?'

'Just a guy trying to make ends meet. You want to come in for some tea? Of course, I don't allow shotguns in the house. Or better still, why don't you all just leave.'

'Hal, we're not going anyplace until you're tied up and waiting for the state police.'

'Well, I simply can't permit that,' Hall said, with disturbing, singsong confidence. 'So I suppose I'm going to have to dispose of you all, beginning with your friend who insists on pointing that gun at me. You're a Slocumb, I presume?'

'Ah surely am,' Lyle said proudly.

The words were barely past his lips when a shot exploded from where Hal's car was parked, driving Lyle backward into the fender of the truck, clutching his belly. He managed a single, wild shot before he dropped the shotgun, stumbled, and fell heavily on his side.

Standing by the garage, smirking, was Larry, the massive killer Matt was supposed to have murdered, then incinerated.

Matt was just turning to help Lyle when Larry shot the man again, this time in the chest. Lyle, who had been up on one elbow, slumped back onto the gravel and was still. Comfortable with his handiwork, the killer turned the gun on Matt.

'I've been waiting for this chance,' he said. 'You'll never know how much I've been waiting.'

Matt felt his heart stop as he saw the man's sausagelike finger tighten on the trigger.

'No!' he cried.

'Larry, wait!' Hal ordered. 'I'll tell you when.'

Matt felt his knees about to buckle, but beside

him, Ellen stood her ground defiantly and even put her arm through his.

'Killing us won't solve any of your problems,' she said to Hal. 'Too many people know.'

'Would you care to give me a list of them, Mrs. Kroft? I didn't think so. But please, don't worry. I can take care of myself. Matthew, I'm sorry about this, really I am. You know I care for you a great deal. Always have. But this is business, and you have become a definite liability. As you see, my man Larry, here, is very much alive. Believe it or not, I conjured up that murder-incineration story on the spot, with you hanging on the other end of the line and Dr. Solari about to visit the FBI. Brilliant, don't you think?'

'You're sick,' Matt said.

'Now, Larry, here, is very anxious to shoot you, but I am a sporting man, as well as one who doesn't want bodies with bullet holes floating around in the lake. That wouldn't appear very accidental. So, I am perfectly willing to have you and Mrs. Kroft step over that fence' – he indicated the split-rail fencing that paralleled the side of the drive – 'and step off the edge. Who knows, maybe you'll miss the rocks.'

'Give it up, Hal,' Matt said, regaining a modicum of composure. 'There're way too many loose ends that are all tied to you. You know, you can still come off looking like a hero in this business by telling the police you are blowing the whistle on Lasaject in order to save all those unborn children from spongiform encephalopathy.'

At that moment, out of the corner of his eye, Matt saw movement from the direction of the truck. *Lyle!*

'The bullet or the drop, Matthew?' Hal was asking. 'Your choice.'

Frantic to stall and keep Hal's and Larry's attention fixed on him, Matt rejected the notion of some sort of outburst in favor of pandering to Hal's ego.

'Hal, tell me one thing,' he said, 'that was you who slipped that note about the toxic dump under my door, wasn't it?'

Hal sighed and nodded with exaggerated modesty.

'If you really must know, yes. I am aware of pretty much everything that goes on around here, and I knew about that unusual – um – storage facility almost as soon as it was established. I sent the note to you figuring that as long as you were chasing after your vendetta against the mine, you were no threat to my interests. Brilliant, no?'

Lyle had moved under the open door of the truck and was pulling himself inside. Matt took a step toward his uncle. Larry moved forward to intervene, his pistol ready.

'Oh, give me a break,' Matt cried, raising his voice angrily. 'You're not nearly as brilliant as you think. You've made one miscalculation after another.' He laughed loudly. 'Man, you must have swallowed your gum when Nikki Solari arrived in town. That's where you and Grimes blew it. You should have just let her go back to Boston. You got worried that if somehow word got to me about Kathy Wilson, there was every chance I'd start looking for explanations other than the mine, and figure out the truth. So you went after her. That was a mistake, Hal. A big mistake.'

More movement. Somehow Lyle had found the strength to drag himself inside the cab.

'Big words for someone in your position,' Hal said, no longer cheery, 'but words for which I have no patience. Now make your choice. Larry, if they don't choose the drop, I want Mrs. Kroft shot first, please.' He pointed to a spot just above his own ear. 'Right here from two feet.'

'You killed all those people for money?' Matt asked stridently, wondering if Lyle was lying dead on the seat of the Ford.

His uncle's smile was coldly patronizing.

'Not for money, nephew,' he said. 'For a great deal of money. I have owned more than forty percent of Columbia Pharmaceuticals for years and I was running out of funds to continue losing on the accursed company. Can you imagine what it's like being my age with my tastes and no money? With what we're being paid per dose of Lasaject, my financial concerns are about to be over. That's over with a capital "O". Now, sir, I have things to do. You have not behaved at all like a respectful godson, and so, from this moment, you have ten seconds to choose your punishment . . . nine.'

'Hal, no, please!' Matt screamed at the moment the truck's engine rumbled to life. 'Stop!'

Larry and Hal whirled toward the noise. Lyle, his eyes virtually closed, the bridge of his nose resting on the steering wheel, threw the Ford into first, floored the accelerator, and popped the clutch. Spewing gravel, the truck shot ahead, straight at Larry. Mouth agape, the massive gunman fired off three shots. The Ford's windshield shattered, and it looked to Matt as if at least one of the bullets had hit Lyle in the forehead. But nothing short of a cement wall was going to stop the truck now. The front bumper caught Larry at the knees. His gun spun to

488

the ground as he was lifted up onto the hood, his moon face not two feet from Lyle, who looked to Matt to be unconscious or dead. Still, Lyle's foot held the gas. The Ford shattered the rail fence, sped through ten feet of shrubbery, and hurtled off the edge of the precipice like a hang glider taking flight. Then, in what seemed like slow motion, the nose of the truck tilted downward, spilling Larry into the void before disappearing. Moments later there was a loud explosion from the rocks below.

By the time Hal Sawyer turned back from the scene, his godson was standing there calmly, with Larry's gun leveled at him.

'Business is very bad, Uncle,' Matt said.

Chapter 37

'Matthew, please, you're not thinking of the greater good. Omnivax will save hundreds of thousands of lives every year. If you block the release of the vaccine, think of all the blood that will be on your hands. Why, you don't even know for certain that Lasaject caused any of those deformities. You're guessing, assuming. . . .'

Hal Sawyer ranted on nonstop as Matt and Ellen used lengths of clothesline to lash him tightly, facedown, on his bed. If someone happened to show up at his home and release him before they had the chance to report things to the state police, so be it. Grimes was gone for good, so were Sutcher and the other killers, Larry and Verne. Hal might try to run, but he wouldn't get very far.

'Darn it, Matthew, this is no way to treat your own flesh and blood! . . . Who's going to visit your mother if I'm not around? . . . *Your mother!* . . . This is going to break her heart, and it's all your fault . . . For crying out loud, Matthew, I'm your godfather. . . . Ellen, Ellen, you're more my generation, explain to my nephew the importance of family. I'm his uncle – genetically, that makes us twenty-five percent of each other. *Twenty-five percent!* That's like selling out a quarter of yourself. . . .'

'We can't make it,' Ellen said, checking Matt's watch. 'We're not even going to be close.'

'We can only do our best,' Matt replied, tightening the cord a bit more than it needed to be. 'We have a shot, depending on the traffic. It'll be closer than you think.'

'Can you do the rest of this yourself?'

'Sure, why?'

'I need to make a phone call before we leave. My friend Rudy will be worried sick about me. Also, he knows people. Maybe there's someone he can call.'

'Quickly, though. I have just another minute or two here, then I want to be on the road. Listen, Hal's girlfriend, Heidi, lives here. Why don't you make a quick rummage through her things for some warm clothes. It can get chilly on the bike.'

It took just seconds for Ellen to appropriate a pair of dark slacks, a sweatshirt, and a leather jacket. She dashed to the kitchen while Matt looped the last length of rope around Hal's ankle, then around the leg at the foot of the bed. He was badly shaken by Lyle Slocumb's death and also by his uncle's remorseless confession. His mother's Alzheimer's disease made her less aware of some things than she once might have been, but she would certainly be aware that her brother no longer came to see her – aware and deeply hurt. In spite of the situation and the urgency of their getting to Washington, he found himself composing explanations that would be gentler on her than the horrible truth.

'You can't leave me here like this,' Hal was bellowing, each plea more desperate, more pathetic than the last. 'What if I have a heart attack? What if I have to pee? In this country we're presumed innocent until proven guilty. Who made you the goddamn judge, jury, and executioner? For Christ's sake, Matthew, listen to me. I've known you since you were born. You can't do this!'

'Hal, where are your car keys?'

'My what?'

'The keys to your car.'

Matt had found his bike in the garage and retrieved the key to it from the kitchen counter. But if he was going to drive 170 miles across Virginia at eighty miles an hour, he would much rather do it in a Mercedes sedan than perched on a Harley with a novice rider, who hated motorcycles, squirming on the seat behind him.

Hal stopped his machine-gun ranting and laughed.

'If I had them you surely wouldn't get them,' he said. 'Not unless you let me go. But thanks to you, I don't have any keys at all.'

'What do you mean?'

'I had only one set – my other one's with Heidi – and my set was in ol' Larry Hogarth's pocket when he made the big swan dive. Too bad.'

'Hal,' Matt said, checking the knots one last time, 'I hope you don't get the pleasure of driving an automobile again for the rest of your life.'

He stopped in the hallway for Hal's fleece-lined leather jacket, hurried to the garage, pulled on his helmet, and revved up the Harley. He had made the drive to Washington in two and a half hours. Cutting fifteen minutes off that time stretched the bounds of possibility, but not past the breaking point. Then he checked the fuel gauge and groaned. Just under half a tank – two and a half gallons at best. At the speed he intended to be going, they would be getting around fifty miles per. There would be no chance to make the trip without stopping. Gassing up would be brief, but rolling into the station, pumping, and rolling out would probably add three minutes, maybe even four. Still, depending on when the actual injection took place and how lucky they were once they reached the clinic, it was still remotely possible.

Ellen raced out of the front door and met him as he was backing the Harley past Hal's Mercedes. Dressed in Heidi's leather jacket and black slacks, she looked every bit the biker.

'Let 'er rip,' she said, climbing up behind him.

'Just pull on your helmet, lean back, relax, hang on, and watch the world go by,' Matt replied, accelerating down the drive. 'Did you reach your friend?'

'No, but I left him a message. Ordinarily he'd be fishing in the pond behind his cabin at this hour. Today I hope he's out pacing about, worrying about why he hasn't heard from me.'

'I'm sure he is. Well, here we go. Second star to the right and straight on 'til morning.'

'Don't worry about me,' Ellen said. 'Just go fast.'

Go fast. . . . Damn you, Hal.

With vivid, lurid images of the victims of the Belinda syndrome in full control of his thoughts, Matt swung onto the highway and hit the gas.

'Sher, the limo's here,' Don called out. 'A white stretch limo, at that. Isn't this something.'

'We're just about ready,' Sherrie called out from the bedroom. 'I want this girl to look her very best for her debut on national TV.'

'*Worldwide* TV,' Don corrected.

He watched as a man and a woman in dress suits, wearing sunglasses, emerged from the limousine

493

and headed up the walk. *Men in Black*, he was thinking.

'Ta-da,' Sherrie sang, holding the baby out to her husband.

'You both look just fine,' Don said, beaming. 'Really fine.' He took the baby and kissed Sherrie on the mouth. 'No one could ever guess you had this baby just four days ago.'

'You're pilin' up some big-time points, sir,' she said, checking out the scene below their window. 'Not every kid has the Secret Service escort them to their baby shots. You ready?'

'Ready as I'll ever be. Even when I was fightin' Golden Gloves, I don't remember being this nervous.'

'You, nervous? What are you nervous about?'

'Believe it or not, the baby.'

Startled, Sherrie turned slowly and looked at him, a shadow of concern darkening her face.

'You mean the shot?'

'Uh-huh.'

She sighed.

'Me, too,' she said. 'I've been afraid to talk with you about it because I was afraid you'd think I was crazy or . . . or ungrateful. I know Mrs. Marquand told us that plenty of people, babies and grown-ups, had received this shot when it was being tested. Still, Donelle's going to be the very first to get it after it's been approved.'

'I know.'

'I was speaking to Andrea last night about her son Randy. He was one in May. He has fits all the time that his doctor says are caused by a reaction he had to one of his baby shots. He has to take medicine, and now Andrea says the medicine is messing him up.'

'I didn't know that. Is the shot one of the ones Donelle's gonna get?'

'It has to be. She's going to get thirty shots at once – all the ones she's ever going to need.'

'I wish we knew more,' Don said.

Sherrie walked across the room and embraced him and their daughter.

'Same here,' she said, just as their Secret Service escorts knocked on the door.

Thankfully, the day was sunny and dry. Matt pushed the Harley as hard as he dared, across the Virginia border, then along rolling two-lane roadways through the lush Shenandoah Mountains and the Appalachians. In less than an hour, they had picked up Route 81 in Staunton, and were headed north toward 66. Matt kept their speed at an even eighty, nudging it up a mile or two when he sensed there were no police around. The windscreen and top-of-the-line shocks made it feel like forty. In Harrisonburg, they took on four gallons and learned that they were about 110 miles from Washington. An hour and thirty minutes remained before the shot heard round the world would be fired.

Depending on the congestion once they hit the city, they had a chance. They picked up I-66 in Middletown and headed east, barreling on through light traffic. Riverton . . . Markham . . . Marshall . . . The Plains . . . bit by bit, they were making up time, closing the gap against the moment when Lara Bolton would trip a switch and inject the first dose of Omnivax into the thigh of a baby girl.

Three percent. Maybe more. Not odds he would ever want to have operating against his child.

On the seat behind him, Ellen sat quietly for most

of the trip, using the handgrips for balance, and occasionally his arms.

'This isn't nearly as unpleasant as I remember,' she yelled as they sped through a particularly spectacular mountain pass.

'I'll help you pick out your first bike,' he hollered back.

For most of the initial hour of their trip, Matt had constantly scanned his rearview mirrors and the road ahead, looking for problems or police. As the day grew brighter and the road more hypnotic, his thoughts drifted to Nikki. He pictured her hunched over Fred Carabetta, battling through the pain of her fractured ankle, using makeshift instruments to perform a delicate procedure that could easily have ripped the man's vein in half. Courage, resourcefulness, compassion, intelligence – over the short time they had known each other, she had shown him so much. He had truly never believed there was a woman who could take Ginny's place in his soul and his heart. Now, at least, he knew it was possible. Perhaps for the first time, he acknowledged the effect that Ginny's death continued to have on him – the indolent and virulent depression that had functioned like a great wall, preventing him from experiencing true joy. Was Nikki the answer? *Maybe*, he said to himself as they rocketed along the interstate. *Maybe she was.*

Catharpin . . . Centerville . . . Fairfax . . . by the time they passed through Arlington, they had ten minutes left. Probably not enough unless there were some preliminaries. There was still going to be the problem of getting in contact with someone with enough power to stop the injection, and doing it without getting killed.

Traffic was heavier now, much heavier, and Matt was forced to slow into the twenties to join the migration along the west bank of the Potomac. To his right he caught a glimpse of Arlington National Cemetery. Joe Keller would never be buried there, nor would Kathy Wilson or Teddy Rideout or any of the others who were victims of Hal Sawyer's war. But Matt knew that thanks to the woman hanging on behind him, the death of every one of them would eventually save lives.

Eight minutes until three.

'Take this exit,' Ellen called out. 'We'll cross the Potomac here and look for signs to Anacostia. We're almost there.'

They headed east on 395, crossed the Anacostia River at Pennsylvania Avenue, and then turned onto Minnesota. This was the tenement, lead paint, hard-scrabble section of the city – a drug-infested, 80 percent unemployed island of violence and despair, situated less than two miles from the Capitol. It was hardly an accident that Lynette Marquand had chosen a community health center here to showcase Omnivax. Her husband was trailing badly among black and Hispanic voters. Matt wondered how long it would take for Lynette to accept the tale of Lasaject and halt the inoculations.

Traffic had slowed to a near-crawl.

Two minutes, if that.

'Are we close enough for you to make it on foot?' Matt asked.

'Maybe. I'm not quite sure where we are relative to – wait! Fenwick Road. Over there! That's the street. I'm certain of it.'

Matt accelerated and swung the Harley up onto the tree belt and across a weedy lawn, onto

Fenwick. Several blocks down the street, they could see broadcast trucks, a number of them, lined up along the side of the road. Then they saw the blue barricade a block ahead.

'What time do you have?' Matt asked, hoping his watch and the one Ellen had taken from Heidi's bureau disagreed.

'After three,' Ellen replied sadly, 'maybe five or six minutes. You gave it a heck of a try.'

How long was the show going to last altogether? Matt wondered. Probably not more than ten or fifteen minutes, with maybe some commentary from the various networks' health gurus after that. If regular broadcasting resumed, it might be hours before they could get their story heard, and get word out to the pediatricians of the country to stop the injections. They had failed to stop the initial injection, but there still might be a chance to get to someone in a position of influence in time to prevent thousands of other exposures.

Three percent.

'Barricade,' Matt announced. 'We're there.'

As they approached the intersection, a young D.C. cop strode lazily toward them. He looked queerly at Granny Biker, perched comfortably on the raised passenger seat behind Matt.

'No admission here,' he said. 'You'll have to head that way two blocks until you see the officer, or else go back to the freeway.'

'Should I say something to him?' Ellen whispered.

'I think we get only one chance at this, and he ain't it. By the time he finishes calling his supervisor, who will call *his* supervisor, it'll be tomorrow.'

'What, then?' Ellen asked.

By now, several other cars had pulled up behind them. The officer walked past the Harley to repeat his instructions to the occupants of a silver minivan.

'I think we have to move up a couple of levels in the chain of command. Hang on.'

'Just pray that kid in the policeman's uniform doesn't start shooting.'

'It's not him I'm worried about,' Matt said. 'Hold tight. I'm going to try to make it up to the front door of the clinic. What time have you got?'

'Ten after.'

'Damn.'

Matt waited until the policeman had moved to yet another car, and then quickly accelerated around the barrier, up over a low curbing, and down the sidewalk. If the cop fired at them, they never heard or felt it. They were closing rapidly on the phalanx of broadcasting vans marking the entrance to the clinic. A hundred yards . . . fifty . . . Matt was entertaining theatrical visions of driving through the glass front door when, from the corner of his eye, he caught rapid movement coming from his left. He slowed and was turning his head when a woman hurled herself at them. Arms outspread, she connected with his and Ellen's shoulders like a missile, sending both of them sprawling off the motorcycle and onto the dirt of a weedy, trash-strewn vacant lot. The riderless Harley skidded on its side along the concrete and came to rest against the base of a tree. The woman, an athletic brunette in her thirties, held them down until two other Secret Service agents arrived, guns drawn.

'Not a move!' one of them snarled, his pistol fixed on them. 'Take those helmets off slowly, you first.'

Ellen and Matt did as he demanded.

'I'm a doctor,' Matt said quickly.

'Please listen to us,' Ellen said. 'I'm a member of the commission that approved the vaccine they just gave to that baby in there. My name's Ellen Kroft. We've just discovered there's a serious problem with Omnivax. We need to speak to someone in authority while they're still on the air so that we can warn the public and keep more kids from being vaccinated. Hundreds of lives may be at stake. Please! I'm telling the truth. There's a dangerous contamination of the vaccine. Mrs. Marquand must be told about it.'

One agent, a lanky black man with a scar across his chin, eyed them suspiciously, then took a silent poll of the other two. Both merely shrugged.

'ID?' he asked.

Ellen shook her head.

'Of course.'

'Wallet, jacket pocket,' Matt said.

'Take it out slowly.'

The agent handed Matt's wallet over to the other man, who scanned the contents,

'West Virginia license. Matthew Rutledge. It says he's a doctor.'

'And I'm the Pope,' the first agent muttered, removing a set of handcuffs from his back pocket. 'On your feet, both of you. Jill, pat 'em down.'

'I'm telling you,' Matt said desperately, as his left wrist was shackled to Ellen's right, 'we have to get down there before they go off the air.'

'Shut up!' The agent turned to the other two. 'Well?'

Jill lifted the two-way radio from her hip.

'Bert, it's Jill. How much longer of a delay before they get the show going?'

'Delay?' Ellen asked.

'I said, shut up!'

'Alan, Bert says ten more minutes,' Jill said to the black agent.

The man sighed.

'Tell him we're bringing down two party crashers for him to talk to. The sooner we get this out of our hands and into his, the better.'

'Thank you,' Ellen said, utterly relieved. 'You're doing the right thing.'

'Why does that sound to me like Find another job?'

'Have they given the shot yet?' Ellen risked asking.

'No, they haven't even gotten on the air.'

'What happened?'

'What happened is, some wacko got in there dressed as an electrician. He used a pair of electrician's shears and cut the pool feed cable from the camera inside the clinic to the truck that transmits the signal to all the networks. We've been on delay for forty-five minutes now. But I think the cable's just about been replaced.'

'Then, hurry,' Matt said. 'Get us to one of Mrs. Marquand's people before they give that shot, and I promise you, you'll be heroes.'

'You better be right.'

With an agent on either side of them, and a sizable crowd jeering from tenement windows, Ellen and Matt were led down the sidewalk, toward the clinic.

'I can't believe we're going to make it,' Matt said.

'I told you not to give up.'

'No, that was me. I told you.'

Ellen turned to Jill.

'Do you have any idea why the man cut the cable?'

'Like Alan said, he's a wack-job. Listen, in case you couldn't tell, we're not having a good day. If you're juicin' us about who you are or this vaccine, we're gonna cuff you to the same tree he's huggin' and leave all three of you there overnight to sample the hospitality of the neighborhood.'

The agent gestured to their right, where the culprit stood, his arms shackled around a good-sized oak.

Ellen grinned as they hurried past him toward the gleaming health center.

Rudy waved with his fingertips.

'Hey, Rudy,' she called out, 'this is my new friend, Matt Rutledge. Matt, this is my . . . significant other, Rudy Peterson.'

Just as they reached the clinic, a couple emerged. The woman was cradling an infant in her arms, holding her so that the child was bathed in the warm afternoon sun. Behind her, just inside the door, Matt could see what looked like more Secret Service people. At the sight of the two of them, handcuffed together, the couple took a wary step backward.

'Hi,' Ellen said cheerily, her smile threatening to escape the bounds of her face. 'Is this the baby who's going to get the vaccination?'

'Yes,' Sherrie replied, glancing down lovingly at her child. 'Her name's Donelle.'

Chapter 38

Late afternoon shadows were stretching across the streets of D.C. when Matt finally fired up the Harley and headed back toward West Virginia. He was riding alone. Ellen and Rudy remained behind to answer more questions from the FBI and to review the evidence Rudy had brought into the city with him. The progression from the Secret Service agent in charge of security at the clinic to his counterpart on Lynette Marquand's staff to Marquand herself had been rapid.

There had simply been too much at stake for anyone to delay.

In a small conference room, Matt and Ellen were being interrogated by former Georgia Congress-woman Joanne Kramer, Marquand's chief of staff, when word was brought in that the feeder cable Rudy had severed had been replaced. It was the moment of truth. Kramer hurried from the room, leaving the two of them with a Secret Service agent. Five interminable minutes passed before the door opened and Kramer reentered. With her was the First Lady of the United States. Beneath her piled-on-for-TV makeup, Marquand was ashen. There was no warmth in her expression as she took stock first of Matt, then Ellen.

'So, Mrs. Kroft,' she said, still standing, 'it would seem that your abstention from the

Omnivax vote did not mean you had lost interest in the vaccine.'

'Hardly,' Ellen said. 'A man had threatened my granddaughter's life if I voted against it. I needed to buy some time.'

'And now that man is dead.'

'Yes. He worked for the owner of Columbia Pharmaceuticals, the manufacturer of the Lassa fever component of Omnivax.'

'And there is something fatally wrong with that component?'

'Yes.'

'And you are convinced it would be a grievous error for us to vaccinate the infant who is out there awaiting her immunizations.'

Ellen sighed in relief at the news. The shot heard round the world still hadn't been fired.

'Yes,' she said again. 'I most emphatically do.'

'And you, Dr. –'

'Rutledge,' Matt said, clearing his throat. 'Matthew Rutledge. People from my community in West Virginia who received test doses of the Lassa fever vaccine ten years ago are dying. I think the agent that is killing them is still in the vaccine.'

Marquand again leveled her gaze at Ellen.

'Mrs. Kroft, my staff has informed me that you have been a financial supporter of my husband's opponent in the upcoming election. Is your miraculous appearance at this moment at all politically motivated?'

Ellen took some time before responding.

'I disapprove of your husband's position on social security,' she said finally. 'That is why I support Mr. Harrison. But our being here now has nothing to do with politics. I assure you of that.'

For fifteen seconds, all was silent as Marquand steadily probed Ellen's eyes with her own.

'Thank you,' she had said finally. Her voice was husky, her expression still gray. 'And you, too, Dr. Rutledge.'

Without another word, she and Kramer then turned and left the room. Fifteen minutes after that, the first of the FBI interrogators had arrived. The child had been sent home; the cameras had been shut down; and no doubt, the administration's spin-doctors had been called in for emergency work.

Before leaving for home, Matt had sat alone in one of the empty clinic examining rooms wrestling with the decision of whether to notify the police about the situation at the toxic dump site or to wait until he had the chance to evaluate things in person. When Lyle didn't return, Lewis and Frank would surely have known there had been trouble at Hal's. He was certain of that. What they would or could do about it, though, was anybody's guess. Their brother was dead. Their beloved old truck was at the bottom of Long Lake. They were several miles from their farm, and Lewis was not in the best of shape for travel. Still, the problems Matt would cause for them by sending the authorities to the scene of such carnage might well destroy them. Nikki and those inside the cave were reasonably stable when Ellen and he had left for Hal's place.

Finally, after a heated internal debate, he had decided to wait on calling for help from anyone until he could ride out to the mountain himself.

Rush-hour traffic was a bear, and Matt took many more chances than he was accustomed to in getting across the Potomac and out of the city. It was seven-thirty by the time he was first able to accelerate past seventy.

Just outside White Sulphur Springs, he glanced down at his pager, which he kept in a plastic holder on the handlebars of the Harley when he was riding, and transferred to his belt loop when he wasn't. It had been on the bike since the evening he followed Bill Grimes up to the mountain cabin. The light indicating a page was flashing. He had no idea how long that had been the case. He pulled off the highway and called the ER at the hospital.

'Dr. Rutledge,' the ward secretary exclaimed, 'we've been trying to find you. There's a disaster drill in progress, only it's not a drill.'

Matt's pulse quickened.

'What's going on?'

'I really don't know. It's confusing. I think there's trouble at the mine. Maybe a cave-in, maybe an explosion. The first two cases are due to arrive by ambulance any minute.'

'Tell whoever's in charge that I'll be there in about an hour.'

Fifty minutes later, Matt swept around a wide, left-hand curve – one of his favorites to ride – and saw the lights of Belinda nestled in the valley below. So beautiful; so deceptively peaceful. Main Street was quieter than usual, but the hospital more than made up for that. One ambulance was in a bay, having just been unloaded, a second, also now empty, stood off to one side of the tarmac, and a third, flashers on, was just rolling up the drive. Matt parked the Harley and hurried over to help.

'I've never seen anything like it. Never,' one of the EMTs was excitedly telling ER nurse Laura Williams. 'We pulled these people out through a hole way up on this rock wall. There were flares marking the entrance to a cave and a rope on the ground leading in to where the trouble was, but no indication who put them there.'

'I know,' Williams said. 'The other crew's still talking about it.'

'And those barrels of chemicals. God, what a stench. That can't possibly be legal. What made those mine people think they could get away with such a thing?'

'Need a hand?' Matt asked, battling back the urge to answer the EMT's question, and peering into the ambulance at the two stretchers.

'Sure. The guy on the left is a load.'

Fred.

Matt stood on his tiptoes and determined that the occupant of the other stretcher was Sara Jane Tinsley.

'How did you guys know where to go?' he asked.

'One of the cops who was on duty when the anonymous call came in knew the area the guy was talking about. We all went out in a caravan.'

Matt took one end of Carabetta's stretcher, hauled it onto the cement platform, and helped pull it up into position to be rolled inside. The OSHA bureaucrat, moaning continuously and lolling his head from side to side, appeared to be in no immediate danger. Matt moved to speak to him, then just as quickly pulled back and raced into the crowded ER. There would be time for Fred.

He easily spotted orthopedist Brian O'Neil, half a head above any of the disaster team.

'Hey, Brian,' he called out, hurrying over.

'Well, Matthew, don't you look like shit. Where were you, at some sort of motocross?'

'Believe it or not, I was in the cave with all of these people when it blew.'

'But – ?'

'Later. Are you taking care of Nikki Solari?'

'The doc?'

'Yes.'

'Sweet woman.'

'Behave. She hurt bad?'

'Trimalleolar fracture. A little displacement, but nothing that a bit o' time in the OR and a few well-placed screws won't fix.'

'Promise to do a good job, and I promise not to tell her your degree is in veterinary medicine. Where is she?'

'Ortho. Please let her know I'll be in with her in two minutes.'

'Make it five,' Matt said.

Eyes closed, an IV draining fluid and antibiotic into her arm, Nikki lay on a stretcher, her swollen, discolored foot and ankle propped up on pillows in a transparent air cast. Her face and arms had been washed clean, but dust and small shards of stone filled her hair. Still, she looked absolutely beautiful.

'Hey you,' Matt whispered, 'lady doctor.'

Nikki smiled broadly before opening her eyes. Matt kissed her on the forehead, then on the mouth.

'Did you make it in time?' she asked.

'No shots today, missy,' he said. 'Come back some other time. So sorry.'

'That's great news. Nice going.'

'It was my Uncle Hal all the time, Nik. He owned most of Columbia Pharmaceuticals. Grimes and the others worked for him.'

Her expression darkened. She immediately understood the implications for him and for his mother.

'I'm really sorry,' she said.

'Yeah. Well, it's quite possible even John Dillinger and Attila the Hun had nephews.'

'I suppose,' she said sadly.

'How did you get out?'

Nikki shrugged. 'While the Slocumbs were doing their thing, I decided to drag myself back into the cave to look after Fred and Morrissey and the rest. A lot of time passed. I was getting worried. Then, all of a sudden, there was noise, then powerful lights shining in, and a few seconds later the Calgary Stampede of EMTs, policemen, and firemen began.'

'The Slocumbs?'

'I have no idea where they are.'

Matt kissed her again.

'I'm worried,' he said. 'I think I'm going to let you rest and go see if I can learn something about what might have happened to them. Brian O'Neil, the orthopedist who's taking care of you, is terrific.'

'Why, Gunner, I didn't know you cared,' O'Neil boomed from the doorway.

'Okay, I care, I care. Just don't make the mistake of thinking my judgment is flawed in other areas as well.' He pressed Nikki's cheek tightly against his. 'I'll be back soon, baby,' he whispered. 'Be brave.'

'After what we've been through, how could anything be scary?'

'We've got an OR right now,' the orthopedist announced, 'and I think we should take it so long as no one else is ready.'

'Might as well get it over,' Nikki said.

'I want you to recuperate at my place,' Matt whispered in her ear.

'You still in the back-rub business?'

509

'We never close.'

Matt patted O'Neil on the arm as he passed, and wandered out into the bustling ER, looking beyond the busy nurses and physicians at their charges. Sid, the security guard, was in Bay 3, the curtained-off area next to Fred. Two bays down, Sara Jane was being cleaned off by an aide, and next to where she lay, Evan Julian, the ENT surgeon, was huddled over Colin Morrissey. Julian was the most meticulous, compulsive physician on the hospital staff, and never started a case unless every instrument was perfectly aligned on the scrub nurse's tray. Matt grinned at the notion of Nikki, her shattered ankle in a bulky makeshift splint, performing a successful emergency tracheotomy by lantern light in a cave filled with dust and toxic fumes.

Matt anxiously checked the other bays and rooms. The woman he had called Tarzana was in a side room, thrashing about wildly, restrained to her litter by leather straps. But no Slocumbs.

If there was dire need for his help with any of the patients, Matt knew he would have pitched in. But at the moment, he was feeling totally drained and more than a little fearful about Frank and Lewis. He left the hospital through the waiting room and headed across to his bike. As he was approaching the Harley, he noticed a tan Mercedes sedan parked not too far away. The driver, his face obscured in the shadows, was beckoning to him. He took several steps in that direction and froze. The car was Hal's.

'Doc, it's me, Frank,' the driver called out in a loud whisper.

Matt hurried over and jumped into the passenger seat. Lewis Slocumb was stretched across the back, apparently none the worse for wear.

'You all right?' Matt asked, gesturing at Lewis's chest tube.

'Ah'm okay,' Lewis said grimly. 'Bastard kilt Lyle.'

'I know. I was there. I'm really sorry, guys. I am. Lyle died saving our lives. And a lot of other lives, too. He was a real hero. How'd you get out and . . . and to Hal's?'

'Yer pal Grimes had one a them phones – ya know, lak a two-way radio. When Lyle dint come rot back, we knowed it 'uz bad. A couple var frands got phones. I tole ya we knowed some people. Frank called Earl Morris – ya know him?'

'No.'

'Well, Earl's moun'n jes lak us. He brought a bunch o'er an' hept us clean up. I don't think no one's gonna find Grimes an' his pals where we put 'em less'n they kin dahve in real deep, real dark water. Cleaned up all the casin's, too.'

'Why was I so worried about you two? What about Hal? How'd you get there?'

'Earl Morris knowed whar he lives. We piled in back a his truck an' went over. Thar yer uncle were, all trussed up lak a hog at bar-bee-que time.'

'Did he try and talk you into untying him?'

'Oh, he tried,' Frank said. 'B'lieve me, he tried.'

'And this car? He told me he didn't have another key.'

'He lied,' Frank said with a twinkle.

'We knowed he 'uz lyin',' Lewis added. 'He ain't vura good at it. Thanks he is, but he ain't. With a l'il hep from us, he tole what hap'ned ta Lyle, then he tole us whar the car key was. Wanted us ta have it in exchange fer untyin' him.'

'Did you kill him?'

'Thought about it.'

'I'm glad you didn't. I need him alive.'

'We may a left some marks, though.'

'Whatever it is, he deserved it. As soon as you can, find someone who'll buy his car and use the cash to get yourselves a new truck.'

'Wer gonna. First we gotta fond Lyle's body. We want ta bury him back ta the farm. Summabitches.'

'We'll get down to the lake at dawn tomorrow. I'll meet you at my uncle's and show you the road down to the water. Lewis, I'm going back into the hospital to get some stuff to pull that tube out of your chest. I don't think you need it anymore and I don't want it to let in an infection.'

'Whute'er ya say. Ya gonna be sendin' the po-lice out ta yer uncle's place?'

'You check those knots I tied?'

'Yep. They ain't comin' loose no tahm soon.'

Matt opened the door and stepped out onto the pavement. The breezy night was cloudless and utterly clear. A West Virginia night.

'Maybe in a few days,' he said.

Epilogue

Six Months Later

The massive Hart Senate office building, more than a million square feet, was built in the late seventies adjacent to the Dirksen Senate Office Building, on Constitution Avenue between First and Second Streets. For four days now, the august central hearing room of the Hart Building had been the scene of the first major hearing of the new, post-election Senate – an investigation into the Omnivax debacle by the Committee on Health, Education, Labor, and Pensions.

Ellen had already testified, as had Rudy and Matt and others, including Lara Bolton, the former Secretary of Health and Human Services in the former Marquand administration. For nearly six hours now, the senators, seated at draped tables beneath a massive, gray marble wall, had been taking turns questioning the star of the proceedings, Dr. Harold Sawyer, currently awaiting trial and being held without bail at the maximum security federal penitentiary in Florence, Colorado. And for nearly six hours, Hal had been sidestepping and evading their queries like an All-American halfback dodging second-string tacklers.

Matt, along with Ellen, and Cheri Sanderson from PAVE, had been present for Hal's entire testimony, and his patience as well as his faith in the system was frayed to near the breaking point. With Grimes, Sutcher, and the hired killer Verne all still missing, and Larry a bloated, fish-eaten corpse, washed up on the shore of Long Lake weeks after his death, there was little in the way of substantive evidence against Hal beyond the testimonies of Matt and Ellen.

'Dr. Sawyer,' Delaware Senator Martin Wells was asking wearily, 'let's get back to your relationship with Dr. George Poulos of the Institute for Vaccine Development. In the six months prior to your arrest, precisely how many meetings – face-to-face or by phone or by e-mail – did the two of you have?'

'I would have to check my appointment book, Senator,' Hal replied, smiling earnestly, 'but from my recollection, as I told Senator Worthington, it couldn't have been more than one or two times.'

'This is really depressing,' Matt whispered. 'He is just so damn slick. If I didn't hear him admit to what he's done, I would probably believe that he was just the unfortunate victim of hiring the wrong people.'

'Matt,' Cheri said, 'I heard that he's in the process of cutting a deal with the federal prosecutors. Is that true?'

'I'm afraid it might be. Once they realized that he was going to be tough to convict on many of the major charges against him, they started going after the bigger fish he was dealing with.'

'George Poulos, for one,' Ellen said. 'I'm convinced he's the link between the Marquand administration and Columbia Pharmaceuticals, which means he's the one who suggested they might send someone like Vinyl Sutcher to pay me a visit.'

'Senator,' Hal was saying, 'I want to cooperate,

really I do, but I feel I have answered your questions regarding my relationship with Dr. Poulos as forthrightly and –'

'Oh, I've had enough of this,' Matt snapped. 'Let's go out for coffee. My treat.'

'Can't,' Cheri said. 'Sally's meeting me at the office in half an hour. She's at a meeting of the commission President Harrison has formed to look at vaccine issues, including funding for increased clinical investigation and public education, as well as debate on the whole business of parental choice. It's a miracle what's happening all over, and it's all thanks to you guys.'

'Oh, pshaw,' Ellen said.

'As long as we don't end up throwing out the baby with the bathwater,' Matt cautioned.

'Even we don't want to do that,' Cheri said. 'We just want to be listened to.'

'So, did someone say coffee?' Ellen asked.

After seeing Cheri into a cab, Matt and Ellen bundled up against the brisk February wind and walked arm in arm around to a diner on C Street. Hal's testimony would be continuing in the morning. Federal prosecutors had asked Matt to attend as long as his uncle was testifying, but today would be Ellen's last day at the hearings. Rudy was back at his cabin, teaching, writing, fishing when the weather permitted, and awaiting her return. She was still living in her place in Glenside, but the two of them had been seeing more and more of each other, and Ellen had mentioned something to Matt almost in passing about a trial period of living together in two places.

They sat across from each other in a booth, watching the traffic inch past, and saying little, but each aware of the bonds that would forever exist between them. Three months after she had helped to save his life, Ellen had returned to Belinda for the burial of Colin Morrissey, who rapidly became incapacitated from his neurologic disease and simply wasted away. Soon, sadly, Sara Jane Tinsley would share a similar fate.

For nearly six months now, the owners of BC&C had been besieged by attorneys, mine agencies, and government investigations. Armand Stevenson had been sent packing and was facing criminal charges. Blaine LeBlanc was gone as well, and latest estimates placed the fines and settlements in the tens of millions. Still, under new management, the operation had remained open, and recently, had even been hiring.

'So,' Ellen asked finally, 'what do you think about your uncle making some sort of plea bargain?'

Matt shrugged. He was thinking about his mother and her brother's many kindnesses to her. Since Hal's imprisonment, Matt had spent even more time with her than before. But she was inching closer and closer to custodial care, and now as often as not called him Hal.

'He hurt a lot of people,' he said finally. 'One minute I want to see him put away forever, and the next I think that he simply went crazy with all the money that was at stake. It's really out of my hands. All I can do now is keep telling the prosecutors what I know.'

'Well, I saw him in action,' Ellen said. 'I hope he gets twenty consecutive life sentences and they let him plea-bargain down to one. When are you headed back?'

'Probably tomorrow night.'

'You miss her.' It was a statement, not a question.

'I miss her,' Matt said.

Nikki had been in D.C. for one day and one night, but her responsibilities as a pathologist at Montgomery County Regional Hospital, and as the new medical examiner for Montgomery County, precluded taking much time off. After having her ankle fixed, she had taken a leave of absence from her Boston position, and had simply never gone back. Six weeks later, with the job offer from MCRH in her pocket, she had sent in her resignation, and a week after that, had flown up to Boston with Matt to pack her things.

'You want to know what she said to me when she was here?' Ellen asked. 'She said that men like you don't come along and resuscitate a girl every day, so she had decided to pay attention to that.'

'I'm paying attention, too,' he said. 'She's really been great to be around. I just have to get accustomed to . . . to having someone in my life.'

'It's just a day at a time.'

At that moment, Matt's cell phone began vibrating. Actually, it was Nikki's. He had never owned one himself, but she insisted they keep in close touch when he was in the big city.

'I'll be back in a minute,' Ellen said as he pulled the phone from his pocket. 'Say hello for me.'

'Hey, good afternoon, Doc,' he said. 'Didn't I just talk to you a little while ago?'

'That was then,' Nikki said. 'How's it going?'

'Hal's performing even as we speak. There're rumblings he's going to cut some sort of a deal with the prosecutors.'

'Well, he can't have his jobs back. I like them.'

'That won't be a problem. I have mixed emotions

about any plea-bargaining. One moment I think there should be some lenience because he was just crazy, and the next I don't want him getting away with anything less than the guillotine.'

'It'll work out the way it works out,' Nikki said.

'I suppose.'

'I know you're in a tough spot, Matt. For what it's worth, I think you're handling things terrifically.'

'I think I needed to hear that.'

'I mean it. You're a great doc and a wonderful man, and I'll tell you that as often as you want to hear it.'

'Thanks. You're pretty terrific yourself.'

'Say, I almost forgot the reason I called. Yes, Virginia, there is a reason. The neatest thing just happened. I was getting ready to go into the office, but I had a little time, so I took my coffee and Kathy's mandolin out to the porch and played a few licks out toward the mountains. I have a ways to go on the thing to even be listenable, but I'm getting better.'

'That's a gross understatement. Remember, I've heard you.'

'But wait, that's not the point. While I was playing, this incredibly beautiful little bird flew down and settled on the railing right in front of me. I've never seen anything like it. I kept playing and playing and it didn't move. It just sat there like it was actually listening to my music. It was small, but so red and ... and so perfect. What do you think it was?'

Matt swallowed back a fullness in his throat and gazed across the street toward the Hart Building.

'I think,' he said, 'it was a tanager. A scarlet tanager.'